3D Books

Two Tears

Rita Smith

With thanks
Rita Smith
Feb. 6/2018

This book is a work of fiction. Any references to historical events, real people, or real locales are used fictitiously. Other names, characters, places, and incidents are the product of the author's imagination, and any resemblance to actual events or locales or persons, living or dead, is entirely coincidental

3D Books
Published by 11th Dimension Press Publishing Services
3D Books is a division of 11th Dimension Press, Canada

First Published in 2014 by 3D Books,
a division of 11th Dimension Press

ISBN 978-0-9939629-6-7

For my family

I

I didn't want to get out of bed today. I could easily cover my head with the blankets, leave the drapes closed, disconnect the telephone and bury myself in my heartache. Must I get up and face the world, a world that had been forever changed for me? Life as I knew it was no more. I didn't care if I ever saw the light of day. I was lost and lonely but I had to make some attempt to carry on, if only for the sake of others. My life would never be the same again for me, but I had to get on with it regardless. I had others to think of.

Slowly and grudgingly I sat up in bed, the one Bob and I had shared for so many wonderful years. As I looked around the beautiful room, I began to remember how much fun and stress we faced when we tore it apart to renovate. We renovated by combining two smaller rooms, giving Bob and me more space. It also gave us doors opening onto a balcony overlooking the garden. This allowed for a lovely breeze mixed with the aroma of many beautiful flowers in the summer, and added to the luxury of this now larger room. In the wintertime we felt cozy inside enjoying the pristine scenery, trees bowed down with heavy snow and the odd track made by some animal walking through the yard. An en-suite was added alongside an enormous walk in closet. Our king size oak bed was centred in the room against the back wall with a cushioned cedar chest sitting at the foot of the bed. Night tables sat on each side of the bed with lamps on top. Even with my triple dresser, and Bob's dresser we had plenty of space. Wall to wall plush beige carpeting covered the floor. The walls were painted a delicate pale beige. Windows the length of the wall opened onto the balcony. Sheer ivory curtains covered all of the windows under coffee damask drapes, matching the bedspread. Drapes were pulled back during the day and closed in the evening for privacy. Many family photographs lined the walls as well as other artwork. This room was warm, happy and full of love.

Okay, enough of this nonsense get up and get ready for the day I said to myself. I noticed that my hair was badly in need of some pampering. With all that I had been through in the last few months, the shock of Bob's all too sudden diagnosis, illness and subsequent death, the last thing on my mind was my weekly visits to the hairdresser. When I was first made aware of just how ill Bob was, I had the good foresight to have my hair trimmed and permed. With all the running around that came with his illness, I was thankful I had done that.

After finally getting out of bed, showering, blow-drying and brushing my hair through, I was able to make it tidy and presentable. Before my last trim, my hair had grown longer than I was normally used to, but it was easy enough to manage, if I combed it through and pulled it back with a clip. However, I knew I would have to do something about it before the funeral.

Veronica's Hair Salon was local and always busy due to Veronica's attention to detail. I couldn't remember how long I had been a client but I was always pleased with the results, no matter what I was having done. Like most of the other clients, I had a regular appointment every week but Veronica always managed to squeeze her clients in if an emergency came up. There were four other hairdressers on staff, all equally dedicated to pleasing their clients.

Veronica's manicurists and facial specialists were always kept busy too. The many different methods of hairdressing always fascinated me, and I loved to see the transformations. I only availed myself of cuts, sets, and perms, no tinting.

Veronica attended to me most often, but if something came up whereby she wasn't available, I wasn't unhappy with any of the other staff. Just to have my hair trimmed and set by a professional gave me a bit of a lift. I enjoyed and found it relaxing to sit in the chair and be pampered. More often than not I dozed off, and today would be no different.

The salon was large and bright. Sage green painted paneling covered the bottom of the walls. The upper half was covered with paper in a large floral design full of greens, pinks and creams. As with any beauty salon, walls facing the chairs were completely covered with mirrors. I hated to look in those mirrors when I first sat down. I think most clients felt the same way. By the end of the session it was a different story. We were happy to see our reflections. I knew it would be different this time. No matter how good a job Veronica did on me, my face was a mess. It was a normal day at the salon, clients talking and laughing, like one big happy family, enjoying coffee and cookies. Someone always brought in snacks for the clients. I tried to hide my envy at their happiness.

Veronica quietly expressed her sadness at Bob's untimely passing. She knew what I was going through. Her husband had passed away a few short months ago. She was still trying to come to terms with it as well. All of the chairs were occupied. There were a couple of these clients that I knew; all of them were still waiting for their pampering. It was a busy little shop and most of my neighbours and friends were clients as Veronica. Her staff always managed to make us feel so much better after a session. She told me she and the staff planned to attend the funeral later. That comforted me somewhat but it wasn't surprising. Veronica and the staff were more like family to their clients. It was typical of the reaction of most of the people we knew.

After Veronica finished, I paid my bill and hugged the staff. As I drove home, all kinds of thoughts swirled around in my head. Were all the funeral arrangements made? Had everyone been notified? I was blessed and grateful for my children, family, my best friend Beth and others around me. Their strength at this time was helping me to get through this. I couldn't have done it without them.

Beth had coffee and sandwiches ready for me when I arrived at home. I didn't feel like eating but she encouraged me, reminding me that we had a long day ahead of us. She was right. I kicked off my shoes and put my jacket in the hall cupboard. We sat at the kitchen table as we so often did. She took hold of my hand but didn't say much. She didn't have to; I could tell by her face that she was hurting for me. Beth had been my friend almost forever. We could anticipate what the other was going to say and could read each other's feelings. We sat quietly sipping our coffee for a short time. One look at the clock a couple minutes later told me it was time to get dressed once again. Beth was already dressed. She would stay with me until the children came to pick me up. That meant a lot to me.

After going upstairs I put on my navy blue open collar dress, dotted with little flowers. Bob had given me a diamond pendant and matching earrings on our 25th anniversary that I wore as well. My shoes were navy blue just like my dress but had a lower heel than I would normally wear. I knew I would be standing greeting guests so my feet needed to be comfortable. There were enough chairs in the visitation room but sitting and chatting wasn't as personal as standing beside guests, perhaps at the casket or just holding hands. I would never get more than a couple minutes to sit down.

The children arrived just as I came downstairs. Beth was going out the door as they came in. We were trying to be strong for each other but just seeing the children brought on the tears. I wiped my eyes with tissue. The children held me close. I put on my coat and before opening the front door, I glanced in the hall mirror. I barely recognized myself. What I chose to wear was fine but my face, oh my poor face. I had aged so much over these past months. I hadn't paid much attention to my face or myself for that matter with all that had gone on recently. I functioned, got out of bed, showered, dressed then moved on to whatever was on the schedule for the day. Now when I took the time to look closely at myself, it was frightening. I had dark circles under my red and puffy eyes and my face was pale, gaunt and much, much thinner than normal. The strain of Bob's illness, his untimely death and most of all, the revelation he made to me and me alone before he died, was almost unbearable. I am not sure I could or would have been so accepting, had he not been so seriously ill. I will never know now.

I was raised during and after the war years. Like most others in Britain, we learned we just had to get on with it.

No time for counsellors. I am not even sure there were counsellors back then. My family and I weren't as unfortunate as a lot of the Brits, many being bombed out of their homes, but we still went through a certain amount of trauma. I remember the sirens going off, being taken out of our beds in the middle of the night, following most of the tenants from our house down to a neighbour's house on the ground floor, gas masks and ear plugs hanging around our necks.

My dad always felt it was more secure than the air raid shelters which were nothing more than brick buildings in the middle of the street. At least on the ground floor of the tenement, we had three floors above us, hopefully giving us a bit more protection. Wooden props lined the close (entrance to the tenement) as a means of supporting the building. In addition to that, at the front of the close, a cement baffle wall about four feet by six or seven feet high was erected. To be honest, I don't think we as young children grasped the reality or gravity of the war but it taught us to be stronger and more able to cope with almost anything.

Bob's need to bare his heart and soul to me before he died, telling me things I could never have imagined, left me heavily burdened and confused. I could not confide in anyone, not even my best friend Beth. It left me feeling alone and in a place I never thought I would be. Beth and I shared everything. Keeping this from her left me feeling guilty but I know she would have understood. At the very least she would have supported me, no matter what. I didn't have time to understand what had happened. I had to be strong for everyone's sake.

Bob's sudden terminal diagnosis came as an unbelievable shock to both of us. We could barely take it in. He was always so healthy. He was organized in every facet of his life. It wasn't surprising that he wanted to tie up any loose ends. There weren't many.

Always considerate of my needs, he wanted to relieve me of the burden of arranging a funeral. It was emotional for both of us but in between planning, we had a few laughs as we remembered some of the happier times. I was determined to follow his wishes to the letter.

Bob had only been ill for a very short time but most family and friends had an opportunity to visit if and when he was up to it. He didn't want a long drawn out visitation but because of our standing in the community, that wasn't possible. We agreed to one evening with the service the next morning, allowing those who might not have heard of his death time to visit.

Bob's family, the Wilsons, were pillars of the community, well respected due to their involvement in the church, charitable foundations, as well as the business community.

There were only a few last minute preparations to be done. Family and friends were wonderful, taking over and leaving our daughter Lisa, son Daniel and me to greet the visitors. I often wondered how the bereaved got through funerals, attending to every detail while at the same time trying to come to terms with a death. I could not have managed on my own. I was blessed and grateful to have family and friends around me.

We prepared ourselves as best we could for the first visit to see Bob before others arrived. Holding hands tightly, we walked slowly over to his casket sitting at the end of a large room, pale peach brocade drapes covering the wall behind. On either side of the casket there were many photographs of Bob and our family. It was quiet, peaceful and serene as most funeral parlours are. Little couches and chairs, complimenting the drapes, were set up around the room, with end tables placed here and there. Bowls of candies and Kleenex were readily available. We chose a light oak wood casket, not the most expensive, not the least, somewhere in between. When we saw Bob, the tears flowed. He had lost weight over his last few months with us although he retained his good looks. I hated it when mourners commented as they looked down of a deceased person, "they did a wonderful job" or "doesn't s/he look so natural?" Now as I looked down on Bob, my soul mate, I understood. He appeared to be sleeping, looking peaceful. In some sense, I don't think that helped. We half expected him to sit up and smile at us. We had discussed what he should wear. The decision was unanimous. He would wear his dark blue blazer, with gleaming brass buttons, a white shirt and his navy tie with the university crest on it. Impeccably dressed as always. He was such a creature of habit. If we doubted that Bob was dead, it passed over quickly. He would never ever lie down in his clothes. Whenever he came home from work he immediately changed into casual clothing before doing anything else. His clothes were neatly hung in his closet. Seeing him lying there, forced us into reality. Bob was dead. He was okay with an open casket provided he didn't look frightening. Seeing him so natural looking, we were happy we made that choice. His death was more than I thought I could bear, a void that would never be filled. I would have to live on through the wonderful memories of the many happy years we shared.

In the obituary we suggested that anyone wishing to do so could donate to a hospice, palliative care, a charity of their choice, or support those with cancer who needed financial assistance. It made more sense to give a gift to help someone rather than flowers that would die and be thrown out, although many floral tributes were delivered to the funeral parlour. I had never seen so many beautiful flowers in such a variety of arrangements from small bouquets to larger baskets, every colour in the rainbow giving off an aroma like that of a summer garden. It helped to brighten up this rather dull and rainy, early spring day in the year 1998. The fragrant aroma from the floral tributes softened and brightened up the dark sorrow felt by family friends, neighbours and business associates who attended the visitation. Large sums of money were donated in Bob's name, a fitting tribute to a man who gave so much during his lifetime. As we greeted visitors, it wasn't easy having to go over every detail of Bob's short illness and death. Fortunately close friends and family already knew the circumstances of his death but there were a few who hadn't heard. Everyone was shocked at the suddenness of his passing. It was difficult for me to come up with words at a time like this. It has been said that if you don't know what to say, don't say anything. The mourners will understand. There were some who couldn't find the words and that was okay too. We hugged, held hands or shared a look that each of us knew what was meant by it.

After the last visitor left, we walked up to the casket and said goodnight to Bob. "Rest well. We'll be back tomorrow for the service. Goodnight."

The children and I went home. Beth was there before us and had the kettle on, not that we needed any more coffee. She wanted to go over the details of the funeral, make sure everything was as we planned. Afterwords she rinsed the cups and went home. "Goodnight Fiona, you are doing amazingly well. You will get through this. See you tomorrow." We hugged and cried. The children stayed with me that night and I was thankful for that.

The next morning a folding partition in the funeral parlour was opened to accommodate the large crowd expected at the service. Slowly the oversized room was filled to capacity, making it necessary for some to stand at the back. Bob was loved and respected by all who knew him personally and even by those who, perhaps, only came in contact with him once or twice. He was just that kind of a guy. It was no surprise to me that the room was filled to capacity.

A harpist sat in the corner playing music Bob had chosen including Dream of Olwen, Barcarolle, Clare de Lune and La Golindrina. Pastor Ken Walker walked up to the podium as the harpist finished her music. He opened with a short prayer. After we sat down he read The Lord is my Shepherd. Bob and Ken grew up together. Ken's father was the pastor at our church. I got to know Ken after I arrived on the scene with Bob. The Wilsons and Walkers were long time members of the congregation. Having a pastor who knows the deceased, makes all the difference when it comes to the eulogy. I have been to funerals where the that wasn't the case and it's obvious from the words they give. In Bob's case, Ken spoke as a friend, pastor and from the heart.

"As most of you know, our families have known each other for years, through church and socially. Bob and his siblings had attended Sunday School. We followed on to Bible Class and attended the same public school and university. We shared many things but not the girlfriends we dated. I married one of the group. Bob was too busy pursuing his goal of becoming a lawyer, the same profession as his dad. However, that all changed when a wee lass from Glasgow caught his eye one evening at a church social. They both loved dancing, tennis, walking and were compatible in every way. The Wilsons welcomed Fiona into the family with open arms, glad that Bob was finally going to settle down. They got a kick out of her accent and often kidded her. She always took it in good fun."

I smiled at some of the remarks while wiping away tears from my eyes.

"Nature took its course and they married. I didn't marry them. My father was proud and happy to perform the ceremony. Lisa was the first child to join the family. She was the apple of her dad's eye. They thought their life was complete and were content but happily Daniel came along a couple of years later. Now their life was not only complete, it was perfect. I didn't know of a happier couple except perhaps Beth's family. These four parents were inseparable. Life was good, the children grew quickly as children do, went off to universities and completed their education. However, just when Bob and Fiona were going to do some travelling, Bob took ill. We were all shocked at his sudden death. He will be sorely missed. Fortunately Fiona and Bob didn't leave all their plans until retirement. They travelled and spent as much time as possible with family and friends. Even as they discussed their life together before he died, they agreed they hadn't missed out on anything. If there was something that they might have wished for, it would have been to have had a little more time together. As Christians, they accepted it as God's will. We have no say in that but it is comforting to all that we know where Bob is and his pain is over. Our deepest sympathies go out to Fiona, Lisa, Daniel and all the family on this sad occasion. We share our deep sorrow at this time and count it an honour that we knew Bob."

Others were invited to speak. A couple of his staff gave short musings of what he was like as a boss. Many shed tears as they spoke of him lovingly. All too often when a person dies, he or she is not privy to the deep thoughts and feelings of family, friends and associates. Many tributes and accolades only come out at a funeral. Unfortunately the deceased can't hear them. This wasn't the case with Bob. He wouldn't hear these words but he had been honoured on many other occasions. He was well aware of how highly regarded and loved he was by those that were close to him. I took great comfort in the fact that this show of love and admiration during his last few months was not just a show but a genuine outpouring of love, respect and admiration for a man who truly deserved it.

Ken led us all in a chorus of:

"How good is the God we adore, our faithful unchangeable friend. Whose love is as great as his power and knows neither measure nor end. In the sweet by and by, we shall meet on that beautiful shore. In the sweet by and by, we shall meet on that beautiful shore."

After he closed in prayer, he invited everyone back to our house for a time of fellowship and refreshments. Those wishing to do so could attend at the committal ceremony.

It was overwhelming standing there shaking hands and listening to words of sympathy. It was such a large crowd.

The graveyard was gray, cold and damp. Mourners huddled close together, trying to keep warm, drawing comfort from each other. Bob's parents were buried on the other side of the pathway. Memories of the time we received the devastating news of their untimely and tragic deaths was in the thoughts of many in attendance, especially the family. Emotions ran high.

I knew Bob never got over their deaths. It was difficult for the whole family, but it seemed to affect him more than anyone. He found it difficult to accept that they were gone. I was thankful today that his parents had gone on before him. I am not sure they would have gotten over it, especially his mother. Mom Wilson always said she had no favourites and mostly that was true, but we all knew she had a soft spot for Bob. He was the closest of his siblings to his mother. Parents never expect to see their children go before them. It's not normal. When they do, it often tears them apart to the point that some never get over it.

As I stood there, listening to the graveside prayers, my mind went back to a time in Scotland when women never attended the graveside ceremony. I half wished that could have been the case today. On the other hand, I was glad I had stayed with Bob right to the end. When the ceremony was over and it was time to leave, I drew back, not wanting to leave him. How could I leave him there alone? How could I go on without him? Daniel and Lisa tightened their hold on me and hugged ever so tightly. We were all unable to stop our tears. Daniel whispered into my ear, "you know mom, gran and gramps are just across the path. Dad's not alone. We can come back tomorrow if you want." His words comforted me. I blew a kiss, turned around and slowly walked towards the waiting car. Most of the others had already gone. I was heartbroken.

Back at the house everything was ready for the guests. Beth wanted to have the tea at her house but I graciously declined her offer, telling her that I wanted to have everyone back at my house where I felt Bob's presence would be with us, if only by the surroundings. Beth, with the help of church friends and neighbours, had prepared everything, leaving nothing for me or the children to do which took a great burden off of us at this time. Everything was prepared but I insisted that we hire people to serve. I wanted everyone to be able to relax and mingle. It would make it easier for us as we tried to cope with the family and friends who wanted to share memories.

I often wondered how the bereaved got through these visitations with people smiling, talking, and sometimes laughing after a funeral. However, this gathering of friends and relatives showed me how much it helped ease some of the pain, even for a short time, because they genuinely cared and shared our pain. Many wonderful stories about Bob and his life were told which I appreciated. It might have been a different story if they had known the truth about Bob, which I only recently found out myself, but everyone loved him so why would anyone think any less of him? After the initial shock I was hurt, confused, and in denial, but I still loved him, and I didn't love him any less. I could never have wished for a better partner or marriage, not even if things had been different and I had married Ian instead, the man I once believed to be my one and only true love in Glasgow.

After a short visit, guests started to leave but before they did, I gathered up my strength to thank everyone. Tears fell, and as my voice shook I said:

"There are no words to adequately express our appreciation and gratitude for all your help and support through this sad journey. You will never know how much this has meant to us. Bob knew his friends and family were genuine and could be relied on and you have shown that and more. He was proud of all of you throughout his illness but not surprised. Thank you."

One by one the guests left but not before giving me, Daniel and Lisa hugs, reminding us we need only call. Tears flowed as friends and family hugged, offering words of comfort and strength. Everyone expressed deep shock at how quickly Bob had deteriorated and offered their help. I need only pick up the telephone at any time, night or day if I felt like talking to someone. I already knew that but I appreciated the offer.

The hired staff cleared everything away with Beth and some of the others helping to put everything in its proper place. No one wanted me to stay by myself that night, but I had been surrounded by so many wonderful friends and family over the past months, I felt I needed to be by myself.

I still hadn't grasped that Bob was gone. I knew he had died, we had the funeral and he was nowhere to be seen, but it still hadn't sunk in. Our marriage had been a happy one and we were inseparable, except for work schedules and other commitments. I could not envision my life without him by my side. Daniel and Lisa insisted they stay with me, at least for this night but I encouraged them to go home. Bob and I adored our children and were proud of them but we agreed adult children needed to live their own lives, just as we had been allowed to do and we tried not to interfere. I knew they would be there for me but no one could ever fill the void left by Bob's death. I didn't think I could come to terms with all that had happened over the past months, his illness and subsequent death and his revelation, as long as I had a lot of company trying to keep my mind occupied. I needed to get my mind around this whole situation and I couldn't do that if I was always being distracted. Beth invited me to stay at her house for the night but again I declined. Beth and the children could see I was adamant; they didn't want to get me any more upset so they reluctantly agreed to go home. "I will call you, if I need you." None of them lived that far away from me and could be here in short order.

After everyone, including my children and Beth left I closed, and locked the big heavy oak door and turned out the porch light. Leaving the hall light on, I walked towards the large kitchen that had been renovated several years ago. Light oak custom-built cupboards covered almost three quarters of the walls. A bay window reached from the back of the sink to the ceiling with an overhead light shining on the plants sitting on the ledge.

Delicate light green marble countertops sat atop the bottom oak cupboards, enhancing the beauty of the oak. An island in the center of the kitchen matched the cupboards and countertop. Stainless steel appliances gleamed, as did the matching vent above the stovetop. Recessed lighting in the ceiling brightened the kitchen, especially on a sunny day. Gray ceramic tiles with a marble effect covered the floor. I remembered the discussions Bob and I had about the renovation. While there were a few little tiffs, we pretty much agreed on the final outcome. I loved my kitchen, and Bob's mission in life was to make me happy.

One opening from the kitchen led into the hall, another into the dining room, across the hallway from the family room. Manicured lawns and landscaped gardens were visible from the wall-to-wall windows. This room was large. No problem fitting in a large china cabinet, a matching oversized corner cabinet and server in the room. Light oak was also the choice for the dining room suite. It blended in with the kitchen cabinets, easily seen from the dining room. I loved fine china and figurines. Several Scottish bone china tea sets, which were gifts to me over the years, were proudly displayed in the china cabinet. Collecting odd china cups and saucers was also my passion. I had accumulated an enviable assortment over the years. When I first arrived in Canada, I was surprised at the amount of odd cups and saucers used at various functions. I thought Canadians must have been very careless, breaking several tea sets, leaving only the odd piece.

Little did I know at that time, they were purchased that way. I loved the idea. Sixteen six-piece place settings of my best china dinnerware were also in that cabinet, along with crystal glasses and assorted dishes. Another passion of mine was Royal Doulton figurines. As with the china, I had collected many figurines over the years. Bob was good at surprising me with a new one for some occasion or other but it didn't always have to be a special occasion. Sometimes he bought them "just because".

Other collectibles were placed in that cabinet too, such as our children's home made gifts. These were my most precious collectibles of all. Swarovski figures sat in a small matching cabinet on the wall. The lights bouncing off each piece gave the impression of a cabinet full of diamonds.

Expensive wallpaper covered the top half of the walls in the dining room, in a beautiful floral pattern with shades of green, pink, red and even blue and gold on a beige background. A corresponding border ran the length of the room, halfway down the walls, with a light green chair rail below the border. Beneath the chair rail, green paneling covered the walls. Pale green baseboards were installed around the edges of the highly polished light hardwood floors. On one wall hung a magnificent large antique mirror. A picture of a lady sitting on a chair, much like one of my Doulton figurines, hung on the other wall. It was a classy but cozy and inviting room.

Beth left some coffee in the pot. I poured myself a cup, moved into the family room and sat down in Bob's special chair covered with soft beige leather.

Although a little worn, he would never hear of getting rid of it, or even recovering it. Looking at it was relaxing and I felt so much closer to him sitting in that chair, almost feeling his big strong arms around me, reminding me of the strength and support he had given me throughout our life together.

As I looked around the fairly large comfortable room, my eyes rested on a beautiful photograph above the fireplace. It was taken on our 25th wedding anniversary some 10 years ago. Bob's face beamed with pride as he stood at the back with Daniel, our son, beside him. My face glistened, a lovely smile showing my pride. I sat in front of them with our daughter Lisa seated beside me. On this special occasion we were supposed to be going out for a family dinner. At the last minute we decided to dress up when Daniel and Lisa told us they were taking us to the club instead, suggesting tuxedos for the men. We knew we wouldn't look out of place because functions were held there every night in one of the many rooms in the private club. Bob wanted to wear a dark suit but Daniel insisted on the tuxedo because none of us got dressed up often. We agreed it would be a nice change on this special occasion. Besides, the children seemed anxious for us to go for it. We were thrilled that they wanted to do this for us. Sitting here now, I was thankful that we gave in to them. Otherwise I might not have this wonderful photograph to remind me of happier times. I could see a lot of Bob in Daniel with his dark hair and magnetic blue eyes. They were both handsome. In the picture I wore a plain but elegant black dress and a matching jacket with a sequinned fuchsia collar. My hair was drawn up in a French roll with soft curls at the front. Bob had given me a beautiful silver diamond pendant and earrings for our anniversary. I wore them that night. Even Lisa dressed for the occasion. She much preferred to dress casually. Seeing her all dressed up was a gift in itself. Her dark hair, also swept upward for this occasion, offset her beautiful smile. On her slim figure she wore an elegant sheer white blouse with frills down the front and a long slim line black skirt. I beamed when I saw how elegant and beautiful she looked. All of this splendour was captured in the photograph and as I gazed on it, I thought that if someone had told me that night what the future held, I would never have believed it.

Tears came ever so easily these days. Now as I looked at the happy family in that picture remembering our total surprise, tears dropped down my cheeks. Instead of the family dinner we were supposed to be having, the club was filled with about 100 of our friends, family members and business associates. We were thrilled and delighted that the children had planned this all by themselves, with quite a bit of help from Beth. We didn't suspect a thing.

What a wonderful night it was, one of many that we shared during our life together. Oh how I wished I could turn back the clock. I knew that wouldn't be happening but I could wish. I dabbed my eyes as I continued to glance around this room that reminded me so much of Bob. Books were such an important part of his life. Shelves were filled with a large and impressive collection. Whenever he got the time to relax, which wasn't as often as he would have liked, he was happy to sit with a book while the rest of us did our thing. Being a successful lawyer kept him busier than he might have wanted to be at times but we made good use of whatever free time we managed to get. I couldn't complain.

We loved this house and were happy raising our family here. It was elegant, tastefully furnished yet homey, a place where friends and family felt our warmth, comfort and love. A large burgundy rug in the center of the room surrounded by hardwood flooring, brought out the warmth of the room and friends always felt relaxed. The oversized bay windows on each side of the enormous stone fireplace overlooked the ravine. When the garden was in bloom, the view was gorgeous. Even in wintertime, the scene from the window was breathtaking, looking more like a Christmas card, while we sat warm and cozy inside the house with the fire glowing. Dusty rose drapes hung by the windows. Rich oak paneling covered the lower walls. Above the paneling, the walls were painted a delicate shade of pink, almost off white. Expensive but welcoming furniture filled the room. It was inviting and comfortable, not too stuffy, giving the appearance of being gently used. An oversized, overstuffed green chesterfield with two wing back chairs coloured to compliment the couch, sat lazily on the floor. An oak coffee table, with marble inserts, sat in front of the chesterfield. Matching side tables were placed near the wing chairs. Large padded leather footstools were placed around the fireplace, mainly used for sitting on.

I could almost hear the happy sounds of the children singing as I thumped out some old Scottish songs on the piano. So many happy hours were spent in this room. If Bob was reading, I sat quietly thumbing through magazines while the children played games or completed puzzles. We enjoyed just being together as a family. These were wonderful memories that would get me through this difficult time.

We had redecorated this room many times over the years. It was a room that invited you in, and begged you to stay a while. Walls were filled with many family pictures and some artwork that the children had done at school, which I had framed. Yes, this was a family room in the truest sense of the word.

I finished my coffee, took the cup into the kitchen and ran some tap water into it. I turned off the lights on the main floor and clicked on the upstairs lights. I wondered if I would be able to sleep in our room tonight. I wanted to feel close to Bob. How would I make it through the night without him? I was alone while he was in the hospital, but I knew he was just away for a bit. This was different. I knew he wasn't coming home. I was now alone. When he died, I stayed over at Beth's, at everyone's insistence. I was too distraught to argue.

I gave myself a little shake and said, "C'mon, you have to start somewhere, you can do this." We had four bedrooms upstairs. I had a choice. I stopped at the master bedroom, hesitated for a few moments then slowly turned the handle. I reached inside to the switch on the wall. The light came on and I gasped at the silence and emptiness of the room. I didn't feel so brave now. Maybe I should have heeded the children and Beth when they suggested I stay with them. At least I should have asked one of them to stay with me. It was tempting and only a telephone call away but I knew I had to do this. If I didn't sleep here alone tonight, then when would I? Putting it off would only make it more difficult if and when I felt I was more ready. No, I had to do this. I decided to sleep on Bob's side of the bed, hoping it would make me feel closer to him.

I threw off my shoes and lay down on the bed. The tears wouldn't stop. I wept uncontrollably. Bob's presence was sorely missed. I was so alone. There was never a time when he was not with me, except when either of us was in the hospital. Even with his busy practice, we always strived to spend our nights together.

When the diagnosis was first given and I was alone, I broke down. Most of the time after that though, I put on a brave front. The strain of it all was now coming to a head. I was a softie at the best of times and could cry at the drop of a hat but during the past months, I knew I had to be strong for Bob's sake. I have always been a woman with a positive and strong personality but I even surprised myself when coping with Bob's illness and subsequent confession.

I was angry that he had left me. How could he do that just when we were going to have more time together, now that the children were more or less established on their own and he could cut back on his workload. I pounded the pillow then quickly scolded myself, knowing that he had no choice. If there were anything he could have done to give us more time, he wouldn't have hesitated for a minute. It was out of our hands, it wasn't to be and I felt guilty thinking the way I did. I was being selfish. We had a wonderful life together, perhaps more so than a lot of other couples that we knew, and I didn't want to see him suffer any more than he already had.

Sleeping on Bob's side of the bed was the right decision. I imagined his big strong arms around me, snuggling up as always. It helped to keep me from feeling alone. We almost always fell asleep in each other's arms. I visualized him coming out of the en-suite after a shower. I even thought I heard the water running. It's amazing how your imagination works. I wanted it to be true, I knew it wasn't but there was nothing to stop me from dreaming and hoping. He should be here with me. I let my often vivid imagination work overtime just to get me through this night but I knew that wouldn't last forever. For now I would use anything to keep me going. I could not imagine my life without him. The loneliness I felt tore at my heart. He was only gone a few days. How could I endure without him? I needed his strength, and his arms. I needed the love we shared. I convinced myself that in some way, somehow, he would be there to give me the strength to get through it.

We had been married for 35 years. Ours was as happy a marriage as any that I knew of, in fact happier than most. We were best friends and confidantes, always had each other's best interests at heart. Fiery, physical love were not words that would describe our marriage but the genuine love we felt for each other more than compensated for it. We had so much in common, it was uncanny. He was such a considerate, caring person who always put me first in his life and I would have done anything for him. There were no secrets between us; at least that's what I thought until near the end of his life when he dropped a bombshell on me. In my wildest imagination, I never expected that. I had also kept something from him but convinced myself it didn't matter. It hadn't hurt our marriage. My love for Ian was in a time past before we met. Under different circumstances, that secret might have been worrisome, but Ian and I broke off long before I met Bob and since he didn't know about it, how could it hurt? Some things are better left unsaid I thought.

I didn't get much sleep that night, tossing and turning into the wee hours, but not because I was afraid of being alone. Thoughts of all that happened lately kept flashing through my mind until I finally drifted off to sleep only to awaken a few minutes later realizing how alone I was. Finally, at about 4:00 a.m., I fell into a deep sleep.

II

I awakened early in the morning but stayed in bed for a while going over everything in my mind, thinking about what had been and what might have been. Did I want to get up to face another day? I didn't, but I had to. I forced myself to get out of bed after about a half hour of contemplating.

Beth telephoned to invite me over for breakfast, which I was more than happy to accept, telling her that I had to shower and dress first. Having my best friend's house so close to my own was great. We shared so much over the years. Beth and I were best friends so too were our husbands and children. Also, although our houses were close to each other we each respected each other's privacy. We were not the types to be in and out of each other's homes for "coffee and gossip". We had our time together, if it was through shopping or partying, and were there for each other but we still had our own "space".

I put on a pair of gray pinstripe slacks and a black long sleeved blouse, brushed my hair, added a bit of make up and headed over to Beth's. Her house was not unlike ours, both being built around the same time. Each house on the street was built on a good-sized lot. Everyone kept their lawns manicured and gardens were spectacular. Most of my neighbours had gardeners and those who didn't, had the gift of gardening. We were happy here. All of the neighbours got along with each other but it wasn't a street where we were in and out of each other's houses all the time.

Beth was still in her yellow terry cloth housecoat when I arrived. If I hadn't been going out I probably would have stayed in mine. As soon as I saw her at the door I started to cry. Where did my strength go? I thought I was doing quite well. Seeing a familiar face, someone or something that brought Bob right to the forefront, jolted everything back again. Beth cried right along with me as we hugged each other. Over coffee, I told Beth that I needed to get away for a bit by myself.

"Where will you go and why alone?"

"I feel so overwhelmed by all that has happened in such a short time, and by the amount of love and support shown to me. I need to be alone with my own thoughts, to try to get some focus on where I go from here."

Although we had shared many confidences, I couldn't bring myself to tell her about the secret Bob had divulged to me before he died. I felt guilty about that but I couldn't tell her, not now, maybe never.

Beth understood my need to get away but said,

"I know what you are saying, but going alone might not be the answer. You know Daniel and Lisa will never hear of it. Are you thinking of going to the cottage?"

The cottage held many happy memories of times spent with family and friends, but I couldn't bring myself to venture up there, not yet anyway.

"Maybe one day when I am more settled, I might take a trip up there with you or the children. No, I am seriously thinking of going on that cruise we booked before Bob got ill. It's a trip we always wanted to take and it's paid for. I would be alone, yet not by myself."

Beth gasped in shock. To think that I would go so far away from home at a time like this. Didn't I realize that I would need the comforting and understanding that only family and friends could give me? She tried to reason with me but if there was one thing most people knew about me, it was that when my mind was made up, that was it, barring unforeseen circumstances and valid arguments.

I had never travelled alone, except when I moved to Canada. Even then I had a friend to travel with. Now that Bob was gone, if I wanted to do any travelling it would have to be on my own. I would have to get used to the idea.

"I can't wait to hear what the children have to say," Beth added.

We sat chatting at Beth's oversized butcher-block kitchen table. Soon it was time for me to go home. I promised to let her know what the children's reaction was, although she knew all too well what it would be, and so did I.

The cruise I was referring to was to Scandinavian countries leaving from and returning to Dover. Bob and I had hoped to take two extra weeks at the end of the trip to travel to Scotland to visit with relatives and friends. We had gone on many cruises before and visited more countries than most of our friends. We loved cruising. It gave us a chance to see more countries on a relatively short holiday. We didn't see all of what the countries had to offer but we got a sampling. If we were tempted to see more, we could always go back for a land tour. Another plus for cruising as far as we were concerned, was the fact we could do all this travelling and come back to the same "hotel" at night. We didn't have to keep packing and unpacking. The major complaint among our friends who went on road trips either by car or bus was the packing and unpacking. Like it or not most bus tours also require travellers to get up early in the morning.

We never managed to get the Scandinavian cruise we wanted. It was either not the right time, the ports of call were not what we wanted, or it was never in and out of the U.K. When this perfect itinerary came up we booked it immediately. With all that had gone on in the past few months, cancelling the trip was the last thing on our minds. Now I had decided I would go on the trip alone. What better way to get away from it all, be alone and yet have people around me? I felt it was meant to be.

Daniel had invited me out for supper that night. Lisa was meeting us at the restaurant. I was happy to accept because I was in no mood to cook for myself. Eating without Bob just wasn't the same, although there were times when he couldn't be at home for mealtimes. On those occasions I kept dinner warm and we still had our little chats at the table while he ate.

During the day I busied myself with telephone calls notifying insurance companies and other businesses about my trip. I made an appointment with our lawyer to go over Bob's affairs. I also had to face the challenge of going through Bob's things and I definitely was not looking forward to that. Clearing cupboards and drawers that Bob used was going to be difficult for me. I felt it would make me feel as though I was throwing him away, but I knew it would have to be done and the sooner the better. Otherwise I wasn't sure I would get back to it.

Daniel picked me up as planned, and off we went to a nice local waterfront restaurant. I was blessed to have these two children with me, especially now. We were always proud of them. They were good children who had grown into loving, caring and considerate adults. Bob and

I had dined in this restaurant many times. It was situated at the end of the pier, right at the edge of the waterfront. The decor was nautical, with wood, ropes, life rings, portholes and all things relating to ships. We always sat at a table at one of the windows where we could watch the various types of boats sail past as we enjoyed a leisurely meal.

Lisa was already seated. She got up to kiss me. During the course of dinner, I told the children of my plans. As expected, their reaction was the same as Beth's, gasping in shock. They were convinced I had taken leave of my senses to even think of it.

"This is not a good idea mom," Daniel said.

"I agree," echoed Lisa.

"Why don't you take Aunt Beth with you? You have two tickets."

"I thought about that but it would defeat my purpose. I need to get away, be on my own, yet not by myself, away from family and friends. This cruise is perfect, I would have people around me but I would be able to choose if and when I wanted company. It's the perfect solution."

"What did Aunt Beth think of your idea?" asked Lisa.

"Much the same as yourselves."

Everyone knew that when I made up my mind, I wasn't easily persuaded. The best they could hope for was that I would change my mind the closer it got to the time of departure.

III

The cruise was still weeks away. In the meantime, I had things to take care of. Family was always first in Bob's heart and being a lawyer, meant that all legal and personal matters were put in order long before his untimely death. Even so, there was still a lot I had to attend to. I met with our lawyer, filing will for probate, and notified insurances as well as other organizations that Bob was a member of. When I saw how much work was involved in settling an estate, I was thankful that Bob had done so much preparatory work. It took a great burden off my shoulders. How do people manage in cases where there's no will or power of attorney?

Going through Bob's clothes and personal belongings also had to be done, but I was not looking forward to that at all. Daniel, Lisa, Beth and other close friends had offered to help but I wanted to, I needed to do this myself. I had to face reality, however much it hurt that Bob was gone. Packing the clothes myself would force me to realize he was not going to phone me to tell me he would be late for supper, come through the door, out of the shower, or even shout upstairs to say the coffee pot was on. As much as it would be upsetting to me and I didn't relish the idea, I knew I had to do it. It was too personal.

Daniel and Lisa helped by dropping boxes off at the house as I needed them and picked them up again for drop off at whatever charity I decided on. Doing that was a huge help. I knew I wouldn't be able to leave his personal things at drop boxes or even inside the charity shops because I would feel I was abandoning him. Bob and I both felt like that when we disposed of his parents' clothes. It is a solemn and heartbreaking feeling.

Daniel and Lisa stopped by the house every day and telephoned every night. Beth had me over for supper and encouraged me to go downtown for lunch to look around the stores. Other friends and relatives kept in touch, making sure everything was okay and I was alright. I had many invitations for outings and meals. Sometimes I met the children for lunch or supper. It helped because I was not ready to start cooking for myself in that big house. Would I ever get back to cooking? A friend who had lost her partner told me that she never turned down an invitation to eat out or away from home. "If you decline, you don't get asked again." That happened to her. Family and friends slowly drifted away and she felt so alone.

I started in the master bedroom. Bob was an impeccable dresser. Everything he wore was in mint condition; shoes, socks, suits, shirts, and underwear, even his handkerchiefs looked as though they had just come out of a box. Bob kept all of his clothes in immaculate condition. Whenever he bought new items, he packed those he was replacing to donate to charity. I had no difficulty in deciding what he would want me to do with his clothes. The Salvation Army was his favourite charity. Some of his clothes could probably have fit Daniel, my father, brother, or even Beth's husband, but I couldn't bear the thought of ever seeing someone close to us wearing them. Was I being a little selfish for not sharing with family and friends? None of them needed anything and they could well afford to buy whatever they wanted. Bob would have understood.

Every jacket I neatly folded had some memory attached to it and every time it brought tears to my eyes. This is the main reason I wanted to do this myself. I needed to be by myself to cry, to grieve and in a way, this was helping me. His tuxedo, which he didn't wear often, immediately took me to the night of our 25th anniversary. He had worn the tux on other occasions after that but the anniversary was such a wonderful surprise, an evening filled with family and friends, that the tux would forever be part of that night. He was meticulous about everything. His closet and dressers were no different. He had special drawers installed in his cupboard. The top third had shoetrees installed in rows. They were secured to the cupboard, leaving the shoes standing in pairs. It resembled a shoe display in an upscale store, especially since they looked brand new, without a mark on them. Before he put the shoes he had worn that day into the cupboard they were polished and neatly put in order. Below the shoes, other drawers were installed and those were sectioned off in little boxes that contained his neatly rolled up ties and socks. His underwear was in the bottom part of this cupboard and everything else, was rolled up in pairs. He had several hooks on the inside of the door where he hung his belts and ties.

I checked every pocket before packing it for charity but I didn’t expect to find anything. He always put any change he had into a little dish on top of the dresser. One of the most difficult tasks was going through his wallet. He had a little cash, credit cards, membership cards, pictures of the children and a picture of our wedding. A piece of paper about the size of a business card fell out of his wallet onto the floor. I picked it up and noticed a scripture written on it. It read, "And God shall wipe away all tears from their eyes; and there shall be no more death, neither sorrow, nor crying, neither shall there be any more pain for the former things are passed away." Rev..21 v.4. I had never seen it before but Bob, being a Christian, would have been strengthened and comforted by that. I had no way of knowing how long it had been in his wallet, but I now knew the reason it was there.

I broke down sobbing. It wasn't so very long ago that he was in this room with me and now as I cleared out his clothes, it tore at my heart. I stopped so often just to wipe the tears from my eyes. This was all part of the grieving process. I had to expect this. I was only at the beginning of this terrible journey without my much-loved husband and partner in life.

Bob wasn't one for jewelry but had a couple of expensive watches. I knew he would want Daniel to have them. His wedding band was the same as mine, a wide filigree gold band with little flowers intricately engraved into it. We had our initials inscribed inside, as well as the date of the wedding. I phoned Lisa to tell her I wanted her to have her dad's wedding band but she was reluctant, saying I should keep it, at least for now, but I had my own ring. I knew Bob would have wanted his little girl to have it. Naturally the ring was too large for her small fingers but she didn't want to change it in any way by sizing it to fit.

I suggested that she wear it on a gold chain around her neck. I told her I would buy a nice one to set off the ring. She thought that was a great idea. I took a break, went downstairs and made a coffee. This big empty house was so lonely. There had been so much happiness and laughter here throughout the years. I sat at the dining room table, looking at the Doultons. Like everything else, everyone had a memory. Most of the memories were of happier occasions but there were a few sad ones too, all part of life. We were truly blessed that we had so many wonderful times with our family and friends. I finished my coffee and walked back upstairs. I knew I had to get this done, fearing that if I left it I might not get back to it.

At one point I sat on the bed sobbing. I missed Bob so much. He was everywhere, in everything I saw or touched. I was strong and held up well but it had been such an emotionally draining time. I wondered if I would ever get rid of the puffy eyes. I had no colour in my face either, but that could be helped with a touch of rouge. Clearing out his things was difficult but it had to be done, and I wanted to be the one to do it. As I continued to empty the closet and dresser drawers, I talked to Bob as though he was sitting on the bed. I wasn't losing my mind, I knew he wasn't there, but somehow it helped me get through it. I held his clothes close to my body, trying to get even a sniff of him before I packed the boxes, losing another connection to him that I so desperately needed to get me through this terrible sense of loss.

For this reason, I felt a deep need to keep some of his clothing for myself. I had to do this. I couldn't completely lose all of him. I chose his beige slacks, brown sports jacket, a pair of loafers, a sweater, a shirt, and a few pairs of socks and underwear. I felt that in some way this would keep him closer to me. Some might think that is crazy but I needed the clothing for me. I could sense his presence with every piece of clothing I packed, with every sniff of his cologne, after-shave, deodorant and even the smell of his leather belts. I wasn't delusional, he was gone but if this was how I was going to get through this, then so be it.

Other than the personal items given to Daniel and Lisa, mementos would be shared by Bob's brother Bill, sister Jenny, Beth and her husband Joe as reminders of Bob. Not that they needed anything to help them with that.

Days flew into weeks. I was kept so busy that I hardly remembered the cruise departure date was coming up fast.

All of my affairs had been taken care of including Bob's wishes and the distribution of his clothes. Beth called or came over every day, as did the children. Whenever the subject of the cruise came up, they tried to talk me out of it but I was as determined to go as they were to stop me. I asked them to try to understand that this was what I needed. It might not be for someone else in the same position but it was right for me. At least I thought it was the right thing for me. The thought of going to the cottage alone was not in the least tempting. I could not have gone there on my own and I didn't want anyone I was close around me.

The cruise was the way to go.

IV

Beth and I went shopping for some cruise wear, although I didn't need any new clothes. She thought the change might give me a much-needed lift.

Finally, the day arrived for the flight to London. I was as ready as I ever would be, but my nervousness was clearly seen in my every move. I was shaking slightly, tears fell easily and I appeared a little confused at times. I wasn't so confident now but I couldn't let my family know of any fears I might have. What was I thinking? Bob and I had always been a twosome. To go on this cruise without him, suddenly seemed scary, but I couldn't and wouldn't back down now. I had to do this, to get away from everyone. Exhaustion was etched on my face. I needed rest and I needed to unwind, to relax and ponder what I might do when I got back home again.

Last minute instructions, including checking the mail, making sure the gardener attended to the yard and taking care of the flowers was given to Beth because she lived so close. The children would also drop by to check the house.

Everything was under control. Knowing that everything would be looked after while I was away gave me the luxury of being able to go off on the cruise with little or no worries. While they were happy to help out, they still had doubts about my sanity. They put on a happy face although knew how they felt deep down. I couldn't blame them.

Daniel and Lisa arrived a little early to take me to the airport, knowing what a stickler I am for promptness. I hated line-ups and would rather go earlier and sit people watching until boarding time. As I locked the front door my heart was pounding leaving without Bob. I looked out at the house from the car, tears falling down my cheeks. Flashbacks of the day we finally moved into our new home ran through my head. Lisa gave me a hug and held me tight. What was I thinking? Could I do this without Bob? How would I feel when I come back to this still empty house? I had doubts but I was determined. I needed this time to myself and I had to start somewhere. The fact that the trip was booked before Bob died was a sign to me that this was what I should do.

Before we got on the highway to go to the airport, Daniel pulled the car into Beth's driveway. She and Joe were at the door. I got out of the car as they met me in the driveway. Again hugs, kisses and lots of tears were exchanged. Although they, like everyone else, weren't convinced I was doing the right thing, they wished me a safe journey. Beth said that I looked tired and weary and had to agree that I needed complete rest away from everything and everyone.

"When you come back, I want to see the old glow on your face. Nothing less will do."

I got back in the car, and waved as we backed out of the driveway. We were finally on our way.

It was an emotional time for all of us. Daniel dropped us off at the departure door as he proceeded to the parking lot. He would catch up with us at the check in counter. Once we were inside the airport Lisa got a trolley, loaded the luggage and we went in the direction of the airline counter. It was extremely busy with many long line-ups. Because I had upgraded, I went directly to the pre-boarding counter where I was immediately taken care of. My luggage was put on the conveyor belt, my passport and ticket were checked, the clerk wished me a pleasant trip then it was off to do whatever we wanted until departure was announced.

At this point Daniel caught up to us and suggested we go for a coffee but I wanted to get through security and get settled in on the other side of it. I wasn't so sure of myself now. I couldn't stop the tears. I knew if I prolonged the goodbye it would only make me worse. I thought it would be better all around if we made the parting sooner rather than later, although I knew it would be difficult no matter when or how it took place. Daniel and Lisa must have felt the same way because they didn't give me the usual arguments when they disagreed. It was obvious I was getting more upset. What am I doing? What am I thinking? Maybe the children were right but it was too late to turn back now. I had never felt so alone as I did at that moment. So much so that I actually thought I might not go through with this trip. I was feeling faint but I had to put on a front. One last tight group hug and I headed for security. I didn't think I was going to make it, as my knees were getting weaker. I couldn't let them see me faint. At that moment the security alarm went off. It was the distraction I needed to take the attention off myself, Daniel and Lisa. Apparently the passenger in front of me had some type of metal object on his clothing that eventually checked out okay. It was perfect timing.

As usual, the duty free shops were full of travellers hoping to purchase alcohol, cigarettes, perfume, jewelry, watches, clothing, and other miscellaneous items. I was never impressed with the prices offered in the duty free. I could get most of the same items at lower prices when they were on sale in the downtown stores. Obviously everyone didn't think like me because business was brisk, but I always enjoyed looking around the shops. It helped to pass some of the waiting time. The displays were set up in such a manner that it was hard to resist. Ladies testing the perfumes sent off overpowering aromas before you even set foot through the door. Cruise ships had well-stocked duty free shops and I found their prices more reasonable.

After browsing I went into the first class lounge to have a coffee and a scone. I wasn't hungry but I needed something to settle my queasy stomach. The noise coming from business people using their computers, telephones or talking amongst themselves filled the room. I picked up a magazine and a newspaper to keep my mind occupied for a while. I busied myself reading, not always taking it in, but looking at the pictures anyway. I did the odd bit of people watching and guessing too, imagining where travellers were going, what the reason was for their trip and what their occupations might be.

I didn't have to wait too long before the announcement came over the p.a. system advising that my flight was pre boarding anyone with children or those who needed assistance. As a first class passenger I was allowed to board at any time. Since Bob's seat was paid for and I had cancellation insurance, they were kind enough to upgrade me. All the first class passengers, myself included were settled nicely in our seats before the rest of the passengers boarded. Immediately the stewardess came around to make sure we were comfortable, took our coats and asked if there was anything we wanted to put in the overhead bins. Also, a choice of cold drinks was offered.

The captain announced we were ready for takeoff. The cabin crew went through the plane making sure everyone was safely fastened in. Everything checked and we were off. At that moment I could not stop the tears as I watched the plane roll down the runway, turn around and take off. Flying away from my city and all that I held dear was too much. I have never experienced such loneliness and sadness except perhaps when I left Glasgow to seek a new life in Canada. I kept my eyes fixed on the window, not looking beyond it to the outside. My reflection in that window was all that I saw. It wasn't a pretty sight.

I could hear the clicking of the buckles as passengers unfastened their seat belts as soon as the warning light went off. Unless I had to get up from my seat, I normally left my belt fastened. A gentleman sitting beside me introduced himself and I responded by saying "hello." After that he wasn't too talkative. As soon as he could, the man opened his computer and was glued to it for most of the flight. He was probably a businessman on his way to some meeting in London. I wasn't unhappy about that because I wasn't in a talkative mood either. We exchanged a few more pleasantries, where our hometown was, where we were going and why. I found it difficult to talk to people without getting emotional. The stewardesses came around with magazines, cool drinks or coffee, doing their best to settle us in for the six or seven hour flight. I was glad I had upgraded because it was much more comfortable and slightly more private. The stewardesses were ever so attentive, fulfilling our every need.

Shortly into the flight, a meal tray was offered. I wasn't the least bit hungry but I managed to eat a little bit of the chicken and vegetables. I was never one to pass up dessert. I ate the little dish of mousse and finished with coffee, biscuits and cheese. A stewardess cleared everything away and shortly after, the screen came down for a movie. Although I had my eyes fixed on the screen, I couldn't recall what the movie was about. All kinds of thoughts danced around in my head. I dozed off several times during the trip, but not for long. It hardly seemed as though any time had passed before the stewardess started putting the lights on and lifting the blinds. Judging from the aroma, breakfast was on its way. I knew we were almost in London. Unbuckling my belt, I excused myself and got out of my seat. There was no lineup at the washroom. I washed my face and hands, put on a little makeup and felt a bit more refreshed. Afterwards the captain announced that we were about one hour out of Heathrow.

When I returned to my seat, the stewardess offered me a breakfast tray. I drank the orange juice and ate the muffin and thoroughly enjoyed the coffee. This was definitely an improvement. I hadn't been eating too well lately. My lack of appetite was unusual for me. All of my life I had to watch what I ate because I had a tendency to gain weight. I was continually on and off one diet or another. Now here I was, losing weight when I wasn't trying to but I knew it wouldn't last.

The plane landed safely at the Heathrow Airport at 12.05 p.m. Once I got through customs with my luggage. I was met by a representative of the cruise line. A couple of other passengers on the plane were also going on the cruise. We were guided to a mini bus that would take us to Dover. The journey to Dover was much longer than I expected it to be, thinking Dover was just outside of London. Most of the passengers, including myself, were still a little tired after the flight and kept having little catnaps. In between snoozes, I enjoyed looking at the countryside as we drove along the highway.

V

The ship was due to sail at 7:00 p.m. When the bus arrived dockside, we were directed to the security area where everything was checked out. Windows covered the outside walls throughout this large area, making it bright and welcoming. We took the escalator to the second floor, which led us onto the gangplank once we had our tickets and passport cleared. Everything was extremely well organized and efficient.

Sailing was not scheduled for another couple of hours, leaving enough time for passengers to get settled in. Guests were arriving continuously, having come from many destinations by different modes of transport. Boarding was smooth and hassle free for all of us.

Cabin staff assigned to passengers escorted them to their decks and cabins. Some went up in the elevator, some down, some had long walks along the fully carpeted decks, and others were closer to the elevator. The walls were covered with a lightly coloured laminate type paneling. When I arrived at my cabin, stewards and maids assigned to servicing the cabins in that area were lined up, smiling and ready for any request that a passenger might have. Luggage would be delivered to the cabins some time during the remainder of the day and even into the night. Most of us knew that and were advised to bring a little overnighter with us, so that we would have toiletries and p.j's for the first night. Casual dress was always allowed for the first night. A change of clothing wasn't necessary.

Compared to some other ships Bob and I had sailed on, this cabin with an outside view through a window rather than a porthole was spacious and luxurious. We had sailed on this ship before so I knew what to expect and wasn't disappointed. Two sofas, one on each side of the cabin, were turned down in the evening into a Queen-sized bed. If a single person occupied the cabin, they had the choice of a single bed, leaving the other sofa as it was.

Most cabins could accommodate from one to four guests. Unfortunately, on this trip the Queen bed wouldn't be needed. I could have requested the Queen anyway but the single was comfortable enough, and I still had the couch to sit on until I went to bed.

Window drapes and couch covers were pale green and pink with a wispy leafy pattern on the fabric, giving the cabin a warm, bright and roomy feel to it. Cabin walls were also in an off white laminate type material. Two colour-coordinated chairs, one positioned under a vanity and the other near a couch were also inside the room. A television set sat on top of the vanity. Normally at sea, there isn't much of a choice on TV. Variety shows from the evening before and some of the other activities were broadcast over it the next day. News from around the world was a regular feature and the Cruise Director always had some instructions on the itinerary. A small refrigerator sat under part of the vanity counter. It didn't contain snacks and drinks normally put in a hotel room fridge. It was more for the convenience of the passengers who might want to keep something cold, perhaps some specialty wine, cheese, chocolates or other food. Bathrooms are compact. A tub and shower, sink, vanity and a toilet were placed strategically to make the most of the available space.

Again making the most of the space, closets were adequate for the many changes required during a cruise. On this trip I would have double that amount, as I was sailing alone. Of all the cruises we had taken and of all the ships we had sailed on, this was definitely our favourite.

After checking everything out, I kicked off my shoes and lay down on the couch to read the shipboard newsletter outlining the activities for the rest of the day. My tired eyes kept closing. I shook my head a couple of times then gave in to a much-needed rest. Engines had been quietly purring but as the ship prepared to leave the dock the noise got louder, waking me up. I sat up with a start. Watching from an upper deck as the ship pulled away from the dockside, was a must when Bob and I travelled. Standing on deck watching other ships, large and small, sail smoothly in and out of the port was exciting. Not wanting to look too bedraggled, my face clearly showing the effects of the strain I had been under over the past year, I splashed some water on my face, smoothed some cream into my skin and added a dash of blush. It didn't give me the effect I had hoped for. Perhaps some fresh air might help. A light jacket would be fine for the short time I would be on deck.

Although I was born in Scotland where I lived until my late teens and had travelled throughout England many times, I had never seen the White Cliffs of Dover. Seeing them was a treat. Bob and I had wanted to go on this cruise for some time. Little pangs of guilt filled me knowing how much we both wanted to take this trip, but it wasn't to be. Perhaps I might have felt less guilty had I chosen to stay home but no matter, I made the decision. In my heart I knew he would approve. I felt his presence as I stood at the rails when the ship got underway. Several other passengers were also up on deck for the departure; always a drawing card on cruises, so I wasn't alone.

As we got underway, hovercrafts were arriving and taking off from the port. A slight breeze filled the air but it was still light enough to see everything. Most passengers stayed there until we were quite a bit out from shore. Dinnertime was fast approaching and gradually everyone left to get ready for our first meal on board.

I made my way back downstairs. Everyone was happy, friendly and excited about the trip. What to wear was not a decision I had to make on this casual night. My hair looked pretty good. The scarf I wore on deck had kept it from blowing all over the place. I took a quick shower, which refreshed me more than I expected. With my clothes back on, the usual "war paint" in place, a dab of perfume and I was good to go. Looking in the mirror, I still appeared withdrawn but maybe not so much.

Strolling along the deck before dinner, I could feel romance in the air all around me. No place like a cruise for romance. Many couples strolled arm in arm or arms around each other's waists. Light music could be heard coming over the p.a. system, colourful ship lights reflected on the water as daylight gave way to darkness, the big ship purring like a kitten as we sailed ever so quietly and calmly through the water. A teensy bit of jealousy crept into my thoughts as I passed other happy couples.

Finding the dining room wouldn't be a problem for me because I knew my way around this ship. Upon entering the dining room, I was met by a member of the staff who took me to my table after I handed him my number. Seating arrangements were arranged when I first boarded.

Sparkling crystal chandeliers hung all over this large dining room. Salmon coloured carpeting with coordinating flowers covered the floor. Window drapes were opened so that diners could enjoy the night scene as we sailed along. Once out to sea, the view was mostly of the ocean, although the sky reflecting on the water at night painted a pretty picture. Sometimes other ships passed, white waves rolled by and in some areas, little flying fish could be seen popping out of the water. Tables were set up in various styles and sizes; square, oblong, and round, seating four, six or eight passengers, with tables for eight being the most popular. When Bob and I travelled, we preferred a table for two but very few ships offered that now.

I was seated at a table for eight beside the window. When my tablemates arrived for dinner we introduced ourselves to each other. No one seemed to notice the empty chair beside me and I didn't volunteer any information. Everyone was excited and a little tired after their respective trips from different places. Noisy chatter from other diners sounded throughout the room. As soon as a passenger sat down at the table, busboys and waiters were right there to fill the water glasses. Wine stewards also arrived at the table after the passengers were seated. Service was excellent.

Dining on cruises is luxurious to say the least and tonight was no different. Food is sumptuous and far too much for anyone to eat, although most of us managed quite well, tasting everything. I usually opted for a salad or soup, a main course, which tonight was either tornadoes of beef tenderloin, grilled medallion in a red wine sauce with square baby carrots or croquette potatoes or rock Cornish hen forestiere, with natural pan gravy and ragout of mixed mushrooms, red beet puree and braised wild rice. Many fish and pasta dishes were also offered. I had beef tenderloin and would be happy if I got through it.

Dessert was always my weakness. Bob got a chuckle out of me when I asked him to order dessert as well for me, even though he was not a dessert person. That wasn't necessary because we could order as many desserts as we wanted. There was no limit but in my mind, it looked better if it at least appeared as though I only ordered one. Tonight I chose the hazelnut chocolate soufflé with Armagnac cream from a choice of orange sorbet, vanilla ice cream, strawberry ice cream, frozen Drambuie with coconut semifreddo, caramelized puff pastry pear tart, and assorted international cheese and crackers. I limited myself to one serving of the freshly baked rolls so that I would be able to finish all that I had ordered. Often diners filled up on the homemade bread or rolls, only to realize later that they hadn't left much room for the rest of their dinner. On the other hand, they always managed to find the space, even if they were totally stuffed. Everyone at my table was excited about the cruise. Most of the others ordered wine. I had the cold and refreshing water. Coffee was the finishing touch for me at the end of the meal.

Dinner over, it was time to leave the dining room. As I excused myself, I wished the others a pleasant evening. Tears filled my eyes as I moved towards the door. Oversized dishes of after dinner mints sat on the table. It was like a magnet to diners and especially me. I loved them and tried to be discreet as I scooped them up. Just as I did with dessert, I managed to convince Bob to take some for me too. In fact, he was so well trained that I didn't have to remind him.

Being the first night on board, most shows weren't extravaganzas. Tonight's offering was a Welcome Aboard Show, starting shortly after dinner in the International Lounge. Normally passengers were tired after their flights.

Many went back to their cabins to unpack, or get caught up on sleep to prepare themselves for the rest of the trip. I didn't feel much like going to see the show that night but I knew if I went to my cabin so early in the evening, I might fall asleep and then be up half the night.

A stroll along the deck, or perhaps a walk through the shops after my meal might suffice for the first night. Many of the first seating diners obviously had the same idea. It was a friendly atmosphere, everyone saying "hi" as they passed each other. Outside a slight breeze blew my hair around. Too many times I forgot to take a scarf with me when I went out on deck. Stars were visible, shining brightly as the big ship sailed ever so smoothly through the water, swishing little whitecaps along the side of the ship. Music coming from inside the ship could be heard everywhere on board. It was obvious love was in the air as many couples strolled along in each other's arms, heads on their partner's shoulders, breathing in the night air. I was a tad envious but I couldn't complain. I had experienced more love and happiness in my marriage than many people experience in a lifetime. Deck chairs were covered to keep them dry in the evening mist. I lifted a cover and sat down, going into a sort of trance. I let my mind travel at will, not taking in the activities around me.

Chilly winds blew across the deck and I was a little cold. Loneliness was getting a bit much. I got up, replaced the cover on the chair and went inside. The casino was on this deck. As I walked past it, Bob was very much on my mind, not that he was ever out of my mind. I didn't go in. Bob wasn't a gambler by any stretch of the imagination but on cruises he liked to play the slots, always limiting himself to $20.00 a night. When that was gone, he was done. Sometimes he won, other times he lost, but in the end he usually broke even. It was his form of entertainment. I got pleasure out of shopping while he played. Stores were always well stocked with exquisite merchandise such as jewelry, crystal, perfumes, and even souvenirs, all duty free. Business was always brisk. Bob bought me a trinket on every trip. I might buy one on this cruise for myself from him, but not tonight.

I felt the strain of everything that had happened over the last several months. Leaving family and friends behind, the travel from Canada to Dover alone only added to my already fragile emotional state. I wasn't totally convinced I was doing the right thing and yet, I had to do it alone. This was the perfect place. I wasn't alone but the people around didn't know me.

Before retiring to my cabin for the evening, I went up for a coffee in the 24 hour Lido Cafe/Pizzeria. Quite a few passengers were wandering about, inside and out. Some walked towards the casino, others going to the lounge show, others just sitting watching the activities or people watching.

The Lido was large and beautifully decorated. Colourful murals and tile accents covered the walls. Bamboo tables were set around the room. Gorgeous tropical flowers filled small vases resting on the glass tabletops. Four matching chairs with comfortable cushions sat under the tables. Lighting was softly dimmed but still bright enough to see everything clearly. Windows surrounded the entire outside wall area of this cafe, giving passengers an excellent view of the ocean as they sat at the tables. A swimming pool was located on this deck just outside of the cafe. A whirlpool and spa were next to the pool area. The Lido was convenient for coffee and/or lunch. Many passengers who couldn't sleep, didn't want to sleep, or were partying into the wee hours of the morning often ended their evening in the Lido. Although there were other passengers seated in the cafe, I managed to get a table beside the windows. I wasn't ready for company and hoped no one would sit beside me. Not being in a mood for conversation, I was just as happy to beat the crowd. As the shows ended, the cafe became much busier and the window tables were always the first to be filled. Pangs of loneliness and sadness, and missing the children and friends kept popping into my mind. Tears came ever so easily. It was difficult to hold them back. Watching the little whitecaps bobbing on the dark ocean as I finished my coffee helped me to relax a bit. With my coffee finished, I went over to the counter to get a refill to take back to the cabin.

Listening to the sounds of happy people dancing and singing coming from various lounges added to my loneliness. Walking past the lounge where the first show was coming to an end, I took a little peak inside the room. Roars of laughter and applause told me everyone was having a good time. As I came to the casino, I could hear the chinking of the slot machines. Music from the lounge enticed couples to dance. Tables in the lobby outside the casino and shops were filled with passengers completing jigsaw puzzles or playing cards while others sat and relaxed over a drink. Waiters were ever so attentive as they took orders from anyone wanting a drink.

Just as I had thought, my luggage had been delivered to my cabin, probably while I was at dinner. Sometimes it took longer for the luggage to arrive. I was happy that I could get unpacked and put my clothes away before going to bed. The maid had been into the cabin to prepare my bed for sleeping. A chocolate candy lay on my pillow, yet another reminder of Bob who wouldn't think of eating his chocolate, knowing I wanted it.

I spent the rest of the evening unpacking and hanging up my clothes. I turned on the TV to catch up on the news. Before popping into bed, I had a shower and fell asleep almost as soon as my head hit the pillow. I awoke during the night expecting to see Bob beside me or coming out of the shower. Would I ever get over the loneliness? I knew it was early and I should expect these feelings to go on for a long time. I would always have them but hopefully I would learn to live with them and carry on in the good old British tradition. Maybe my family was right when they suggested I travel with someone. Whenever I thought of Bob tears easily filled my eyes. I put his photograph on the dresser beside my bed. I glanced towards it and told him that I loved him. Since his death I found great comfort in talking to him in the photograph. His good looks still mesmerized me. I could never believe that he had sought me out, not with all the gorgeous women we both knew.

Spending the entire cruise weeping wasn't going to help anything, it would be such a waste. Being a fairly strong person, I made up my mind that I would pull myself together and at least try to enjoy the trip. When thoughts or memories of Bob came to me, that's when my strength was at its weakest. I said, “good night,” again and slowly drifted back to sleep. This time, I made it through to morning.

VI

I felt surprisingly rested when I awakened and was ready to face the day. I pulled back the drapes to catch the sun starting to peep through the sky. It was getting lighter and lighter, not yet at its brightest but I could tell it was going to be a gorgeous day. The water was calm as the ship sailed ever so gently and smoothly on her way. It always brought a sense of wonderment to me. Looking outside at the water swishing by, I noticed some adorable tiny flying fish popping in and out of the water. They appeared to be playing some kind of game with each other. I knew the basic principle of how ships stayed afloat but I found it difficult to take in how a giant heavy ship managed it. I felt the same way about airplanes. I knew the dynamics of how they stayed in the air but couldn't take it in. I just believed it.

I laid out a tracksuit to wear to breakfast before getting into the shower. After drying off, I dressed, brushed my hair and added a little lipstick. My hair was normally as straight as a poker, giving me too many bad hair days although I got many compliments on my thick head of hair. The perm in my hair made it a little easier to manage, but there were times when the sea air turned my hair to frizz. Having a perm meant I could put in a couple of rollers for a quick set if I was going out in the evening.

I locked the cabin door and walked upstairs to have breakfast in the Lido Cafe buffet. When Bob and I travelled, we always ate breakfast and lunch in the buffets or pizzerias rather than the dining room. It was casual and in this case, I could sit by myself if I wanted to. There were no designated tables in the Lido; passengers could sit wherever they chose. Dining room tables for breakfast and lunch were not designated either, but a waiter usually directed passengers to specific tables, making sure each table was filled before starting to fill another. This ensured different passengers sat beside each other every day which was a good idea, but not if you didn't feel like talking. I wasn't hungry nor had I been for some time but I knew I had to eat something, at least to keep my strength up. When a passenger opened the sliding door from the outside deck, a gentle warm breeze blew in letting those inside the cafe know it wasn't too hot, perfect for sitting outside. Joggers who had been running around the ship on the deck below came up the back stairs and into the buffet. It was quite busy at that early hour. Jogging was in my plans but not today, maybe tomorrow, maybe not.

Cruising is an ideal way to travel. There's so much to do if you want to, or you can relax by yourself for the whole trip. There was never any pressure from the entertainment staff who were more than willing to help you get involved with others, but only if that's what you wanted. Among the daily activities on board each and every day were deck quoits, bridge, ping pong, arts and crafts, bridge, bingo, cards and games, discussions on the ports of call, line dancing, slot lessons, hair and beauty demonstrations, backgammon, scrabble, hearts, pinochle, canasta, shuffleboard and many other things, as well as talks on everything from precious gems to fine art. A well-stocked library was on board this ship as well as a movie theatre showing a different movie every night. There was something for everyone.

A boat drill is mandatory at the start of the cruises so that passengers know what to do in case of an emergency. Passengers are shown how to put on lifejackets and where their muster stations are located. This exercise, while extremely serious, is actually quite funny. Most passengers can't help laughing at the antics of others trying to get their lifejackets on. Photographers are always on hand as they are at every activity, taking photographs for mementos. Instructions for this exercise are listed on the back of the cabin doors for reference. I often wondered if anyone would remember the instructions and their muster station, should the ship run into difficulties.

Thankfully, I never had occasion to find out. All of these activities and other information regarding shore excursions, safety, etc. are also listed in the ship's newsletter delivered to every cabin in the evening. These activities are repeated several times on the TV as well.

The line in the Lido moved slowly along, mainly because breakfast buffets and the other meals in the cafe were well stocked. Passengers had a difficult time choosing what to eat; there were too many choices. I moved my tray along, wondering what to have. Something light appealed to me. Perhaps I'd have orange juice, yogurt and cereal. Finishing that would help me feel as if I might be getting back to normal, at least as far as eating was concerned. Selections ranged from fried, scrambled, poached, boiled or specially ordered eggs, French toast, croissants, muffins, scones, pancakes, bacon, ham, sausages, hash browns, every kind of cereal imaginable, yogurt, fruit, juices, and the usual tea, coffee, milk and cream.

Not everyone liked to have breakfast and lunch in the dining room. A surprising amount of passengers like myself preferred the buffet. For that reason it was abnormally busy. Looking around the room for an empty table, or at least an empty seat, I saw one table occupied by a lady who appeared to be alone. The other three chairs were empty. On the off chance she was reserving the chairs for friends, I approached her to ask if she was waiting for friends. She was not holding the chairs for anyone. She motioned for me to sit down. We introduced ourselves to each other and shook hands. Other than chitchat about the weather, the ship and what our plans were for the day we didn’t say much else. She was just finishing off her coffee. Shortly after I sat down, June, the lady I sat down with, excused herself and left the cafe.

This was a day at sea, meaning there were no ports of call. I didn't see much point in going down to the cabin to change out of my tracksuit. Besides, everyone else was dressed casually. I brought a copy of the ship's newsletter with me outlining the days events, hoping to decide what I might do after breakfast and lunch, if anything at all.

With my breakfast finished I took my coffee outside to the open deck. I sat down at an empty table by the pool. As I sat sipping my coffee and scanning the ship’s newsletter, someone asked me if anyone was coming to fill the seats. When I looked, it was June who was by herself again. I invited her to join me. We started chatting. She told me that she was on this cruise by herself and had never sailed before, admitting she was a little nervous and apprehensive about travelling alone. I told her I knew how she felt as this was also my first trip alone, although I had previously travelled on several other cruises with my husband. I didn’t say I was a widow and she didn’t ask. I admitted to being a little nervous myself even though I knew my way around this ship and what to expect in the days ahead.

Surprisingly, I was glad to have her company. Up until now I wasn't in the mood for conversation. She gave her surname as Fyffe and said she was originally from a small town outside Glasgow, Scotland. That town just happened to be the same town where my old boyfriend Ian lived. She moved to England shortly after she got married, saying work prospects for her husband were much better there. My heart skipped a beat at the mention of the town. It was a small town but it was large enough that residents might not necessarily know each other. I never asked if she knew him.

I had never gone back to Glasgow after moving to Canada. I listened intently as she brought me up to date on many of the changes that had taken place over the years. For some unknown reason, I was drawn to her and I felt a kinship between us. She must have felt the same way because we hit it off right from the start. We chatted all the way through to lunchtime. It was as though we had known each other forever. Perhaps we were destined to meet. It just felt that way.

"I am having my lunch in the Lido Cafe. I prefer the casual buffet where the selection is excellent. Where are you eating lunch?" I asked.

"I hadn't thought about it much. I don't have any preference. If you aren't meeting someone and you don't mind, I would love to join you".

"Sounds good to me." I went on, "I am always amazed at the lineups for the dining room or the buffet. You would think people were starving, which is not possible on a cruise unless it's your choice." We laughed.

Food is one of the main attractions on cruises. It's everywhere and in abundance at all times. After the dining room closes, the all night buffet is open as well as the pizzeria. If you don't want to go anywhere, just phone for room service. No chance to go hungry. I think people feel that since they have paid for the trip, which includes the food, they have to get their money's worth.

Lunchtime had sneaked up on us and just as I had predicted, there was a lineup at the buffet but it moved along quickly. I was happy to be able to show June the ropes, so to speak. It took my mind off my feelings and being alone. When we moved inside, we each picked up a tray and moved along the counters filled to capacity with sumptuous offerings. So much to choose from and the way it was presented, was enough to whet your appetite, not that anyone ever needed an incentive to eat. What would we have today? There were so many choices from pasta, stew, fried or boiled fish, beef, ham, fried chicken, roast chicken, chicken salad, tuna salad, vegetable and fruit salads, roast potatoes, mashed potatoes, vegetables, chips, hamburgers, hot dogs, sliced tomatoes, several varieties of cheese, crackers, rolls and bread. Large bowls of fresh fruit, apples, oranges, bananas, grapes and pears were also put out on a little side table. Equally tempting were the dessert selections including pastries, cakes and an ice cream bar where passengers could make their own sundaes. Tea, coffee, milk, juices and soft drinks were also offered.

I opted for a salad with a side helping of penne and sauce as well as some fruit salad and coffee. June took the stew and a piece of cake. We carried our trays outside to sit at a table by the swimming pool. It was not a hot day but it was still comfortable. The weather didn't seem to bother the swimmers, some of whom were playing water badminton and other aquatic games. Large windows all around the pool area helped to keep a bit of the cool air off them. The sun was shining, which helped to warm us up a bit. Several passengers were having fun in the whirlpools beside the swimming pool.

We had no problem talking as we ate lunch. We were comfortable with each other but we didn't get into any heavy conversations and were surprisingly relaxed in each other's company. I didn't want to ask June anything about her personal life because we had just met. Besides, I didn't want to be in a position where she might ask me some things that I wasn't prepared to talk about. She must have felt the same way because she didn't ask me any personal questions either. We shared how many children we had and discovered we were both widows. However, the circumstances of our lives and our husbands' deaths were so different from each other but we wouldn't discover that until much later on in the cruise. We were about the same age, both originally born in Scotland, both widows and both on a vacation by ourselves for the first time. Even if this meeting had been orchestrated by the cruise, it couldn't have worked out better. We had so much in common. Just how much could never have been imagined, even in our wildest dreams.

June had dark blonde hair with no sign of gray but I thought it was probably tinted. She was an attractive slim lady about the same height as me, 5' 7". Her blue eyes sparkled, she smiled easily, and her face showed little sign that she wasn't as young any more. By contrast, I had considered tinting my dark hair but decided against it. I have a good head of hair but the gray was coming in, especially around the temples. It gave me a look of elegance, or so I was told.

My eyes are hazel. I had worked all my life to keep my weight stable and at the moment I was holding my own. I had dropped several pounds over the last while but on a trip like this, I knew I would easily gain it back.

"By the way," I asked, "what sitting are you for dinner?"

"I have first," she replied.

"Why don't you change and join me at my table?" There was a spare seat for Bob at my table, which meant she could take it over.

June didn't have to think twice about it. She jumped at the opportunity, saying the passengers at her table were friendly enough, but they were all couples which made her feel like a fifth wheel. However, she also didn't want to hurt anyone's feelings by requesting a change. I told her not to worry about that. Passengers often change tables if there was space. Dining room staff were always happy to accommodate when possible.

After lunch we made our way down to the dining room where we spoke to the Maître D', who was happy to oblige. It was hard to say who was happier, June or me. One thing was abundantly clear; this was the beginning of a strong friendship.

Seating arrangements settled, we were both happy and relaxed as we walked together along the decks to our respective cabins. We exchanged telephone and room numbers. Our cabins were one deck apart but in approximately the same area of the ship. As we parted company at the stairs, we told each other how happy we were to have met and arranged to meet again in the lounge close to the dining room before dinner.

VII

I took off my track shoes and lay down in bed with the intention of relaxing until dinnertime. My eyelids kept closing but I didn't want to fall asleep. Every now and then I opened my eyes wide and sat up. Maybe it was the soft rolling motion of the ship as it sailed on its way, maybe it was because I felt happier and more relaxed at having found a travel companion, or maybe it was because I was finally coming to terms with being alone. Whatever the reason, I gave in, and laid back down, still trying to keep my eyes open. I couldn't fight the sleep. I drifted off into a deep sleep, so deep that I found myself on board a train heading south to England. The year was 1952.

Moira, my best friend, and I were once again on the train travelling to see our favourite quartet, the Blue Rays. Moira and I loved dancing. We met the group when they played at our favourite dance hall in Glasgow. After that, we began following them wherever they played in the U.K. We became good friends. The group also played on the radio during intermissions on shows and two of the boys also acted in radio comedy shows. The group was extremely popular with all ages of dancers as well with people who just loved their style of music.

Moira was a flaming redhead with green eyes, but she didn't have the temper that supposedly goes with the hair colour. Freckles were in abundance on her face and body. She had more than I did, if that was possible. We were both about the same height and build. Moira had two brothers. She could play the boogie on the piano with the best of them. We were inseparable, although we had other friends who often joined us for some escapade or another. When it came to following the Blue Rays, it was us alone. Everyone else thought we were crazy but we didn't care a whit.

London, England, was our destination this time around. We boarded an overnight train in Glasgow Central Station travelling to Euston Station.

We both worked for British Railways. Employees were entitled to a free pass once a year and as many one-third off the fare privilege tickets as we wanted. It encouraged us to travel on the train as often as we could. Many of the other employees didn't take advantage of this concession. Not us, every chance we got, we were off to somewhere new.

It wasn't always to see the group. Sometimes we travelled to Edinburgh or some other city for the day. Our motto was why not? We wouldn't have been able to afford such travel otherwise. We were rarely far enough away from home that we would have to book a room, which cut down on expenses.

Whenever we travelled, we wore casual slacks and flat shoes. This often drew surprised looks from older women, sometimes younger ones. "Ladies" didn't wear "trousers", and especially not the "drainpipe" style, which had become so popular. We didn't mind the attention. In fact, we enjoyed it. “There just jealous,” we would say to each other.

We were too excited to sleep on the train. Berths were not part of the "freebies" we were allowed from the Railway, nor was it a luxury we could afford. We didn’t mind a bit and probably wouldn’t have slept much even if we had a berth, because we were always a little wound up with excitement and usually talked during the whole trip, wherever we went. If we managed to get a few winks on the trip, we were happy. There were a couple of empty seats in the first coach on the train but once we pulled out of the station, we were off along the corridor hoping to find an empty coach, although we knew that wasn’t very likely. The overnighter was always packed full but it was worth a try. As we reached the entrance to the next coach, several good looking young football fans blocked our way. Judging by their attire they were definitely from Scotland on their way to see their team play in London or thereabouts.

"No point in going up any further," one of them said to us.

"We’ve been through all the other coaches right up to the end and there are no empty seats,” said another.

"Might as well sit here with us," a third chipped in.

They looked to be about the same age as we were. I looked at Moira and she looked at me, smiled and said “why not?” Their duffel bags were spread all over the floor, making it difficult to pass anyway. Their bags were not too uncomfortable to sit on, much better than sitting on the floor.

Once we got through the formalities of introducing ourselves, we chatted away as though we had been life long friends. For some unknown and unbelievable reason, I found myself particularly drawn to one chap named Ian. His eyes were a magnetic blue colour and as I looked into them, I was hooked. I shivered from head to toe. Sparks between us were obvious. He was about 6 ft. 2 inches tall, with dirty blonde hair and a little growth on his chin. When he smiled, his dimples added to his exceptional good looks. He looked like a big, lanky schoolboy although he was 19 years old and an apprentice. Moira sat beside Ian's friend George, who was about the same height as Ian. His hair was dark with natural waves in it and his eyes were a dark brown. He had thick eyebrows and was a little heavier than Ian although far from overweight. It was easy to tell who they were rooting for with the team shirts, scarves, rosettes, socks and all the usual football fan regalia.

Each of us had brought along sandwiches, biscuits and cold drinks, which we laid out on a makeshift table, giving us a variety. Alex and Henry were the names of the remaining two of the group. All of them were roughly the same height and weight, not an unattractive one among them. Their bodies were lean and muscular and obviously in good physical condition, probably because of playing on football teams. After we finished eating, we cleared off the table and put what was left in our respective bags. Alex brought out a deck of cards to play silly games like SNAP. We got into fits of laughing. In between laughing and playing cards, they asked us where we lived, if we were still at school, or where we worked.

Moira took it upon herself to do the answering.

"We are both from Glasgow, and live a few closes away from each other. We have been pals forever. We went to the same schools, and now work in the British Railways Head Office."

"What about you?" I asked.

Ian took the lead. "We also live near each other in Mossblown, a little town in Ayrshire. Like yourselves we grew up together, went to the same schools and played on the same football team. We are all in apprenticeships now, but apprenticing in different trades. Our fathers worked down the mines. It's a hard life and our parents encouraged us to take a different route. Obviously you can see why we are going to London, but why are you two travelling?"

When we told them the reason, they were like most of the others we told, they thought we were nuts. They liked the quartet all right and even went to the local dance halls when they were in town, but following the quartet wasn't for them.

Moira piped in with, "Maybe we think the same about following football teams."

We laughed, as she was dead on.

Because the Glasgow to London train was an overnighter, many of the other passengers were sleeping or trying to. Sleepers or berths were expensive. Many passengers tried to catch a few winks in the coaches. If they were lucky they might even be able to stretch out, but that was doubtful because this particular train was always filled to capacity. With the important football game, it was virtually impossible to get a seat. We occupied the space between the coaches. It was not too uncomfortable but it was quite rickety which kept us laughing. We tried to keep the noise to a minimum while having a great time, laughing, and telling silly jokes. Every so often one of us would start singing and before long, we were all into it singing silly songs like "One man went to Mow," "Ten Green Bottles" and so on. We also sang, or tried to sing, a few of the popular songs of the day, made popular by Johnnie Ray, Frankie Laine, Guy Mitchell, Rosemary Clooney, Nat King Cole and others. Our renditions proved that the stars had nothing to worry about when it came to competition.

We tried to keep the noise to a minimum, conscious of the fact people would be trying to sleep. One thing in our favour was the chickitika, chickitika, chickitika sound of the train passing over the rails, covering up some of our noise. No one complained, either because the noise of the train drowned us out or they were enjoying it and singing along with us. The odd passenger passing through stopped to chat or join in the singing. I felt like we were on a picnic, this being a rolling one with all the markings of a day in the park. No one slept and before we knew it, we were entering Euston Station in London. This had been one of the most enjoyable train rides Moira and I had been on. We had fun and the time passed quickly, too quickly under the circumstances of meeting the fans.

Moira asked Ian, "Do you think you might get to the dance hall after the fitba' match?"

"If we had known you sooner, we could have made other arrangements but our time, like yours, is pretty much spoken for," he answered.

Before we went our separate ways, we exchanged addresses and telephone numbers.

Ian told us the time of their return trip and when we realized we were taking the same train, or at least we were hoping to catch it, they seemed as happy as we were knowing we might meet again. I was especially happy about that bit of information because I had fallen for Ian. I could feel the blood rushing from my neck to my face when I thought about seeing him again. I sensed he felt the same way, just by the expressions on his face and little things he said to me. When he touched my arm, it was magic. My hair stood up on end.

Alex's cousin met the boys at the train station to take them to his house for their overnight stay. As they drove away, they waved out of the window at us. Ian gave a wink as he waved to me. He shouted out of the window,

“If we don’t see you on the return trip, I’ll get a hold of you when we get back and maybe we can all go out somewhere.”

"Sure you will," said Moira.

I knew I would be devastated if we didn’t meet again. I had never felt like this about anyone before, as crazy as it was, it was true.

As we walked towards the exit in the station, we shivered at the cold air as it came through the open space. A dull sky greeted us but it was still quite early in the morning, lots of time for the sun to come out and we hoped it would. We had reservations at a B&B a short distance from the station. We hailed a taxi and drove off to our digs. Moira and I had travelled to London many times so we knew our way around the city. We loved London, who didn’t? We often revisited the same places, enjoying every minute of our time there. The main reason for our trip was the Blue Rays. Any other adventures would be a bonus.

It was a short ride to the B&B, the same one we always stayed at when we were in London. It was reasonably priced, clean and convenient to most touristy places. The landlady was a lovely woman who always made us and other guests feel right at home. When we arrived at the breathtakingly beautiful and immaculate Victorian house, we walked up the few steps to the front door and rang the old fashioned doorbell. Mrs. Galloway, the landlady opened the large solid oak door with stained glass inserts. Brass on the door shone so brightly we could see our reflections in it. Her natural smile was a treat. She gave us a warm hug, greeting us like the old friends we were and after a few minutes of chatting, we checked in. Our room this time was on the third floor. Getting up the stairs two at a time, was no problem for us and it was good exercise, which we didn’t mind. This time though, our gait had a little more lilt to it, after our chance meeting with the football fans.

I was surprised at how much I was thinking about Ian. I couldn't get him off my mind. There was something magnetic about him. Could this be a case of love at first sight? It had never happened for me before, so it likely wasn't now. It was probably just the excitement of the trip but I didn't believe that and I didn't want to get too worked up about him not knowing if I would even see him again.

Brightly coloured Victorian wallpaper covered the walls in the gorgeous old-fashioned room Moira and I would be staying in. It was large and spotless. Off white lace curtains edged the windows with a shade underneath for privacy. An overstuffed quilt lay on top of heavy blankets, topped with a bedspread that matched the curtains. The bed was begging us to bounce on it and that's exactly what we did. It was so soft; we sank right down into it. Comfort was a plus. Two upholstered chairs sat lazily in the room, one beside a desk and another at the window. Booking this particular room was a first for us, even though we had been to this same B&B many times before. We agreed to splurge this time around, mainly for the reason that the bathroom was just outside of the room and for our exclusive use. Other bathrooms were shared and central to the rooms, meaning they were a little walk down the hallways. Mrs. Galloway's was nearly always fully booked and getting into the bathroom could take a bit of a wait and a lot of patience. We had learned a few tricks during our many weekend travels and paying a little extra for this comfort and privacy was one of them.

Whenever we followed the Blue Rays it was usually a day trip, returning to our own houses at night. London is a good 500 miles from Glasgow, therefore, we needed to get accommodation for the night. We could have taken an overnight train back to Glasgow and saved on the B&B but by the time we got home from the dancing, getting that train was out of the question. Besides, it was an adventure for us and we enjoyed getting away from home and out on our own for a couple of days.

We thought we might get a few hours of sleep on the way down, but it didn't happen, although we weren't unhappy about that this time. We were a little tired but we didn't want to waste any of our precious holiday weekend. We could make up for it that night, and sleep in a little longer next morning, if we wanted to. Sunday was not as busy as regular workdays in London, or anywhere in the U.K. for that matter. Most stores were not open but at least in England, the pubs, markets and a few other tourist places were open. Suitcases dropped, a quick bath and into some clean casual slacks, sweaters, and walking shoes and out the door we went.

We set off this Saturday morning to take in a few of the shops, although shopping was secondary. London is a fascinating city, one that we could never get tired of visiting. Window-shopping would pass some time and we might get bargains in the meantime. We didn't have many time restraints other than we wanted to be at the dance hall as it opened, but we were game for anything until then.

The sky had brightened up and it wasn't so cool. Tourists and Londoners brought the streets to life, with hustle and bustle everywhere. After a couple of hours wandering around, it was time to have a cup of tea in a little cafe across the street which we had noticed as we wandered around. Lucky for us, it wasn't crowded. We opted for a light lunch, a sandwich, and a little cake and coffee. I glanced at my watch and realized we had lost track of time as we sat chatting, enjoying our lunch. We hadn't intended to roam so far from the B&B.

"I think we should take a taxi back instead of a bus. It will be quicker and it will give us a bit more time to relax before we go out tonight. Besides, the buses will be crammed with shoppers and we don't have time to wait for another one which could be just as busy." I said

"Sounds good to me," Moira agreed.

It was still early enough when we arrived back at the B&B. We knew it would be another late night for us so once in our room we dropped the parcels, took off our coats and bounced on the bed. We hoped to catch a few winks and get our batteries charged so to speak, before getting ready to go dancing. Lying in bed quietly going over the day's events and again remembering the train ride and how much fun we had with the boys, we got the giggles, as we often did, at some of the antics on the train. No sleeping for us, and by the time we finished laughing, we were sore.

"Okay that's it," I said sternly, trying to stop the giggles. "Time to get ready. I will take the first bath while you decide what you are going to wear tonight."

It was a treat to get into this old fashioned bath with its Victorian fixtures. As with everywhere else in the house, the wall coverings were exquisite. Standing under the shower, I imagined myself back in the turn of the century. That's how realistic the decor was. Gorgeous didn't do it justice. When I returned to the room, Moira had her clothes hanging up, ready to put on. When she was in the bath, I decided on which outfit I would wear. Afterwards, we both sat in our robes and put on our make up as we sipped some juice and ate snacks we had purchased. We weren't hungry, just needed a little something to tide us over. We had nothing left to do but get dressed and head out the door.

Although we brought enough clothes with us to choose from, knowing that we often changed our minds at the last minute about what to wear, we bought a couple of new dresses. We could never resist a bargain. These dresses were too nice and too reasonable to pass up. Naturally we chose to wear them instead of what we brought with us. No surprise there. My dress was powder blue with short sleeves, with a little lace collar and box pleats all around the front and back. Moira's dress was floral taffeta, also with short sleeves, but her dress had a flared skirt. Luckily we brought light coats with us just in case we needed them, and we did.

It wasn't cold but going out dancing in dresses alone would have been a bit chilly. A couple of smashers we said at the same time and then laughed. We hoped others might think that. We were drop dead gorgeous.

The Savoy dance hall was located just a short distance from the B&B, the main reason we stayed there, that along with the fact that it was charming, the food was good and the landlady treated us like daughters. It was a lovely evening. We enjoyed walking, so off we went to the hall. It wasn't surprising to see a queue when we arrived at the hall. The Blue Rays always attracted a large audience anywhere they were playing. It never entered our heads that we might not get in. We had "connections" after all. The cashier's booth was at the entrance to the foyer but we waited in line like everyone else. The mood was happy, chatty and the crowed revved up and rarin' to go. Finally we reached the cashier. When she heard our names, she smiled and handed us the two passes that we knew would be waiting for us to pick up. We walked right in.

The entrance to this dance hall was large, much the same as most of the others belonging to the same chain spread throughout the U.K. Colourful floral carpeting covered the floors. Two doors opened at the end of the foyer, leading onto the dance floor. This particular ballroom was as large as any in the chain, except that the dance floor in the middle of the room was probably much larger. Tables and chairs were set on a carpeted area all around the dance floor. Lighting was dim with a crystal ball in the center. Bands were set up on the revolving stage. When one group was finished, the other band or group waiting to come around played their signature tune as the stage slowly turned around. Not one beat was missed in this turnaround, the old left and the new was ready to play for the eager dancers.

The usher showed us to our table, which had been reserved for us at the front of the hall beside the stage. Just as we arrived at our table, the familiar sound of the signature tune of the Blue Rays was heard, signalling that the groups were changing and our favourite group was coming around. Perfect timing. We were excited to see them again. Everyone started clapping in expectation, possibly led by us. A long round of applause continued as they rotated, all the while playing their signature tune. Members of the group were looking for us, wondering if we had arrived. When they caught a glimpse of us, we got waves and winks. We were chuffed at being treated like celebrities. Real celebrities couldn't have been more honoured than we were, acknowledged by a group of renown in front of the whole audience.

What was this? Who was that lady? Where did she come from? How come we didn't know about her? We asked each other these questions as our eyes caught sight of a beautiful young lady up there with our band. There had never been a female in their group before. It came as a shock and surprise to us, their biggest fans, and we wondered why we hadn't seen an announcement about her in the music magazines we bought each week. The woman's name was Janine. She was stunningly beautiful and could sing too. Her hair was longish, and copper in colour, much like Rita Hayworth's tresses. She changed gowns a couple of times during the evening, each one more beautiful than the other. One was a deep royal blue, covered in sequins with white organza around her tiny waist. A diamond or diamonte necklace, earrings and bracelet sparkled ever so brightly. She changed from that into a pale peach tulle type of dress, which was plainer than the blue one, and her final dress of the evening was sequinned and emerald green, highlighting her red hair. All of the gowns were strapless and form fitting. We felt a teensy weensy bit jealous in a nice way at the sight of her standing up front with our boys. The tinge of envy was only because she would be travelling all over the country with them while we could only see them now and then. We thought she was lucky but we probably couldn't have handled travelling around with them anyway. We had a lot going on in our own lives. It wasn't envy, our interest in the group was purely their music, dancing and we considered them friends who took an interest in us and treated us nicely.

All members of the Blue Rays were happily married, some with families and most importantly, much too old for us. If we didn't have the cheap rail travel, we wouldn't have been following them all over the country as much as we did. Dancing was a very popular means of entertainment for a lot of us and people of all ages enjoyed going to the dancing during the week but Saturday was the most popular evening. Many went dancing in couples but most went on their own. Ladies usually went with girlfriends and fellows with chums. To most, it was the love of dancing to various popular bands or groups that attracted them to the dance halls every week. Many met life partners at the dancing. Some went out on casual dates afterwards but most times it never amounted to anything. No matter what the plan or hope was, everyone was comfortable and no one ever felt out of place going alone, that's the way it was and that's the way the dancers liked it. To each his/her own.

We had been following this group for a long time becoming friends as well as their No. 1 fans. One night on one of their trips to Glasgow, two members of the group visited my parent's house for tea. That was quite a memorable night. Moira and I were driven home in the leader's expensive, luxurious Bentley car. I nearly drove mom crazy cleaning up the house and removing the clothes from the pulley. I asked dad to bake something special for them because with their continuous touring around the country, they seldom got home baked food.

Like most people who travel for work or other reasons, restaurant and hotel food soon gets tiring. Neighbours were peeking from behind their curtains to see the "stars" arrive. It was the talk of "the Steamie" as we say, the "Steamie being the old wash house where women washed the family clothes and caught up on all the local gossip. Moira and I felt more like the celebrities than they did. Mom made steak pie, mashed potatoes and steeped peas, normally served on Hogmanay, a very special meal. My dad a former baker, baked rolls, shortbread and black bun, also usually reserved for a traditional Scottish New Year. It was a special night for Moira, my parents and I but it was also a special evening for the neighbours who got caught up in the excitement of having celebrities visit our street.

When the stage came to a halt and the music started, we were asked by some of the male patrons to dance and we were up for almost every dance. Soon it was time for intermission, a time when dancers went for a drink, outside for a breath of fresh air or perhaps a visit to the "cludgie" (toilet). The lights went up in the ballroom. Some dancers preferred to sit at their tables and give their feet a rest. We headed back stage where refreshments were waiting for us. Janine was officially introduced to us and we immediately loved her. Apparently she had heard about us, hopefully good stuff. She was as nice as she was gorgeous. She was looking for the name of a good hairdresser. We gave her the name of a trendy salon in town where all those in the know frequented. I think that cemented our relationship and we all became friends forever. Janine gave us a copy of the tour schedule so we could keep tabs on them, and make our plans if we were planning another visit. She also gave us copies of the new promo photos, which included her. They were fabulous.

As always, we enjoyed ourselves and were happy we made the trip. We could have paired up with some chaps but that was not in our plans. When we went dancing at home, it was an unwritten law that we went together and went home together. If one of us was interested in seeing someone on a date, that would be set up but we never let anyone take us home. Our minds were always on having a good time dancing. Getting involved with someone, especially from London, was definitely out of the question. For us it was too far for any kind of relationship.

The Blue Rays ended the night playing Tenderly for the last dance. We went back stage to say good night. Since Glasgow was on the itinerary, it wouldn't be too long before we all met again. Contentment was written all over our faces as we left the Savoy. The night couldn't have been any better. It was well worth the trip and more so because we met the boys, maybe more so for me than Moira.

Once outside the Savoy, the night air felt a little cool on our faces. Many of the dance hall patrons were walking along the street, heading home. We hadn't taken many steps along the road when the aroma from a local fish and chip shop was too much of a temptation. We stopped dead in our tracks.

Chippies are popular in both Scotland and England so it was no surprise that it was packed. The sound of the battered fish and chips being dropped into the hot fat only tempted the patrons all the more, not that they needed any encouragement for fish and chips. Fish and chips should definitely be considered the national meal. It was always a favourite Friday night meal and definitely when coming home from dancing, the movies or just after a walk. I liked the fish and chips. My favourite was pie and chips, but I wouldn't be able to get the Scotch pie here in London. Fish and chips were always my secondary choice and that's what I would have. No matter how delicious these fish and chips might be, they could never compare to ours in Scotland. Nothing could equal that taste, nothing.

There was an empty table over by the window. We always went for the window seating. Moira went up to the counter to order and I sat at the table where we had a bird's eye view of all the action in the chippie and the street. Chippies were busy most nights but Saturday night was a biggie. Most of the dancers and patrons ended up in these establishments for a snack or meal before going home. It was a happy atmosphere with everyone chatting, laughing and joking around. Some of the patrons of the chippie, struck up conversations with us. Once they realized we were from Scotland, we got some friendly kidding, but we didn't mind that a bit and gave back as much as we got. After we finished our meal, we moved towards the door and wished everyone a good night. Lots of people were wandering in the well-lit streets even though it was around 2:00 a.m. but it was Saturday when the streets were always busier. We felt safe as we walked back to the B&B. There were lots of Bobbies (policemen) patrolling the area, keeping an eye on things.

We let ourselves into the house as quietly as possible; tip toeing up the stairs, trying hard not to let the stairs creak. Every time there was a slight creak, we had to cover our mouths to stifle a giggle and the more we tried to stifle it, the more it squeezed out. It was difficult to keep the giggles in. We were bursting to let it all go. But we couldn't do it, it wouldn't be fair to the other residents who were most likely asleep by now. Once inside the room, we kicked off our shoes, feet slightly aching, got into our "goonies" (nightgowns,) put pillows over our mouths and roared and roared with laughter. Something was definitely tickling us. After we got control, we chatted animatedly about the events of the train ride, and the fabulous evening at the dancing with our favourite group. Our giggles started again, so we covered our mouths, snorting and giggling. The more we tried to cover our giggles, the more we burst out laughing. The more we tried to stop, the more we couldn't. We pulled the heavy covers over us. I don't know what the neighbours must have thought if they heard us.

I broached the subject of Ian again telling Moira that he was the one for me. She gulped, "What? Are you nuts? You don't even know him."

"I hope we meet them on the train because I know for sure he is the one." Moira was okay with meeting them on the train because they were good company and helped to make the trip go by quickly, but that was all. "I won't be shattered if they get another train." Whatever our reasons, we had to admit that the train trip down was good fun and it would be nice to see them again.

VIII

We had planned on sleeping in the next morning but because we were only in London for the weekend, and our train was not scheduled to leave until 2:00 p.m., we wanted to make the most of our morning. Reluctantly, we got out of bed, bathed and dressed before packing our suitcases and going downstairs for breakfast.

It was a large and bright dining room in keeping with the Victorian decor. Travellers filled the room. There were two empty seats at a larger table where an Australian family sat. The waitress motioned us over to join them. Breakfasts in most B&B's are substantial. In fact, tourists can sustain themselves on that for most of the day, with maybe a light snack before supper. Choices were cereal, bacon, eggs, sausage, toast and jam, scones and cream, pancakes and tea. We ordered the same breakfast of cereal, bacon, eggs, toast and tea. It was delicious and filling, enough to keep us going through to supper time, although we always managed to get a snack in somewhere in between.

It was like the League of Nations in the dining room, guests from a variety of backgrounds and countries. The mood was happy and enthusiastic as everyone anticipated their next adventure. We enjoyed meeting other travellers whenever and wherever we travelled. It was always interesting to learn of other countries and travellers were usually friendly and willing to share information. While we ate our breakfast, we chatted with the Aussies, telling them I had relatives who emigrated there and loved it. Other guests included travellers from France, Belgium, Germany and Italy, countries close to Britain. A young couple from America told us they were on an extended honeymoon. We exchanged what our plans were for the day, some asked for tips and others were glad to help out in any way they could. It was such a friendly, happy place to be at this favourite B&B of ours. As guests finished breakfast, they picked up their luggage and set off full of hope and expectancy.

Moira and I had travelled from Lands End to John O'Groats but it wasn't always in pursuit of the group. We often took off on Saturdays and holidays, sometimes with other friends, other times on our own. One of the nice things about travelling in Scotland, England or Wales was that most places were not too far from Glasgow. We could take many day trips, saving us money because we didn't have to stay overnight. While we thought the scenery and history of most places in England and Wales were the best to be found anywhere in the world, we were a little prejudiced, preferring the beautiful scenery in Scotland. Our train fare concessions made these trips doable for us and we took advantage of every opportunity we got.

On this trip, it would have been nice if we had been able to take a later train, giving us more time in London where there was so much to see and do, no matter how many times we visited. Unfortunately we had to be at work the next day and taking a later train would mean we wouldn't get into Glasgow until the next morning, with no time to go home first. The plus side on this particular trip was that we might see the boys but we still had a few hours before we had to head for the train station. We were eager to get going. Another trip to Speakers' Corner in Hyde Park was always worth our time. Stopping along the way whenever we saw something that piqued our attention was also in our plans. Many vendors set up around outside Hyde Park. It was a tourist paradise with all sorts of weird and wonderful souvenirs for sale.

Carrying our suitcases around London would have been awkward as well as slowing us down. Since we often stayed at Mrs. Galloway's, we knew it wouldn't be a problem to leave our suitcases with the landlady until we were ready to go to the train station. She was only too happy to oblige. She liked us although she, like most people we knew, thought we were nuts.

Hyde Park was a must, but other than that, we didn't care where we went or what we saw. Our main reason for the trip was to see the Blue Rays but why waste the rest of our visit by sleeping in?

It was early summer and the weather was reasonably good. Sunny but not too hot, nice enough for walking to Hyde Park and walking around to watch the various "entertainers".

Soapbox preachers were always in abundance in Hyde Park. Sometimes listening to them drew spectators into discussions, which could get testy. We were no different. More than once we had been drawn into the discussions, but it wouldn't keep us from going back. It was at the very least invigorating and highly entertaining. Even at this time of the day, the park was busy. Political pundits by the dozen, already in position, spouted off about something, with hecklers in the crowd yelling back.

The place was alive. “The End is Near” written on sandwich boards, carried by a couple of men walking through the park, always attracted attention. Carriers of these boards were probably the quietest of all the speakers, but every now and again someone would challenge them and when that happened, the Bible was opened and the arguments began. No one in Speakers' Corner ever won the arguments, but they never came to blows either, That in itself was pretty amazing because it often got hot and heavy. London Bobbies were everywhere but unless the characters got out of hand, they usually let the orators spout off. Bobbies could often be seen shaking their heads or smiling at the antics, as they walked around the park making sure everything was okay. It was a popular tourist attraction as well as a must for the locals.

Moira and I could never understand how these speakers, many of whom were originally from other countries, could get up on their soap boxes and run down the British Government, the Royal Family, and many of the other established British organizations and get away with it. Hadn't Britain allowed them to come into the country? Hadn't they been able to make a good living here? Weren't they better off in Britain? If the answer was no, then why would they want to stay?

To be sure, there were always two or more opposing views and although it could get testy at times, we never saw any fights any time we were there. We just enjoyed walking around.

After an hour or so of watching and listening to the various characters and spectators, we walked over to the gate and outside the park, passing souvenir stands. We weren’t interested in any souvenirs but we glanced at the merchandise as we slowly walked past each stall. It was enjoyable to listen to the patter of the sellers. Sometimes they were just as entertaining as the ones inside the park.

"Oy, c'mon get your souvenirs of London. Best prices in town, best quality, something for everyone."

We were still full from our huge breakfast but felt a little peckish for a cup of tea. Perfect, we spotted a little restaurant on the corner. Carefully watching traffic and the lights, we crossed over quickly. A peek in the window told us it wasn't too busy and the smell from freshly baked scones being baked in the back room, wafting outside, beckoned us to go in. It was too much of a temptation for us. We were so weak when it came to avoiding bakeries or restaurants where the aroma almost wrapped around your neck and pulled you in. Not surprisingly, we went in even though we were not the least bit hungry. We ordered fresh baked scones with Devon cream and tea. Eating again, not hungry, we took one look at each other and burst out laughing. It didn't take much.

We were usually lucky enough to get a table by a window when eating in cafes, that way we could watch the antics of the folks coming and going from Hyde Park or wherever we were. Who needed to see a film or stage show with all that was going on around here and it was free to boot! We had plenty of time to get back to the B&B for our luggage and make it to the station.

After eating we decided that a walk would do us good and might work off some of the food we had eaten. Mrs. Galloway's was ideally centrally located to most of the places we wanted to visit, this being the main reason we always stayed there. We walked briskly the rest of the way home.

We found our suitcases just inside the door where Mrs. Galloway had left them. She gave each of us a hug and wished us a safe trip home saying she hoped to see us again soon. She gave us a little bag with some of her homemade scones, along with a container of Devon cream. As we moved the suitcases outside to the end of the pavement, we kept an eagle eye out for the bus, which would stop at the door if someone was getting off, or waiting for it, otherwise it would drive on. The service on this route was excellent, so we knew we wouldn't have to wait too long. Sure enough, we hardly got the suitcases outside before the bus which would take us right into Euston Station, pulled up to the sidewalk. Most businesses were closed on Sunday, leaving the buses fairly empty; otherwise we might have decided on a taxi to reach the station on time. We couldn't afford to wait until an empty bus came along knowing we had to be at work the next morning. I personally didn't want to miss the train this time around. I was hoping to see Ian again. On the ride to Euston I told Moira the butterflies were back in my stomach at the thought of seeing Ian again.

"Well don't get too excited pal o' mine, it might not happen. Remember, you don't even know these fellows."

"I know, you're right. It's totally crazy and not like me at all, but I can't help it, I know I will be devastated if we don't see them. I don't believe it myself."

By the time we finally reached the station, I could hardly contain my excitement; I was so jittery and flushed. With my hands shaking, I couldn't find my ticket. I dropped my handbag and was just about ready to keel over with anxiety. I enjoyed the weekend immensely as Moira and I always did, but I couldn't get Ian out of my mind.

The odd time he wasn't foremost in mind was when I was otherwise preoccupied. Moira and I talked about my crazy, sudden feelings a few times but I tried not to go on and on about him. She had already told me to slow down; otherwise I was going to be disappointed if we didn't see them on the train. Even if we did meet up with them, there was no guarantee they would want to notice us. I knew she was right, but I couldn't help it. I told myself that I would get over it but deep down I didn't believe that. I would be shattered if we didn't see them again. As we headed towards the gate I kept looking around searching for any sign of them.

Euston was a main station in London, always busy but on this particular Sunday, it was busier than ever mostly on account of all the football fans catching their train back home. Fans were clearly distinguishable by the team colours on their shirts and scarves blowing in the breeze as they as they ran to catch their trains. Trying to single out any one person was almost impossible with the mass of people and colours everywhere. I wondered if they might already be further down the platform or if they were even on the train. We walked towards the gate, glancing over the crowd as we moved along, looking to see if we saw familiar faces. There was no sign of them. It was possible Ian and his friends had changed their plans if, after the game, they were celebrating a win or drowning their sorrows due to a loss and they didn't have the strength to get out of bed early enough to make it to the station. I didn't think they would want to take the overnighter because they, like us, had to be back for work in the morning but circumstances can change plans.

Passing through the gate, with our tickets punched, we walked up the platform, looking for an empty coach. The train engines faced outwards with the last coach at the buffers beside the ticket takers. We got on the train at the second to last coach and walked the rest of the way towards the engine. Rather than walk up the platform to check for empty coaches, it was much easier to see them from inside as we walked through the corridor. Every time we passed a coach, a quick look inside let us know the boys were not there. Passengers were quickly filling up the empty seats. It looked as though the train might be filled to capacity. If the boys were not sitting somewhere down the train, they might be out of luck and have to sit in the corridor like they did on the way down, providing they got on the train.

We continued on through the train corridor, searching for an elusive empty coach, hoping to find at least one of them empty but as we got closer to the engine, I was losing hope that we would meet up with them on this trip. At the second to last coach, we hit pay dirt, a coach with not a passenger in it. Now if the boys would only appear before anyone came along to fill the other seats that would be great. We staked our claim, lifted our luggage up onto the racks and put our jackets on the seats. It was close to departure time, and there was still no sight of the boys, but I kept a lookout from the window. I could see up the platform, but with the crowds running up to find an empty coach and others getting on the train, it was not a clear view. I was beginning to give up. I kept looking out just in case, all the while trying to look nonchalant, taking in the action. If they did come along the platform, I didn't want them to think I was waiting for them, even if I was.

The porter blew the whistle signalling that the train was about to leave the station. The steam came rolling past the coaches as the engine prepared to leave. The porter began walking along the platform, through the light steam haze, shutting the coach doors as he passed them. Before he reached our coach, I decided I would take one last look before I brought my head back inside. Just as I was about to pull in I noticed them rushing for the train. I shouted excitedly to Moira, "They're rushing like mad to get in before it moves."

She came over to the door and stuck her head out beside me. Sure enough it was them, or should I say we saw their scarves blowing about as they bobbed in and out of the other passengers, making a last minute dash for the train. We waved our arms to get their attention, to let them know where we were, hoping they would know to jump on anywhere, then walk along the corridor to our coach. Had they kept running up the platform to our coach there was no way they would make it before the train moved. They must have seen us because they got into the coach nearest them and once on the train, they walked towards our coach. The porter gave his final whistle and the train ever so slowly started moving out of the station. He continued walking alongside the train checking and making sure all the doors were shut and secure. By the time the boys reached us, they were out of breath and flopped down on the seats laughing. They sat there for a few minutes, catching their breath, before they threw their luggage up on the rack beside ours. There was plenty of room on both sides of the coach.

"Boy, we're glad you looked out for us. It's great to have an empty coach. This train is jam packed," Ian said. "Much better than sitting in the corridors."

This was a huge improvement over spending the whole trip sitting on duffle bags, although I didn't think that was so bad, considering the fun we had.

It wasn't too difficult to tell which team won the cup. These guys were ecstatic. Once they caught their breath, they started into the team song, waving the rattlers and scarves. They weren't alone; other fans on the train were doing the same thing. I didn't know if any fans from the opposing team were on the train although I am sure there must have been a few. But they might have put their colours away and would definitely not be singing. We had to listen to the play-by-play of the game, including demonstrations. Lucky they didn't have a football or it might have gone out the window. We also heard about their night on the town. All in all they were happy with their weekend. They were so excited they never thought to ask us how we enjoyed our weekend but truth be told, they thought we were nuts anyway. Hmmm! The way they were acting after a football game and they thought we were crazy? They were just as crazy, dressing up in the colours, making noises and following their team around. We couldn't see the difference, but to each his own.

We were all psyched up from our busy respective trips but it was a happy tired. Sleeping would be a waste of time. No one would have been able to settle down enough to sleep anyway. Besides, we would be home in time to catch some sleep before work called in the morning. Comfortably seated on the brightly patterned velour seats with lots more space than we had in the corridor on the trip down, we were set for a fun trip home. Plus, this time we didn't have to keep moving when someone came along the corridor to use the toilet or to check the other coaches.

We carried on from where we left off with what colleges we attended, work, families, girlfriends, boyfriends (if any), movies and what we did in our spare time. Our backgrounds were quite similar, coming from working class families, none of us going to university. I attended college. We had a lot in common being movie buffs, and loved dancing with the only difference being our love for the Blue Rays and their love for their football team.

Ian reached up to the luggage rack and brought down one of the suitcases to use as a table for playing cards. Rummy and pontoons were a cert to be played sometime during the evening, if they ever got to them. SNAP, the game where you just play cards until someone drops a similar card on top then it's a race to yell "SNAP", always gets everyone wound up. Some shouted before their time, others were itching to go. This is the game we played on the way down and caused us to go into hysterics. In our hurry to win, it often sounded like "snip, snope, or snipe" and so on. It was hilarious, not only this time but any time it was played. We almost ended up on the floor laughing our heads off. It was great fun and the hours flew by.

After a couple of hours playing cards, Alex brought out the mouth organ and the ever popular sing along began. Because this was not an overnighter, passengers weren't apt to be sleeping but the sleeper coach was further up the train anyway. I suppose some might have booked them for a sleep on the way. If anyone needed a snooze, it would most likely be in the regular coach on the seats, if there was enough room. Some passengers might just stay in town and go straight to work the next day, others might have the day off and yet others might not have anything to do when they returned to Glasgow. There were quite a lot of seniors on the train, mostly soccer fans. We tried to keep the noise down as much as possible. A few of the other travellers walking through the corridors, popped in and joined the sing along. Everyone was in such a happy mood.

Ian sat next to me the whole time. I had goose bumps all over. I couldn't have been happier. I wasn't sure what was happening to me. I was shaky and silly, just like a schoolgirl. I had never felt like this before. George and Moira sat together again, I think more or less as a convenience rather than because she fancied him, although neither seemed to mind.

As the boys had all grown up together it was natural they would support the same team. They had remained close friends throughout their lives in the same neighbourhood. The travel distance between their small town outside of Glasgow, and where we lived took about an hour or so on the bus, not far but far enough. They did everything and went everywhere together, the same as we did. That's the way it was with young people, friends were friends for life and pretty much did everything together.

The trip back to Glasgow seemed to be the fastest we had ever taken because of the fun we had, the boys helping to pass the time quickly. Otherwise we might have slept on the way home or been bored. In one way, it was nice that the time had passed quickly. The downside was that we would be leaving our newfound friends, and at this point, we didn't know if we would meet up again.

The train came to a stop at the buffers. We could hear the familiar announcement "Glasgow Central Station." Ian and George brought our suitcases down from the rack. We left the coach and headed up the mobbed platform trying to juggle our way through the crowds. Moira and I would walk the short distance from the station to the tram stop to wait for our tram home. Ian and his pals would have to walk along several streets to the station to get a bus home. It would be another hour and a half before they reached their hometown, if they were in time for the last bus. If they missed it, they would be out of luck and would have to wait until next morning. We stopped before we headed in different directions and as we were saying our goodbyes, we all agreed that we had a great time and were glad to have met each other. Ian asked me if it would be okay if he called on me sometime. Perhaps he could visit me one weekend. I was breathless and almost speechless but I managed to say, "sounds good to me."

None of us had a telephone nor did any of our neighbours. As a matter of fact, I didn't know anyone who had a telephone. People contacted each other by way of a little note in the mail, if they didn't live close to each other. There were telephone boxes at most street corners that people could use, if needed. Phones were always busy. Several neighbours could be seen daily standing at the phone box waiting for a call or waiting to make a call.

Most of the calls were important, not just for idle chat. We had telephones at work but no one was allowed to use them for personal calls or any calls for that matter. The telephones were strictly for business purposes and bosses. I suggested to Ian that he drop me a note, as was the custom, if and when he decided to visit Glasgow. We could then make arrangements for me to wait by the box for his call. I gave him the number of the telephone at our corner. Everyone knew the corner box numbers.

Ian put his arm around me, drew me to him and gave me a peck on the cheek. Wow! What was that? How could a peck on the cheek weaken my knees so much that I thought I might drop to the ground? My face flushed. He turned to walk out of the train station with the rest of the boys and kept turning to look back, waving as did the others. We went in the direction of the George Square tram stop. We were sure we were in time to get the last tram for the night but if we had missed it, it wasn't too far for us to walk home. We were in a much better position that Ian and his friends. On the way home, I told Moira how I felt after the peck on the cheek. She looked at me with a surprised and stunned look.

"You can't be serious. You don't even know him. He's a nice fellow okay, but you better slow down pal o' mine."

Moira was happy for me but she didn't want to see me getting hurt. Besides, who knew if I would even hear from him again. The peaceful smile on my face let her know that I was serious, more serious than I ever felt about any boy I had met before.

"He does seem like a genuine chap and he was definitely interested in you but who knows, he might just have been friendly, passing the time. You might be reading more into it than is there. I am not saying that's the way it is only that it could be. I don't want you to get your hopes built up, and then be let down. Wait and see what happens," Moira said to me.

I could feel a tear come into my eye and I didn't want Moira to see that. I quickly turned the conversation on to her.

"How about you and George? Do you fancy him? Would you like to see him again?" I asked.

"He's alright, seems nice enough. I wouldn't say no if he asked me out but I won't be shattered if he doesn't. Besides, these four seem to go everywhere together and two girlfriends might throw a spanner into the works. Let's wait to see what happens. If Ian calls you, we could set up a foursome if George wanted to. Let's not get ahead of ourselves. They don't live very close by and we still have our other friends here."

We got off that subject and chatted the rest of the way home, going over the Savoy, Janine and where we would likely travel next time. By the time we arrived at our stop, it was almost 2:00 a.m. and getting on that last tram was a stroke of luck. We made it in the nick of time. We only lived a couple of closes apart. I stood at my close and watched until Moira reached hers. When I saw that she had gone in, I headed upstairs to my house.

Mom and dad were already in bed when I got into the house but they were still awake, or at least mom was. Until I got home after an evening out, mom could never go to sleep. She got up and put the kettle on, always interested to hear the tales of our escapades. The fire had been backed up for the night but it was still burning a bit in the fireplace. Coming in from the night air, it was a welcoming warmth. I was always excited to tell mom everything about our trips.

I told her of our surprise when we saw Janine as part of the group but added that she was beautiful, friendly and a great singer. I said everyone was well and happy to see us, sent their regards and mentioned they were booked to be back up to Glasgow again before too long. "Oh, that's nice," my mother replied.

Mom asked her if we managed to get to Speakers' Corner this time but she probably knew the answer before I told her. She knew it would take something special for us to miss that.

"Silly question, mom. Bugs me to see all these people complaining but if they didn't, I suppose there might not be a Speakers' Corner which would be a shame, since it's a great draw for the tourists as well as the Londoners."

"I know, just checking." We smiled at each other.

Mom wanted to hear all the details about the soapbox preachers and what they were spouting this time. I told her that we met some football fans on the train going down to London and again on the way back home. I could feel my face getting a little flushed as I told her about our new friends and also about the fun we had on the journeys. She looked at me and said: "Well judging by the look on your face, you seem pretty interested in this Ian. Do you think you will ever see him again?"

"I gave him my address and the number of the box at the corner so if he wants to, he can call to set something up. He will write to let me know when to be at the box, at least that's what he said. If he does write, and I hope he does. Maybe he can come over for supper. That way you and dad will get to meet him and he you. Would that be okay?"

"You know it's okay. Your dad and I are always happy to meet your friends. It gives us a chance to get to know them."

Tomorrow, being Monday, meant that we had to be up and off to work early in the morning. As was the case with most companies, rules and regulations were strictly enforced. Our employer, British Railways, was no different and in fact, most of us who worked there thought it was a lot worse than other companies. Strict was an understatement. Absolutely no lateness or any other tardiness was acceptable.

Mom and I called it a night and went off to bed. Mom made sure the fire was safe, rinsed out the cups and turned out the lights.

I tried to convince myself that if Ian didn't call, it wouldn't bother me but I knew in my heart I would be disappointed. Moira and I were popular and had many dates but nothing serious ever developed. We did what most of the other young people did, went to the pictures, dancing, or on walks, often in a foursome, sometimes by ourselves. On Sundays several of us went to the swimming pool then out for breakfast. I enjoyed the company of friends and looked forward to the times when we were all together. The chaps we hung around with were friends, just good friends, nothing more. This time it was different with Ian. There was something special, a spark I had never felt before. I couldn't get him out of my mind.

My stomach did cartwheels at the very thought of him, and blood rushed up my neck to my face. The feelings I was having totally took my breath away, never having experienced anything like it before, especially since I didn't know him. Love at first sight was not possible in my opinion. I didn't believe there was such a thing. Now I wondered, is this what they call love at first sight? Finally I dropped off to sleep, with Ian on my mind.

IX

Monday morning rolled around all too quickly, signalling the start of another week at the British Railways. I felt like sleeping in but taking a day off from the Railway, especially when some knew where we were on the weekend, was not an option. I made myself get out of bed, picked out clothes for the day, washed and dressed. I grabbed a piece of toast to eat on my way out of the door. Dad had already gone to work. Mom had long ago given up trying to convince me to sit at the table and have a proper breakfast before heading out. She knew all too well how strict they were at the Railway. Lateness was absolutely not tolerated for any reason. Moira and I always made sure we left in time to get on a tram into town. If one was too full, we could afford the time to wait for the next one. Mom never pushed me but she would have felt better if I gave myself a little more time to relax before going out to work.

Both Moira and I worked in the typing pool. It was a pretty good job and the money wasn't bad, by normal standards. Getting travel concessions was an added perk, especially for us as we always made good use of them. We worked in a huge bare, drab room. The wall facing the street was all windows from waist height to the ceiling. An opaque covering was over the bottom half of the windows; just enough to let the light in and enough too keep anyone from outside looking into the office. This was to keep us from being distracted by anyone passing by. With the daylight coming in from the windows and the overhead bulbs, there was enough like to work but it was a dreary room. The walls were bare, except for a clock that faced the supervisors' desks. On a rare sunny day in Glasgow, the sun peaked through the glass, giving the room a bit of brightness. On days when it was raining, and it rained a lot in Glasgow, it could be miserable and depressing.

The area surrounding the room was busy mainly because of a bus terminal across the street, the one where the boys would have taken the bus to go home. People were always coming and going from all parts of Scotland, even tourists from other parts of the world, travelling north or south from Glasgow.

Three long rows of desks that were joined together ran to the middle, with an aisle going down the center of the room. The rows were on either side of the aisle. Typists were seated at these desks with just enough working space between them. Several shorter desks ran down from the longer rows. Little shelves were pulled out to house the typewriters, making sure we all faced the front of the room.

It was important that we all faced the front where two supervisors sat, supposedly typing too. In actuality, they never took their eyes off the typists and at the first sign of any laxity, one of the supervisors marched like a soldier to the spot to see what was going on. Every so often one of them walked around the entire room, to make sure we knew who was boss. We could barely turn around without a supervisor being right at our backs.

This building was the head office of the British Railways and all of the typing, other than what was done by personal secretaries of which there were very few, passed through this typing pool. The volume was continuous and huge. Wicker baskets filled the many shelves along the wall behind the supervisors. If and when one of us finished our work, we went back to that basket, and took more work back to our desk to type. It was almost impossible to slack off but if one of us did, a severe reprimand was in order. These supervisors were like jail guards and we the prisoners. Much of the work that had to be typed was done in shorthand. This meant we had to be able to decipher someone else's work, no easy feat. That being said, much of the longhand wasn't much better. But it was great experience for us. If any of us had a problem deciphering some word or sentence, we could ask another typist or God forbid a supervisor, to look at it. The supervisors took turns going around the room, picking up the finished products to check over, looking for errors. If an error was found, the typist was called to the front to pick it up for retyping, while at the same time being scolded for carelessness. It was better for all concerned if mistakes were not made. No one was allowed to talk.

Neither Moira nor I had a newer typewriter. Whenever new typewriters were purchased, they were given to the seniors in the pool, and theirs were then passed down to the next in line. We never expected in our working life to be in line for a new one. We could only dream but we not so secretly hoped we would be out of there before becoming a senior. Getting a new typewriter was not enough of an incentive for anyone to stay on.

Moira was not in the same row as me, but if either of us had forgotten to find out what the other was doing that night, she would take a piece of work over to the other and pretend to ask her to decipher a particular word, at the same time asking, "are you going to the pictures tonight?" No sooner did we put our heads together than the supervisor got up from her seat and made a beeline to the desk, pretending it was time to pick up finished work. When that happened, it was a signal to us that the "jig was up!"

I was one of the lucky ones, though. I had applied for, and was successful in getting a position in another department, the office of which was across the street from the typing pool. Every afternoon I went over there, and visited the various offices to take dictation from the supervisors. It was staffed by men who treated me like a human being. The atmosphere was more relaxed, sometimes even having a laugh or two. The work still got done, even with such levity. When I finished taking dictation, I went back to the typing pool, usually close to quitting time, and got things organized for the next morning. The next day, I worked on what I had been given. I tried to stretch it out as long as I could, not because I didn't want to work, but because I didn't want to come under the close scrutiny of the supervisors. We were never free of their scrutiny, no matter. Sometimes though, when I didn't have as much work, I had to go back to the basket for more. No one could ever be out of work. I didn't mind though, because I knew I would be out of there after lunch.

Tea breaks were short and smokers jammed the washroom to get a quick puff. Before long, the supervisor came barging in the door, almost knocking the person behind it into the toilet. There was no stretching the break. The supervisors were always referred to as Miss, and each person had to sign in and sign out every day, as well as at lunchtime. I pity the person who was ever late. No one could fudge the time because each person passed the supervisors' desks to get to the sign in book. There was at least one of the supervisors at her desk at all times.

Moira and I were inseparable friends, we went everywhere together, had lunch together, shopped, danced and just hung out together. Lunch times we ate our sandwiches then walked over to Marks and Spencers or Woolworths to see if there were any bargains that day, maybe picking up a chocolate bar. We both loved Jerry Lewis and Dean Martin, and saw every one of their movies. Moira was crazy about Dean Martin. On her birthday, I splurged on one of Dean's records. Money wasn't too plentiful, but I always managed to wangle the price of the pictures from my dad. I often made arrangements with Moira for the night, even though I had no money. I knew my dad would spring for it. When I got home and started getting ready to go out my dad would ask where I was going. I always had the same reply, which he already knew, "Nowhere, but if I had the money I would go to the pictures."

It worked like magic every time.

I took on a part time job as a waitress in a nearby cafe one year to earn extra money for a trip to Paris. It was easy to get there on time after I was finished work at the Railway. Another friend from the Railway also worked there. It was basically a coffee and ice cream cafe, with no main meals. When patrons came out of the pictures, we were mobbed, no writing slips, we had to remember the orders in our heads. We had a good time at the cafe but we were no better off financially. I never did get my trip to Paris. Most of my money went to nylons, which I couldn't keep from ripping. That was another great experience too.

Monday was an unusually nice day. Instead of eating in the lunchroom, we ate outside. My whole conversation was about Ian. Poor Moira had to listen but didn't seem to mind. I knew it was crazy. I was crazy. I couldn't help it, I wanted to meet him again, see where it might lead. The thought of seeing him made me weak at the knees.

"You know, I don't want to rain on your parade or hurt your feelings, pal o' mine, but aren't you putting the cart before the horse just a little? You are letting yourself in for bitter disappointment if he doesn't contact you. I know what you are saying, how you are feeling but it takes two and we don't know about him yet. For your sake I hope he does come through, even if it's just to confirm how you feel but you have to admit, it's sudden. I don't want to see you hurt. I am not saying you will be, I am saying don't get overly anxious, please. He seemed to be interested, so who knows? Wait and see, okay?"

Moira was only looking out for me, not wanting to see me hurt, but of all the fellows we hung around with, she had never seen a reaction like this. Truth be told, I was probably more surprised at myself than she was.

We didn't plan on doing much that night, as we were still a tired from our trip. I had to wash my hair and look out my clothes for work. It was a good night to stay in for both of us.

Tuesday followed our usual routine. Moira and I got the tram and went off to work. It was too early to hear from Ian so I wasn't worried. We went into town after work, where I bought a cardigan on sale, Moira bought a pair of shoes, nattering all the way. Moira did not mention Ian. After supper, we met up with a couple of other pals and off we went to see The Quiet Man, a lovely story. Afterwards we splurged on a coffee. Once at home again, I fell asleep, Ian on my mind wondering about him and me.

Wednesday also followed our regular routine. Maybe today there would be a note from Ian when I got home but I was trying not to get too worked up. My excitement quickly disappeared when mom told me there was no letter.

"You seem overly anxious to hear from this Ian," mom said. "It's only been a few days, hardly time for a note to get here, providing he wrote one as soon as he got home. Don't get your hopes built up too much. If it's to be, it will be."

That was mom, always sensible but it was not what I wanted to hear.

On Thursday, I waited for Moira at the close. She knew instantly that I hadn't heard from Ian. I wasn't looking for her coming down the street; my eyes were staring at the ground. I could tell she didn't want to get into the situation between Ian and me. She only said: "You didn't get a letter but honestly, it has only been a few days, give the guy a chance. You are too anxious."

"Oh well, if he doesn't write to tell me to be at the phone box, he will be the loser," showing phony bravado.

We both knew I didn't mean it.

"You know what the mail is like when you are waiting for something, it seems to take forever," Moira said, trying to make me feel better.

Back home from work, my mother smiled as she handed me a note from Ian. My hands were shaking, my heart thumping as I tried to open the envelope. When I finally opened it, I read,

"Fiona: I hope this note finds you well. I haven't been able to get you out of my mind. I didn't know if you would still be interested in hearing from me. I would love to see you again. If you feel the same way, I could come to Glasgow on Saturday and meet you at the bus station. We could go to the dancing if you like or whatever else you might be interested in doing. I will call you on Saturday morning at about 9:00 a.m. We can make arrangements then. I hope you will be waiting for my call. I am looking forward to seeing you. Until then, love Ian."

"Love, Ian." That sent a tingle through me. Why did he say that? Does it mean he loves me? I was being silly, acting like a schoolgirl but I so wanted him to have the same feelings for me, as I was sure I had for him. How will I get through the week until Saturday? I could hardly contain myself.

I started humming and immediately mom said, "I suppose we will be having company for tea on Saturday? I don't think I have ever seen you as taken with a boy before."

I told mom I was running up to see Moira for a few minutes. She knew I wanted to tell her about the letter. My tea was ready but I told mom I wouldn't be too long. Moira's family had just sat down to tea. When I told her about the letter, she couldn't have been happier but she was still worried about me being disappointed.

"I can't wait for Saturday, how will I get through the rest of the week?" I said to her.

"You don't have long to wait, only a couple of days, you'll make it" she said, giving me a hug. I let her get back to tea and went home, singing all the way.

I don't know how I managed to get my work done on Friday. I was especially glad that I had the job around the corner. I took the dictation alright but wondered if I would be able to read it on Monday. "Oh well, I'll worry about that on Monday." I kept busy but the day dragged by ever so slowly. At last it was Friday night. Saturday was almost here. I set my alarm for the next morning. I never had a problem getting up for work, but I wasn't taking any chances. I was too excited to sleep and afraid that if and when I did doze off, I might sleep in. I let mom know that Ian was going to call me on Saturday morning.

" I think he might come through here, I hope so anyway.

X

Finally, Saturday morning arrived. Mom wasn't surprised to see me getting ready so early on my day off. Lightheartedly, she remarked on my excitement adding that she didn't remember me being so nervous about a date before. I tried to fluff it off, but mom was very discerning. She could read me like a book; she wasn't easy to fool and knew I was a little more than interested. My nervous chatter was one thing that gave me away. I was humming some tunes as I thought about getting ready to go down the corner to await the call.

"Ask Ian to come over for tea?"

Parents always liked to meet new friends and especially of the male persuasion, even a casual date. This was a good way to get to know who their children were going out with, to see if he was worthy of their child. Most children didn't seem to mind that.

"That's a good idea mom, I'll ask him. That way you can get to meet each other. Thanks."

I knew in my heart that Ian could very well be the one, Mr. Right. It was important he meet my family and they him. I hardly knew him, but other people have known instantly how they felt about someone. Many had happy marriages, some maybe not so much but the same could be said about long term relationships before marriage. I have known couples that lived together for years, had a good relationship and decided to tie the knot. It was the undoing of the relationship. So who knows, it could go either way.

My heart was fluttering. I felt faint at the thought of hearing Ian's voice again. I couldn't make up my mind what to wear. I went through my closet with a fine tooth comb, checking this outfit and that outfit. Would this blouse match this skirt, or pants? I tried on several outfits before the penny dropped. Boink! What an idiot. I was only going to the phone box, not the bus station. He wouldn't see me anyway. I could go down in my goonie (nightgown) for that matter. Looking in the mirror I said to myself, "C'mon, get a grip, smarten up. If this is how you are with a telephone call, what will you be like tomorrow, if he comes through?"

I closed my eyes, counted to 10, took a deep breath and relaxed my body. I got washed and threw on some baggy pants and a sweater.

Mom and I had a little chat over a cup of tea before I went down to the telephone box at the corner. We had a good relationship, as good as any mother/daughter could be. She was easy to talk to and was genuinely interested in everything I did. I would never keep anything from her, or at least I hadn't up until now. That being said, there are always some little things daughters don't discuss with or tell their mothers. That's what close girlfriends are for. If it was important I knew my mother would want to know.

Being the discerning lady she was, mom knew this new friend I had met, was special to me, different from most of the boys that I had brought home. I had many boyfriends, all of whom my parents had met but they were just that, friends who happened to be male. Knowing how I had reacted with others, she could tell this time it was different. They always encouraged me to bring friends home. Seeing for themselves who I was hanging out with was better than being told but by now they knew most of my friends very well. Moira's parents were the same.

I was out bright and early well before the time Ian said he would call. Even then, there were two people waiting at the box and one on the telephone. Most of the people waiting knew each other, we were neighbours. Jim had to make a call. He was next after the lady in the box finishing her call.

Jennie, the next in line, suggested I use the telephone first because she was waiting for a call. I told her I was waiting for a call too. The lady in the booth finished her call and Jim moved in. Now the two of us were waiting and hoping Jim wouldn't take too long. We didn't want our callers to get a busy signal. Good, Jim's call was short. Now the box was empty again. We moved a little closer to reach the phone when it rang. After a few minutes, the telephone rang. Jennie suggested I take it because it was a little early for her call. I wasn't expecting Ian's call for several minutes and told her to pick up the phone. Sure enough the call was for her. I hoped she wouldn't be too long either but didn't want to be selfish because if Ian called, I wouldn't want to be rushed. Telephones in private homes were rare unless you were quite well to do. In our working class neighbourhood, it would be rare for someone to have a telephone. Even if they did, most people wouldn't ask to use them because it wasn't a flat rate. There was a charge for each call, even local calls. Everyone was considerate of those waiting and tried to make their calls as short as possible so that others wouldn't have to wait too long or miss their call. Besides that, unless you had a lot of extra change with you, when your time was up, the operator let you know. If you didn't have the extra change, you were cut off. As a rule, telephones were used for emergency or important calls, not for idle chitchat.

Jennie finished her call, gave me a wave and left for home. Now I was getting edgy wondering if he had called when someone was on the phone or even if he would phone at all. Anyone passing me must have thought I had to go to the bathroom as I was fidgeting so much. "Will he phone, won't he phone?" I hoped no one else would come to use the phone in the meantime.

Many of the neighbours were already out on the street shopping for their groceries. Little groups gathered here and there, stopping for a chat with a neighbour, catching up on the local news. It was a typical Saturday morning in Glasgow, and it was one of the ways homemakers socialized and caught up on the local news of the day.

After what seemed like an eternity during which time I questioned whether or not I should wait, the telephone rang. It was about 10 minutes past 9:00 a.m. I was already inside the box holding the door open with my foot just in case someone else needed to use the phone. I couldn't commandeer it.

"Bring, bring - bring, bring - bring, bring." The ring startled me. I reached for the phone, hands shaking, and dropped the phone. But since it was attached with a metal cord, it didn't fall to the ground. I put the phone to my ear and said,

"Hello, Pollock 2316."

My knees buckled when I heard Ian say,

"It's me, Ian."

I tried not to let my nervousness show in my voice. I cleared my throat.

"Hi Ian, I am glad you got through okay, the phone has been busy this morning. Did you get a busy signal?"

"Nope, I got through on my first try. I was wondering if you got my note, if you would be at the telephone, or if you might have changed your mind. It's great to hear your voice again. If it's okay and you don't have any other plans, I thought I might meet you later on at the bus station on Killermont Street."

"No, I haven't any plans for the day and would love to meet you. Just say what time your bus is coming in. Mom has invited you over for tea, if you would like to come".

"Sounds like a good idea to me, I would love to meet your family." Maybe you can think up something for us to do, or someplace to go. We can talk about it when I get there."

Ian gave me the information on the estimated time of arrival of the bus he would take to come to Glasgow. We could always take a walk around the shops in town, visit George Square, maybe get a coffee in a cafe and then decide what to do for the rest of the day. I didn't think either of us was bothered about what we did; we just wanted to see each other again. I know I did. About the only sure thing for the day was we had to be at my house for tea. The telephone operator interrupted the call:

"Time is up, please place money in the box".

Ian popped in some more change, but we knew we had to get off the line before that money was used up too. Since we were going to meet up later on and spend the day together, we could talk all we wanted then. We said goodbye and hung up the telephone.

I had to run up the street to Moira's house. She lived three flights up but I didn't hesitate a minute, taking the stairs two at a time, singing all the way. I knew she would be up, as we were all pretty early risers, even on the weekends. I chapped on the door, waited a minute or two and Moira's mom came to the door.

"You're up and about early this morning my lass. What's the reason?"

"I had to be at the phone to get Ian's call. I wanted to let Moira know."

At that Moira came to the door. She could tell by the huge smile on my face that the call must have come in.

"Well?" she said.

"Yup, he called and I am meeting him in town later. Mom invited him to tea and he said that was okay. I am so excited Moira I could scream and I might have, if it hadn't been so early in the morning. I just wanted to let you know. Our plans for Sunday are still on and I will tell you all about it then, okay?"

"I am happy for you and am glad he phoned. Good luck, see you tomorrow, same time as always."

I skipped back down to my close, ran up the stairs two at a time to my house. We lived on the first floor, which wasn't such a challenge. The door wasn't locked. I opened it and went into the house. Mom looked at me questioningly,

"Well?"

"He called, la de dah, he called and he is coming to Glasgow this afternoon. I don't know what we will do yet but he says he would like to meet you and is looking forward to tea," I said breathlessly.

"Good. I am glad you aren't disappointed. I'll go out to the shops later and get something nice in for tea. Why don't you settle down, relax and have something to eat, even a slice of toast."

I wasn't hungry. Eating was the last thing on my mind but I knew mom would be worried if I didn't have something. I made a bit of toast and had some tea. That kept her happy.

Saturday was an unusually nice day, weather wise. Wearing a light coat or jacket would be the sensible thing to do. In Scotland you can never tell what the weather will be like before the day is out. Starts nice, ends up terrible or vice versa. Almost everyone carried umbrellas with them,just in case. Sometimes there were four seasons in one day.

Now I was in a dither about what to wear. Ian would actually see me this time and I wanted to make a good impression. Wearing slacks and casual clothes was not particularly common but it was Saturday and wearing slacks was a bit more acceptable, among the young folks anyway, in spite of the stares we might get. Moira and I often bucked the trend in the clothing department. Besides, after a week of strict supervision and dress code at the British Railways, we found it much more relaxing in casual clothes and we didn't have to worry about supervisors breathing down our necks.

Most of the morning was spent trying on this and trying on that. I finally chose a pair of gray pinstripe slacks with the ever-popular drainpipe bottoms. A pink mock turtleneck sweater would go quite nicely with that. I chose my light black jacket to finish off the outfit. Jewelry wasn't a big priority with me although I liked it but seldom wore any. My aunt had given me a gold pendant with a small drop pearl and a little diamond above it. It was delicate and very special to me, reminding me of an aunt that I dearly loved. My plain black loafers, also popular with young folks, were comfortable for walking. That was my choice. A quick glance in the mirror and I felt comfortable with my decision.

"Not bad, I'll do."

I went into the other room and stood in front of mom and dad.

"What do you think?"

"You look braw (lovely) lass. Lucky chap Ian".

My natural hair colour was a mousy brown but Moira and I had played around with tints too many times to count. This latest attempt turned my hair from a mousy brown to a sparkly gingery colour, probably because of the many natural red highlights in my hair. It was easy to see that I was excited and shaky with nerves. My dad noticed it and said,

"I hope this fella's worth it hen."

I smiled and said, "cheerio," and skipped out the door, my head in the clouds.

XI

Surprisingly, for a Saturday when service was cut and trams were fewer and father between, I didn't have to wait too long for a tram. It was only about a 15-minute drive and a few steps walk from where I got off the tram to the bus station. Saturday was a big day in Glasgow. Shoppers came from many smaller towns outside of Glasgow where the shopping was good. Glaswegians filled the shops as well on their day off. Argyle and Buchanan Streets were favourites with the shoppers, lots of excellent shops with wide varieties of merchandise. Marks & Spencers was probably the number one shop, with Lewis's, Littlewoods, and C & A running close behind. Sauchiehall Street had many beautiful shops too, a little more upscale. There were several good shoe shops on Argyle Street, most were busy and streets crowded as shoppers bustled from shop to shop trying to find the best bargains.

Not many people owned their own cars and the mode of transportation was either a tram, bus or train. Service was excellent. The terminal would be especially busy today as this was a hub for travellers from all over Scotland who were coming to Glasgow for one reason or another, mostly for the shopping. Some travellers transferred to other buses for other destinations. I gave myself plenty of time by leaving home earlier than necessary. Crowds were already in the terminal. My stomach got queasy as I walked from the tram stop to the bus terminal. Goose bumps were forming on my skin and my palms were getting sweaty. I was shaking, actually feeling a little faint.

Waiting for Ian's bus was agony, in a pleasant way. I watched intently as buses drove in and out, carrying so many people from out of town. At long last, the bus I was waiting for drove into the platform. I could feel those butterflies again. An older man got off the bus first, followed by a woman. A couple with children came next. Where was Ian? Did he miss the bus? Did he change his mind? A few more passengers got off and then I saw him. I was so excited. He looked more handsome than I remembered, but slightly different without his scarf and tam in the team colours. He wore a navy blue bird's eye suit, which was all the rage. It was called bird's eye because of the tiny white dots all over it. A plain light blue shirt with a tiny slivery fleck was the perfect match. His light blue tie had a small navy pattern on it. Shining on his feet like the sun was a pair of ox blood coloured slip-on shoes, very popular these days. His eyes darted back and forth looking for me. When he saw me, he waved. I melted.

We both picked up our pace as we headed towards each other. My legs were weak but I carried on and as we came together, Ian gave me a little peck on the cheek. I was putty. I had to get control. I didn't know what Ian's feelings were, if he even had any, hence I didn't want to show my feelings first and maybe end up looking like a fool. This could be a casual friendship to him, but my instincts told me differently although when you want something to be true, the mind can convince you of something that's not there. Ian gently took hold of my hand as we moved slowly out of the bus station, in the direction of city center. We stopped at the booth first so Ian could double check the time of the last bus home. My hands trembled and I could feel a slight tremble in his too, which gave me some encouragement. It was entirely possible that he felt as I did, there definitely was magnetism between us, no getting away from it. I told him how much I had been looking forward to seeing him again. He said I was never out of his mind since we met. He could hardly wait for Saturday either to see me again. These were more reassurance for me, just what I needed.

We left the terminal on the side opposite to the Railway offices where Moira and I worked. I guided him across the street to let him see the office but with the covering on the inside of the windows, he would have had to climb up on the ledge for a peek. He wasn't about to do that, especially with his suit on. We crossed the street again to the terminal side and dawdled down the street heading for the city center where all the activity was, especially on Saturdays. Our chatter was animated because we were each a little nervous. I would start to say something just as he did and vice versa. After a few instances, we started to laugh. We stopped in at the little tearoom where Moira and I often had tea, if we had any money. It was mostly on paydays that we treated ourselves to lunch. The food was good and the prices were reasonable. It was spotless with little square tables here and there, all covered with fresh white linen tablecloths. The servers were friendly as were most of the customers who wandered in. It wasn't quite as busy today. Most of their business came from the offices around which were normally closed on the weekend. Today there were a couple of employees catching up on work. As for shoppers, a few ventured up the street as far as the station, their main goal being down in the city center. I thought a tea break might be just the thing to relax us, help us to settle down for the rest of the day. Again we both started to say something at the same time, it was hilarious and it broke the nervousness until finally, we both relaxed and lightened up. We each ordered a tea and scone. Soon we were catching up on what we had been up to since our trip to London. I told him that it was work as usual for Moira and me. We went to the pictures one night during the week. This was our normal routine, work, pictures and dancing.

"How is Moira anyway?" He asked.

"She is great and said to tell you she was asking for you."

It was pretty much the same scenario for Ian and the others but instead of going to the pictures, they played soccer a couple of nights after work. That was about it for him.

"Any idea what you want to do today?" he asked.

"I haven't made any plans because I wasn't sure what you might want to do. I told my mother we would be back home about 6:00 p.m. for tea if it's okay with you."

It was still early enough on this pleasant day.

"Why don't we follow the rest of the crowd and walk over to town to check out some of the shops? You don't come up here very often, do you?" I asked him.

"No, we rarely come up here except for the odd soccer game. It's mostly for shopping anyway and we are not into that. Let's dawdle down to the main area, look around, see what might take our fancy, then have a bite of lunch."

"Deal. Depending on time, we can either walk home or take the tram, it's not that far from here."

"Okay, fine with me."

It wasn't far to walk down to town and since the weather was pleasant, we decided to walk. We could have waited for a tram but there wasn't much point in that since they were usually packed with shoppers. We weren't in any great hurry to do anything so whatever happened, happened. Ian reached for my hand as we walked down to Argyle Street. I was in seventh heaven.

We stopped in at some of the shops. I tried on sandals that I had been looking for. I didn't buy them but at least I had an idea what was available. Ian said he was looking to buy a new shirt for work. We checked them out but he didn't fancy anything or just wasn't in the mood for shopping. We stopped along the way and bought an ice cream cone then sat down on a bench licking our cones, watching the comings and goings of all the shoppers. There were a few of the street entertainers here and there, singers, an accordion player and even the piper who drew a great crowd as the onlookers hooted and hollered while twirling around.

It was a typical Saturday afternoon in Glasgow City Centre, everyone was in fine tune and friendly as they walked along the street, or sat taking in the entertainment and sights while getting a much-needed rest for their feet.

After we had enough of the shopping, we decided to walk home, weather was still good and trams were packed anyway. We had plenty of time and while it was getting a little cooler, it was a nice enough for walking. As we walked hand in hand, we chatted about everything and anything, feeling more relaxed now. I told Ian I had gone to college then when I graduated, I worked for an engineering firm before joining the Railway. I had one brother, Andrew, who had emigrated to Canada. Ian shared his family information telling me he was an apprentice electrician. As we got closer to my house, several of the neighbours were still standing at the corner or at the closes. It was almost closing time and since nothing was opened on Sundays, the women had to make sure they had enough supplies to tide them over until Monday. Some of the women might have been delayed longer than they anticipated as they chatted with neighbours. This was also a typical Saturday scene in most Glasgow neighbourhoods and cities throughout Scotland.

We lived in a tenement in a working class area of the city. The original sandstone was just that, a sandy colour. Not many people knew that after years of industrial smoke and soot from the fireplace chimneys these tenements were now a dirty dark gray colour, almost black. Some buildings just up the street were a beautiful red brick colour, more modern and a little more upscale than the older gray ones. There was no door on the front or back of the close. On cold days the wind blew right through it. In our building, the close itself had three flats, as did the other three floors, or landings as they were called. Some buildings had four landings. Our close was made of stone, painted on the bottom half, and whitewash (a kind of white thin paint) on the top half. Landings were also stone, as were the stairs. Tenants took turns washing the stairs. When it was our turn, the chore fell to me.

The stone was very cold and hard, definitely not good for the knees. Pipe clay (a sort of chalky substance) was used to make designs on the landings and down the sides of the stairs. I earned some extra cash from neighbours who didn't want to or couldn't do the stairs when it was their turn. I could always use extra cash for the pictures or to buy something for myself. Although I earned a fair salary at the Railway, I had to turn all of my pay over to my mother who in turn gave me pocket money. It was never enough for me. Most people worked under that system until they were 21 years of age. After that you went on your "own can" as it was called, then you paid your mother room and board. Sometimes it worked out for the better, sometimes not. This is when I had to try and wangle a few bob (shillings) from my dad for the pictures.

My close and the area in general, was a lot better than some of the other areas around. Our house was up one flight of stairs in the building, and consisted of a room and kitchen to the front with an inside toilet, without a bath or sink in it. A pull chain hung down from the toilet tank. We never complained about that because many closes, including some across the street, had outside toilets that were situated on the landing. These were shared by three families. Toilets had no windows in them, which made them dark and dingy. It was a scary place for children, especially at night, but I never had to contend with that. The landings between floors had large windows, which gave some light on the way up to the respective houses. I can still remember the days when the landings had gas mantles to light the way. Every evening the leery (lamplighter) would come around and light the mantles. As children, it was exciting to follow him and watch while he lit the lamps on the street. When he emptied the carbide in the stank (drain), we could poke at it and watch it fizz and spit. I think some of the boys put some of the carbide in cans or bottles, dropped a match in and watched it explode. Such fun.

Our house wasn't posh by any means but it was warm and cozy. The kitchen also doubled as a bedroom for my parents who slept in the recessed bed, or hole in the wall bed as it was sometimes called. The room was brightly papered. A small dinette set, with four chairs, and a sideboard, with a Westminster chiming clock on top, filled the room. This is where we sat down for our meals. Most of the neighbours, including us, had newer interior fireplaces installed. A stand-alone gas cooker was placed against the wall on the other side of the room. We only had cold water and that came out of a Gooseneck type tap. The sink was lead and very deep set atop a cupboard. My father always referred to the sink as a "jaw box". Attached to the ceiling hung a pulley, as it was called. It consisted of two outside lengths of wood, almost the length of the room, with about four lengths of rope inside the frame. At the end of the pulley a rope hung down, that was used to lift and drop the pulley. The rope was anchored on a hook on the wall. These "pulleys" were in all of the houses. On washdays, if it was cold or wet outside, the clothes were hung on the pulley. It was annoying when anyone came into the kitchen. There was no way around it, they had to come under that pulley and if a person forgot to duck, the damp clothes smacked them in the face. I insisted that my mother clear the pulley that day, as I always did when company was coming. I didn't want any clothes hanging down, although it wouldn't have mattered to Ian because his family probably had the same thing.

Before having the interior fireplace installed, we, like everyone else in the building, had an old time lead grate containing a fireplace, plus an oven. The cooking unit on top could be folded back, leaving a space to keep pots or a kettle warm, providing the fire was lit. I wasn't too unhappy when my mother decided to renovate, because I was the one who had to put the black polish on the grate every Friday, and shine the stainless steel until it glowed. It was hard work. Interior fireplace was the name given to the modern tiled unit. It was about five feet long by about four feet high. Tiles were about six to nine inches deep, and the depth allowed a mantle piece along the top, with a step down on each side where an ornament could be placed. Tiles also formed a fender of about 18 inches with the fireplace in the middle. It was a vast improvement over the older ones, took up less room and easier to clean.

What was known as "the room" was much the same size as the kitchen. It too had an interior fireplace. Two recessed beds were in that room, one of which I slept in. We had a piano, placed along the wall between the two recessed beds. When we had company, which was often, we all gathered around the piano for a singsong. A large wardrobe sat in one corner. On the same wall as the fireplace, close to the corner, there was a built in cupboard that was called a press, filled to the brim with books that my dad kept buying at the Barras (flea market) every Saturday. A recessed bed actually looked like a cupboard from the outside, it had a door on it and when it was closed, it could be mistaken for a cupboard. Once opened, it was evident that it was long enough and deep enough for a mattress to be fitted in there on top of a frame. Since most people used these areas as beds, the doors were nearly always removed. My dad used the other recessed bed area on the other side of the piano, as a den for himself.

My dad was a very talented artist. His den walls were covered with his work. When he was a young man, he earned a free session at the Glasgow School of Art but when it was over, he could not afford to continue, even though his teacher, who saw his talent, tried his best to help out. This was one of the tragedies of the poorer classes.

Fireplaces provided the only heat source in these houses but they usually did a good job, except when someone left the room door open. Those sitting huddled in front of the fire, not wanting to get up and out of the range of the heat, could be heard yelling, "shut the door". Often on a cold winter's night, families huddled around the fireplace until their legs got badly marked or marley as it was called, with the heat.

This room was also brightly wallpapered and had a multi coloured Axminster rug on the floor. Many of dad's drawings were hanging on the walls, giving the whole place a homey feel. We had a lobby between the two rooms and the toilet. The only entrance/exit in the house was the front door, which opened into the lobby. In the middle of one wall sat the coal bunker filled regularly by the local coal man who used a horse drawn cart. He carried the bags of coal on his back, even up to the third and sometimes fourth storeys. His face, hands and clothes were always black from the coal. Many a time my brother and I, when we were younger, hid the carpet beater in the coal bunker before the coal man arrived to fill it. When he did, the carpet beater would be lost but not for long. It didn't take long for our parents to find the beater. The carpet beater was used to beat the dirt out of carpets, hanging on a clothesline in the backyard. They were also often used to smack the children on the behind as a punishment. It wasn't used to beat, more like a tap but the threat of it was usually enough to smarten us up, until we forgot again. The second use being the reason the carpet beater was hidden, when possible.

Dad and I had done most of the wallpapering in the house. Every time I thought about it, I laughed because I could always envision him up the ladder, cursing and swearing like a Dragoon Guard when things were not going right. On one such occasion, mom was trying to catch the bottom of the roll while dad held onto the top. This, they hoped, would allow them to paste the paper evenly all the way to the top at the same time. On this particular occasion, mom was trying to get under the ladder to catch the now pasted paper so she could spread it in place, while dad spread the top at the same time, each smoothing out the air bubbles as they went along. Mom was a little larger than the center of the ladder making it shake as she struggled to get under it. Dad almost fell off the ladder, which only increased his "choice" vocabulary. The paper began to rip just below his hands and with all the movement; it finally split across the width, leaving him with a strip of about three inches in his hands. The rest of the wallpaper dropped from his hands and landed on top of mom, pasting itself to her. She scrambled to get out from under the ladder, which didn't help matters. I was paralyzed laughing, and couldn't help her but I finally managed to reach for the ladder to steady it enough for her to get out and when she did, dad got down. We all took one look at each other and went into fits of laughter. Needless to say, that particular strip of paper was useless. I have to admit dad did use swear words but it was never in an angry way or directed at anyone, it just seemed to be part of his conversation.

I smiled and gave a little wave to a couple of the neighbours who were standing chatting at the close. When I introduced Ian to them, I could tell by their smiles and wide-open eyes that they were impressed. No surprise there! We went upstairs, opened the door and went inside. We rarely locked our doors when someone was home. We shut the door behind us and walked through the lobby into the kitchen. Ian was understandably nervous about meeting my parents. He needn't have been because when I introduced them to each other, they shook hands and formed an immediate bond. Mom asked Ian if he had a pleasant trip up and if he managed to get a seat on the bus. He told her he got on an empty bus at his terminal so there was no problem getting a seat. He told my parents he was glad to meet them. Dad with his usual sense of humour which he thought was funny but not everyone did, made some crack about getting fed up waiting for us to come home so that he could get his tea. He also told Ian he had better be on his best behaviour. The smile left Ian's face until he saw my dad was trying to be funny. That took the edge off and it was smooth sailing from then on.

I could tell my parents were happy with their first impression of him. What wasn't to be impressed with? He was, after all, a tall good-looking fellow who was an apprentice electrician. He not only looked good, his prospects were nothing to sneeze at either, should this friendship blossom. It didn't hurt that Ian was polite, had good manners and gave mom a lovely box of chocolates. I felt we were all off to a very good start.

Mom bought some of the best gammon (ham) for teatime. I asked if she would make some of her fantastic fritters to add to whatever she was getting for tea. We all loved fritters and I knew Ian would like them too. Fritters are made from thinly sliced potatoes, dipped in batter and deep fried. They were definitely not good for weight control but too good to resist. Everyone loved them. Dad made some shortbread and empire biscuits to go along with cream cakes which mom bought especially for tonight. Our family, like most of our neighbours, didn't often eat this fancy but this was a special occasion. Our family probably had more sweets than most of our neighbours, because my dad baked them.

Sometimes I baked cakes and biscuits, which I thoroughly enjoyed doing. Chip off the old block.

We had a lovely tea time, all relaxed and talkative. Naturally my parents tried to get as much information out of Ian as possible, not to be nosey but because he was taking their daughter out and it was also a means of conversation. He didn't seem to mind when dad asked where his father worked and how many siblings he had. He also asked how far along he was in his apprenticeship. Nothing too deep, thank goodness. Ian complimented mom on the lovely meal and told dad he loved the shortbread and especially the empire biscuits. He thanked them for the lovely meal. He was on a roll for sure, saying the right things at the right time.

Supper over, we moved to the fireplace chairs with a second cup of tea and a biscuit. My parents were going to see a film, a normal activity on Saturday night. We told them to go ahead and we would clear the dishes and the table. They gave their okay to that arrangement. In my mind I could pretend to be Ian's wife while cleaning up together. We thought it would be a good idea if we stayed in on this first date, to get to know each other a little more and maybe play a game or two or just listen to some of the records on the radiogram. Ian had to get back into town for the last bus home, but we still had a few hours before that. Dishes done and put away, we picked out some of our favourite records, including The Blue Rays, of course, Johnnie Ray (my favourite, not his), Frankie Laine, Guy Mitchell, etc. I put the music on and we played a few games of cards.

We talked as we played. I mentioned again that my brother had immigrated to Canada a year ago and I was now the only one living at home. Ian said,

"Quite a few of our neighbours have also emigrated to Canada, some to Australia but I don't fancy doing that. Do you think you might join him at some time in the future?"

"Nope, not in my plans at all. I am happy with my life, my job and the friends I have. I have never had any notion of leaving Glasgow and only concentrated on getting a good job after finishing college. There are good opportunities for advancement in the British Railways but when I left college, there were no vacancies. I put in an application and took a position with an engineering firm, hoping a job with them would come up soon. When I finally got accepted, there was only a vacancy in the typing pool but it got my foot in the door. I am hoping some day to get an executive private secretary's job but they are few and far between. Most of the people in those jobs stay until retirement. The other good thing about the job with the Railway is the travel concessions. That's how Moira and I can travel all over to see the group. Nope, I am quite happy with my life and have no other plans at the moment."

He was an apprentice electrician, which meant he was committed for about five years until he finished his time. I asked him about his future plans, if he had any.

"Well first of all I have to complete my apprenticeship. After that I will have to find a job and will probably start at the bottom. I don't think there will be any problem getting a job. My long range plan is to have my own business but that is a long way down the road."

When dad questioned Ian about his dad and family, he told us that he had a brother and two sisters all at home, with him coming in the middle. They lived in a larger council house, with a lot more room than we had. Council houses were provided to families whose homes were over crowded. Mixed families, meaning male and female, were given priority when Council houses became available. The larger the family, the quicker they got the new house. Many inner city families moved to outlying areas where the newer houses were built. My parents had applied to get a larger home on the basis of a mixed family, but we never got the approval and now that we were adults, my brother no longer living with us, it didn't matter much anymore.

The time flew by and before we knew it, it was time for Ian to take the bus home. Before he left though, we had a cup of tea and some of the cakes that were left over from supper. I offered to go into town with him to see him off, but he didn't want me coming back home by myself. It was safe enough where I lived, but he didn't like the idea anyway. When we went downstairs to the street, Ian slipped his arm around my waist. My body tingled and I liked it. I took the hint and put my arm around his waist. We dawdled along to the bus stop, chatting about this and that and about when we might meet again.

The first tram came along the street and passed the shelter without stopping. There was no one waiting in the shelter. We hadn't reached it yet but the driver would have stopped, had we signalled him to do so. Ian would have to take the next one for sure; otherwise he would miss the last bus home from the town center. We had the shelter all to ourselves, which suited us just fine. We cuddled up to each other and kissed, and I could feel the blood rush to my face. Ian looked at me and said,
"You will probably think I am nuts. I'm even surprised at myself, but I am falling in love with you. I haven't felt like this for anyone else. I hope we can continue to see each other, see how things move along. How do you feel about that?"

I knew my feelings for Ian were strong, knew I hadn't felt like this before either, but it scared me a little because it was too fast. I didn't want to tell him how I felt just yet but I definitely wanted to continue seeing him.

"I like you a lot Ian and I hope we can continue to see each other. It won't be as easy as if you lived in Glasgow but we can at least get together on weekends. During the week will be more difficult for you than me. We can work something out. I know I want to see you again and can't wait until you come back. I can always visit your home too. Let's see what happens, okay?"

Just at that, another tram stopped. Ian hugged and kissed me goodnight, got on the tram and waved until he was out of sight.

I floated home with my head in the clouds. I couldn't wait to tell Moira but it would have to wait until tomorrow when we got together for our Sunday venture to the Baths.

I was back in the house before my parents came home.

"Well how was your evening with Ian?" Mom asked when they came in. "I can see by your beaming face that it must have worked out nicely."

"We sat by the fire and got to know each other a little bit better, had some tea and finished the cakes. He told me all about his family, his friends and what he hopes to do in the future after he finishes his apprenticeship. He enjoyed meeting you and said to thank you again for being so nice to him"

"Will you be seeing him again?"

"Hopefully, but we have to figure out when he is able to come to Glasgow or when I might be able to visit his family. We like each other and have a lot in common except they follow football teams and we follow The Blue Rays. He will call again next week" I replied.

Mom said that he seemed like a decent, clean-cut fellow and that he would be welcome any time. He was polite with good manners. Dad didn't say too much, except that he thought he was okay. Mom and dad didn't have to give me any of the usual lectures because we had gone over that in the past. They knew they could trust me.

XII

It was Sunday morning again. Weather permitting, Moira and I followed the same routine unless something else more important came up. We met up and headed off to the local swimming pool just up the road. As with everything, there was always a queue. Swimmers were allowed so much time then they got turfed and others were let in. It wasn't often that there weren't any people waiting to get in but on the odd occasion it happened. When it did, there was no time limit put on swimmers. The Baths, as they were called, consisted of two swimming ponds, a large one and a smaller one that was affectionately called the baby pond. By its very name, you can tell it was for the little ones. Along the walls around the pool were cubicles for swimmers to change into their bathing suits. After changing, swimmers had to go through showers before getting into the water. Swimmers didn't waste any time getting into the water because before long, the sound of the whistle told those in the pond that their time was up and they had to get out of the water immediately. No dithering, no fooling around, just get out and get out now.

Upstairs in the same building there were hot baths where residents who didn't have baths in their houses, and that was the majority of people around the area, paid sixpence for a hot bath. Saturdays were especially busy for the hot baths. Tickets were purchased at the front desk after which patrons were sent to a large waiting room where they waited until their number was called. Baths for men and women were in different sections of the floor. Ladies baths consisted of two rows of approximately 10 cubicles facing each other, housing bathtubs. It was probably the same for the men. An attendant, more like a prison guard on duty, called out a number when there was an empty bath. She turned on the bath water with a large key bar. She let the water run to an amount she thought you should have and you dare not say a word. You weren't allowed to complain. If the level of the water was too low, too bad, it was never too high, if it was too hot, too bad and if it was too cold, too bad again. When the guard thought bathers had enough time, she banged on the door, yelling it was time to get out, and again, no dilly-dallying.

Moira usually called in for me because our close was next to the road leading to the baths. I could hardly wait to tell her about Ian's visit. She was just as anxious to hear about it, knowing how much I was looking forward to seeing him again. She was also curious to know what my parents thought of him.

'Hello Moira, how are you this morning? Time for a cuppa?" Mom asked her.

"I am okay thanks. How about yourself? Thanks very much but I just had my tea before I came down the road. I'll pass on it for now."

She turned to Moira and said, "I suppose you will be getting all the gossip on Ian? How come you didn't find a fellow on the train?"

"I did meet Ian's pal George and the other two chaps but I am not put out that he didn't call me. I am not as star struck as your loonie daughter. Maybe you should start saving for a wedding soon," she laughed.

"Nice Moira thanks a lot," I said with a whiney upset voice. "C'mon, we should get going, don't want to keep the gang waiting. There'll likely be a queue by now. Hopefully they will keep a place for us if they are there first. Remember mom, we will be going to the cafe for a snack before we come home so don't worry about lunch."

Once outside and walking up the road, Moira couldn't wait any longer. "Okay let's have it, how did it go? Do you still think he is the one or? C'mon, tell me all about it, did you go out or stay in?"

"I met him at the bus. We walked through town, went into some shops, had a snack. Later we had some ice cream cones and sat on the bench people watching. I was a bit nervous at first, he was too but after a while we relaxed and had a lovely time. We came home, had tea and stayed in as mom and dad went to the pictures. We played some records and a couple of card games but mainly we talked about our families, work and what plans we had, if any. When I told him that Andrew had gone to Canada, he asked if I was planning to emigrate. It worked out better than going out because we got to know each other a little more. I agree it's crazy and as fast as this is happening Moira, I think he is the one for me. He told me he thought he was falling in love with me. Even tho' I am pretty sure he is the one, I only said I liked him a lot, but didn't want to commit myself to any relationship just yet. He totally understood and agreed we should continue seeing each other anyway, as often as possible and see where it takes us. After all there is no rush and there is the distance between us. I suggested that I could take the bus to his hometown sometimes. We made a cuppa and had something to eat before he had to get the tram. When he put his arms around me, I went weak. We kissed and I could see stars. You know me Moira, always platonic friendships, but not this time. I am sure he is the one. We'll see."

"I'm happy for you kiddo, I am but I just want you to go slow, don't move too fast. There's lots of time. Get to know each other well, meet his family and friends and, like you say, see where it goes."

"I know, I know, you are right as usual but we just seem to click. There definitely was magic in the air. It feels right and if it's to be, it will be. Time will tell. At least we both seem to be on the same wavelength so that's a start. I promise I won't do anything foolish. You know me. I get all fluttery just talking about him."

The pond, the only one in the neighbourhood, was busy as usual, especially on Sundays when most people had time off from work or school. Many of the swimmers were friends of ours. We had been meeting every Sunday for years. Sometimes we met during the week but not that often. Afterwards we went to a nearby cafe for lunch. It was sort of a ritual with us. The cafe was at the corner of the same street as the pond. We didn't have far to walk. After lunch some of us went for a walk up to one of the big parks where we listened to the bands playing at the band shell. The park was always busy on Sundays too. It was a great place for young families to relax, have a picnic and listen to the music. Children could jump around as much as they wanted to.

We sat on the grass with the gang for a while, then left them behind and walked back down the road. An ice cream parlour, that had great ice cream, was on the way home, so naturally we stopped in. Passing that cafe was almost impossible for us. A nougat wafer is made with two thin wafers with a bit of marshmallow inside. The edges are sealed with chocolate. Double nougat meant two of these wafers with ice cream in the middle. Naturally double nougats were our choice, if we could afford it. Walking the rest of the way home, we ate and talked, but all I could talk about was Ian, how I felt about him, even though I had to admit I was surprised at the suddenness of the attraction and perhaps a little wary. His words, "I think I love you" kept repeating over and over in my mind. When we reached my close, Moira said “cheerio” and headed up the street a bit to her close. Monday morning would come soon enough and back to the prison camp and the commandants. Early to bed and early to rise it would be.

Mom, dad and I had some hot chocolate before getting ready for bed. I picked out my clothes for the morning. Naturally I went to sleep with Ian on my mind.

Moira called in for me on the way to the tramcar stop. This was our arrangement every day. We didn’t need to contact each other; we just met by my close. I was always ready and waiting for her. Neighbours, who went out to work were also on their way to the tram. Ours was a friendly working class neighbourhood where neighbours knew each other and were always on hand to help each other. If there was time while waiting for the tram folks got caught up in the local news of the day.

XIII

Not surprisingly, the week seemed to drag by. Normal routines followed, pictures one night, Moira's or my house to listen to records another night. On the nights that our favourite quartet played on the weekly radio show, we were glued to the set. It was one of the best comedy shows on the air but we only started listening to it because the quartet played on it. On other nights, we might have other friends in or go to one of their homes where we listened to the radiogram or played cards. On winter nights when the fire was lit, although many summer nights it still had to be lit, we stared into the red coals and tried to read them, the same as we did with tealeaves. Amazing what the imagination can see. Saturdays were mostly for dancing and Sundays the swimming pool and walks up to the park. I didn't stay out to late on Sunday, work called early in the morning. Basically that was our lives. We were happy and had no real complaints. If a well-known star from the U.S. was in town to do a show, we usually got tickets for that.

In the wintertime when the Pantomimes were playing, we took in one of them.

Moira knew I hadn't heard from Ian because I would have told her during the day. She was always the first to hear but she could probably tell by the look on my face before I said anything. I tried not to get disillusioned or read too much into this but it was difficult to do. Moira didn't bring up the subject and wouldn't until I did.

We went to the pictures straight from work one night during the week, not knowing there was another note at home for me. Just as well. I might have cancelled the picture show with Moira. That wouldn't have been fair. As soon as I walked in the house, mom, with a big smile on her face, handed me the note. Excitedly, I opened the envelope. He apologized for not writing sooner but he had to work a lot of overtime during the week and he couldn't manage to get over this weekend. If it was okay with me, he would meet me next weekend, same time same place and would phone on Friday around 8:00 p.m. to confirm that I was free and it was okay for him to come through. He apologized again for not being able to come through, hoped I would understand, and said he would make it up to me next time. He added that he hadn't been able to get me out of his mind all week and couldn't wait to see me again. At the bottom of the note was a

P.S. "I meant what I said last week. I love you and I hope you feel the same way."

Mom knew it was good news because I was smiling. I didn't show her the note but told her that he had to work extra hours this week. At least I knew he felt the same way about me as I did about him, which was good news for me. We had clicked, there was magic between us, I knew it, but it was nice to hear it from him. Knowing how we felt about each other meant we could be open and honest with our feelings, move slowly and see where it all lead. Even though it was love at first sight, I wasn't in any rush to get in too deep. We got along extremely well, but what about in the longer term? Anyway, there was no great rush. We were both young. Sometimes there is that special person for you and it's like magic. I never believed in love at first sight. Now I was a true believer.

Another week dragged ever so slowly by. Moira and I went through our usual activities but my heart and mind was on Saturday. Friday night I was front and center at the phone box. No one else was there. It wasn't long before the phone rang and it was Ian. We didn't talk on the phone too long except to say we couldn't wait for Saturday.

Finally it was Saturday again. I was rushing my life away, but it was a good rush. Waiting nervously in the same spot for the arrival of the bus, I watched all the usual activity; people coming empty handed and going laden with parcels. Moving up the platform to where passengers got off the bus, I got there just as the bus rolled in. Once the bus stopped I stood back a bit to let the passengers get off. " I wonder if he made it to the bus in time," I though. Just at that, off he came, the first one this time.

As soon as I saw him, my knees were weak again and I was tingly all over. Gosh he was handsome, wearing a navy sports jacket, gray pants and a pale gray shirt. His shirt collar was opened over his jacket collar. I wore a brown wrap around skirt that I had made myself with a heavier cardigan over a pale yellow short-sleeved shirt. He walked towards me, a few steps away, and as we came together, he put out his arms to hug me. We wrapped our arms around each other and whispered how happy we were to be together again. I melted.

As we walked hand in hand down the street to the same cafe where we had gone two weeks ago, we shared with each other what kind of week it had been for us and what we had done. I was the one who did most of the talking because he pretty much worked all week, with no leisure time. We ordered scones, jam and tea, and then another. While we were excited, we were not as nervous with each other this time. We were getting more relaxed and comfortable with each other. Reaching across the table, he held my hand and told me it was torture waiting for Saturday. I put my hand on top of his and said "ditto," (me too!)

Downtown was our destination again. It was where the action was and since it was early afternoon, there was no point in going to the pictures or dancing so early. Shopping was on the agenda. We didn't wish to purchase anything in particular, just to see if anything took our fancy. Instead of going to my house for tea, we planned to get a meal at one of the local pubs after wandering around town. There were some nice pubs in town and most served good meals quite reasonably. After we finished our tea, we strolled over go Argyle Street arm in arm, like a married couple, which I pretended we were. It was mobbed but that was part of the ambiance of the place. It was alive with people and of course, the usual assortment of entertainers.

As we walked in and out of the shops and along the street, we kept bumping into many shoppers, now loaded up with parcels. The town center of Glasgow was as nice a shopping area as could be found anywhere. That's the main reason a lot of people came from smaller towns outside of Glasgow where they might not have the larger department stores. It was also a days outing for families, getting new clothes, shoes or whatever. Prices were better in Glasgow. It was a great place to shop, vibrant and full of excitement.

We stopped in front of one of the largest, best and most popular shops in the heart of the town, looked in the windows and decided to go inside. Downstairs and right to the record department in the basement was our first stop. Shoppers could request clerk to have a particular record played before making a choice as to whether or not they might buy it. It was also a gathering place for the younger set where they hung around listening to all the popular music of the day being played, while searching the crowd, possibly hoping to meet someone of the opposite sex, or an acquaintance. A friend of mine, one of the group that regularly hung out together, was there. We stopped and chatted with her for a bit. I beamed as I proudly introduced Ian to my friend. She looked at me smiled and gave an approving wink. I knew she was giving me the okay. Ian had been planning to buy a new Frankie Laine record that was currently popular on the radio. He asked the clerk to play it and then bought it.

When we felt we had spent enough time down there listening to the music and looking around the other goods for sale in the basement, we took the escalator upstairs to the clothing department, housewares department and don't ask me why, but the toy department. We held hands as we walked around the shop, the picture of contentment. I silently imagined we were married and looking for items for the house. I liked the feeling of being married to Ian and could easily get used to it.

After all browsing was over; we strolled further along the street, stopping at windows to see what they had for sale. Although we hadn't intended to buy anything, we had managed to purchase a few odds and ends along the way. There was a nice little pub at the corner, close to the railway station. Ian liked the look of it. We went inside. Like everywhere else in the center of town on Saturdays, the pub was crowded with shoppers who needed to sit down and have a refreshment or meal before heading home with their parcels. Fortunately we didn't have to wait too long before we were seated in a booth. A booth was perfect for us. It was a little more private, if any table could be private in a pub.

This pub, like all pubs, had a long wooden bar with brass rails. Several patrons were standing at the bar having a drink. The decor was woody with beautiful panels all around the bottom half of the walls. Royal Stewart Tartan wallpaper covered the upper part of the walls above the wood. Many pictures of castles and other scenes from Scotland, along with Scottish artifacts hung on the walls. A large mirror hung behind the bar with a huge selection of liquor bottles neatly displayed on shelves underneath it. Beer taps were made of brass with white porcelain knobs on them. Bartenders were working non-stop to feed the thirsty shoppers. The atmosphere was noisy but light and lively.

Ian ordered a beer. I asked for a shandy (half beer and half lemonade), and we both ordered steak pie and chips. Ian reached across the table and held my hand. Tiny specks of perspiration peeped out along my forehead. He couldn't take his eyes off me and again said he had never felt like this about any girl before.

“We both know this is quick, we hardly know each other but I think what we feel is real and this doesn’t happen every day. We were meant for each other, we both feel it and I don’t want to waste any more time wondering. I know you are the one for me and I think you feel the same way so why don’t we make the commitment. I want you to be my steady girl and I hope you will say yes to marrying me,” Ian said.

“I feel the same way about you. I couldn’t wait to see you again. You are all I think about but do we know each other well enough to make such a serious commitment so soon? I love you and wouldn’t want to lose you either but doesn’t it take more than a few meetings to be sure? I have had boyfriends but it was always platonic, nothing serious, just friends. I never had any feelings for any one of them such as I have with you. Is that love or something else?" I replied.

"I know, but you have to admit there is something magical going on here and I don't want to risk losing you to someone else."

"The way I feel, I can't see that happening but it's early. We both seem to be saying the same thing, that we love each other. If that is true and we genuinely love each other and want to spend the rest of our lives together, then nothing will come between us. Nothing will change our love. Let's see each other exclusively as often as we can and see where that takes us."

Ian squeezed my hand and nodded his head in agreement, mouthing to me, "I love you."

The waiter brought our order. We were in no mood for eating but we both loved the steak pie and chips, so we forced ourselves. We were content just sitting there holding hands, looking into each other's eyes and enjoying being together for this short visit because at the end of the day, Ian would have to go back home. It wasn't like we would see each other every day

We couldn't sit there all night. After we finished our drinks and discussed what we might do now, going to see a movie seemed like the best choice. It was still early and Ian wouldn't have to catch his bus until much later on. We didn't have a television and even if we did, there was not much worth watching on it. There were a few cinemas over town with a variety of films on screen. Moulin Rouge was showing at one of the theatres. It won out. I loved musicals with Fred Astaire, Ginger Rogers, Gene Kelly, Judy Garland, Peter Lawford, Donald O'Connor, Mitzi Gaynor, Betty Grable, June Haver and Carmen Miranda. Ian was not all that keen on musicals, preferring some of the gangster movies with James Cagney,

Humphrey Bogart, Edward G. Robinson and George Raft, to name a few. I also enjoyed those actors and gangster movies but there wasn't one playing in town so Moulin Rouge it was.

Every time Moira and I went to see a musical, we floated into the huge foyers of the picture houses. Then after we came out from seeing the movie, we waltzed or tap-danced around the floor, depending on what movie we had just seen. We danced the whole way home, singing the songs of the movie, all the while pretending to be movie stars.

Staying in town to see the movie suited us because it was easier for Ian to get the bus. The early show was just about to start. We were in luck. Afterwards we could go to some little cafe nearby and have a cuppa or cold drink.

Once inside the cinema and once settled in our seats, Ian put his arm around me. I lay my head on his shoulder. My heart was purring like a kitten and I was as happy and content as a little puppy. It was pure magic. If there was a downside to this relationship, it was the distance between our homes but if that was the only hurdle to conquer, it could easily be overcome.

I was sorry to see the picture end. It was a great film and we both enjoyed it, but it meant that it was closer to the time when Ian would have to go home. The closeness I felt with him only confirmed my feelings for him. In between concentrating on the film, I let my mind wander and pretended we were married and had a baby sitter minding the children so that we could have a little break. I wouldn't be waltzing or tap dancing in the foyer tonight. I couldn't imagine what he would say if I did, but I felt like doing some fancy foot work, maybe a split or two. I was so in love and happy. I was on Cloud 9.

The cafe where I had a part time job at was just up the road. Different people owned it now but it remained pretty much the same. That's where we went to have a cuppa, scones and a bit of time to relax and chat some more. It was busy as always on Saturdays. Everyone else was so busy chatting with the people at their tables that they didn't pay much attention to other tables.

Ian again broached the subject of us making a commitment to each other and said he would like to give me a ring. I was ready for a commitment but I wanted to take a little time to be sure, give it more thought.

Too soon it was time to head for the bus station. I could catch the tram home after I saw him off. He said it was better if he took me to the tram. That way he wouldn't worry about my safety. While we waited for the tram, we sat on the bench. We snuggled up in each other's arms. There were lots of people in around the square, couples walking hand in hand, groups of chaps heading home after a night of whatever, while laughing. Watching all the antics of the different people was as good as a movie. I turned my face up to Ian and he kissed me. It wasn't a peck on the cheek this time but a real honest to goodness kiss with all the emotions that went along with it. Being in such a public place kept us from getting carried away, which we could easily have done. Was this love at first sight or was it something else, a feeling we might not be able to control? Whatever this magic between us was, no matter how we felt, it could not get out of hand. It might be easier to say than do it but that's the way it had to be as far as I was concerned.

Marriage was sacred. Anything more should and would wait until such times as I got married. I, like most of my contemporaries, totally believed in the sanctity of marriage, As I thought about that perhaps the distance between us might be a blessing after all instead of a problem. We would probably only see each other on Saturdays, which could make the situation worse, but at least it wouldn't be a daily battle. Ian knew how I felt and while he might not have been totally in agreement, he respected my feelings. We discussed the possibility of at the very least getting engaged, and even marriage. We knew that if we made that decision, it was still a long way off but at least we could think along those lines. In the meantime, the more we saw of each other, the better we would get to know each other and see where that took us. We made plans for next weekend.

Rumbling and rattling along the rails was my tram. By now there were a few more people at the stop. We hugged and kissed again, I stepped out and onto the tram. I made a beeline for the upstairs seats in the little box. Moira and I always made a dash for that spot. Ian still had enough time to catch his bus. It wasn't easy to watch him walk away through the square in the direction of the bus terminal. He turned to wave and then he was off. I had tears in my eyes. I wished we lived closer and yet I didn't.

The city was alive, even at this time of night. Couples walking hand in hand made me a little envious. Cheery, singing patrons were filling the streets as they left the pubs. Some of the antics of the ones who were just a little bit tipsy brought a smile to my face, even a chuckle. When the car moved away from all the activity of the center of town, I stared blankly out the window, not seeing anything but daydreaming of Ian and what, if anything, might become of us.

Mom was still awake, as usual, when I came home. She always pretended she wasn't waiting for me, that she had just got up to go to the bathroom or some other lame excuse. Truth be told, she wouldn't have rested until I got home safely. The kettle was on a peep on the gas, ready for whatever. She made a cup of tea and we both sat down by the fire to talk about what Ian and I had been up to. I told her about the shopping, pub lunch, the Moulin Rouge, how much we enjoyed it, how comfortable we were in each other's company and also that he would be coming back next weekend. I didn't go any further into detail than that because she would have thought I was crazy, as did Moira and everyone else I knew. If circumstances had been different, I might well have married him right away, which wouldn't have been a smart thing to do. With our tea finished and cups rinsed out, we went to bed.

It didn't take me too long to drift off. I was happy, excited and yet amazingly calm. I dreamed that I was walking down the aisle in a beautiful old church. The sun was streaming through the stained glass windows. Pews were half filled with family and friends awaiting the arrival of the bride. Moira appeared first, dressed in a pale blue bridesmaid's gown, then came the bride, me, stunning in a beautiful white wedding gown, exquisitely beaded with pearls and rhinestones. As my father and I walked down the aisle, I could see Ian at the altar with his good friend and best man George at his side. Both were resplendent in highland dress. I appeared overly anxious to reach Ian. I was moving like those films shown in slow motion. Would I ever get down to meet him at the alter? Finally I reached him, his face beaming at the sight of his bride. He smiled as he stretched out to clasp his hand in mine. "Who giveth this bride?" The minister asked. As my father, also looking magnificent in highland dress, stepped forward to say "I do", someone entered the church. The door shut with a loud bang. Everyone in the congregation turned to see who came in. I woke up. What a disappointment to learn I had only been dreaming. The noise caused by a door banging was actually dad shutting the toilet door. I felt like killing him. Hopefully one day it would be real. I drifted off to sleep again, all snuggly and warm with Ian on my mind.

XIV

Next morning, Sunday, when I awoke, I was still warm and cuddly from the dream. I didn't want this wonderful feeling to end as I snuggled up inside the blankets, stretching and snuggling. I lay in bed for some time, feeling good, reminiscing and dreaming of a future with Ian. My mind was all over the place, thinking about married life together. I had no doubt that he was the one for me.

I didn't want to leave those thoughts but being Sunday, Moira would be calling shortly for our walk to the baths, meeting up with friends and doing what we always did on Sundays.

I gave a yawn and a stretch then got out of bed. I had a light breakfast, put my towel, bathing suit and everything else I needed into my bag. Moira was just at the close edge, about to come up for me but I got there before she came any further. Two of the regulars in our swimming group were not able to make it. It happens, and that's okay. We do the best we can to get together every

Sunday but often there are other commitments that come up. Everyone got along extremely well together. We had been doing this Sunday thing for a long, long time. Moira and I enjoyed the company of the others but we were not unhappy when we were by ourselves, leaving us to talk on a more personal level.

I knew Moira was dying to know about my night with Ian. She was surprised when I told her that marriage had been discussed. I quickly added that it wasn't if but when. We both had the same feelings for each other; we were in love and didn't want to lose one another. I told her about my dream which made her laugh, and took away that too serious look from her face. She asked if she looked nice in her bridesmaid dress. Everything was Ian, Ian, Ian. I thought I should cool it a bit before Moira belted me one but I knew she was genuinely happy for me. I could see it in her face. She didn't want to see me getting hurt. I agreed, things were moving too quickly but it confirmed our feelings for each other. No matter, I had no plans to rush into any marriage. She voiced her concerns like a true friend although she admitted she didn't have any reason to doubt our feelings. Getting involved with one person, even thinking about marriage at our age, was something we always thought was a joke. We were having too much fun and were in no rush to settle down with anyone. Maybe someday but definitely not now. Besides, up to this time, there hadn't been anyone either of us felt we wanted to spend the rest of our lives with. Love does strange things for sure, and I was in love. Moira couldn't deny the radiance she saw in my face, something she had never seen before. I sensed she had doubt even though she was happy for me. I sensed that something was bothering her and asked her what it was. We were so close, we could tell each other anything and counted on the other to be honest in all things. We trusted each other's opinions.

"What is it Moira? Do you have some sixth sense or something? You know how happy I am. I believe you when you say you are happy for me, but I feel there is something else. Am I missing something?"

"No, I am truly happy for you if he is the one and you finally have someone in your life. I can honestly say I have no reason to doubt him. You seem to be as sure of your feelings as he his of is. I respect that and hope everything works out for you. If there is a slight doubt, it is that you don't know him, his family, what his life is like. This has all happened suddenly. I am not saying it can't happen, it has happened to others, but pal o' mine, just go slow, don't rush into anything. You are both young, have your whole lives ahead of you and if this is as genuine as you both believe, it will survive. Only time will tell. You know you are my dearest and best friend and I wouldn't hurt you for the world but I don't want to see anyone else hurting you either. I am not saying Ian will hurt you, he probably won't, just take your time is all I ask."

"I know, I know. I appreciate what you are saying. Believe it or not, I agree with you and don't intend to do anything foolish."

We left it at that as Moira told me I was the most levelheaded person she knew. If anyone would tread carefully, it was me.

During the weeks following, Moira and I were still inseparable as usual, meeting at the close to go to work, gabbing all the way, lunching and gabbing, shopping and gabbing and going to the pictures together. We didn't go back to the dancing over town though. That had been a regular Friday or Saturday outing for us but now that Ian was in the picture, the dancing was out, except when George occasionally joined us for a foursome on a weekend visit. It was so romantic dancing to the slower music snuggled in each other's arms, Ian whispering in my ears and me happily laying my head on his shoulders, eyes closed. When the music stopped, we just stood on the floor for a while, hoping for another slow dance that sometimes played, and sometimes did not. When we finally had to get off the floor, Ian wrapped his arm around my waist as we walked over to the table where George and Moira were sitting waiting for us. Both of them were happy in each other's company, being with us. While I secretly hoped something would develop between them, it was not to be. We enjoyed double dating no matter where we went but it was obvious they didn't click, although they developed a great friendship.

Ian and I kept in touch during the week by letter or telephone calls to the corner box. Sometimes he would stay over until Sunday, which was great for us. It gave us more time together. Mom made up a little cot in dad's den for him to sleep on. It worked out just great.

We saw each other as often as possible. On the odd occasion, Ian managed to come up to Glasgow for a short visit when we stayed around the area of the bus terminal, usually window shopping or having a cuppa in a cafe. Other times we caught another bus at the terminal travelling to seaside towns close to Glasgow such as Largs, Saltcoats, Ayr, Portobello where we had a picnic while enjoying the beautiful scenery all around us. When I knew the plans, I packed a lunch. Sometimes we got on the tram and went to the end of the line for our little picnic.

We didn't care what we did, so long as we were together. We treasured these times because it gave us time to get to know each other better. We agreed on almost everything. If we did have a difference of opinion, it was always resolved to our mutual satisfaction. We were so in love and enjoyed every minute we shared. Other than nights when we stayed in at my house, we tried to spend some time with our mutual friends, safety in numbers we thought. Although we discussed marriage, I was surprised when he seriously proposed to me one evening. Before I said anything, he let me know he wasn't rushing me into anything. He was not planning on marriage for some time yet. He was only 20, and had to finish his apprenticeship then find a decent job so that he could afford to support a family. He wanted everyone to know we were committed to each other and wanted me to wear an engagement ring. I was never surer of anything in my life. He was the love of my life, the one for me. I knew this was a once in a lifetime love that didn't happen often, but I still wasn't in a rush to get married either, preferring to enjoy the courtship and all that went with it. My parents totally accepted Ian and were happy for us. They too encouraged us to take our time. Marriage was serious business, and besides we were both still young.

XV

There was one slight problem for me, or perhaps a nagging doubt. I had not yet met Ian's family. To save him from having to come through to Glasgow, especially during the week, I told him I wouldn't mind making the trip to his home. I worked beside the bus terminal. It would have been easier for me to travel to see him. He always had an excuse; his folks were away for a wedding, out of town for the night or busy at some function or another. I didn't pay too much attention to it at the time, people do have other commitments but now that Ian wanted to formally establish our engagement, I sensed something might be amiss. At this stage of the courtship, I should have met his family and they should certainly have wanted to meet me.

He wanted me to wear an engagement ring and I had no real objection, if that would make him happy. I wasn't opposed to the idea of the ring but engagement rings cost a lot of money, which he didn't have. Besides, when we decided on a wedding date, we would have to start saving for the wedding and setting up house.

Traditionally the bride's parents paid for the wedding but while we were not poor, a decent wedding would still be costly. I was prepared to at least share in the costs, which meant I would have to save up some money too.

As far as an engagement ring was concerned, it wouldn't make any difference to me anyway. I didn't need a ring to honour my commitment to him. He knew I was right, but he wanted to let the whole world know we were "taken". He wore a beautiful gold signet ring with the family crest on it. It belonged to his grandfather and had been left to him when he died. It meant the world to him. He removed the ring from his finger, and asked me if I would consider wearing that as a symbol of our love. This gesture touched me deeply, knowing how much he treasured the ring. How could I not accept it? A huge diamond ring wouldn't have been more thrilling to me. Our strong commitment to each other didn't need to be sealed, but giving me the ring made him happier. Just being together made us happy. Sometimes we went dancing, to the pictures or sat by the fire alone, whenever we got the chance. We were comfortable with each other.

Everyone was happy that I had found the man of my dreams, although I often wondered when the bubble might burst. Everything was perfect, perhaps too perfect. I remembered hearing somewhere that if something seems too good to be true, it probably is, but I had no real reason to think that, although the thought crossed my mind now and then.

There was no way to hide it. I was bothered by the fact that I had never been invited to Ian's house to meet his family. It didn't have to be a big thing, such as dinner, a cup of tea or nothing at all would have been fine with me. Meeting each other's parents, even early on in relationships was expected in courtships. The distance between us was a bother rather than a barrier. I didn't believe the reasons he had given me so far. Not inviting me had nothing to do with distance as far as I was concerned. I would have been happy to travel to meet them. Besides, they didn't live that far away. After all, he didn't mind coming through to Glasgow every weekend and many times during the week. Why would he think I feel any differently? He had already met my family and most of my friends.

To be honest, I never doubted him but I began to think something was amiss in the family, more so now when we had made this commitment to each other. I couldn't shake the feeling that there was some reason he didn't want to share and I didn't know why. If we were to marry, we shouldn't have any secrets. Most times I didn't pay too much attention to it but with this seal of our intentions, it kept creeping into my mind. What could be wrong, if anything? I needed to know and thought Ian at least owed me an explanation.

During one of his visits to Glasgow, I broached the subject again and asked him when I could visit his hometown to meet his family. He said I could come down one weekend soon. I asked him when, to make a date but when I kept pushing for a time, he admitted that both his father and mother were alcoholics who were unpredictable. He said he didn't want me to be subjected to their mood swings. I was shocked by that revelation because neither of my parents ever took a drink, except maybe Hogmanay and perhaps at the odd social function now and then. That was the extent of it. I told him I was sorry to hear that and tried to convince him that it wouldn't make any difference to our relationship. I was marrying him, not his mother, father or his family. He added that his mother did not drink at all for a very long time but after years of his father's alcoholism and all it entailed, she just seemed to give up and started drinking herself, perhaps to lose herself in her drunkenness.

It was a coping mechanism for his father's drunkenness but it didn't help the family. It was worse. The children mostly tried to keep out of her way. No one was ever there for the family. He knew I would have to meet them some time, but he was hoping against hope, that they would get the help they needed, especially before the wedding. They had both joined A.A. and quit drinking several times. Life was good during those times and during those times his parents tried to make up to the family for all the hurt they knew they had inflicted upon them. Sober they were good people but unfortunately it didn't last and as one started drinking, the other soon followed.

I tried to understand how he must have felt but unless someone has lived through it, no one can grasp the depths of anger, hurt even depravity that alcoholism inflicts on others. I tried to reassure him that it wasn't his fault, and said it wouldn't make any difference to the way I felt about him.

He offered to invite his mother, who was the better of the two, to visit us in Glasgow one weekend. At least my family could meet her but I didn't like that idea, and insisted that his dad come along, suggesting he might just be on his best behaviour. Ian got a little testy at my urging so I dropped the subject, but was secretly hoping things would turn around with his dad. After that, I began to doubt more and more. I tried to understand how he must feel. I knew of other families who had alcoholic relatives, who didn't shut themselves off from others.

Often, family and friends were the reason people got through a situation like this. They needed support to enable them to cope.

As time went on, I couldn't understand Ian's reluctance to take me to his hometown and I began to get a little annoyed. If we were going to get married, I would have to meet his family eventually. I tried to put myself in his position, to understand what it would be like if my father was an alcoholic. Maybe he thought I would be concerned that he might end up like his father, but he didn't seem that interested in drinking. Any time we were together in a pub, he only had one beer, sometimes a glass of wine. Each time I brought the subject up; it was always the same story. No matter how he felt about his father and mother, he should have had more faith in me. Something wasn't right, but what? Moira and my parents had also asked why I had not been down to meet his family but what could I tell them? Was this the chink in the perfect armour? Nothing is perfect.

We had been going together for a few months and other than the situation with his parents, we were happy. On a visit over town one day, Ian suggested looking at rings. He wasn't planning to purchase one just yet; he wanted to find out what kind of ring I might want when we did buy one. I was happy to go along with that, but first I had to get the situation with his parents cleared up before we went any further. I insisted I had to meet them.

I had started collecting some little items for our future home. Mom also picked up any items when she saw them on sale. I bought magazines to check out wedding fashions and other items, just to get some ideas. We liked the same things and never had arguments about purchases,. Whatever I decided for a wedding was okay with him. Maybe the odd little disagreement, which was quickly resolved but never anything serious. We talked about having children and how many, whether or not I would work, where we might live and so on. All of this was wonderful, and I could hardly wait for the day. When we were apart during the week, I missed him so much but weekends were wonderful and we made the most of whatever time we had together. Our emotions and feelings ran wild, but I held fast to my belief that I would wait until we were married. It wasn't easy on either of us, but that's the way it had to be. Meeting his family was about the only stumbling block in this otherwise perfect relationship but every time I broached the subject, it caused friction.

On one of Ian's stay over weekends, I brought up the subject again and again he tried to avoid it every time. This time I would not be deterred. I sensed, or knew there was something not quite right here. I was determined to find what it was before we went any further. I couldn't believe it was only on account of his parents' drinking. It had to be more. Was he ashamed of where he lived? It happens, but that wouldn't have bothered me. How bad could it be? He lived in a Council house. Most of them were newer and nicer than the tenements that I lived in. Some developments were a little rougher as were many other places, not only in Glasgow but elsewhere.

He tried to reassure me that there was nothing wrong and kept saying he didn't want to talk about it. I persisted, telling him that whatever it was, I loved him with all my heart. I couldn't envision anything being so bad that would change my mind. I begged him to trust me. I had to know what was going on. If he couldn't trust or confide in me now, what would it be like when we got married? There is something coming between us and I didn't want us to start our life together with it unresolved. I knew there had to be more to it than his parents' alcoholism. I hoped I was wrong but I had to know and was not prepared to go on any longer without me meeting with his family. He knew I was determined.

My parents were going out for the evening. I suggested we stay in instead of going out that night, although we had planned to go to see a picture. A nice relaxing evening by the fire might help Ian to unwind, to trust me and let go of whatever problem that was upsetting for him. He seemed terrified, or at least apprehensive at the thought of being open and honest with me. What it was, I didn't know, but I didn't believe it was the alcoholism, there had to be more to it. If we were going to share our lives, we must be able to communicate with each other. He knew I was right.

I put the kettle on to make tea. We took up our usual spots in front of the fire. I tried to encourage him by saying the best way to tell me whatever was bothering him, was just to get it out and off his chest. Didn't he believe I loved him enough to weather anything and would do anything for him? Didn't he love me and wouldn't he have done anything for me? Unprepared, shocked, devastated and completely in disbelief, did not describe how I felt when Ian finally opened up.

Right off the bat he assured me that he loved me and only me. Nothing would ever change that. He had never loved anyone else the way he loved me. He was so looking forward to us spending the rest of our lives together. It was all that mattered to him. I must believe that, no matter what. Surely he knew I believed that. Then came the heart-wrenching story that tore at the very fabric of my being.

"Before I met you I had a girlfriend who lived beside me. We grew up together. After I met you, I knew what true love was, and I broke it off as soon as I saw her again. We have always been friends and as we grew older, we became a couple. I suppose we might have eventually married. I think the world of her, but I do not love her. I know now that I have found you, that I never truly loved her. I love you, and couldn't continue the relationship. She was very upset with me. She didn't want to believe me. She told me she had noticed a change in me when I came back from London with the boys but didn't think much of it, knowing how much partying would have gone on plus all the overtime I put in when I came back. I told her that had nothing to do with anything. She wondered if we just needed a break from each other. After all, we had been a couple for so long, it might do us both some good. I told her that it was over. I was sorry to hurt her but better now than later. She would always have a special place in my heart. Naturally, she was upset, but she didn't say much. She just walked away. I felt badly but she seemed to take it surprisingly well."

He never told me about her because he knew he would be breaking it off with her after he met me. He knew I was the one for him. He didn't see her after that night, except on the odd occasion when they passed in the street. She lived in the next close to him so it was only natural they would run into each other. When they did, it was just "hello" as they passed in the street.

Ian continued, "once she realized it was finally over between us, she called in at my house one evening. She left a message with my mother, asking me to meet. I thought she might try to get us back together again. I didn't want that. It was better to leave it the way it was but I felt at the very least, I owed her the chance to say what she wanted to, considering she didn't say anything when I broke it off. Maybe she thought it over and realized it was actually finished."

"I met her at a little parkette across the street. You cannot imagine my shock when she blurted out that she was expecting a baby. Was she trying to trap me? I wondered. No, it was true she convinced me. The baby was definitely mine. We had been intimate only once when her parents were away for the weekend, which happened to be before we went to London. It just happened, it wasn't planned. I knew she was telling the truth. I trusted her. As I looked more closely at her, which I hadn't done any time we met in the street, I could see she had put on a bit of weight but she did not look like she was having a baby. I didn't want to believe it or accept it, especially now but I knew I was the one. I didn't know what to say or do, I was in shock. I asked her if she was sure. She said she had a suspicion before I broke it off with her but wanted to give me time, hoping I would get back with her. She didn't want the baby to be a reason for reconciliation."

"My reaction was not what she wanted or expected. I couldn't pretend. I told her how sorry I was, sorry that this had happened. I would take full responsibility and help out as much as possible but I could not marry her. I didn't love her. I didn't want to hurt her. I wished this hadn't happened, but it had and we had to try to make the best of the situation. She is a wonderful person. I knew she would bear the brunt of this, but I didn't think marrying her was the answer. It was no way to start out married life. I knew people would talk. There wasn't anything I could do about that. She was very upset but didn't say much. I wished there was something I could have said to make her happy, but I don't love her, I love you. I knew the difficulties she would face, the stigma that would follow her, people could be mean, but her parents were good people. I felt sure they would be there for her. I asked if I could walk her home. She refused. I didn't know what else to do I am so sorry."

My eyes were wide with disbelief. This was totally unexpected. I started to cry. I saw the tears in his eyes too as he told me. I knew it wasn't easy for him being the kind of person he was. I knew he would honour his commitment to her to fulfill his obligations, but that didn't help me. Something like this happening never entered my mind. He hadn't even mentioned having a girlfriend and he hadn't pushed me to be intimate. Yes, we had come close, but we were committed to waiting until we were married.

This was the real reason I hadn't been invited to Ian's house. His parents were alcoholics alright, life was miserable for the family, but the main reason was crystal clear, he didn't want me to run into his ex-girlfriend which could easily have happened had I visited the neighbourhood. He didn't want his ex to come face to face with me either.

"I don't understand Ian, you never said anything about a girlfriend, even on the train when we were all talking about friends including girlfriends or boyfriends. Why didn't you say something about her before?"

"I'm sorry, I don't know why I didn't mention her, maybe I thought you might not be interested in seeing me again. I definitely knew I wanted to see you again. Nothing has changed between us. I love you. I want to marry you. I never loved her, I thought I did, but we just grew up together. As difficult as this is, I don't want it to come between us. Maybe we can work something out. This is all a shock to me too."

He didn't tell me her name and that was fine with me. I didn't want to put a name or face to this person who I thought had destroyed my life.

"I wasn't unfaithful to you Fiona, all of this happened before we met. When I came home after meeting you, I broke it off. That's the honest truth but now I wish I had told you, especially now. I wish I had."

I couldn't take this in. I became angry, feeling he had misled me. This was my perfect match, we were so in tune with each other and here he was dropping this bombshell on me. I couldn't think, my mind was numb. I was shaking, crying, staring at him but in a trance like state. What should I do, what should I say? He kept trying to convince me that everything was the same, I was the one he wanted but admitted this situation changed some things. I couldn't handle this right now, I couldn't breathe, and I had to get him out of here. He reached out to hold me but I pushed him away. He looked surprised at my reaction but what did he expect? I didn't want to listen to him anymore. I wanted him to leave. He realized it was futile to try to reason with me now. He left saying he would call later when we both had a chance to think this through. He let himself out of the house, walked to the tram stop and waited for a tram.

I was glad my parents were not coming home until later because I wouldn't know what to say. They would wonder where he had gone. My eyes were red and swollen from crying. There was no way they wouldn't notice that. The one man in my life I was crazy about, who stirred up feelings in me that I didn't know I had, committed to marriage believing we had a once in a lifetime miracle, had just drained the very life out of me with this revelation. I slipped into bed before my parents came home. I couldn't face them now and I didn't know what I would say to them in the morning. Maybe something would come to me when I was alone.

All night long I kept thinking about this poor girl having a baby with no one beside her for support. Not having Ian in my life now was unimaginable. What must it be like for her, having a baby alone with the man she probably loved, engaged to another person? I was angry at him but my heart went out to the girl. What a situation to find yourself in. I kept wondering why he had never mentioned her. Was it because he saw her only as a good friend? Why would they be intimate if that's all it was? I couldn't fault him for not knowing about the baby if he broke it off and hadn't seen her since, but he should have told me about a girl from his past, especially under the circumstances, the intimacy. I was angry at him but in some way, understood how he felt.

All kinds of scenarios swirled around in my head. What would married life be like for us with a child somewhere else? Financially, it would be a drain on us too, but we could live with that. If Ian and I had children how would his girlfriend's baby fit in with all of that? Could I accept the child if he had visitation rights? Would I wonder what Ian was up to every time he went to visit them? My head was in a spin. One minute I thought we could get through this because of our love for each other. Next minute I felt it would put a real strain on our marriage. All night long it continued, yes we could, no we couldn't. Could I see myself living without him, now that we had met each other? I fell asleep.

In the morning it started all over. I never told my parents or Moira anything. This had to be my decision alone. I tried to put myself in the other girl's place. It didn't help. He must have loved the girl or thought he did at one time. What if he stopped loving me too?

Moira knew Ian was staying for the weekend. The swimming was not on. She wasn't expecting to see me until Monday. When mom asked why Ian hadn't stayed over as planned, I told her that he had to go to some family function the next day. She asked why I couldn't go with him. I made up the excuse that I thought I was coming down with a cold and decided to stay in. My eyes hadn't gone down much, which gave some credence to my story. It also gave me the excuse to stay in bed all day. How was I going to face everyone and what would I say?

XVI

Monday morning I was back up for work. Mom had a cuppa ready for me and, as usual, a slice of toast. I drank the tea and took the toast with me.

"Feeling any better this morning, hen?"

"A bit but you know the Railway, we have to go in whether we feel like it or not."

Moira was waiting at the close for me. I didn't feel like going to work or facing Moira either. How will I get through this day?

Moira took one look at my face and said,

"What happened to you? Your eyes are all puffy."

"A bit of a cold coming on I think."

Moira wasn't buying that excuse. It was obvious to Moira that something was wrong. Normally perky and talkative, especially after a weekend with Ian, I was just too quiet. Moira asked if we did anything special on Saturday. I told her we stayed in; I wasn't feeling that great and didn't feel much like talking. Moira was as discerning with me as I was with her. We knew each other that well. It was a quiet ride on the tram to work. We took our coats off and headed to our sign in before sitting down at our desks. At tea break, some of the coworkers noticed I was unusually quiet and asked if I was o.k. I gave them all the same excuse, "coming down with a cold."

I went over to the other office, took my dictation and again everyone wondered what was wrong. This was such an upbeat office with lots of laughs that I enjoyed, but not today. I wasn't up to it and I gave the same story, "coming down with a cold." Thankfully, it was almost closing time when I got back to the typing pool. Not long to wait until I could go home. Moira was putting her coat on with mine in her hands, ready to go. I put my work on the desk for typing tomorrow, headed out of the office, walked to the tram stop and only waited a few minutes until a tram arrived. Moira didn't talk on the way home, she knew I wasn't up to chitchat for whatever reason and didn't bug me. She left me at my close and waved as she walked up the street. I wouldn't have been surprised if she had clued in that something was wrong between Ian and me.

I could always confide in my mother, as we had a close relationship, but as is often the case with mothers and daughters, there are some things we only share with our best friend. When I got home from work at the end of the day, mom asked how I was feeling and I couldn't help it, I started to cry, which startled her.

I told her that Ian and I had our first disagreement and that I didn't feel like talking. She let it go at that and didn't enquire any further, knowing or thinking it would all be over by night. Ian would somehow contact me. She knew that if I wanted to confide in her I would.

Ian wrote to me every day asking me to accept a call on the telephone. His letters remained unanswered. Why was this happening to me? How could I have missed this? Why didn't I see it? How could I possibly not see something like this coming? I didn't even know he had a serious girlfriend. I trusted him completely and hung on to his every word. I was deeply hurt.

During the days I did my job as I was expected to, but the change in me was obvious. Coworkers were concerned about me but knew enough not to intrude. If I wanted to discuss anything, I would in my own time. Once I told them I didn't want to talk about it they left me alone. The same was true of my parents and Moira. In the evenings, I stayed home, mostly in my room where I could only think of Ian, wondering how this situation could be resolved. I was broken hearted. My parents weren't overly concerned. They figured given time, all would be well again.

After much soul searching, I came to a decision. I wrote a letter to Ian telling him that I could not be happy as his wife under the circumstances. Somehow I would always feel responsible if anything happened to that child. Whether or not he married the girl was irrelevant, I only knew that I couldn't live with that knowledge and, therefore, it was over. It was not an easy decision for me to make. I loved him and would never love anyone else the way I loved him. We had our once in a lifetime chance, this was it and we missed it. I couldn't be the one to take away this child's father. I told him not to try to contact me in any way. I added that this was the most difficult decision I had ever made. Seeing him again or hearing from him would only make me feel worse. I asked him to respect my wishes. My heart was breaking, tears just wouldn't stop running down my cheeks but I knew this was the right decision for me.

I wrapped his grandfather's ring in tissue and enclosed it with the letter. I registered the package so that the ring would be safe. The ring was no sparkling diamond but it meant everything to me because I knew how very much it meant to him.

Ian didn't take the note seriously. When I left the office one day he was waiting outside for me. My heart started pounding when I saw him standing there. I was angry that he hadn't respected my request to leave me alone. Seeing him there weakened me but I knew I had to be strong.

When I saw him there, I asked Moira if she wouldn't mind going home by herself. I didn't want to get into any kind of confrontation in front of her, or anyone else for that matter. I asked if she would drop up to my house and tell mom I would be a bit later and tell her why. She said a quick hello to Ian and took off to get the tram home.

I told him I was not pleased that he had turned up at the office and that I meant everything I wrote. There was no turning back for me. It was difficult enough for me without having to see him. He said he thought about going to my house but wasn't sure if my parents knew or whether or not he would be welcomed. He asked if I had told Moira and what her reaction might be.

He begged me to at least give him the opportunity to try to explain things and asked me if we could go for a cup of tea or something. I was not strong when it came to him, deep down I wanted him to take me in his arms and tell me it was all a mistake but I knew if I listened to him, I would weaken and perhaps give in.

My hands were shaking, the tingles were there and I broke out in a cold sweat when he touched my hand. I was afraid I would lose control. That was the last thing I wanted. I could feel myself weakening already. How could I let him go?

I agreed to go to the pub for a little while, simply because I thought I owed him that much at least, or was I secretly hoping we could come up with a solution, a compromise. I didn't want to lose him. In my heart I wanted him to explain it all away and make everything right. Going to the pub might be the best place; it would be crowded which could help me to stay in control. As luck or fate would have it, the only seats available were in the same booth, in the same pub we always went to. It was the closest place. I didn't feel like wandering all over the city. As we entered the pub, the familiar strains of the popular "Your Cheatin' Heart" were playing. I had to be strong. I had to do this. Ian ordered a beer and I ordered a shandy, the usual.

It was difficult to say who was more emotional. We both had tears in our eyes, we both trembled, the magic we felt was still there. He reached across the table for my hand. I didn't pull back but it only made me feel worse. I was putty in his hands. How could I be strong? I loved him so much. He told me that regardless of what happened between us, he could not marry the girl. He didn't love her, probably never did, and it was no way to start out married life.

He cared for her and always would, but after he met me, he knew instantly what real true love was. He was sorry for the mess, for the girlfriend, for the soon coming baby and most of all, for me, whom he truly loved. He never wanted to hurt me and he certainly didn't envision this turn of events. He tried to convince me to change my mind by stressing that all this had happened before he met me. He begged me to take some time to think about it, before making the breakup final. Wasn't our love strong enough to get through this? Didn't we each deserve that much?

Regardless of what he decided to do, I didn't think it would work out. I was not sure how I could cope with this strain being put on our married life. Maybe I should have been a stronger, but that was how I felt. Every night in bed I thought it over, thought it might work, then I thought it wouldn't. In the end, I realized that if these were the kind of doubts I had now, what would it be in the future? It broke my heart, but I couldn't continue the relationship with him. I felt myself weakening, but I held my ground. I drank some shandy and rose up to leave, telling him not to follow me. I strongly emphasized that I did not want him to contact me again, either directly or through my friends. I didn't know how strong I would be if he kept trying to contact me.

As I left the pub, I turned to look back at him, his hurt clearly showing in his face, as tears ran down his cheeks. I don't remember ever seeing someone so sad and it tore at my heart. I hesitated, my eyes filled with tears, but I knew I had to do this. I was extremely upset, but I had to keep control and I had to get out of the pub.

I didn't want to go into any details of what happened between Ian and myself. My family and friends knew something was wrong. After this length of time everyone knew it wasn't a lovers' quarrel. I hadn't said anything before because I wasn't sure what my decision would be. The only thing I ever told anyone was that it was over. I didn't want to talk about it. Ian kept writing to me but I never opened the letters. I destroyed them as soon as I got them.

Eventually the letters stopped coming. I was devastated and knew I would never feel the same way about anyone else ever again. I appreciated the fact my family never questioned me; they knew how difficult it was. Everyone was as upset as I was because they thought we were perfectly matched and were looking forward to the day when we got married. Mom often told me she saw the hurt in my eyes and wished there was something she could do. They got quite attached to Ian. Their hearts were breaking for me but they knew I would tell them the whole story one day, if I wanted to.

Moira was the only person I ever told the whole story to because she was more than my best friend, she was my confidante, loyal to the core, plain and simply, she was "ma pal for life". I asked her not to tell anyone I but I didn't need to do that, I could trust her completely. She was as upset as I was, but didn't know how to comfort me, knowing how much Ian meant to me. Just being there for me was appreciated. She had cautioned me several times as did my parents, not because they saw something in Ian or they didn't like him, but because it was all so sudden and perhaps too good to be true. That's not to say it wouldn't have worked out. Sometimes people just click. Circumstances we couldn't have imagined were responsible. While Moira told me to slow down, she never imagined anything like this in her wildest dreams. She never tried to influence my decision in any way and only commented that she didn't know how she would have handled it. It wasn't the end of the world and possibly our love could have overcome it but I didn't want to take that chance and I didn't want to take the baby's father away. Would it have worked? We will never know. I asked Moira not to let me know ever, if Ian tried to contact her or if she saw him or heard about him. It was over. We never discussed Ian again.

XVII

I knew I would have to make some major changes in my life if I was to get on with it. Everything had happened so quickly, the unbelievable attraction between Ian and me and now this equally unbelievable confession leading to the breakup. I was traumatized but went about my normal routines like a robot. Ian had completely captured my very being. Getting over him would not be easy, Dimming or turning out the torch I carried for him seemed almost impossible right now. Knowing how much I loved him and how weak I was when it came to him, the thought of some chance meeting was a concern for me. In my heart of hearts I fantasized about leaving the office and finding him waiting for me outside, or perhaps waiting for me at the close when I got home. I almost hoped that it would happen, but I knew I wouldn't be able to cope with that. Why wasn't this a dream, like the one I had about walking down the aisle to meet him? Why couldn't I wake up from this one? I knew with absolute certainty there would never be anyone I could love the way I loved Ian. He had totally and completely stolen my heart.

Life went on as it has a habit of doing. After the war, we were told to just get on with it and amazingly we did. We picked up the pieces and went on. Not to say everything was forgotten but we persevered.

Moira and I carried on with our swimming on Sundays, pictures during the week, sometimes dancing, whatever. We had our group of friends and met others along the way. We were a happy young group but there were no serious attachments among us, just good friends. Every time I came home, I secretly hoped there was a letter from him or that he would be around the corner. It wouldn't have helped but I could dream.

In the early fifties, many Scots were migrating to Australia, the U.S. and Canada in search of new lives. Even though the war had been over for some time, many folks found life in general could be a challenge. An aunt and uncle of mine became the pioneers of emigration, moving to Australia with their two young children. They were known as ten quid immigrants, meaning that's all they paid. I think the government funded the rest. It was designed to encourage people to start anew in that country and increase the population. Around that time, a few of my cousins and their families decided to try their luck in Canada. Over time several other relatives moved to Australia while others relocated to Canada. My brother Andrew joined the throng to Toronto. He had been after me for some time to join him. I wasn't interested. I was quite happy with my life. I had the same offer from rellies (relatives) in Australia but I never considered that move. For a start it was too far away and it took six weeks sailing to get there. Getting back to Scotland for a visit wouldn't be easy and my parents wouldn't have been able to visit me in Australia. Truth be told, I wasn't interested in going anywhere. I had a good life, good friends and was happy until I met Ian and our subsequent break up.

After the breakup, things changed. I needed to get away, make a new start. I wrote to my brother telling him I might be interested in moving to Toronto. He didn't waste any time writing. He sent a telegram and suggested a time for me to go to the good old telephone box. He knew the number well because my parents phoned him every week from there when he was in the army. Mom, dad and I were at the phone as planned. Andrew said he would send me the money for my fare if I was seriously interested in moving. This, like the romance with Ian, was rather quick but I learned something from it. I told Andrew that I was interested but asked him to give me some time to think it out. I didn't want to make any mistakes that I might regret. That was okay by him. If he paid my fare it would be a real incentive because with what I earned at the Railway, saving for such a trip wouldn't have happened. My parents were not in a position to help out either but they were happy for me if I wanted to take Andrew up on his offer, although it meant their last child would also be moving some distance away. However, they would not stand in my way or put up a fuss to dissuade me. I was not the same person after the breakup; it hurt them greatly to see how sad I had become.

I didn't bounce upstairs, sing a song here or there, tell a wee joke and basically stopped talking as much. That was a sure sign something was amiss. It wasn't only the breakup that affected me, I found it very difficult to accept that Ian had misled me and I didn't see it. It didn't change how I felt about him. I didn't think my love for him would ever die.

I made an application to go overseas, and passed all the necessary criteria, including the medical. I was approved for emigration to Canada and booked my passage. I was looking forward to my adventure but I was not looking forward to leaving family and friends. I wasn't too worried about getting a job in my new country. I knew my skills were in demand. With Andrew and the rellies I would have around me in Toronto, it meant I wouldn't have to be anxious about anything. Leaving my parents was another matter and one that I was not looking forward to. What would I possibly do without Moira, my best friend, my confidante, and my rock? Leaving the country I was born and raised in was not an easy decision either. There was another downside, leaving also meant I would be ending any opportunity I might have to meet up with Ian again some day, even though I didn't want that to happen. Every time I thought about it, every time I heard a song that reminded me of him, every time I saw football supporters and so many other things we shared, I broke down. In my heart I knew this was the right thing to do and the worst-case scenario, which wasn't so bad, would be that I returned to Scotland.

Coworkers at the Railway gave me a farewell tea and bought me a new set of suitcases. My parents rented a hall for a party and invited all of my friends, college mates and family. Ian was not included. Mom asked me if I would like him to be invited, as a sort of farewell. Absolutely not I told her. I meant that, but I visualized that someone might ask him anyway to surprise me.

Everyone had a great time, singing, dancing and sharing memories until it was time for the guests to leave. There is nothing like a chorus or two of "Auld Lang Syne" to bring on the tears. Why is it that Scots always insist on singing that on such occasions or at New Year? It's a real tearjerker.

Moira and I bawled our eyes out. As sad as I was, nothing could compare to the hurt I felt at the loss of Ian. Never a day passed when I didn't think of him, never a day passed when I didn't shed a tear for him, and never a day passed that I didn't hope to see him coming around the corner. He knew I meant it when I told him to stay away, he would honour that, but it didn't stop me from thinking about him, wondering if I had made the right decision. Thinking of him made my toes tingle. Perhaps we could have worked around the situation. The chances of that now were gone. Maybe in time, my broken heart would heal, time has a habit of doing that, but I was sure I would never forget him, never find someone to love as I did him. That doesn't happen twice in a lifetime.

When my father realized I was definitely going away, he placed an ad in a newspaper to find someone else who might also be going on the same ship, someone that could befriend me. As luck would have it, we got a reply. My parents and I went to meet the other girl and her family who lived in a small town outside of Glasgow. Both families bonded immediately. Patricia, (Trish) had two sisters and a brother in Canada that she was going out to live with. Trish was the same age and about the same build as me. That was a relief, most of my friends, except Moira, were shorter than me. Anyway we hit it off right from the start. Both sets of parents shared a great sense of relief knowing we found each other to start out on our journey.

Sailing was set for spring, departing from Southampton. Moira, being the friend she was, and having free transportation, travelled on the train to Southampton with us. I was thrilled, but knew we were only delaying the inevitable. My parents were happy that Moira was making the trip on the train with us, possibly thinking it might ease things a bit. I waved a very tearful goodbye to my parents and others who were there to see me off. Trish's family and friends were there too. I was so upset that I almost wished Moira wasn't going on the train. I knew the tears would start all over again in Southampton, not that I thought they would ever stop on the way down on the train. As the train pulled out of the station, mom was standing on the platform, dabbing away at her eyes, while my dad tried so hard to be brave. He put his arms around her and pulled her close to him. Trish's parents weren't much stronger. The scene inside the train carriage was not any better. Unbelievable as it sounds, I still hoped in my heart to see Ian running down the platform to see me. "Parting is such sweet sorrow," they say, only I didn't think it was so sweet.

Moira, Trish and I managed to gather our composure and settled down to the long ride. We were lucky enough to have a coach to ourselves. As the train chugged along the tracks towards Southampton, it took Moira and I back to our last long trip to London and our chance meeting with Ian and his friends.

Everything seemed to center around Ian. We told Trish about the trip, but didn't go into details about Ian. We managed a few laughs too. Our parents had packed lunch for us and about half way down to Southampton we got out the food. Again I thought about the memories of sharing food with Ian.

The rest of the time I looked out of the window at the passing scenery although I wasn’t taking it in. I was daydreaming. Moira and I promised each other that we would be friends forever and never ever forget one another. Could I be strong enough to do this? Could I move away and leave it all behind? The only way I could find out was if I actually gave it a try, and the worst case scenario was that I would return to Scotland. Even though I was sad, I was also filled with a great sense of adventure at the thought of what lay ahead. I wasn't going out to live with strangers, I had relatives in Toronto. I had a nice home to go to with an English landlady and her Canadian husband. My brother stayed there too. That made a huge difference.

When the train pulled into the station at Southampton I had to say my final goodbyes to Moira. It was the saddest, well almost the saddest day of my life. We hugged each other so tight, but finally had to let go. As I moved forward through the loading area to board the ship, I kept waving to her and she waved back until we lost sight of each other. She was taking the next train back home by herself. That wouldn't be an easy trip either. What a friend! If only she could have wanted to go to Canada with me. Maybe someday in the future she would.

She had instructions to keep me posted on our favourite quartet. I had told them of my plans. Before I left home, I received a lovely card and a copy of their latest record from them.

Although Trish and I paid for our own travel and were not funded by the government as some were, we didn't have our own cabins on the ship. We each shared our cabins with three other ladies. It certainly wasn't luxurious by any stretch of the imagination, but it was clean and comfortable, with two sets of bunk type beds and a couple of dressers. It would have been nice if we could have shared the same cabin. Perhaps if we had booked our tickets together that might have been arranged, but we were happy enough to be on the same deck just down the hall from each other. There wasn't a bathroom in either of our cabins. We, like the rest of the third class, had to share a communal bathroom further down the deck. We were thankful that we had good roomies. It was nice that we were all about the same age and full of excitement about the new life ahead.

Once we got settled in we wandered around the ship, checking it out, and finding out where everything was located. We soon found out we were in "Tourist Class".

Clearly marked areas, (First Class Passengers Only) in bold letters, advised all they were not allowed to go in. That was okay by us, we were happy with our own accommodations but we were curious and managed to get a peak through one of the windows on the doors. The door wasn't open, it was unlocked so we pushed the door slightly open and saw all that we wanted to see. Just as we thought, it didn't look all that much different from our tourist area maybe a little classier but basically the same amenities.

Our lounges were quite large and bright with windows all around the rooms and a small bar in one corner where the passengers could buy various drinks. There was no problem finding a chair in the lounge, as it had lots of tables and chairs to accommodate all of the passengers. Several of the tables had games and cards laid out for anyone who wanted to pass away some time. Meals were served in a fairly small dining room. Food wasn't bad and every night there was a bottle of wine in the center of the table. This was, after all, an Italian owned ship. A variety of movies were shown throughout the trip in the theatre on board.

We soon met up with other emigrants, all eagerly awaiting their new lives in a new land, full of hope and enthusiasm. Some were going out to friends or relatives, some were striking out on their own. Others were actually returning to Canada after a trip home. When one returning passenger said she had not been home in so many years, we both vowed that wouldn't happen to us. We wouldn't wait too long until we took a trip back home, little did we know.

Most of the crew members were Italian, some of whom spoke very little English. Whenever we took the elevator down to our cabins, a very handsome Italian who was operating the elevator attended us to. Antonio was his name. He immediately set his eyes on me and every time I was near the elevator Antonio asked me to come in so he could talk to me. I was not interested in another romance, although I was flattered by his attention, his good looks and accent. Fraternization was not allowed between crew and passengers but it did go on and Antonio was no different, paying little attention to that ruling. Whenever he got the chance, he cornered me.

We filled most of our time on the trip by going to the movies, dancing, playing cards and so on. Sometimes we strolled along the deck but it was an Atlantic crossing in May, so it was actually quite chilly. Enjoying the trip as much as we did surprised us. Being at sea for seven days was something we were not looking forward to when we first got on board, but the trip was so much fun and time flew so fast, that we wished we were sailing on a longer trip of six weeks to Australia.

Other passengers seemed to be enjoying their time at sea as well, getting in a vacation so to speak, before the reality of having to work set in. I was relaxed and happy, my mind occupied with other things. There were actually spaces of time when I didn't think of Ian. Those lapses didn't last too long. I sometimes wondered what kind of turnaround Ian's life had taken. Did he marry his girlfriend?

Neither Trish nor I got sick on the trip. Other passengers didn't fare so well. In fact, several of them were not seen outside of their cabins after boarding, while others could be seen at the rails, holding on for dear life. We didn’t find the sailing that rough, but just the thought of sailing was enough to make some people sick. One of my uncles told me to eat on the trip, even if I didn't feel like it, because if I got sea sick, I would have something in my stomach to bring up. I wouldn’t experience the pain of throwing up all the time. We followed his suggestion and had no trouble at all.

On the last night of the trip, before we docked in Quebec, Antonio tried desperately to get me alone but every time he saw me, other passengers were in the elevator. While he was helping staff pick up the passengers' luggage he saw me along the corridor but again, he couldn't get a chance to talk to me because there were too many cabin helpers working alongside of him. When he finally managed to talk to me, he asked for my address in Canada because he wanted to write to me. He was interested in applying to emigrate to Canada himself and hoped he could get in touch with me, if and when he was successful. I gave him my address, but made it perfectly clear that I was only interested in a pen pal. One other relative came over on that ship after I did and in the course of conversations, Antonio found out she was related to me. He told her he hadn't been successful so far in getting travel documents but he wasn't giving up.

XVIII

Many of the passengers, including us, gathered on the deck, hoping to get a bird's eye view of the ship's arrival in Quebec City. What a perfect docking, slow, steady and ever so gentle. We were dancing with excitement but it was also tinged with a little sadness, remembering our families and friends back home. On the trip we met many new friends, some of whom were going to places other than Toronto. That was a little sad too. The night before we were to dock we exchanged addresses, hoping to keep in touch with each other, maybe even meet up again one day.

We were awestruck at the view as we approached Quebec City. The magnificent Chateau Frontenac sat regally up on the hill in the heart of the historic district with its towers, turrets and cone shaped roofs looking like a huge castle. I read in a brochure on the resort that it was built in the late 19th century by William Van Horne of the Canadian Pacific Railway, and was intended for a stopover for Canadian Pacific travellers. Emily Post's father, Bruce Price, who had designed Montreal's Windsor Station, was the architect, his style reflecting the middle ages and Renaissance. Many famous people stayed there, including royalty and movie stars. In 1943-1944 Winston Churchill, President Roosevelt and Canadian Prime Minister William Lyon Mackenzie King met there to plan Canada's war strategy. It wasn't difficult to imagine why they chose that location. It was breathtakingly majestic.

The port was busy. The whole area looked rather festive with all kinds of colourful streamers blowing in the breeze. Trish's sisters met us at the dockside after we got clearance. We had a few hours to spare before heading to Toronto by train. We passed the time by taking a quick walking tour of Quebec City. The upper part of town overlooks the St. Lawrence River, with a walled section in the core. Streets are narrow and covered with cobblestones, reminding us of streets back home. Walking around the beautiful grounds of the Frontenac was enjoyable for us but too soon it was time to make our way to the train station.

The station was almost as magnificent as the Chateau Frontenac and looked quite similar. It was designed that way with beautiful brick and turrets, giving it the appearance of a smaller version of an 18th century castle. Huge windows sat over the front entrance with a large clock built in above the windows. It was a magnificently impressive building and the hall inside was no less beautiful with a canopy type of roof and gorgeous lighting.

We were surprised at the size of the trains in the station. We hadn't realized Canadian trains were so much larger than the trains we were used to seeing in the British Railways. In fact, they were gigantic. We just had time to get a coffee and a donut in a "diner" inside the station. We had never seen a diner, except in the movies. We were beginning to feel quite "American", only this was Canada.

Travelling on the train to Toronto was fairly uneventful. We enjoyed the scenery all along the way. Everywhere we looked we saw those same colourful streamers that were visible from the ship. We were chuffed, thinking our new country was welcoming us in such a manner. It was only much later that we learned those streamers were actually decorations in gas stations or used car lots to attract attention and customers. Welcoming new immigrants was not their purpose.

Andrew was waiting for us when we arrived in Union Station in Toronto. He worked for the Canadian National Railways and was quite the railway buff. He was only too eager and happy to give anyone a rundown on the station itself, which covered a large city block between two main streets. Huge stone columns that were turned from Bedford limestone towered in the center block, possibly about 40 feet high. They complimented the Indiana and Queenston limestone used for parts of the exterior. A beautifully designed ceiling graced the Great Hall, about 250 feet long and 84 feet wide. Rising way above the floor sat the centre of the arch. Arched type windows were at either end of the Great Hall, easily well over 40 feet. Andrew told the eager listeners that the station had been opened by the Prince of Wales in 1927.

I got all teary eyed when I saw Andrew again as it had been some time since I had seen him. We were both emotional but happy. He had been in Canada for a couple of years and looked very Canadian in his wind breaker jacket and jeans. He was acclimatized. He had also managed to scrape up enough money to buy a 1947 Ford car in which he took me to my new home in the east end of Toronto.

I wasn't used to this kind of luxury. Hardly anyone in Scotland owned cars, at least no one that I knew. Beryl, my new landlady, was originally from London and had married a Canadian during the war after which she relocated to Canada as a bride. They had no children. Beryl took me upstairs to my room. It had a single bed with iron head and foot rails that sat on one side of the room against the wall in the corner. On the opposite side of the room sat a double dresser with an attached mirror. Along from that a good sized window overlooking the back yard allowed the daylight in. Frilly covered orange crates, standing end up, one at each side of the bed, were used as little cupboards. I never had a room of my own in Glasgow. My hole in the wall bed was part of the living room with a piano for singsongs if anyone visited. It wasn't very private. Being able now to look out into a private yard was much more than I expected. A full bathroom in the hall, next to my room, was pure luxury. I thought of Moira and our friends going up to the baths to get our sixpenny bath. I just had to go along the hall and could stay in as long as I wanted to. Having a bathroom in the house was a dream. No sergeant major banging on the door telling me to get out.

Beryl was good to me. She took me to downtown Toronto to find a job. My office experience was a definite asset and in no time I managed to get a position with a large insurance company, located on one of the main streets in Toronto. My boarding house was very close to a streetcar line. All I had to do was walk a short distance to the stop. When I got off the streetcar at the other end, I only had a few steps to walk to my job. It was perfect.

Beryl and I spent the following week shopping in the major department stores. I wasn't in a financial position to buy much, but I was surprised at the variety of goods that were on sale. They didn't seem to be all that expensive either.

Beryl's husband, Charlie, often drove his car to work. When he did, he offered me a ride downtown with him. I was in la la land. Charlie's car was a new Chrysler, large and oh so luxurious. I felt like a movie star sitting up front with him. Maybe one day I might be able to afford a car but if I did, it was unlikely it would be a top of the line model like Charlie's. If my friends could only see me now!

I settled in easily. I missed Moira and my parents terribly. Ian was in my thoughts every day. When I was alone in my room, lying in bed, my mind often wandered back to happier times when I believed that I would be planning a wedding and life together with Ian right about now. We never know what is around the corner, which is just as well. How quickly things can change.

My employer was exceptionally kind to me. I loved my job and was happy there. I couldn't get over the difference in attitudes between the British Railways and this job. No stern supervisors, no eagle eyes always peering at me. In no time at all, I was promoted to secretary for the personnel manager, a lovely man. I had always been a hard worker and didn't need the commandants in the Railway to make me work. I always felt that keeping busy made the time go by but we never got the chance to slack off in the Railway. It was never an option. People told me I had a great personality because I laughed a lot and never got stressed out. The past months had changed me somewhat but I was beginning to get back to my old self. My new coworkers did everything they could to make me feel welcome and helped me greatly whenever I had a problem.

During lunch hours I got into the habit of going over to the department stores. My company's building was located a couple of streets over from the main shopping area where I loved going into the big stores. I was blown away with the selections and prices. I didn't always buy something. I enjoyed looking around. One of the major stores had a bargain basement and that was mainly where I spent my time and money, picking up some good buys to send home to my parents and Moira.

Even though the war had been over for a few years there were still plenty of shortages in Scotland. Anything I sent home was appreciated. Glass nylons, as they were called because of their sheerness, were in short supply, almost impossible to buy. If you were lucky enough to get a pair, the cost was high. While I was still living in Glasgow my brother sent me nylons. At that time he put one pair in a letter and a second one in another letter. I loved it when friends remarked on the sheerness of the nylons. Unfortunately, they were very delicate and I never got much wear out of them. Andrew sent some to Moira as well. Now that I was in Canada, whenever I had a few dollars to spare, I bought nylons for Moira and enclosed them in a parcel to my parents. Tins of ham were appreciated by my mom and dad.

Often in the evenings my brother took me for a ride in the car down to the waterfront, to the pictures or to visit some relatives. Other times my cousins picked me up in their cars to go for a drive, stopping in at cafes to get my favourite, a chocolate ice cream soda. It was just like in the pictures Moira and I drooled over. Life was different no doubt but I adjusted well, although I missed my family, friends and, of course, Ian.

Trish got a job at the other end of the city and she, like me, made new friends. We often got together on a Saturday. Sometimes we went dancing but it wasn't the same as in Scotland either. Everything was different. Most of the dancers attended with partners, with a few singles "stag" as they were called. In Glasgow more dancers went on their own so we seldom sat out many dances. Although there were fewer singles in Toronto, we still didn't sit out many dances. During the weeks, we kept in touch by telephone. That was a plus for sure. Everyone had a telephone and we were allowed to use them. We quickly saw the convenience of that.

XIX

Even though I had adjusted very well to life in Canada, I still missed home and in the beginning I wished I could afford a trip back. That was out of the question, for the time being anyway. I had to settle for the odd telephone call. International calls were expensive ($15.00 for three minutes,) and for that reason, calls were few and far between. Besides when I got a call from home, I was drained emotionally. It was good to hear their voices but it was upsetting. I made friends easily. My life was busy socially and as time passed, I thought less about going back home, although returning home to see my parents and Moira was something I hoped to do in the not too distant future. Having them visit Canada would have been great, but I knew they couldn't afford that either.

I was invited to parties, dances, theatre, dining and life was treating me very well. I still kept in touch with several people in the old country but as it often happens, each finds a new life, marries and has a family or whatever. Slowly they drift away. That wasn't the case with Moira. We remained best friends, although the letters weren't as often as before. Moira had a new boyfriend, new job, and was extremely happy. I tried to coax her into moving to Canada, but she had absolutely no notion of that. Besides, she had no one in Toronto, except me.

Now that she had a new boyfriend, that move didn't seem very likely, unless he wanted to relocate. I held onto the hope she might visit sometime.

Moira always respected my wishes and never discussed Ian in any of her letters although I secretly wished she would break the pledge and let me know if she had heard anything about him. I was curious as to what happened to him, the girlfriend and his baby. She wouldn't tell me even if she knew. There wasn't a day that went by that I didn't think of him in some small way. I considered that we might get together. I believed our love was meant to be. In my saner thoughts, I knew it wouldn’t happen but I was still very much carrying the torch for him, although the flame was not so bright with each passing day. This was the only void in my otherwise great life. I never knew a heart could ache so much.

One day, I received devastating news from home that Moira was seriously injured in a traffic accident. The extent of her injuries was never revealed other than she had severe brain damage, along with other injuries. Mom tried to visit her, but although both sets of parents were friendly and often went out to dances together, mom was never allowed to visit. We were never told what actually happened other than she was in a coma. It was obvious her mother, Mrs. MacDougall, didn't want anyone to see her daughter like that. Several other friends were also denied visits. Even Moira's new boyfriend was not allowed to visit. Apparently there was no chance of recovery. It was only a matter of time. Everyone copes with sickness, death and other tragedies in different ways.

Perhaps Mrs. MacDougall could not cope seeing Moira's friends because they were so healthy. Who knows? Those were the wishes of the family and everyone had to respect that. There was nothing anyone could do. Friends were upset and hurt but I felt sure Mrs. MacDougall was hurting so much more.

I wrote to Mrs. MacDougall. She didn't respond. I knew her days were taken up caring for Moira and they didn't have a telephone, which meant I couldn't reach them. I understood her actions but I was hurt. Moira and I were like sisters. Each mother was a second mother to the other. We were inseparable. With all due respect, we bowed to Mrs. MacDougall's wishes. I felt helpless being so far away. If I could just have been there for her maybe she would have felt my presence and strength. I doubt it would have made a difference to her health but she would know I was there for her, just as she was for me.

Everyone was still trying to come to terms with the news of Moira's tragic accident when I got the devastating news that she had died. I so wanted to return for the funeral of my best friend but her death, as with her accident, was strictly private. A trip home would serve no purpose. Again my heart was broken. At least when she was alive there was a chance we might meet again, either in Glasgow or Canada. Now with her death, that wouldn't happen. I couldn't accept that I would never see my beloved Moira ever again. It was too much. She was my rock. Even though Ian was never mentioned again, we always had that bond between us. We had shared so much in life, worked together, followed the band together, danced, went to the pictures and so on. I just couldn't believe she was gone and I would never see her again.

I wrote another letter to Mrs. MacDougall and this time she replied. She thanked me for caring but never discussed Moira, other than to say she died peacefully.

Every year after that, I sent a card at Christmas time to the MacDougalls and I received one. One time she thanked me for being so faithful over the years. That meant the world to me. Eventually the cards stopped coming and I learned that Moira's parents had died too.

Sadly or gladly, life does go on. I got back into the swing of things with my new friends. I knew I would never ever forget Moira. To this day I still think of the happy times we shared, as well as the not so happy times, which always bring Ian into the picture.

XX

I was an outgoing type of person. I was popular everywhere I went and received many invitations to one thing or another. One night at one of these parties, which were more or less just gatherings, I met a nice, young Canadian named Bob. He was tall, medium build and drop dead gorgeous. His hazel eyes sparkled; he had eyelashes that any girl would give her eye teeth for and eyebrows that matched his gently waved dark brown hair. He looked like he had just come home from the barbershop. When he smiled, the dimples on his cheeks added to his exceptionally good looks. He was dressed in light gray slacks with a darker gray coordinating jacket. One of my new friends introduced him to me. I couldn't believe it when he sat beside me. He told me his name, where he lived and that he was studying to be a lawyer. Once I opened my mouth he knew I was not from Canada. He made the same mistake many people make. He thought I was Irish but I was used to that. It didn't bother me; after all, my grandfather came from County Cork, as did much of Scotland's ancestry. Bob was a little embarrassed by the mistake, but we laughed it off.

I told him a little of my life to that point, that I had come to Canada from Scotland, that my brother and a few relatives lived here, and that I had a job I liked with a major insurance company. I purposely left out the reason I came to Canada. I didn't think it would be of any particular benefit to mention that. However, as I thought about it, I realized Ian had done the same thing to me. I remembered how upset I was when I found out about the girlfriend. I rationalized that I had not been intimate with Ian. There was no possible chance of that coming back to haunt me, so to speak. I had just met Bob and might never see him again anyway. It made me think that perhaps I had been a little too harsh on Ian and he might not have been so deceitful after all. It was too late to worry about that now but it wouldn't have changed things. I couldn't see marriage under those circumstances.

Bob and I had a couple of dances together. Afterwards he asked me if I would like to go somewhere for a coffee, although there were light refreshments served at the hall. We stopped in at a little restaurant close by. I had a soft drink. Bob ordered a coffee. We talked easily to each other, no nervousness or lack of things to talk about. He asked if he could drive me home and I accepted his invitation with a friendly smile. He drove a 1949 Ford that he was extremely proud of. The house where I boarded was not too far from the dance hall. Looking at this gorgeous hunk of a man, I wondered why he picked me out but I wasn't unhappy, in fact I was quite chuffed. We hit it off immediately and chatted away as though we had known each other for years. We were very comfortable and relaxed with each other. I didn't go into the house right away but sat outside in the car talking about this and that.

He told me he didn't have a lot of money at the moment but said he would really like to see me again, if that was okay with me. Being wined and dined wasn't important to me. Going for a walk along the beach, sitting in the park or perhaps having a picnic with someone whose company I enjoyed, might be nice and wouldn't cost much. He had a lot of studying to do and leisure time was at a premium.

We met as often as we could. Sometimes it was only outside my office building where we ate our lunch together. My office was practically next door to Osgoode Hall where he was studying or researching so it worked out perfectly. We took in the odd movie. Between the odd movie, walk, picnic and church socials, we had a lot going on. We were compatible, had the same interests, laughed at the same jokes and enjoyed being in each other's company immensely. Although we hadn't been seeing each other for a long time, we felt as though we were lifelong friends, in fact we became best friends and shared a special bond.

Beryl and Charlie liked Bob, who didn't? She kept telling me that he was a good catch and I should latch onto him. Although I still thought of Ian and "what if", he wasn't always on my mind. More and more I didn't look back but when I did, it still hurt and probably always would. Because of this, I didn't see Bob as a prospective partner, more as a trusted friend. Besides, I wasn't interested in a love relationship, not yet anyway. Any girl that Bob chose to marry would be very lucky. He had a great nature, was considerate, kind and so easy to be with.

After several weeks, Bob invited me to his meet his parents and family. I was reluctant but again, I remembered the time when I pleaded with Ian to meet his family and how upset I was when he changed the subject.

I accepted the invitation. What harm could it do? We were just good friends and it meant so much to him.

I was nervous about meeting his family, mainly because they were quite well off. They lived in a beautiful home in an upscale neighbourhood. His father had a successful and prestigious law practice and their standing in the community was well established.

I came from a respectable hard working family but we were definitely not in the same league as they were. Coming from a country that still had class distinction, it was all a bit unnerving. I stammered my way through the introductions but the Wilsons instantly put me at ease and my nervousness disappeared. They were down to earth people.

Bob had an older brother Bill and a younger sister Jenny. Bill was in pre-med school and Jenny was still at University, hoping to graduate as a teacher. His mother was a stay at home mom and after the children were pretty much on their own, she filled her time with charity work and church activities.

I had never been in such a large house in all my life. A long driveway lead up to the front door of the Tudor style home, which was as close to a mansion with spectacular gardens, as I had ever seen. Bob's mother was credited with their upkeep. Among her many other endeavours, she was an avid gardener. The living room was bright, comfortable and inviting with a large dining room, which was much bigger than my whole house. I felt like I was in Buckingham Palace. I had only seen houses like this in the pictures yet this one definitely wasn't the largest in this neighbourhood. For all their apparent wealth though, the house had a very homey feel to it and I felt completely at ease.

Bob's mother, who was an excellent cook, had prepared the meal but had someone serve it, giving her the opportunity to enjoy her company. After dinner we all retired to the family room to relax over a coffee. This too was a large, bright and comfortable room. The fire was lit, reminding me of back home but in this room, unlike Glasgow, they didn't all huddle around the fireplace trying to keep warm. Two large plush couches sat facing each other with a square coffee table in the middle. Shelves along one wall were filled with books, a gorgeous mahogany desk sat on one side of the room and a baby grand piano sat in another corner. Bob's parents did not drink or smoke and neither did the children, at least not at home.

I told the Wilsons about my family and how well I was settling in here in Canada. I missed my family but with my relatives and the many new friends I had made, it helped me to settle in fairly easily. The Wilsons told me they hoped they would see me again, and invited me to attend their church service with them some time. I didn't mention that Bob had already invited me. They were not pushy and I felt the invitation was sincere. They were Born Again Christians in every sense of the word and attended church regularly. While I didn't commit to anything, I thanked them for asking. When Bob drove me home after the visit, he asked what I thought of his family.

"I think you are very lucky to have such a nice, friendly family. I was a little nervous as you saw, but your mom and the others made me feel very much at home. I have to tell you though, my family is definitely not in the same league."

"Why would that matter? You like them and I know they like you. That's all that matters."

"For one thing, class distinction is alive and well in Glasgow and elsewhere in the British Isles. In fact where I live, the people who live at the top of the street think they are above the ones on the lower part of the street, if you can believe it."

"Well you are not in Glasgow now and my parents are definitely not class conscious as you saw."

After sitting talking in the car outside of my boarding house Bob leaned over and kissed me goodnight. I was surprised by that, but not unhappy. The bells, whistles and tingles didn't happen but then I never expected that to happen ever again. It was more a friendly kiss, for me anyway. I liked Bob and I was happy and comfortable with the friendly kiss.

XXI

This special friendship and bond between Bob and I continued to blossom. We met whenever we could. I attended services with him and his family on Sundays. Afterwards we usually went back to his parents for the remainder of the day, or to some other friend's home for dinner. In between times with Bob, I kept in close contact with my brother and cousins. Bob met them all. He got a seal of approval from each one. Everyone had the same opinion as Beryl, he was an extremely nice guy, a gorgeous hunk and a great catch to boot.

I was happy and content most of the time. Bob and I were comfortable with each other. I still thought about Ian and when I did, the tingle was still with me. It was not very likely that I would ever hear about him again, especially now that Moira was gone.

Bob finished University and passed his bar exam. He secured a position with the well-established firm where he had articled. His father had expressed hope that he would join him in his firm, to carry on if and when something happened to him. He didn't want to hurt his dad's feelings, however, he wanted to start somewhere else and make it on his own. His father was naturally disappointed, but he understood how his son felt and didn't press him into doing anything he didn't want to do.

As we continued to spend more and more time together, the friendship slowly grew into something more. I adored Bob and didn't think I could be without his friendship, but I didn't have the same feelings for him as I had for Ian.

Two people could not have been more suited to each other in every way, except for the bells, whistles and tingles. Ian was still a part of my quiet hours. Bob was loving, tender and considerate. He was not a passionate man but that didn't particularly bother me because the passion I felt for Ian would never happen again, of that I was sure.

On Valentine's night, as we sat in the car in front of my house, Bob asked me if I would consider being his wife. He handed me a beautiful blue box. When I opened it, a very large marquis diamond ring sparkled ever so brightly, even in the darkness. I was surprised to say the least. The sight of such a beautiful ring touched me deeply. I knew it must have cost him most, if not all, of any savings he had. I couldn't understand why he hadn't discussed it with me first, before getting the ring. We had talked about marriage in general terms, such as whether we wanted to marry and have a family. We both agreed we would like to marry some day when the right person came along. Our relationship was heading in that direction, but nothing definite was ever said. My eyes filled up. His eyes, those beautiful hazel eyes, were moist with tears when I looked into them. I knew he would always be there for me. When I was with him, I always felt safe and secure. He could offer me everything and I knew he loved me tenderly and deeply. Was this enough to sustain a marriage? Could I make it work? My love for him was deep, but it wasn't the same kind of love that I had felt for Ian. He was my best friend. I would have given my life for him, but the passion that I felt for Ian wasn't there. Was it enough? What could I say? I knew I would never find such a caring, loving, tender man again. I accepted his proposal. We wrapped our arms around each other, kissing between the tears.

Bob had previously told his family, before buying the ring. They were delighted, hoping I would accept. He had first planned for a more romantic setting to pop the question, perhaps dinner at the club or some other restaurant, but he wasn't sure of my reaction and so he decided to keep it private. A wedding date was set for September, which was about seven months away. No sooner had the date been set than we were caught up in all the hoopla that goes with weddings. I invited my parents over for the wedding. Bob's parents offered to have them stay at their home but Andrew had a house of his own now and had enough room for them. My parents would stay with him.

It was to be a large wedding because of the many friends and associates of Bob's family. There were several members of my family and friends who would be attending but the majority of guests would be from Bob's side. His parents very generously paid for the wedding. His sister Jenny was a bridesmaid, Beth, whom I met at one of the gatherings where I met Bob and who had become my best friend, was my maid of honour. Trish, my sailing partner, was also a bridesmaid.

Trish was now married with a little family of her own. She lived out of town. We didn't see each other all that often, but I could not conceive of getting married without her in attendance and she was only too happy to get away for the weekend with her husband, while his parents baby sat.

When I chose my bridesmaids, my thoughts went back to my old pal Moira. Oh how I wished she could be here to share this special day with me. We had been so close over the years, and even though miles separated us, the bond was still there until, of course, her untimely death. It would have given her such pleasure to see how happy I was. Although she wouldn't be there in person, she would always be with me in my heart. Bob asked his brother Bill to be best man, Andrew and his friend John were ushers.

I couldn't believe the generosity of family and friends. I was given several showers, which were unheard of in my native Scotland. In addition to that, the wedding gifts were beautiful. By the time the wedding day rolled around, there was little that we needed to buy, except larger pieces of furniture. Substantial amounts of money were also given to us. Bob and I hoped to use that money towards the purchase of some of the furniture. I felt a little guilty when I thought, for only a moment, what it might have been like had I married Ian. I knew it definitely wouldn't have been as extravagant. Guilt filled me as I also pondered what our married life might have been like. Bob's parents gave us enough money to make a down payment on a small two-bedroom bungalow in the east end of the city. In addition to the two bedrooms, there was a good-sized living room and dining room. The bathroom wasn't huge, but it was all we needed. The basement was the size of the house, it wasn't finished but that wasn't a problem as we could fix it up the way we wanted to although there was no rush to do that.

If and when we did renovate, it would give us another room and bathroom. The house was in a nice quiet neighbourhood. A well-kept lawn sat in front with a small garden area in the backyard. The house itself was in pretty good condition and was perfect as a starter home for us. The previous owners had taken good care of it, but we would probably make some changes, as people tend to do when they buy a house.

My family was not as financially able to give such a generous gift as the Wilsons, but they brought over some beautiful fine bone china and lace from Scotland. They also brought over the traditional Good Luck horseshoe that brides attach to the bouquet, and a sprig of heather to be added to it as well.

If the weather on our wedding day in September was any indication of things to come, we were in for smooth sailing along life's way. It was a beautiful sunny warm day, not too hot, almost perfect. The church where the family worshipped was filled to capacity. Bob's mother looked stunning in a gorgeous dusty rose gown. My mother was equally beautiful in delicate pale green. I was radiant (so I was told,) in a very simple but elegant white brocade gown with a full skirt. The long sleeves were narrow at the wrist with several tiny pearl buttons at the cuff.

A diamanté tiara adorned my longish hair, done in such a way that the hair rose up through the middle of the tiara. Gently flowing from that was a full-length veil. My maid of honour and bridesmaids also had very simple but elegant dresses made of a lighter brocade material. The maid of honour's dress was mauve, the bridesmaids in lavender. Floral tiaras adorned their heads and each posey had the tiniest bit of tartan showing. The men wore black tuxedos with a touch of tartan in the form of handkerchiefs peeping out of their pockets. Colourful vibrant floral arrangements filled the altars.

As the organ began to play the bridal march, the guests arose and all heads turned to the back to watch the procession. I remembered the dream I had when I was marrying Ian. Everyone looked lovely and happy. When I appeared holding on to my dad's arm many of the female guests could be seen wiping tears from their eyes. Tears could also be seen glistening under my veil. I was a little nervous but I had a steady grip of dad's arm. Bob's eyes said it all as he saw me approach. Once the marriage ceremony was performed and the register signed, the bridal party led the guests out of the church to the sound of bagpipes. We stood outside for a bit to give guests an opportunity to congratulate us before we headed off to have photographs taken. A limousine was waiting for us at the end of the pathway. We got in, rolled down the windows and had the traditional Scottish "scramble" or as we call it "scrammel". This is when the bridal party threw coins out for people to pick up. It's supposed to be for the children but some adults have been known on occasion to get right down on their knees with the children and madly move around trying to scoop up as much of the change as possible from this treasure trove. On most Fridays and Saturdays in Glasgow, crowds of youngsters hang around various churches waiting for the scrammel.

Having photographs taken was a bit tedious but it had to be done. The bride and groom, the bridal party and the families all had to be photographed. At least it was a lovely day and the park we chose for the pictures was a beautiful backdrop. When that was over we made our way to the private club, where the Wilsons were members, for the reception.

Everyone had already gathered in a room off the main banquet hall, sipping champagne and cocktails until dinner was announced. Our reception line was formed outside of the ballroom. Guests passed through the line before taking their places at the tables. Once the guests were seated, we were again piped into the reception to the clapping of hands in time to the music. The head table was quickly filled and dinner was served. We chose juice, fresh fruit cup, tossed salad and a choice of beef or chicken served with pearl potatoes, glazed carrots and asparagus tips. Baked Alaska was our choice for dessert, which was also piped in with our guests clapping enthusiastically. What a sight! My dad had baked the three-tiered cake in Glasgow and transported it over for the wedding. Tartan ribbon adorned the cake. Our initials were embroidered on the satin banners (a Scottish tradition), and inserted into the beautifully decorated cake. Favours were placed all around it. Favours are tiny floral pieces that are removed by the bride and given to special people in her life, such as friends, aunts, grandparents etc. It is considered an honour to be given a favour.

Speeches were short and sweet at our request. Cutting the cake was next. Once the photographer took all of the photographs he wanted, others started clicking cameras for their mementos of us cutting the cake. All formalities over, it was time to dance. We started it off but only made it through part of the first dance together. After that, we were in great demand by the other guests.

At about 10:00 p.m. we tried to make our getaway but unbeknown to us, others were waiting for the same moment. Promising the guests we would return, we climbed the stairs to the room set out for us to change into our regular clothes. Our guests didn't believe us, thinking we would sneak out but reluctantly, they allowed us to go upstairs.

Once inside the room we put our arms around each other, expressing how happy we were and how much we loved each other. We couldn't stay away too long from the guests, otherwise they would have been up and pounding on the door. My choice for going away clothes was a pale yellow coat with a dress to match and a little pill box hat. Anticipating some skullduggery, we previously took our luggage out to the airport hotel, only keeping our change of clothes at the club. Bob wore a navy blue suit, white shirt and navy tie with little flecks on it. Gosh he was handsome.

Upon arrival at the bottom of the stairs, we were cheered by a number of guests who had gathered there. The piper played as we were ushered into the center of the ballroom, while the other guest formed a circle around us. Again with the tearjerker, "Auld Lang Syne". Tears on this occasion were happy tears.

Bob and I went around the circle hugging as many guests as we could. Confetti and rice was showered over us as we left the hall, heading to the door. Our reserved limo was parked outside waiting to take us to the airport, where we were spending the night before taking a flight south the next morning.

XXII

At long last we were alone in the car, still a little nervous but excited. There could never have been a more perfect wedding. Everything went off like clockwork. Months before were taken up with planning, showers, fixing the house and other details. Finally we were alone and happy to be so, heading for some needed rest and relaxation.

Bob slipped his arm around me and I lay my head on his shoulder. He told me how happy he was and how much he loved me. I told him I loved him too with all my heart. I was honest and sincere but the love was different from my love for Ian. Bob must never know that even though my feelings were different, I truly loved this man.

Luxury could only describe the room, or mini suite at the hotel where we spent our first night as husband and wife. A large bed, two night tables with lamps, an ottoman at the bottom of the bed, and a desk and chair just beside a small alcove area set the tone for the room. A small floral covered sofa with a coffee table in front, and an end table with lamp beside it were inside the alcove. An en-suite bathroom with a long counter and double sinks, as well as a tub and shower, was just outside of the alcove. Patterned blue shades in the bedspread and drapes complimented the darker blue rug throughout, except in the bathroom where the floor was a light gray tile. Tiles around the tub were also light gray, with flowers dotted here and there. Sliding glass doors closed off the tub area. Flowers had been delivered to our room, and a beautiful large bouquet of red roses, along with a bottle of champagne, had been placed beside two fine crystal glasses on the coffee table. This was a far cry from anything I had ever seen in Glasgow or could have ever imagined. Any honeymoon with Ian would have paled in comparison to this luxury. Obviously Bob, who tried so hard to make everything perfect for me, had planned all of this luxury on his own.

Although we were not drinkers, this was such a special occasion and because the champagne was provided, we opened the bubbly and poured a glass, hoping it would take a little of the edge off our nervousness.

He handed me a beautifully wrapped gift as we sat down on the little sofa. Inside the box a large diamond pendant sparkled brightly. I reached over to kiss him while passing my gift to him at the same time. Choosing something special for him wasn't easy, but I finally settled on a gold Cross pen, engraved with our wedding date and "I Love You". I told him I had the date engraved to make sure he would have no excuse for forgetting our anniversary date, although I didn’t think for one moment he would ever forget such a special occasion. He was caring, methodical and remembered everything important to him.

When our glasses of champagne were empty, we took turns in the bathroom getting changed into our nightclothes. We were both tired and our flight was bright and early the next morning. As we snuggled up to each other, it was obvious we were both a little nervous but love overcame, and that night we two became as one. Bob couldn't have been more considerate, loving and tender. We drifted off to sleep in each other's arms, sharing how much we loved each other and how we were the luckiest people in the world, looking forward to a long and happy life together.

At 7:00 a.m. the clerk at the front desk rang the telephone according to instructions we left the night before. Shortly afterwards, the porter knocked on the door, delivering breakfast, which we had ordered when we checked in. Bob opened the door to let the porter and his cart in the room. He gave him a nice tip and closed the door. He brought my breakfast over to me while I was still in bed thinking about getting up. What a way to start married life I thought, a great husband and breakfast in bed. Bob showered and dressed in light slacks with a coordinating jacket and an open neck sports type shirt. I finished my breakfast, got up, showered and dressed. I wore a light summer floral dress with a matching sweater over it. Shuttle services were provided by the hotel to take us the short distance to the airport terminal. Departure time was 12:00 noon and we arrived with a bit of time to spare. The fairly short trip to Acapulco was pleasant. We held hands most of the way.

Arriving at our destination on time, we got in line as each passenger deplaned. Almost immediately all of the travellers removed their jackets or sweaters as the hot weather hit them. While the weather back home wasn't too bad, it wasn't as warm as Mexico and the sun was shining brightly. After clearing customs, we walked outside where the hotel shuttle was waiting to pick up arriving passengers. Several other passengers were going to the same hotel as we were, others that were going to different hotels, got on other shuttles. It was easy to tell the newly arrived tourists by the differences in the skin colour. Most of the tourists who had been there for a while sported nice tans while the new arrivals were quite pale.

Bob had booked an ocean front hotel but he hadn't shown the brochure to me as he wanted to surprise me. Our hotel was only about a half hour's drive from the airport. We were happy, relaxed and glad to be on our own for a couple of weeks and had been so looking forward to this time away by ourselves. Doors did not grace the entrance of the hotel, just very large marble pillars marking the entry. Marble flooring covered the entire area. Marble pillars, stucco walls and marble accents were everywhere in this palatial hotel.

A huge winding swimming pool, snuggled in amongst the most gorgeous tropical plants was visible from the hotel lobby. Plenty of shaded areas surrounded the pool and patios for those who didn't want to sit out in the sun all day. Guests looked relaxed and tanned as they sat sipping fancy cool drinks, served by the ever-attentive waiters and waitresses. Some of the guests were sitting on stools at a bar located in the center of the pool.

What a life I thought. I wonder how the poor are living? I knew a honeymoon in Scotland would have been very different. Tourists were laughing, some dancing on the deck to the Mexican band strolling the grounds while others sat enjoying their people watching. It was a happy, relaxing sight. We were met at the entrance by a porter who carried our luggage inside to the desk area. We received two keys at sign in and the same porter picked up our luggage and escorted us to our room. His name was Manuel. He didn't speak much English, just enough to welcome us but he sure was a happy fellow and very good looking. From what I had observed, the Mexicans were a happy, attractive race. Bob tipped Manuel and thanked him for his help.

Once alone, we opened our suitcases and took out some shorts and tops. Even our summer clothes seemed too warm in this climate. We decided to leave the unpacking until later on. Bob took me in his arms and told me how happy he was, and how much he loved me. I couldn't have been happier and deep in my heart, I knew this man would love and cherish me for the rest of our lives together. I hadn't felt this happy, relaxed and content in such a long time.

For a light snack we ordered room service, which we ate on the balcony furnished with white wicker chairs and a table. Brightly coloured drapes and bedspreads gave the room a warm, tropical look. Unless we were desperate for a cold drink, we wouldn't be using the mini bar in the corner of the room, most items being overly expensive.

From our balcony the view was spectacular, sunbathers laying on the sand, the ocean glistening in the hot sun and traders busily trying to sell their goods. Guests were having fun swimming in the ocean, or in the pool, while others sat under umbrellas, little children played with their pails and spades, all the while being waited on by the ever attentive waiters and waitresses. Some of the tourists must have been out there for some time because their bodies sported a brown tan, while others were quite red.. I wouldn't be sitting under the sun for very long, if at all because I burn easily, and apart from the fact it can be very painful, I didn't want to spoil my time here with Bob. It would also encourage my gazillions of freckles to appear, freckles that I hated. I never understood why people said freckles were a sign of beauty. Obviously they didn't have any. I hated them. There wasn't much I could do except try to keep them at a minimum.

Mexican traders were everywhere traipsing up and down the beach, trying to sell their wares. Some very young children travelled with their parents, but they seemed to be more interested in playing than in selling. Mexican children are adorable and photogenic. Perhaps the parents know that it helped make more sales for them. Some traders sold little Mexican puppet dancers and others had tablecloths, hats, shawls, leather purses, sandals, shells etc. Little children went along helping out or trying to sell their own supply of chewing gum. It was a happy scene, traders joking with tourists and with each other. No one appeared upset, even if a sale couldn't be made. They just stood back and watched other Mexicans trying to make a deal. They seemed happy and enjoying what they were doing.

All the pre wedding preparing, showers, etc., had left us happily tired. An early evening for us after dinner was in the plans. We just needed to relax and unwind. With our snack finished, it was time to go back into the room and unpack the suitcases. Every now and then Bob would give me a hug and tell me how much he loved me. As I looked into his sparkling big hazel eyes, I could see the love he had for me and I knew it was deep and true.

"I love you too Bob. I know we are going to be very happy."

We freshened up and changed into casual clothes for dinner downstairs in the hotel. I put on a pair of lightweight white slacks and a sleeveless floral blouse. My sandals were quite open, keeping my feet from getting too hot. Bob wore a beige pair of slacks with a cream coloured short sleeve shirt. Depending on how we felt, a stroll along the street might be nice before retiring for the night.

The dining room was busy. It was a hive of activity with the Mexican musicians strolling through the restaurant, stopping at tables and taking any requests from patrons. We didn't have to wait too long to be seated but we didn't mind anyway, it was entertaining just watching all that was going on. The headwaiter directed us to a table by a window overlooking the ocean. There wasn't an actual window there, just an open space, although I am sure they must have had some type of covering for evenings when it wasn't too warm or if a storm came up. Cool evening air gently breezed through the space and the aroma of the tropical flowers filled the entire area. How much more romantic could a setting be? What a great place for a honeymoon.

Looking around the room, it was obvious we were not the only honeymooners there. Acapulco was a popular place for honeymoons and it was easy to see why in this tropical paradise. Many young couples went to the so-called honeymoon capital of the world, Niagara Falls, which is also very beautiful, perhaps not so romantic, and definitely not as warm. We had considered the Falls but because we lived within driving distance of it, and had travelled there many times for an outing or picnic. We loved Niagara Falls but wanted somewhere different for our honeymoon and it was clear we had made the right choice.

One of the reasons we visited Niagara Falls often was because Moira and I had seen the picture "Niagara" years before, starring Marilyn Monroe. Filming was done in Niagara Falls. A special song "For the lovers" in the film, was played on the tower bells. When I moved to Canada, I promised Moira that if I ever got to Niagara Falls, I would visit the tower and request that special tune be played. The Blue Rays also played that tune. I never did get it played on the bells, but every time I visited Niagara, I thought of Moira, even to this day.

After a leisurely romantic dinner, aromatic breezes and Mexican musicians moving around the room, we left for a short stroll before retiring for the night. Even at that time of the night, young girls who were little more than babies themselves sat on the sidewalks begging with a baby wrapped up beside them. It was pitiful. We found this quite depressing. While we gladly put some coins in their hands, we knew it wouldn't solve anything. Beggars would be back the next night, with the same faces every night and even during the day. I wondered if they even had homes to go to, or if this was their home right where they sat. Back in our gorgeous room in our expensive, beautiful marble hotel, we felt guilty because we had such luxurious accommodations. Nothing we could do would erase the poverty, except to give what we could, when we could.

Even in Glasgow I had never seen such poverty. I got very upset whenever I saw tourists walk past these young beggars, without as much as a turn of the head, all the while spending lots of money on unnecessary things, yet couldn't or wouldn't spend a few dollars on these poor unfortunate people. Not all of the tourists passed the beggars, but far too many did. Others nickel and dimed the traders to get their wares for next to nothing, while laughing and making a joke of it all. I didn't like to haggle with them. Whenever I saw something I wanted, I gave what they asked. Besides it was still very reasonable.

Back at the hotel, we changed into our night attire then went out onto the balcony to take in the evening air, lovely sights, moonlit sky shining on the water and an amazing aroma from the tropical flowers reaching up to us. Soft romantic music drifted up from some of the lounges. Bob put his arm around me as we sat there for a little while, watching the activities below. Couples strolled along the beach, arm in arm, while others sat at tables chatting, yet others were dancing on the outdoor patio. It was time for us to retire. Before slipping into bed, we took turns in the shower. Bob couldn't be called a passionate man by any stretch of the imagination, but he was a gentle, kind, tender and a very considerate lover. I was not disappointed with our intimacy, but wondered what it might have been like with Ian. Guilt filled me as these thoughts surfaced. Bob would have been so hurt had he known. I was angry at myself for allowing these thoughts to come into my mind. Maybe the sparks I felt for Ian wouldn't have been what I expected after all, and from what I have learned, those sparks can sometimes die out or fade away after couples live together for some time.

Ian and I never consummated our love, it just wasn't done. Perhaps if we had, I might not have felt so passionately about him. Could it be more passion or lust than love? The unknown? Maybe I had built it up in my mind because of the feelings he stirred up inside me when we held each other and kissed. Maybe it would have dimmed after a time but I would never know. Possibly because I built this up in my mind, I never expected to feel like that with anyone else. I was not disappointed in Bob. How could I be? He was the most wonderful person in every other way.

The honeymoon went by all too quickly but we enjoyed strolling the beach, swimming and dancing in the evening. This vacation was what we needed to relax after all the pre marriage activities. We also did a little shopping, picking up some souvenirs for the folks back home and a trinket or two for our house. Every evening we ate dinner at a different restaurant, some in other hotels and some along the promenade. After dinner we strolled along the street or beach, stopping in for a dance on the patio when we felt like it, before retiring. We fell asleep in each other's arms every night. I was truly happy and content. Bob seemed to be too.

Starting our life together in our new house filled us with anticipation and excitement. We were anxious to get home, although a little sad at having to leave this idyllic place and get back into the everyday trials and tribulations of life. Our honeymoon would fill us with happy memories for years to come, and we were totally ready for the challenges ahead. When the porter picked up our luggage and put it on board the bus, which would take us to the airport, we felt a little sad at leaving the hotel and the staff who were wonderful. After we paid the bill and checked out, we thanked everyone for the wonderful service and left tips for those who had taken excellent care of us.

Travelling out of the driveway, we saw the newest lot of tourists coming in. They were now the distinguishable pale ones and we had a little tan. This time next week or so, they would be the ones leaving. We waved to them and they to us. Ah well, all good times come to an end, and it was time to get back to "purrich and auld claes" (porridge and old clothes) as we would say in Scotland.

XXIII

The flight was uneventful but pleasant enough. Passengers were excitedly discussing their vacations and planning for next year. Bob's brother picked us up at the airport. It was early fall which usually meant reasonably mild weather but we felt the coolness after the hot Mexican sunshine. My parents had a few weeks remaining on their vacation. They were still at Andrew's house. He, along with the Wilsons, had taken them just about everywhere they wanted to visit. The loved Canada and were not looking forward to going back to Scotland. It would be especially difficult now that their two children had settled here. I wasn't looking forward to their leaving either. We discussed the possibility of getting permission for them to come over after they retired. Dad said he would enquire into it. There was nothing to lose and hopefully everything to gain.

On my parents' last night in Canada the Wilsons threw a farewell party for them in their home. It wasn't a large celebration but it was filled with love and happiness. Mom and dad were so relieved to see me settled in and happy, remembering the difficult time I had after I broke it off with Ian. They both loved Bob's family and knew they looked out for us, which helped to take a bit of the strain off them leaving us here. Both of my parents enjoyed good health, but they weren't getting any younger, anything could happen. No one could predict the future. It helped somewhat to know they would enquire about emigrating. Their leaving was like a repeat of the time I left Glasgow to move to Canada. We were a sentimental lot and it didn't take much for the tears to flow.

We spent the next several months renovating our little house the way Bob and I wanted it. We were both overwhelmed and grateful for all the beautiful gifts we received. Not many newlyweds started off their married life as well as we did. Bob progressed in the law practice and was soon promoted to partner. It kept him busy. Meanwhile, I continued on at my job. We discussed having children and both agreed that if and when I got pregnant, I would leave my job and stay at home. There wasn't much we didn't agree on, but if ever a difference of opinion came up, we settled it amicably so that each of us would be happy with whatever outcome was reached. I wasn't interested in a career anyway, preferring to stay home and raise any children we might be blessed with. Bob was more than able to support us financially.

Christmas together the first year was like everything else, wonderful. Our little house was seasonally decorated outside and inside. We bought a silver tree for the inside with a light beam shining on it as it turned around. As the tree revolved, the beam shining on the silver tree and colourful decorations, resembled a picture on a Christmas card, warm, welcoming, setting the tone for Christmas.

On Christmas morning we exchanged gifts to each other before having breakfast. Christmas was held at the Wilsons with all of the family there. We had the traditional turkey with cranberry sauce and gravy, stuffing, potatoes, vegetables and fresh baked rolls. Andrew was always invited to any social event at their house. Maybe one day we might have our own Christmas dinner with our family, starting our own tradition. Although the Wilsons were in a comfortable financial position, no one over indulged at Christmas. Yes, gifts were exchanged but they were mostly token. Everyone was encouraged to share their good fortune with those less fortunate. We had lots of laughs, sang a few songs and enjoyed being with each other. We never stayed overnight which we could have easily done. We enjoyed going home to our own wee but 'n ben.

While I thoroughly enjoyed these family gatherings, it was difficult and a bit sad because I missed my parents so much. Andrew missed them as well but somehow men seem to be able to control their emotions at times like these. However, we always telephoned them at the good old corner box, but in many ways that made me feel worse.

Moira's death was also a void in my life. I often wondered if she would have come over for a holiday or perhaps I might have visited her in Glasgow. Christmas was never a big celebration in Glasgow, although we exchanged gifts. New Year's was the highlight of our lives, along with travelling to see the quartet. As soon as one New Year's celebration was over, we were already looking forward to the next year. Tradition dictated that everyone stayed in their own houses until after midnight when the bottles were opened and the toasts were made. Houses had to be spic and span. Women could be seen cleaning until very late on Hogmanay (New year's eve).

Whisky, wine and other alcoholic drinks for the adults, plus ginger beer, raspberry wine, blackberry wine and other non-alcoholic beverages for children, were set out on the table. Dad made the black bun and shortbread, but nothing was touched until after "the bells" at midnight. Dad always said that the five minutes before midnight was the longest five minutes he ever put in. Once the bottles were opened and the family celebrated together, it was off to other parties or perhaps the party might be in our house. When Moira and I were "grown up", the party was at my house and soon after the bells, the young guests arrived with the party continuing on until the wee hours of the morning. Celebrations of this type went on for days, as families visited other family members and friends, to wish them well.

There is a tradition that the first person over the door in the New Year must be a tall, dark man. He was to bring with him a piece of coal, something to eat, something to drink and some money, ensuring the family being visited would have, warmth, food and drink, and enough money for the year. When I was in college, one of our friends was well over six feet and had the required dark hair. He was in great demand for the job. A lot people were superstitious about this and would not let anyone else in until their tall, dark man arrived. Dad never turned anyone away from the door as a first foot because when he was younger, he was turned away because of his red hair.

Life for us was good, but we were not newlyweds anymore. Not being great partygoers or heavy on the nightlife, we preferred to spend most of our evenings at home by ourselves or with family. Sometimes we went out for dinner and a movie. Church and other activities that we were involved in kept us busy.

As the years rolled by, Bob and I got a little concerned that there were no children on the way. We made an appointment so see the family doctor. After careful examinations, he assured both of us that we were in good health, and there was no reason why I couldn't conceive. It was just a matter of waiting. Sensing that we were a little over anxious, he suggested we try to put it out of our minds and relax, enjoy life and when it was time, a little one would surely come along. Relaxing about having children was not as easy as the doctor suggested. Neither of us thought we were overly preoccupied with having a baby, but we had to admit it was seldom out of our minds. We considered what we might do if I didn't get pregnant. We weren't getting any younger and didn't want too many more years to pass before starting a family. Thinking about that could have added to the anxiety.

Another year passed and there was still no baby. We began to think about adoption. Friends and family tried to reassure us that there was plenty of time, but we had made up our minds to start the procedure. Applications could take a long time before any adoption was finalized, if we were approved, and for that reason we didn't want to waste any more time. Both sets of parents, while they thought there was plenty of time, gave us their total support in whatever we chose to do.

Dad had been made redundant on his job not long after the wedding, although he was still a relatively young man. He tried unsuccessfully to get another job, but there were too many younger, available men looking for work, which put him at the bottom of the list. Mom and Dad were at an age where they could take early retirement and although money would not be plentiful, they could live on what they made. It was around that time they decided to apply for emigration to Canada, to learn whether or not they would be accepted. This wasn't a situation where there was any danger of them taking a job in Canada because we were here and could well afford to look after them. Sponsorship by Andrew and me helped immensely in getting their application approved reasonably quickly. They would not become a burden to the country because dad wouldn't be actively looking for employment. Mom and dad moving to Canada was what Andrew and I had wanted ever since we had settled here. With the passing years and mom and dad getting older, it was a worry to us should anything happen to them. It would be difficult for us to properly take care of them while we were in Canada and they were in Scotland. We could take turns going back to help but at best it would only be a temporary solution.

Andrew hadn't married. Although he had several girlfriends, none had won his heart. He owned his own house and there was plenty of room for mom and dad. Naturally it was a difficult time for them to leave all they had ever known, family, friends, the neighbourhood that they had lived in since they were married and where they raised their family. Moving to Canada was what they wanted to do because Andrew and I were here. They had no doubts about their decision, just that in a way, it put an end to all they had ever known and they would dearly miss their friends. Fortunately their application was accepted and we were a whole family once more.

Bob and I started the adoption procedure, which was lengthy, with so many forms, balances and checks to be done. Waiting was agony for us but one day we got the telephone call that a baby girl was waiting for us. Had I been pregnant and delivered a little girl, I couldn't have been more excited. Our parents were overjoyed and couldn't wait to see their new granddaughter. Turning back or changing our minds was not an option, but it wasn't even a consideration when we saw the little doll that was waiting for us.

Lisa, the name we had chosen for her, had been given up for adoption as a new born, but had been in foster care until a suitable permanent home could be found for her. She had Bob's dark hair and dimples. Her nose and mouth were replicas of mine, or at least we thought so. She was perfect and we couldn't wait to take her home.

Lisa was a good baby who never gave us any problems whatsoever. I often thought I was in a dream and that one-day the bubble would burst. Life seemed to be just too perfect. When a song was played that reminded me of Ian, my mind rolled back to him. I wondered just how perfect my life would have been with him, and whether or not he had married. Breaking off with him was the right decision. I knew that in my heart. Bob couldn't have been a better husband and I knew he loved me but the passion wasn't there. I always believed that was a once in a lifetime thing.

The grandparents were ecstatic with this, their first grandchild. Giving up my job was easy, although I could easily have continued on because there was no shortage of baby-sitters. I wanted to be the one to raise my children and have the grandparents as just that, grandparents. That way they were never put in a position where they were actually raising their grandchildren. Fortunately, we could afford to do that.

The first Christmas with little Lisa was so special and although she was too young to realize what was happening, the joy she brought to us and everyone else was obvious. She was the icing on the cake of our marriage and life together. How could anyone give her up? However, circumstances cause people to do things they may not want to do. I felt sadness for the mother who had to give her up. What must it have been like for her? I will be forever grateful to her that she gave us this beautiful child.

Bob was well established in his firm now. Lisa was growing up quickly and we felt we needed a bigger house.

If we were to buy a new house, it had to be before Lisa went to school so that she wouldn't have to move away from her friends. Adoption of another child was discussed. It was with mixed emotions that we sold our house and started the packing for the move to the new one. This lovely little home had so many wonderful memories for us. It was our first home, we put a lot of love and work into it and our marriage grew stronger as the years passed by.

Fortunately for us, our house wasn't on the market long before it sold. Our new home was considerably larger than our current one, containing four bedrooms, one with an en suite bathroom, another bathroom in the hall, a much larger living room, dining room and kitchen as well as a family room. The basement in the new house was already finished, and was used as a games room by the current owner. A much larger backyard overlooked a ravine, in a beautiful setting. Even the front yard was much larger. A double driveway with an attached double garage ensured parking wouldn't be a problem.

Lisa was growing like a weed, walking and trying to say sentences. She was about three years old when we thought it was time to get a brother or sister for her. Having an only child was not our preference but since I still hadn't gotten pregnant, another adoption was the answer. Lisa couldn't have been more loved if she had been biologically our own. Before we actually got down to the business of applying for adoption I hadn't been feeling too well. I reasoned it was because we were contemplating adopting another child. I didn't understand it, I was always in good health. When I started being sick in the morning, I was in total disbelief. I couldn't be pregnant, not after all this time. I waited a few more days. When the sickness continued, I made an appointment with the doctor without telling anyone. After the doctor examined me, I could tell by the look on his face that I was finally pregnant. He said I was in great health, he didn't anticipate any problems and handed me an appointment schedule

Lisa couldn't understand why I was getting all fancy that evening in the dining room. She knew we usually ate meals in the kitchen unless we were expecting company and asked if nana was coming over. I told her I was going to give daddy a nice surprise. Lisa liked surprises, but what about this one? Bob loved my Scottish style steak pie. I got busy in the kitchen and prepared the meal.

Lucky for me, he was going to be a little late. I got the potatoes ready for mashing and since there was no time to soak the hard peas, I just used canned peas. My good china was brought out of the cabinet and set on the table, with a couple of candles in the center, ready to light. Lisa was mesmerized by all of this because it wasn't her birthday. She kept asking what the surprise was, but I told her she would have to wait until daddy came home.

When I heard Bob's key go into the door lock, I started to shake. His face lit up when he came into the house and smelled the familiar aroma of steak pie. Since it wasn't regularly on the menu, he knew something was going on. When he saw the dining room table set with the fine china and candles lit, his first thought was that he had forgotten some special occasion or like Lisa, wondered if my parents or his parents were coming for dinner. A worried look came over his face. Lisa was bouncing up and down waiting to get her kiss, hardly giving Bob time to take off his coat. He asked her what she and mommy had been up to that day. All Lisa could say was that mommy had a surprise for daddy. When I came out of the kitchen I jokingly yelled "bon appetito". He asked "what's going on?"

“Relax, we are not having company and no, you didn’t forget any special occasion.”

“What’s this surprise that Lisa is talking about?”

I was just bursting at the seams to tell him but I wanted to toy with him for a bit and said, "If I asked you what was missing in your life, what would you say?"

He gave me a strange look and said there was nothing missing in his life. "What would make you extremely happy?" I continued.

"I don't think I could be any happier. I love my wife and daughter and I don't know of anything that would make me happier."

"Is there something you feel you have missed out on, something you could change, if possible?"

“Fiona, what are you rambling on about? What happened today and what brought this on. It has to be something good because I smell steak pie.”

"What about another baby? How would that make you feel?"

His first thought was that I had probably gone down to the agency but why the celebration? It couldn’t be that because we hadn’t applied yet.

I couldn’t tease him any longer.

“As unbelievable as this sounds, I am pregnant.”

Why didn’t I think about having a camera to capture the absolute look of shock

“What do you mean you are pregnant?”

“I’ve known for some time now that I might be pregnant, but I didn’t want to tell anyone until I was sure. Today the doctor confirmed it. He said I am in good health and I should have a safe delivery. Can you believe it?”

Meanwhile Lisa was tugging at us waiting for the surprise.

"Where's the surprise mommy, where's the surprise?"

When Bob finally took it in and realized what I was saying, he threw his arms around me. We were both overcome with emotion and cried. Lisa tried to get between us. We took her in our arms between us and told her the surprise was that she was going to have a baby brother or sister. Somehow Lisa might have been happier if we had told her she was getting a new doll or bike or some other toy. She didn't seem to think too much of this surprise.

Once I told Bob the good news, we took turns on the telephone to let the rest of the family and friends in on it. They too were surprised considering I had never been able to get pregnant before. Everyone was happy for us. My pregnancy was reasonably uneventful, except that I gained an enormous amount of weight. Family and friends told me not to worry about it. They assured me I would soon take it off again, running after two children. My appetite was ferocious and I seemed to be eating just for the sake of eating.

Little Daniel, although he wasn't so little, was born at 6:00 a.m. in the morning. I had been in the hospital for some time before his delivery, which wasn't real easy, but taking everything into consideration, it went well. Daniel was almost 9 pounds and the image of his father. Lisa wanted a little girl but when we told her we had to take whatever came along, she just shook her head. She loved her little brother but as is normal, they had their moments. Sometimes she got a little jealous of the attention showered on Daniel, but we all tried our utmost to make sure she was included in everything. Bathing and changing Daniel was one way she was included. That made her feel quite grown up and like a little mommy herself. Life was golden, our life complete.

I adored Bob and every day I thanked God for this wonderful man, but the magic I felt for Ian was not there.

Anytime one of the songs that was popular when Ian and I were going together was played on the radio, I couldn't help but wonder about him. It wasn't because I regretted my decision or regretted marrying Bob, it was more or less because it brought memories of years gone by and that included Ian. I felt guilty about that but he wasn't the only one I thought about. At these times it was only natural to go down memory lane and that included Ian. There was no way another man, whoever he was, could have made a better husband than Bob. Our marriage was built on a solid foundation of love, trust and consideration, for each other. I rationalized that people who get married with fire and passion, very often lose that after years together. If that was the only basis of their marriage, it was doomed from the start because the flame does dim eventually. Often couples found out too late that they had little else in common. Not all, but many. On top of all of the other qualities in our marriage, ours was warm, gentle and even intimate, but never fiery.

Our friendship with Beth and Joe grew as strong as our marriages. They were friends of Bob and his family before I came on the scene and when I appeared, I was introduced to them. All four of us became fast and best friends. Beth and Joe got married a year before we did, they had two children about the same ages as Lisa and Daniel, and they moved into a newer house before we did. It was one of the reasons we chose that location for our new home. As the children grew up together, they attended the same schools. Beth, Joe, Bob and I were involved in all the activities associated with our children but sometimes Bob and Joe couldn't attend because of work commitments. When at all possible, they attended the functions with us. Many weekends we got together to play cards or go to a movie.

Grandparents were more than anxious to sit with the children. Beth and I loved to shop too while our hubbies sat with the children during those girls day out shopping trips. Both Bob and Joe, an accountant, had extremely busy practices. Any chance they got, they left the office to join us wherever we might be with the children. We tried to make the most of any free time they managed to get.

Trish and I tried to stay in touch but as the years went by and our families and responsibilities grew, we saw less and less of each other. We always made a point of getting in touch at Christmas time. Trish married well too. Although it was a great sacrifice leaving family and friends to immigrate to Canada, we knew it was the right decision for us. I suppose we were young and carefree, not worried about much and filled with a sense of adventure. Often when looking back and thinking about old friends and good times, it brought to mind that it was a huge sacrifice, but for us, it was the right thing to do. We never regretted it.

The years seemed to fly by, the children grew up and our marriage got stronger, if that was possible. Daniel learned to play the bagpipes. I had a set sent over from Scotland. Lisa took tap and highland dancing. We attended every recital. When they joined the cubs/scouts and brownies/guides, we tried to make time to volunteer in any way we could. It wasn't always easy for Bob, but at least one parent and always the grandparents, attended any function our children were involved in. It was important for them to know we supported them. Beth and Joe did the same.

Other than normal little everyday problems, children falling out with their friends, sometimes not too eager to do homework or practice whatever they were involved in, this was a well-adjusted family. I always felt that their involvement in the church and Sunday school helped focus their daily lives.

It seemed as though no time at all had passed when Lisa graduated from high school and was accepted into university. Next it was Daniel's turn to graduate from high school. Choosing universities at home pleased us. It meant they could stay at home a little longer, and it also cut back on expenses. We knew that one day they would most likely want to get a place of their own or at the very least, an apartment to share with some other students. The decision would be theirs. We wouldn’t stand in their way but we would not be unhappy if they decided to stay at home, as long as they wanted to.

XXIV

Our parents were getting on in years but fortunately, they all enjoyed good health and were active in various activities. Although Andrew had a string of girlfriends, he never married. Mom and dad were still living with him, an arrangement that suited all of them. There was no reason why they should move out on their own. Andrew was happy, why wouldn't he be? His meals were cooked for him, his laundry done and even some of the lighter housework was taken care of.

Bob was getting ready to go to the office one morning when he received a telephone call from a doctor in an out of town hospital. His parents had been involved in an automobile accident on their way home from the cottage where they had been staying for the weekend. He wouldn't tell Bob the extent of their injuries over the telephone, but that fact alone, told us it must be bad. Bob couldn't believe what he was hearing and was on the verge of breaking down.

He was advised to get up there as soon as possible, along with any other siblings. He immediately telephoned his brother and sister who agreed to meet him at the hospital. I couldn't reach the children. Daniel was now a lawyer like his father and Lisa was a high school teacher. Although they both had positions downtown, and could have stayed at home, they chose to move into their own apartments. I left a message for them suggesting they call my mom. Sometimes the children dropped by the house and on the off chance they might do that, I left a note on the fridge. I called my parents with the news and they, like everyone else, were in total shock.

It wasn't difficult for Bob to find the small hospital. It was close to their family cottage and over the years, they spent most of their summers there. On many occasions one or more of the children had to go to the emergency room for stitches or some other patch up. When we arrived at the hospital we knew by the look on the faces of staff, that it was not good news. An attending physician took us into his office and told us as gently as possible, that both parents had been killed by a driver who had apparently fallen asleep at the wheel, and had crossed the line.

Unfortunately, they were dead on arrival. None of us was prepared for something like this. The Wilsons were vibrant active people and to die in such a tragic manner was almost more than this family could bear. Bob was inconsolable, more so than the other two siblings, but everyone deals with grief in different ways. Although Bob's siblings were married and raising families of their own, we had all tried to spend as much time as possible with each other and our parents. We were a close family who took time for each other. Now we had to face the task of arranging a funeral, disposing of the estate and all the other matters that had to be taken care of. It awakened me to the sad fact that, unfortunately, my own parents would not always be with me either. Sometimes it takes another person's death to bring home the reality that loved ones won't always be with us.

Bob's father had all the legal papers in order. The big house was sold. Anyone in the family, who might have wanted to live in the house, had that option but by now everyone was established in their own homes and content to stay there. Everyone agreed that the family home would always have been just that, the family home with all its memories, and they preferred to leave it that way. Other items, collectibles, trinkets and treasures were distributed evenly. Most of the furniture was shared among the many grandchildren who were newly in or setting up their own apartments.

Bob's father's practice would have to be sold or dissolved but no one wanted to see the practice leave the family. Mr. Wilson had worked so hard to build it up to the highly respected firm that it was. The obvious solution would be for Bob to take over. His dad always hoped he would join the firm but never pushed it. Bob wanted to make his own mark and he had, but he gave a lot of consideration to this suggestion. As was the case with his dad, everyone left it up to Bob and Bob alone. When he made the decision to take over the practice, he knew it was the right thing to do, but he wished his dad was around to see him take over. He was now a senior partner in another firm. Before he could make the move, he would have to sever his ties with the other partners. He had a meeting with the others and while they were sorry to see him leave, they totally understood and wished him the best of luck. When all of the legal documents were prepared and signed, Bob took over his dad's practice.

Several months passed, the legalities all completed and life was slowly returning to normal, but I couldn't help but notice the change that had come over Bob. At first I put it down to grief and shock, or the enormous amount of work involved in taking over the practice, although I am not sure I believed that. He was devastated at his parents' tragic death for sure, but he was much stronger than that. He was putting in an awful lot of extra time at the office. I thought he was pushing himself too much. A great change had come over him but being involved with another woman was not even a consideration for me. I knew him too well, and I was secure in our marriage. Besides, any time I tried to reach him at the office, he always took my calls. If I was going downtown to shop by myself, I phoned and he met me for lunch. Sometimes I took a sandwich into the office and we ate lunch there. After shopping Bob would pick me up at an arranged spot and we drove home together. Whatever the problem was, it was not another woman. I knew without a doubt that he still loved me. Even after all these years, he still snuggled up to me in bed. We fell asleep in each other's arms every night.

Bob wasn't picking up. I was concerned. He should have come to terms with his parents' death by now, the practice was reorganized, and he should not be working so hard. He was the boss, he owned the practice, he didn't have to be in working all the time. Also, we were well established and money was not a problem. We had discussed the possibility of him retiring while we were young enough to enjoy it. Maybe that thought scared him a little. Sometimes it can do that. We had travelled a bit and hoped to do more when he retired. Spending our golden years together when we were still fit and healthy to enjoy it was our goal.

Even at his age, Bob continued to be a handsome man who was aging well. Now he was beginning to look pale, haggard and his eyes weren't sparkling. I was worried. I urged him to visit the doctor, but he insisted he was fine. I busied myself with my daily routines and some volunteer work. Whenever we had family dinners or had Beth and Joe or other friends over, someone would comment on Bob's appearance and ask if he was all right. He wasn't our Bob. I didn't know what to do. I couldn't drag him to the doctor like a little child.

I had just arrived home after shopping with Beth when the telephone rang. Probably Bob calling me to say he is staying late again, I thought. I had become used to that. When I picked up his voice sounded weak and far away. I sensed something was wrong. I asked him where he was.

"Don't panic," he said. "I am in the hospital."

I screamed into the telephone,

"What do you mean you are in the hospital? Were you in a car accident? Are you alright?"

"No," he replied. "Can you come to the hospital? Don't worry. Please be careful driving and keep your mind on the road."

How could I not worry? I was already shaking and out of breathe. Bob had never been in hospital. I hadn't taken my coat off yet. I locked the front door, and got in the car, glad that I hadn't parked it in the garage. Then I drove straight to the hospital. I was trying to keep my concentration on the roads but my hands were now sweaty on the wheel. Why didn't he say what the problem was? Does that mean it wasn't much or it was too much?

Bob had never been ill and in fact enjoyed excellent health, due to the fact that he ate well and kept fit. It seemed like an eternity before I reached the parking lot. I ran inside and headed for the room number that Bob had given me. My legs almost gave way. I leaned on the bed as I steadied myself. Seeing Bob sitting up in the bed with a gown on absolutely floored me.

"What on earth happened?" I asked him.

We were alone in the room. There was another bed beside him but no one was in it. Thank goodness.

"What is going on?"

Bob put out his hand, reaching for mine.

"Why don't you pull up a chair and sit on it instead of the bed? You will be more comfortable."

Would my weak legs take me to the chair?

"I know, I know you have been after me for a while about the change in me. I was wrong; I should have consulted a doctor. I haven't been feeling good for some time. I wasn't in any pain, just a feeling of not being a hundred percent. I thought I was coming down with some kind of bug, but the feeling didn't go away. When you suggested I see a doctor, I thought it best to have it checked out by Paul, (the family doctor who is a friend of Bob's brother Bill). Before you get angry, I didn't want to call you because I still thought it was nothing more than an upset stomach or maybe even the stress of all that has gone on recently. I didn't want to worry you. I made an appointment with Paul. It's great having a friend who is a doctor because he fit me in right away. After a good examination in the office, he suggested I book into the hospital so that he could run a series of tests. This would enable him to get quicker results. Some of the results came in fairly quickly. Paul suggested I might have a problem, but didn't elaborate. He wanted to wait for the rest of the results. I didn't press him but I knew by the tone of his voice and the look on his face, that it was more than a bug."

I couldn't believe what I was hearing. There must have been some mistake. I knew he hadn't been the same since his parents' accident, but being that sick never entered my mind. He had gone to work every day, put his parents affairs in order and carried on in the practice. I thought the same as Bob that it was probably the stress of everything. After a little vacation, he would return to normal. As I listened to Bob and looked closer at his face and eyes, they appeared a little yellowish. I knew it was more serious than I originally thought.

Paul suggested that Bob stay in at least overnight and maybe a full day or so, in order to make sure that all the available tests could be done. He didn't want to do that, he wanted to go home, but he was so tired and between Paul and me, he agreed to stay. Paul assured us that it would be much easier and quicker getting the tests done while he was in the hospital.

I waited until Bob got settled for the night, then left the hospital. Always thinking about me, he reminded me to be careful, not to worry the children, at least until all the tests were done. He tried to reassure me that he would be alright. I wasn't so sure. I had a terrible feeling in the pit of my stomach. Bob was going to be in and out of his room the next day, and he promised to call me the minute he had any news. I told him I would not visit in the morning, but would see him after lunch sometime, giving time for tests, scans and so on. Hopefully everything would be completed by the afternoon.

I was in a daze, almost staggering, as I walked through the corridor to go home. It was eerily quiet now that visiting hours were over. Nurses were buzzing around. A lady came along the corridor wheeling a cart with juices, coffee and tea for the patients' nightcap. My legs were weak as I struggled to walk to the front door.

Neither of us had been in hospital before, except me when Daniel was born. Over the years we were blessed with good health. This was a major shock. I finally reached my car in the parking lot, unlocked the door and sat in the seat, staring ahead. Tears slowly filled my eyes. I had to get home. Sometimes the children called us to make sure we were alright. Beth might also wonder where we were. If we had a night out planned, she was usually the first to know. I shook as I tried to put the key in the ignition. I took a deep breath, made sure I had the right key, turned on the ignition and slowly backed out of the parking spot. I headed for the exit, paid my ticket and left the hospital area.

My overactive mind was working overtime, going over every possible scenario. While I am normally a calm person, this was such a shock to me that I was acting out of character, thinking the worst and not considering the positive side. Maybe it is easier to be positive and upbeat in such matters when you are not so emotionally attached. As a Hospice volunteer, I was are emotionally involved to a certain extent. I felt the pain and anguish and I hurt for them, but I could be a little less attached and more objective for the patient and the family. This was Bob who was in hospital for tests, a man who was the picture of health until after the death of his parents. Total exhaustion I thought. Paul will prescribe time off work and perhaps a vacation. That's it.

I felt so alone as I drove home. I convinced myself it was exhaustion, but in the pit of my stomach I didn't believe it. Something was definitely wrong here, I knew it. I tried to keep focused on the roads. I turned on the radio station to a radio program that played older records. I tried to hum along as I usually did, but my heart was not in it. It did help a bit to keep my mind and eyes on the road.

I turned into the driveway, shut the engine off and just sat in the car, not knowing how I got there. I didn't bother opening the garage to put the car in, leaving it in the driveway instead. Normally the timer would turn on some lights, but it was still early for that, leaving the whole house in darkness.

Once inside the house, I checked the telephone to see if anyone had left a message. On her way from picking up some groceries, Beth had stopped in at the house, and she telephoned several times, eventually leaving a message asking where I was. Would I call her when I got home? We always shared everything.

I took my jacket off and hung it in the hall closet. I put the kettle on after that and called Beth, asking her to come over for coffee. She didn't question that because we often called the other when the kettle was on for no other reason than wanting a wee chat. Beth was at the door in minutes and as soon as I saw her, the tears came. Instantly she knew something was wrong. She came close, put her arms around me and hugged me tightly, even though she didn't know what was wrong. I made a pot of coffee, put out the cups and we sat down at the kitchen table. I told Beth the story so far. She breathed in deeply, with shock registered on her face, yet trying to reassure me by suggesting it was probably a bug going around or the enormous pressure he'd been under since his parent's deaths. It also may have been a combination of everything, nothing that a good vacation wouldn't fix. She reminded me that he was in very good health and said,

"How bad could it be?"

We stayed up into the wee hours of the morning going over the events of the day, laughing and crying over some of the adventures we got up to when the children were younger. She called Joe to tell him she was staying over with me, telling him that Bob was in hospital and said she would fill him in later. Having a good friend for company, especially at times like this, was what I needed. I felt so much better in the morning, thinking that perhaps I had over reacted.

I was relieved that the children were not at home. I didn't think I could hide the news from them. I didn't want to say anything until I knew something for sure. Obviously neither Lisa nor Daniel had dropped in earlier in the evening. If they had, they would have left a note on the fridge. For that I was thankful. If they hadn't found me home, they definitely would be on the phone later to find out where I was, then what would I have said? Bob didn't want me telling anyone anything at the moment but he would have understood my need to tell Beth and knew I needed my friend now.

In the morning, Beth had toast and coffee ready for me when I came downstairs after showering and dressing. After finishing the meal we cleared the table, putting dishes in the dishwasher. Beth wanted to go with me to the hospital but not knowing what I would learn when I got there, I felt it was better if I went alone. She totally understood. I had calmed down considerably but when I thought about it, I didn't have a good feeling about the news I was about to hear. I felt it would be better if Bob and I had a chance to consult with the doctors first and try to absorb what they were telling us, before we told anyone else. We were always there for each other and understood when we needed time to be alone and when we needed company, not that we ever had any major problems in our lives. I promised to call her the minute I knew anything. I asked her not to say anything to anyone just yet.

The drive to the hospital seemed to take forever as the roads were busy but it forced me to concentrate on my driving, taking my mind off Bob. He was not in his room when I got there. I needed a coffee and went down to the cafeteria, planning to get one for Bob as well. Under the circumstances, I thought it better if I sat for a bit drinking my coffee, to give me some time to unwind from the drive in and the anxiety I was feeling about Bob's prognosis. I couldn't fool myself; I had a sinking feeling that it was bad. My volunteering with Hospice had educated me in types of cancers and symptoms although unfortunately, symptoms often don't show until it is far advanced. I didn't like the colour of Bob's skin,.

It is a sad state of facts that too many times cancer doesn't show it's ugly head in a way that causes concern. Often people disregard little pains or illnesses thinking it's strain or age or some other reason, simply because they don't feel they are that ill. I didn't know how long Bob might be away for tests. Sitting in the cafeteria was better than sitting alone in his room, waiting, thinking, waiting, thinking. Bob and I drank far too much coffee at the best of times but the amount I was drinking since Bob went into hospital was ridiculous. Although experts say it doesn't calm you down, I felt it helped me to cope. I couldn't get my thoughts together and I couldn't stop the weakness in my stomach and knees. When I finally went back to the room he hadn't returned. I went out to the lobby, picked up some magazines and thumbed through them. Why is it that doctors' offices, hospitals and other such places have terrible magazines?

From where I was seated I could see his room. About an hour later I saw the orderly pushing him in the wheelchair. That was hard to take. My big, handsome, healthy man, reduced to a wheelchair but it was obviously for convenience, not because he needed one. I returned the magazine back to the table and walked shakily down to the room. Bob was back in bed with the orderly fussing over him, making him comfortable. That shocked me. I felt sure he would be sitting on the chair waiting to get dressed and go home. About a half hour later, Paul came into the room. He asked me if I would mind waiting outside while he spoke to Bob. That was not good.

Before I could say anything, Bob told the doctor that anything he had to say to him should be said in front of me. As with everything in our lives, we were in it together, no matter what. Apparently he told Paul that he didn't want any sugar coating, he wanted the truth, good or bad, and that there was to be no glossing anything over. Paul didn't have to tell us, we could sense it, but we were not prepared for how bad it was. Bob had been fairly relaxed and resting while he was in the hospital, but he still looked tired and seemed to have aged overnight, the colour in his skin and eyes frightening.I sat down on the bed beside Bob and held his hand. Then we listened to the devastating report and prognosis:

"All the tests show that you have Stage 4 liver cancer. Unfortunately, it is aggressive, has spread and will continue to spread rapidly. Surgery is not an option. We can start you on chemo to give you more time and of course we will control any pain you might have. You have to know that the chemo is not a cure. If you had checked in sooner chemo may have been more helpful. Unfortunately, we have too many patients that miss the symptoms which is easily done. Getting here sooner may not have helped much considering the aggressive nature of this cancer. You need to understand that."

"Are you absolutely sure there wasn't a mix up in the tests? It does happen, right?"

"Yes you are right, mistakes have been made but not in this case. Your case was checked and rechecked and I personally oversaw everything that was done."

"What about a second opinion," I asked.

"Certainly you can get a second opinion, it is your right and I wouldn't be upset if you did, but I can tell you that we had the top specialists look at your scans and we are all in agreement. I am so sorry."

"How long do I have?" Bob asked.

I quickly spoke up, "Do you really want to know that?" No one knows, not the doctors, not the specialists, no one except God. They can give you a guesstimate, but they have been wrong before. Why lose hope? Please think about this Bob."

"If you don't want to hear this Fiona I understand, but I need to know. I just need to know."

"If that's your decision, I will go along with it. I am not backing away now. We are in this together all the way, right?"

The doctor spoke next, "If you are sure Bob. While we can't be a hundred percent sure, I would give an estimate of anything from six months to a year. Chemo could give you a bit more time. Go home, think about it and call me. You don't have to decide today. Like Fiona said, no one can say with certainty how much time anyone has."

My heart was pumping so fast and loud, I am sure it was evident through my blouse. I could hardly breathe but I would have to be strong for Bob. He didn't seem to be overly phased by this overwhelming news. He had sheer disbelief written all over his face, but he was calm and in control of his emotions, no shaking. He could be emotional, could shed tears easily and felt everyone's hurt, but for some reason he actually looked stoic. Perhaps it was for my benefit just as I was trying to be strong for his.

This diagnosis was hard to digest. He was never sick, never had any pain and took good care of himself. It almost makes one wonder at times like this if doing the right things and living the right way is worth it. It didn't seem to make any difference to the outcome of life. He didn't smoke, didn't drink, didn't overeat and exercised whenever he could. He was active. None of that mattered, he got the big "C" and nothing could change that. I wish I could say I wasn't angry but I was very angry.

Unfortunately, we knew of people who were fine one minute then got a deadly diagnosis. A good friend wasn't feeling too well, went to hospital, had a stint put in and about four weeks later he was gone. No treatment, no surgery, nothing. Another person we knew went into hospital and never came back out. She was gone within a week. Symptoms were never noticed or realized, and she lived a normal daily life, then poof, just like that, she was gone.

While we questioned this diagnosis for Bob, we knew it wasn't all that unusual. Unlike some, we had noticed changes in Bob, but we all put it down to his parent's death, the workload of the estate and taking over the law firm. So much for early detection, other than some tests that can predict cancer, too many have no symptoms until it is too late.

To satisfy everyone's mind and to be absolutely sure nothing was missed, the doctor convinced Bob to stay in hospital for another day or two. However, he wanted to go home. I begged him to get the tests done, just in case there was something that was missed. He was too tired to argue and agreed to stay. I stayed with him for the rest of the day and when he finally fell asleep, I quietly slipped out of the room.

After exiting the hospital I got into the car and sat there for a while. What was I going to tell the children, our families, friends, and colleagues? Should I wait for the second round of tests or should I try to prepare them now? Whatever I did, it would have to wait until morning. I was too exhausted by the time I finally pulled into the driveway. I picked up the telephone to call Beth and as soon as I heard her voice, I broke down. She came over to the house immediately.

I was so glad to have a friend like her. She reminded me of Moira in so many ways. I know they would have been the best of friends too. Both were dependable, trustworthy and a joy to be with. I was blessed and lucky to have had two such good friends in my lifetime.

I had many friends and acquaintances, but these two went above and beyond. I could count on the children and Bob's siblings, any one of them would have come right over, but I wanted to wait for the second round of tests, even though in my heart I knew the Paul was right. I needed confirmation. I needed to be stronger too, hopefully let the news settle in before I said anything to anyone.

Beth knocked as she opened the door. She put her arms around me, giving me a much needed hug. We both cried, although Beth didn't know the results. She instinctively knew it was not good news, but she couldn't have imagined how bad it was, just as Bob and I couldn't. I was trying to be brave for Bob's sake, putting on a face but now I could let it all come out. When I finally got the whole story out Beth stood there, eyes wide, mouth open in sheer disbelief. She tried to reassure me about wrong diagnosis, new treatments and operations but I told her everything we had discussed with Paul. Both of us knew only too well what was in store. We were regular volunteers at a local Hospice and had seen far too many of our friends and family succumb to various forms of cancer. It is the scourge of the modern age as far as I am concerned.

Talking openly and honestly with Beth helped me to settle down a bit. There was too much coffee consumed again that night. It was late; we could hardly keep our eyes open. Beth suggested she stay over again. I didn't argue with that. I was glad of her company. She called Joe again to say she was staying over. He asked if there was any news on Bob. She told him we were tired and she would talk to him in he morning. Having Beth and Joe know the diagnosis was in a way a bit of release from the burden I was feeling. They would never betray a confidence. People would find out soon enough but I had to be sure that our children, my family and Bob's family were told first by me, not a stranger, should it get around, and it would.

First thing in the morning I telephoned Bob's office to let them know that he wouldn't be in for a few days. The staff, like everyone else, knew how poorly he had been looking of late so it wasn't a total surprise when I let them know. He was the boss after all, so there wasn't any problem with him taking time off. If there was a problem with any file and they needed to talk to him, they could call him at home, but I stressed it had to be something no one else could handle.

Bob was so good and never complained about all the tests that were being redone. He wasn't comfortable, but he persevered. The tests all had the same results, nothing could be done. Paul was especially upset and shocked. He was not only his doctor; he was a family friend and as such was in our company from time to time. If he could miss it, it was no surprise that most of us missed it too. It was more than the shock of knowing Bob had terminal cancer, none of us couldn't understand how it had happened so quickly. In actual fact, the cancer had been inside Bob for some time.

As Christians, we knew we were in for a trying time and would have to draw on our faith to see us through whatever lay ahead. It's one thing to say you have a strong faith, it's another to live it, especially when facing what we had to face. Even with the time frame given to Bob, we didn't allow it to let us lose hope. We knew God could over rule and would do what was in His will and in His time, which gave us great comfort. The most important thing now was to see that Bob got the very best of care and that he would not suffer, if I had anything to do with it. We were quite comfortable and could afford to give him all the care he needed.

Paul told Bob to go home and do whatever he wanted, if he felt up to it, and added that if there was anything he wanted, any questions he needed answered, help with care, anything, he just had to call him. He encouraged him to make the most of each and every day, as long as he felt up to it.

It was late afternoon before we arrived home. Bob was as tired as was I, but he didn't want to lie down just yet. I could see he was weak and shaky as he slowly walked towards out favourite room, the family room. All of the tests and the devastating news had taken a toll on him while he tried to be brave and strong, but he seemed to be letting it down a bit now that he was in the comfort of his own home. We sat down on the big comfy couch, held hands and sat quietly enjoying him being home and the many memories this room always brought back any time we were in here. Out of the blue, Bob said he wanted to get away, just the two of us. We had a cruise planned, but that was not for a few months yet, and the thought crossed my mind that he might not be around. I wasn't going to worry about that now. That didn't seem to be what he meant. Going up to the cottage, just the two of us, for a couple of days appealed to him. As long as he felt up to it, I was going to do everything and anything he wanted to and make the most of whatever time we had.

"How about a cuppa?" I asked him but he wasn't interested. Not too long after we sat in the family room, he wanted to go upstairs. I noticed how slowly he climbed the stairs but wasn't overly concerned at this change because he had been through so much upheaval. He would probably perk up now that he was home. He lay down on the top of our bed, exhausted. I lay down beside him and we both dozed off with our arms around each other.

I awoke about an hour later but Bob was still asleep. I quietly got up, went downstairs and phoned Beth. I wanted her to know Bob was home. When I told her we were both exhausted, she understood and said we would chat in the morning. I called Daniel and Lisa, as I always did. I let them know we were okay but since they were both out, I left a message on their machines. I always say what time I am calling and what day it is. I told them I would touch bases with them tomorrow.

I checked the mail, had a glance at the newspaper and returned upstairs to the bedroom. Bob was still asleep but I gently nudged him to ask if he needed anything before we settled in for the night. I also suggested he change into his p.j.'s for a more comfortable night. This alone told me he wasn't his old self; he would never lie down in his clothes. Once he was settled, I got changed too and we lay in each other's arms, as always, both of us telling the other we were so happy he was back home.

Surprisingly, or maybe not so, we both fell sound asleep and actually slept in later than we normally did. When both of us awoke, we slipped on our dressing gowns and headed downstairs to the kitchen. I put on the coffee pot but although neither of us was hungry. I made some toast anyway and we each managed to eat a couple of slices with a bit of peanut butter, which we both loved. How were we going to tell the children, family and friends? They would be as shocked as we were but it had to be done and by us. I had a couple of suggestions but told Bob it was his decision if and when and how. We also discussed the options that the doctor had given us. I let Bob know I wanted him with me as long as possible and thought the chemo might be worth trying, but whatever he decided, and it must be his decision. I would accept and be there by his side every step of the way. He thought for a moment and said,

"I don't think I will opt for chemo, especially since it is only giving me time and not a cure. From what I've seen, the quality of whatever time I might have, could be less than pleasant. You and I know we have seen too many go through chemo, either as a means of some gaining some extra time or hopefully a cure, only to end up back at square one after having lost a lot of valuable time that could have been used to enjoy whatever time they did have. I don't see me going down that road. I will take whatever time I have, enjoy it to the fullest with you, family and friends, and let the chips fall where they may. Paul said I should be well enough for a while and I should do whatever I feel like doing as long as I can. You better than anyone should know what I mean with your volunteering. If people have a choice, they choose what they think is best for them and this is best for me, and hopefully for you too."

"I want you with me as long as possible but I don't want you to just be existing. You are right; we will make the most of whatever time we have. I love you so much."

"Okay now that it's settled, what are we to do about telling everyone? I sure don't feel like having to tell everyone individually. I don't think I am up to that and neither are you. I couldn't take relaying the story over and over again, people feeling sorry for me and all the tears."

"Why don't we invite all of the family and friends over for one of your famous dinners? We could tell everyone at the same time while they are together to support each other and it might make it easier for all of us. Some might not think this is a good idea but for me, it is the right thing to do. We will try to be calm, not appear anxious and hopefully they will take their lead from our demeanour."

Everyone liked my dinner parties. No one ever turned down an invitation unless they had a prior engagement. Sometimes they cancelled other not too important engagements they might have. I telephoned Beth and invited her to the dinner on Saturday, two days away. True to form she offered to help in any way she could. She didn't ask about Bob, knowing I would tell her when I was able to. It had been a while since all of our family and friends had been together so it was perfect. We used to have these dinners more often but with families growing and other responsibilities, we couldn't seem to find the time as often as we would have liked. Everyone thought it was good timing, knowing Bob had been extremely busy and probably needed the night to socialize. No one knew the real reason. I decided to cater the meal but baked all the favourites I was known for. It kept my mind occupied and it let Bob rest without me fussing over him.

He called the office to see if there were any problems. During this time, he stayed in his robe, a very unusual thing for him, but he relaxed and that's all that mattered. I confided in Beth the reason for the dinner party so she would know what to expect. It was selfish of me in a way but I needed her support.

We asked Daniel and Lisa to come over after work as we had something important to discuss with them. Daniel picked Lisa up at work and they arrived together. They almost knocked the door down rushing in yelling "what's the matter, is everything alright?"

We all sat around the kitchen table while Bob tried to tell them in the gentlest way. It wasn't easy and we could hear the emotion in his voice, tears glistening in his eyes. I helped him when he needed it. The children were devastated and like most people do, they offered second opinions, more tests, going somewhere else for treatments and other things they had heard about. We hushed them and said we had been through all of that with Paul who offered chemo, but told them that their dad didn't want to go down that road. We were going to make the most of whatever time we had. They had noticed a change in him, but they didn't know their dad had such a severe problem. "Why didn't you tell us he was in hospital?" They asked. I told them we wanted to be sure of the diagnosis before we told anyone. We cried in each other's arms then told them of our plan for the dinner. They thought we had lost our senses but once we explained the reason behind it, they understood in some small way. "How can we help? The kids asked.

On Saturday the guests started arriving. We had cocktails before dinner. The atmosphere was upbeat and happy, just what we had hoped for. Beth and I kept looking at each other but I don't think anyone was paying attention to us; they were too busy catching up with each other on all the news. Dinner was a success as usual. No one complained about the catered food. After dinner and dessert, we all retired to the family room with coffee or tea. I sat beside Bob as he was about to make one of the most difficult speeches of his life. He was an excellent orator, used to speaking engagements, but this was different. Would he be able to carry it off?

"As some of you know, I haven't been feeling at my best lately but I put it down to the stress of my parents deaths, the way they died, settling up my partnership with the firm and taking over my dad's law firm. Fiona kept telling me to see a doctor, maybe get a tonic or something but like most of us men, I didn't listen. Last week I was quite weak and had to admit that I didn't look too good. I called Paul, went to see him and he admitted me to the hospital for some tests.

Long story short, I have stage 4 terminal cancer that is inoperable. Paul suggested chemo as a means of giving me some more time and to alleviate some of the discomfort. It is not a cure. As you can imagine, we were shocked and couldn't think clearly. After I came home, Fiona and I discussed our options, opinions and what we thought was the best way to proceed but in the end, I decided I would not have the chemo. Fiona wanted me to give it a chance, but I was confident my decision was the right one. In the end she agreed with me. To do otherwise would only delay the inevitable.

This may be an unorthodox way of sharing this news with you, but we couldn't bear the thought of having to tell each one separately and this was the best way for us. We knew we could draw strength from you, we knew you would strengthen each other. We don't want tears or sadness, although there will be some. We need you to be strong for us.

At the moment I am feeling okay. Paul suggested we do what we want, when we want and that's exactly what we intend to do as long as I am able. Paul said there is no reason why we can't go on the cruise that we have booked. When the time comes to sail, and I am well enough to travel, we will be on our way. We also hope to go up to the cottage for a few days by ourselves at some point to clear our minds, put things in order and enjoy being away together. You know how much we love the cottage and its wonderful memories. We know this is an unusual way to tell you. I see your shock. Try to understand, it was not only for us but you too."

Bob's voice trembled with emotion as he struggled with the words, but he did it in his own way. No one said anything for a few minutes, we were all in a sort of group hug, giving the strength that we so needed.

Bob's brother Bill knew that his friend Paul would have researched every possible avenue available, but he asked Bob if he was sure he didn't want to try something else. He told Bill that he and Paul had discussed everything at length and this was our decision. Lisa couldn't help herself; she was a daddy's girl, and naturally she broke down. This tugged at the hearts of others, but it was also cathartic. This is what we hoped for. Everyone was teary eyed yet strong. No one asked if Bob was given a timeline. Just as well, because Bob wouldn't have revealed that information. Most people know what the prognosis is in these cases anyway. Each person there had a different story about someone they knew, and how they tried various alternative treatments. Bob let them know his decision was based on his doctor's opinion. Whatever time he was given, would be spent doing what he and I wanted to do, and not wasting time running all over the place in search of a magic potion. He had every confidence that his doctor knew what he was talking about, telling them he had every test available. "God is in control," he reminded them, "it was in His hands and He will see us through this, no matter the outcome."

A neighbour, John, stood up, cleared his throat and said, "We know how difficult this must be for you Bob and can appreciate your need to gather us here together. It goes without saying, but I will say it anyway, you know we are all behind both of you. If there is anything any one of us can do, all you have to do is lift the phone. We are here for you."

That drew applause but it touched me so deeply that I broke down. Beth and Lisa came over to me and we hugged together. Beth said something funny in our ears and we all started to laugh. It was perfect. Good old Beth.

"O.K. guys, Fiona had someone cater this dinner but she baked some of the goodies we all love. Let's get some more coffee and get started on them. You know she won't invite us back again if we don't finish everything. She might think we didn't like her goodies." That broke the ice. After refreshments were served and we all had our fill, some of the ladies started to pick up the cups and saucers. I told them it wasn't necessary but I think they needed to do it. We cleared everything out of the family and dining rooms, got the dishwasher running and any food left over was put out on plates for anyone wanting to pick up some for doggie bags. One by one our guests left. At the door as we hugged them goodnight, we were reminded once again that they were there for us. Andrew took my parent's home and Bob's family left. Beth and Joe were the last to leave except for Lisa and Daniel. Beth knew we needed time to ourselves.

Lisa put on another pot of coffee. We sat at the kitchen table and tried to reassure them we would be fine and told them as much as we knew. They wanted to move in, or at least one of them for a while. We declined saying that somewhere down the road as the disease progressed, it might be necessary in order to allow their dad to stay at home until the end. We would do everything to keep him home with family. Right now, we needed time to ourselves and would take it one day at a time. News that their father was dying was not only a shock but difficult to understand, given how healthy he was.

As Christians we assured the children that we would be trusting in the Lord as always, no matter where the road ahead led. We knew they would also draw strength from God. It's in God's hands and He will not let us down no matter what. He always answers our prayers but sometimes it's not the answer we want, but it will be the right answer. We must trust and leave it in His hands. What else do we have? It's God's will. He never makes mistakes. Lisa took it very hard which upset her dad, but he understood and hoped time would strengthen her. Daniel too was obviously devastated but being a man and it being expected of them, he tried to be stronger.

Bob had made all the necessary financial arrangements years ago. The old tale of shoemaker's children needing their shoes repaired, didn't apply to him. He was meticulous about everything. He had all of the legal documents in order long before he got ill. In fact he had much of it in place after we got married but had updated everything throughout the years. Now with this diagnosis and his soon coming death, he wanted to be sure everything was as it should be. We went over everything together. Too many wives are left in the dark when the husband dies. Bob made sure that wouldn't happen to me and it was a relief now. I didn't think I would be happy going over all of this knowing he was dying. I've known people who didn't have their affairs in order such as a cousin who was diagnosed with terminal cancer and who on top of that shocking news had to get his will, powers of attorney and all legal matters attended to before he passed away. I think that would be quite traumatic.

Before Bob's illness, we received a brochure from a cruise line that we had travelled on frequently. It advertised a trip we had always wanted to take, Scandinavia and Russia sailing out of Dover and back to Dover. After the cruise, we hoped to spend a couple of extra weeks in Scotland to visit friends and some relatives. We usually added some time at the end of any cruise we sailed on so that we could tour to the port where we docked before going home. Bob suggested we book the trip and I didn't argue but now we might not be able to take the cruise. To cancel would seem like I didn't think Bob would be here or it might take away any hope he had. I couldn't do that. Paul had told Bob he could travel if he felt up to it, and I hoped he would be well enough to sail. On the other hand, if he was up to it, the cruise would be just the thing for both of us to unwind, relax and be together.

In the meantime, any discomfort Bob had was well taken care of. At times he actually seemed better, possibly in some way relieved that he knew what was wrong with him. Some days were good and others were not so good.

XXV

Bob seemed unusually stressed about our proposed trip up to the cottage for a few days. Since it was his suggestion, I thought it odd that he would be fretting over it. As calm as he tried to be, he was sick and it was perfectly understandable if he changed his mind or stressed over who knows what.

The family cottage was beautifully nestled among the trees, facing the beach. Bob's parents had bought it years ago when the children were young, but it was a far cry from what it is today. After they tore the original cabin down, they built a large wooden log structure. Over the years many upgrades and changes were made and it was now a beautiful large house sitting on the shore of a small, peaceful lake, with a sandy beach right at the doorstep.

Other cottages lined the beach all around the bay, visible to each other, but still allowing cottagers a sense of privacy. A wall-to-wall natural stone fireplace in the large family room covered the entire wall. The log house consisted of four bedrooms, a bathroom, a two piece toilet on the main floor, and a large kitchen beside the dining room. Huge wooden logs were used in the construction of the home so that the inside looked much the same as it did on the outside. A verandah was constructed all around the entire cottage, with steps at the front, side and rear of the house.

When Bob's parents were killed, the property was left to the children equally and we all continued to use it as we always had. Sometimes the whole family and our group of friends went up together, other times we each took our separate vacations. Most of our family friends had access to the cottage whenever they wanted, if no one else was using it.

Traffic on the highways on weekends, especially if it was a long weekend, could be exasperating but we tried to leave earlier than the crowd and come home later, if it was at all possible. It was about a two-hour drive up there. During school vacations, Bob and his siblings spent their holidays up at the cottage with their mother. Mr. Wilson went up on weekends. We did the same with our children along with Beth and her children. Bob and Joe came up on the weekends. It was a place that held so many wonderful memories for all of us and it was understandable that Bob would want to go up there for a bit of a getaway.

The weather had been holding up recently but the further north, the cooler it got although at this time it was comfortable, maybe not for swimming in the lake. We packed a few clothes, some food and drove off to the cottage. By the time we got there, it was getting dark and it was a little cool. We unpacked and lit the fire. I always loved to sit by the fire, even at home, because it reminded me so much of Scotland, and the many nights we all huddled around the fire.

In Scotland no one ever wanted to move away from the fire, because the rest of the room was cold. Sitting for so long at the fire gave us all red markings, similar to mesh stockings on our legs which we called marly. It was always easy to tell who had been sitting to close to the fire and unfortunately, some had those marks permanently.

Another memory by the fire was when we looked deep into the coals or wood in the cottage, our imaginations running wild as we envisioned various scenes. It could be romantic too. I rustled up some supper, pulled out some little T.V. tables and we sat by the fire relaxing as we ate our meal. It was just what we needed.

We talked about all the wonderful times we had shared at the cottage, corn roasts, water skiing, swimming and children playing in the sand, along with friends from the city. Over the years we became close to the other cottagers most of whom had families like us and whose parents had bought the original properties. We all looked forward to our times up there and although many lived elsewhere in the city, we got together on occasion.

I made sure Bob was feeling okay and asked if he was tired. No, he felt fine and just wanted to savour the moment. We talked about our life together, his illness, alternative medicine, other opinions and so on. Mostly we just enjoyed being with each other, reminiscing about life in general, family, memories and giving thanks to God for the good fortune that blessed us.

I noticed, on a few occasions, that Bob's mind seemed to be somewhere else as he stared ahead. He started to say something, then stopped. His mouth seemed to be moving but there was no sound. Maybe he was talking to himself under his breath. I wondered if something was bothering him. As well as I knew him, I couldn't possibly imagine how he felt, or what must be going through his mind after finding out his life was almost over. He knew he didn't have very long. I am not sure that he would be distraught about his own passing, his concern would center around those he was leaving behind.

Was he fearing death? I didn't think so. He was a true believing Christian and had the assurance of where he was going. While it's true that no one wants to die or leave families behind, for a Christian, death doesn't hold the same fear. We never expected Bob to die so young, but then we didn't expect his parents to die suddenly and tragically either. Life can hand out some real curves.

We had talked about and looked forward to his retiring early and doing some more travelling to places we hadn't visited yet. Grandchildren might be in the future too. There were many unfulfilled wishes and dreams but neither of us could or would complain. We could never have foreseen this sudden end to all of our plans and hopes. That's why it's so important for people to do things when they are able. As Robbie Burns, Scotland's greatest poet said "The best laid plans o' mice and men gang aft agley." Truer words were never written or spoken.

Picture windows had been installed in the cottage, covering most of the surrounding walls, allowing a spectacular view of the lake, quiet and serene. Most of the cottagers had closed up for the year, the quiet was almost deafening. The odd light from a cottage could be seen across the bay and path lights around the lake were on to help anyone who might be out in a boat. It was a beautiful scene,lights reflecting on the calm water. I could almost hear the children, friends or relatives up on water skis, gliding along behind the boat, laughing all the way.

I was never a swimmer and, in fact, was not that fond of water. I was happy to sit on the beach with friends or with a good book, taking in all that was going on around me.

Our time together over the weekend was wonderful, strolling through the lovely property by day, sometimes bundled up sitting on the porch or by the fire at night. We laughed often as we travelled down memory lane and even with this staggering blow, we knew we had been blessed so many times over in our lives together. Yes, we wanted it to go on longer and I didn't know how I could live without him, but we were grateful for the wonderful life we shared. Bob seemed to be at ease, enjoying the time, but there were times when I looked at him, his mind seemed to be a million miles away, his face vague. Apart from that which was understandable, it was a perfect, peaceful weekend and it was welcomed after the difficult time we had gone through.

Too soon it was time to go home. Bob appeared a little more down than usual as we started to pack for the trip home. I asked him if he was feeling alright, if he was in pain, or if there was anything I could do for him. He said he was fine but I sensed something was troubling but what? Something was different about him, something was happening to him and I couldn't imagine what it might be. Often when I looked at him he appeared to be mouthing something but I never heard what it was. He wasn't mumbling, he was just mouthing words. I didn't want to push. We had always been so close, if he had anything to say, it would eventually get said. It looked as though he was practicing something without saying it out loud. It was strange.

Bob changed his mind and wanted to stay at the cottage for a few more days. He was enjoying this time together. It wasn't a problem. I had no appointments and even if I had, I would have cancelled them. Bob didn't need to go back to work ever if he didn't want to. I phoned Daniel to let him know we would be staying up for a bit longer. He asked how his dad was and was happy to know we were enjoying our retreat.

As soon as I hung up the telephone Bob changed his mind again and wanted to go home. He had work to do and things to settle at the office. That wasn't true and I knew it, but I went along with him. He was slightly agitated, something I have never seen in Bob. He assured me he was not in pain. We had the meds with us if he needed them. This was so unlike him. He seemed at odds but who wouldn't be? Out of the blue he asked me if I had been happy being married to him. Where did that come from? He knew how happy I was. I told him often enough. Did I think he could have done any more for me? Being less than a passionate lover bothered him. I could always tell, but in my mind no one could ever make me tingle like Ian did anyway. Bob couldn't have been more considerate and tender. Perhaps he was going over our lives together in his mind and wanted assurance that I loved him and that he made me happy. I didn't know but I went along with whatever he came up with.

Volunteering with Palliative over the years had given me insight into some of the things terminally ill patients think about. It wasn't easy accepting one's death and often the ill wonder if they could have done things differently, if they have offended people, what more they could have done. They want to wipe the slate clean, so to speak, before they die. I wasn't aware of anything unsaid or undone between us. He knew he could talk to me about anything. I put it all down to his illness.

He changed his mind again and decided to stay over one more night. It must have been difficult for him knowing he would probably never be back up at the cottage that held so many wonderful memories for him. We snuggled up at the fire with hot chocolate, gazing into the cinders. I didn't know how I would ever live without him. I didn't know if I would ever go back to the cottage after he was gone. It would be too difficult with the memories I shared since becoming part of the Wilson family. How must he have felt, knowing he likely wouldn't see it again? Whatever the problem was, he would tell me in his own time.

Maybe he was playing everything over in his mind to get it right, whatever it was. Our marriage was an open book. Whatever was on his mind could probably wait until he was ready.

Next morning, after breakfast and making sure everything was left in a safe condition, we packed up the car and headed for home. Not much was said between us as we drove along the highway. I drove because Bob wasn't up to it. He looked pitifully sad, his eyes puffed as he stared straight ahead. My heart was breaking but I had to be the strong one now. I convinced myself that he was sad leaving the cottage, possibly for the last time.

He had been going to the cottage every summer for as long as he could remember, why wouldn't he be sad? He must be remembering the wonderful times his family had, before I appeared on the scene. The Wilsons were a loving, caring family and their bonds ran deep. When I came into the family, the children and I plus my own family, spent many wonderful summers up there too and so the traditions and bonds continued on.

Traffic was light at this time of the year, which was a blessing. When we neared the spot where Bob's parents were killed, he asked me to pull over onto the side of the road. The suddenness and trauma of that accident remained with Bob over the years. He didn't say anything, just closed his eyes as he remembered them for a moment.

There was a lovely little restaurant just a little further down the highway where we often stopped in on the way home. We were both ready for a coffee and stopped in. Sitting by the window, the view all around reminded us why we loved the area. It was pure cottage country with a view of trees, bushes and sometimes the lake. Bob's hand trembled as he reached across the table for mine. I put my other hand over his and squeezed. Everything we did or said was charged with emotion. To see him now, the illness clearly visible on his face, was almost too much to bear, although his handsome looks still shone through his thinning face. I believed that was because of his inner beauty and strength.

He was obviously tired, drained and exhausted by the time we pulled into the driveway. I unpacked the trunk. It was something he would always do but now didn't have the strength. Bob unlocked the door and went into the house. He didn't take off his coat, just went straight upstairs to bed. He lay there with his coat on, something he never did, except the time he came home from the hospital. It was not a good sign.

Apart from the effects of his illness, I sensed something else was bothering him but what could it be? After I settled in, I shouted up to him to ask if he wanted a cuppa, but there was no response. He must have fallen asleep as soon as he hit the bed. I busied myself with other things around the house, called the children and Beth to let them know we were home, and told them we had enjoyed the time away. Knowing that rest was good for Bob, I didn't bother him. It was almost suppertime and there was still no sound from upstairs. That gave me a start.

I went up just as he was awakening. He could hardly believe he had fallen asleep with his coat on, but he felt better for having the rest. I asked if he was ready to come downstairs or if he preferred me to bring a tray up to him. He seemed more relaxed, and said he would come down to the kitchen. He asked me not to make a big supper, something light. I asked if he had a preference. He said that he didn't but suggested I make something that would strike his fancy. Now what? "How about some scrambled eggs and toast?"

"Sounds good to me," he answered.

I could hear him moving about slowly upstairs and after a bit he came down to the kitchen with his coat still on. He said it was easier to carry it down that way. Neither of us could believe he had slept in it, not our neat, organized, meticulous Bob. We had a chuckle as he hung the coat in the hall cupboard.

When we finished supper, I cleared the dishes and put them in the sink. It was hardly worth putting them in the dishwasher. I would wash them later. I took a cuppa and shortbread cookies, which he loved, into the family room and turned on the telly to catch up on the news. We always liked to watch the news. He was looking more relaxed than I had seen him in a while and I was happy, although I caught him a couple of times looking as though he was going to say something. When I asked him if he had something on his mind or if he wanted to tell me something, he nodded his head "no".

Beth and Joe called to ask if they could drop in for a short visit. I asked Bob how he felt about that, and he was okay with it. Shortly afterwards, Daniel and Lisa asked if they could drop in for a short visit. No need to ask Bob how he felt about that and I told them to come on over. We all sat in our favourite family room, put the fire on and reminisced about old times. Seems as though we were doing a lot of that these days.

True to their word, Beth and Joe left after coffee and dessert. Daniel and Lisa waited a little longer but not much, knowing their dad was tired. We enjoyed their visit, it took our minds off the illness.

By now there was enough dishes to justify turning on the dishwasher so I stacked it and turned it on. Next I wiped up the counter and put away the cookies. Then we both headed upstairs.

XXVI

Time didn't stand still. Days turned into weeks and they passed too quickly. By now everyone knew and saw how ill Bob was. Most had a difficult time believing it. His weight had dropped slightly, his face was a more yellowish colour but he still continued to drop in to the office for an hour or two. He put on such a brave front that some of the staff couldn't believe he was that ill, and insisted he was stressed out rather than having cancer. Eventually even the few hours he worked began to take too much out of him and I insisted it was enough. He didn't need to do it. I wanted him to conserve whatever strength he had to spend with us. He was tired enough not to argue and had staff bring work to him at home but only the absolute necessities. In one way, working gave him a lift but it was physically exhausting, and I hated to see what it was doing to him. I would have been happier if he didn't do anything, but he had always been a hard worker, and he wanted to make sure everything was left in order for those coming after him.

Having him at home was better for me because I could encourage him to have a rest, cup of tea or coffee, whatever, just to ease his way. It meant we could spend more time together and time was precious. Bob asked Daniel how he felt about taking over the practice, just as Bob's father had done. He remembered only too well how he felt at that time, wanting to make it on his own. He told Daniel he would understand if he wanted to do the same thing. Whatever he decided his dad would accept, but he wanted to give him the option, without pressuring him. Daniel didn't want to discuss it, preferring to think his dad would be always be there. Like many, he was still somewhat in denial. Bob asked only that he give it some thought. Daniel didn't want his dad worrying about anything and to please him he agreed to take over the firm, if and when it came to that, adding that he didn't think it would come to that.

It was heartbreaking to see Bob make arrangements for the files to be transferred to another lawyer or multiple lawyers. This was his life. When colleagues dropped in to discuss some legal matter, tears filled his eyes. He knew it was nearing the end. He didn't want to give in and tried so hard to keep up the appearance of being better than he was, but I assured him that he didn't have to pretend for me or anyone else.

Cruise time was coming up quickly and it was obvious that Bob wasn't going to be taking it. The energy alone and the stress of it all would take too much of a toll on him. He continued to take phone calls from the office on legal matters and advised lawyers when asked. Being needed gave him some incentive to carry on. He hadn't experienced a great deal of pain, which was surprising for someone with terminal cancer. When he did, painkillers worked very effectively while at the same time leaving him able to function. Bob took it easy and we cherished every moment we shared.

I continued to have family and close friends over for lunch, dinner or just refreshments as long as it was alright with Bob. He enjoyed having the company, but we made sure the visits were not overly long, to conserve his strength. We wanted him with us as long as possible.

Every so often that same feeling came over me, that he wanted to tell me something. So many times I caught him staring at me or into space. Sometimes it looked as though he wanted to say something, and then stopped. This was so unlike him. I wanted him to feel comfortable enough to tell me any of his innermost fears or thoughts if he had any, but I didn't want to put any pressure on him either. I knew only too well how terminally ill patients sometimes felt uncomfortable talking with loved ones. Unbelievable as that seems, it is true.

That's where my role as a volunteer came in. Patients felt much more comfortable discussing thoughts, problems, questions or doubts with a volunteer because they didn't want to burden their families or friends. Often patients put on a brave front for the family and vice versa. It was difficult to talk about their fears or thoughts. That was my worry with Bob; maybe he would have been more open to a volunteer. I asked if he would like someone to visit him from the Hospice but he declined, saying I was all he needed. For all my Hospice training, I didn't know what to do. Approach him or help him to open up if that's what he needed? From the moment we met we were always close. I tried to understand and not feel hurt.

Laying in bed one night, he asked me, "have you ever held anything back from me, something you wish you hadn't?"

What on earth is this? I was surprised but relieved that at least he was saying something.

"What do you mean, holding something back?"

"I don't know. Secrets, disappointments, unfulfilled dreams, whatever?" Instantly my mind went back to Ian, but I couldn't believe he meant that. How could he, he didn't even know about Ian?

I said jokingly, "why are you asking me? Is this a time for true confessions? Do you have some deep dark secret that you are hiding from me?"

A worried look came over his face, which kind of threw me for a loop. Surely I wasn't going to find out now about some girl in his past, some affair or one night stand that he had, then regretted. Or some child born because of it. This would be too much to bear and especially now. He couldn't have had an affair without me knowing about it. Could he? It's said the wife is always the last to know, but I quickly dismissed the thought. I knew Bob. I trusted him and I knew he loved me. I was his best friend and he mine.

"The only confession I have is that the real reason I came to Canada was because of a broken romance. I never heard of or from him again, and it made no difference to our lives together. Is this truth and consequences? If so, it's your turn. I am all ears," I said jokingly as I smiled.

He took my hand in his, looked me straight in the eyes and said, "I do have a hidden past and I don't want to leave you without being completely honest."

He wasn't smiling. His face was somber and I was worried. Surely this wasn't going to be a repeat of Ian's story or something similar. It couldn't be, I would have known. Again I thought of Ian and his confession, which stunned me then and which I didn't have a clue about at the time.

I answered him with, “maybe I don’t want to know. I don’t need to know, not now. Besides, what purpose will it serve?”

“ I could take this to my grave, but I love you too much and I need you to know. I need someone to know. Maybe I just need to finally confide in someone and hope that person will tell me it's okay. I can't carry this with me to the grave, it's just too much of a burden, especially now. There is no one else in this world that I care for more than you, or can trust as much as you. You are not only my wife, you are my best friend, my soul mate."

This conversation was kind of creeping me out but when I looked at him, I knew he wasn't joking. I didn't have a clue but I was scared. I tried to conceal my fear. What could he be talking about?

He said, "I love you more than life itself, and could never have wanted a better wife or family. You must believe that."

I thought history was going to repeat itself, as I remembered that night in in Glasgow with Ian telling me how much he loved me.

He continued, "I don't know how to make this easy, there is no way. I don't want to hurt you especially now, but I have such deep guilt within me because I never told my parents. I always hoped to tell them someday, but the opportunity never came up. When they died so suddenly I was devastated at the loss, but more so because of the guilt I felt at not being honest with them. They deserved that much. I have lived a lie all of my life and I am tired of the charade. I have to be free of this guilt now, somehow."

I was nervous. "Maybe if in your mind it's so bad, wouldn’t it be better if you didn't tell me, especially now? Perhaps it might be better if I don't know. Whatever it is, it won't change how I feel about you. How could it?"

Surely nothing could taint our lives together. Did he want or need to bring up some old story now? He pleaded with me but the more he said, the more I did not want to hear this story. No matter what it was. I did not want to hear it.

"I want to die and rest in peace with my conscience clear, and nothing between us. I have to do this, even though it's the hardest thing I have ever had to do. I wish there was another way, but there isn't."

The more he talked, the more upset and agitated he got, and the more nervous I got. I didn't want him getting upset. He didn't need any more stress at this time in his life.

"I do not want to hear it, no matter what it is. But, if it will help you, will ease your mind in some way, go ahead. I will listen. I will understand, believe me. I love you too much for anything to come between us."

He stuttered and stammered, trying to find the right words that wouldn't come. He cleared his throat, took a drink of water and blurted out, "I am homosexual."

He could not say the word "gay", because the word stuck in his throat, knowing all too well that many homosexuals were anything but gay. I burst out laughing. “Oh you are so funny aren’t you,” I said.

I knew by his expression that he was deadly serious. He was trying to make it easier for me to cope with his death, make me turn against him and not feel the pain of losing him. I didn’t know his reason. I didn’t believe him and I didn't appreciate it. Did he think I wouldn’t have known if it was true?

“Would I or anyone joke about this? I’ve lived with this, covered this up. No, this is definitely not a joke, quite the opposite. You have to know that I could never have had a happier life than the one I shared with you and the children but there was always a void in my life as well as an unbelievable guilt which had nothing to do with you in any way."

He was extremely emotional and upset. I tried to calm him down. Why is he doing this to himself, never mind me?

I was speechless. I could see he was searching my face, looking for any sign of disbelief, rejection, hate, repulsion, disgust, anger, or all of them. Scarlett O'Hara's retort came to my mind, "I'll think about that tomorrow" but I knew that comment wouldn't do. I didn't have time to think what my reaction was. I only knew that I couldn't let him down. I couldn't show any repulsion. I had to be there for him. What else could I do? Gay? It wasn't possible. Maybe the pain pills are giving him hallucinations. Yes, that was it.

Our marriage and life together was the best of any of our friends. We were best friends and shared everything. Intimacy between us was never passionate, but that didn't bother me. I never thought I would ever have that kind of feeling again after Ian. Maybe if I hadn't loved Ian, it might have been questioned, but I never felt I had missed out on anything. Bob was so much more in every other way. He was tender and considerate. Was he testing me? Why would he make up a story like this?

He continued, "the fact that I couldn't ever be honest with my family, especially my parents, has haunted me most of my life. I couldn't stand the thought of their rejection. It would have killed me."

I told him that wouldn't have happened. We knew of cases where children were actually disowned after disclosing the truth but his parents were not the type of people that would disown their son. True, they were Born Again Christians and as such, didn't accept that lifestyle, but they were also the kind of people who didn't judge.

They wouldn't have treated anyone any differently than they themselves would want to be treated.

Bob said, "I couldn't take the chance. I couldn't have coped. I did what was expected, I acted like a heterosexual and blended in. That only added to my guilt, that I didn't have the courage to stand up and be counted. I felt I let others down who were homosexual. I took the easy way out, although it was far from easy."

My mind was boggled. How could he have married, had a good marriage, raised children and been a pillar of the community, without any of this coming out. Maybe I was the one hallucinating. I couldn't take it in. He said he didn't understand at first, but when he was attracted to men and not women, he questioned it. It was an overwhelming burden growing up like that in an atmosphere of fear and hate. He always knew he was different, but he hoped it was a phase he was going through.

That's how society saw it, a phase, or a choice, but it never went away. There were men that he had been attracted to, but he could never pursue it out of fear of his dark secret coming out. He was born into a family that was well known. He couldn’t risk anyone finding out and telling his parents. He could not take the chance. He knew he would have been ostracized. The guilt, the fears, the questions he had, were so bad that there were actually times when he contemplated suicide. He couldn't see how he could continue on living the lie. The pain and shame were too much, but most of the time he covered it up.

Being a Christian,he was taught, and believed that it was the sin of homosexuality that was condemned, and not the person. He knew that he could never live a homosexual lifestyle. He knew as a Christian, he could not commit suicide. He would have to suppress any feelings he had, or risk being cast out by both his family and church. He could never hurt his family that way, so he fell into the pattern that was expected of him, and kept away from any place that was associated with homosexuality, or anything that would have given the slightest hint of his darkest secret. The toll on him was huge. He felt cheated, dirty, guilty, perverted and often when these thoughts entered his head, is was when he thought about ending it all. He didn't choose this life, of that he was certain, but he did choose to live a celibate life as far as another man was concerned.

What bothered Bob most was the fact people said it was a choice of lifestyle. How could or would anyone in their right mind choose such a life that was hated so much? How could anyone choose a lifestyle where they could never marry and have a normal life with children? How could anyone choose a lifestyle where they were disowned by family and friends? No, it was not a choice. He was born that way but in order to survive in the world we lived in, he had to hide it. He had been raised by bible believing parents who saw to it, that he attended church regularly. He knew homosexuality was a sin, he heard it often enough.

He began to believe he was an evil person. He just didn't understand why God made him this way. He honestly believed God made him that way. He knew he would get the answer some day but he had to live today. He wouldn't have chosen that lifestyle for anything, and neither would anyone else. Unfortunately, that was not the way society saw it. He never went near any homosexual venue, although he was at the very least curious. He was attracted to a particular person early on in his life, contemplated pursuing it and living his life as he thought he should. Immense guilt took over. His family who were pillars of society, would be devastated. He might even be shunned. It would not be accepted or tolerated. At that time he threw himself into his education and tried to put it out of his mind, thinking there was something wrong with him. He was sick. As much as he knew his family was tolerant, he never felt he could share his feelings with them. Besides, he convinced himself he was sick.

He felt more guilt, even today, for the fact that in order to cast suspicion away from himself, he never let anyone think he approved of the homosexual lifestyle. He often agreed with others who voiced the same opinion. This only added to his enormous guilt. He was brought up to believe that not only was it a sin, it was perverted. His parents were not judgmental, but they made it very clear that it was wrong. How could he ever let anyone know how he felt? When he read about homosexual bashings, or beatings, or some other hatred towards that community, it made him sick. It made him even sicker because he didn't have the courage to stand up and be counted, or come out in support. Dreadful things happened to that community, which no one, regardless of any preference, religion or otherwise, should have to endure. He couldn't understand why people didn't just live and let live.

As he grew older, friends were always setting him up with girlfriends. He dated several of them, but he could never get serious. Pretending he was too involved in his work to commit. He knew it wasn't fair to the girls either, but it was expected of him.

He excelled in school, college, sports, work, whatever, because he totally buried himself in all of these activities, to the point of not leaving much time for thinking about anything else. Many, many nights though when he was alone, he was tormented by what he was told were improper thoughts. The more guilty and vile he felt, the more he threw himself into his school, work or play. It was a very unhappy time for him but he was masterful at covering it up.

Being so involved in many activities, coming from a prominent family and excelling at everything he touched, made him seem like a good "catch". Truth was, there was no one he was remotely interested in, and he resigned himself to living a bachelor life. That is until he met me. There was just something about me that attracted him, possibly because it was more platonic than physical. Maybe he was wrong all of these years; maybe he could have a successful relationship with a woman. As time proved, we were best friends, and shared a unique bond. We had a wonderful marriage but there was always something missing, the intense passion.

My head was spinning; I couldn't grasp all of this. The conversation I had with Ian all those years ago, now seemed insignificant in comparison to this revelation.

Bob didn't know how his parents would have reacted. He knew they loved him and supported him in everything he did in his life, but this was a total reversal to all their beliefs. They would have been mortified and embarrassed. Although he could never conceive of them disowning him, they probably would have tried to change him. Unfortunately, he would never know the answer, not on this earth anyway. He regretted that very much which only added to his guilt. That is why he had to tell me and hope, even though this was a lot to lay on me at this time, that I could in some small way understand. He wanted to reassure me that his love for me was genuine. We both had to agree our marriage was not the most sexually fulfilling. It was adequate. He filled the role that was expected of him.

What could I do or say now? I loved him. Had he betrayed me? What would have happened if he had told me before? Would I have accepted it and gone on? Why didn't he trust me enough before he got sick? Perhaps if I had not been so sure that the fire I felt for Ian could not be repeated, I might have wondered. In actual fact I was perfectly content the way our lives blended together.

I was totally oblivious to any sign that he was homosexual. How could I have missed it all these years? What did that say about me? There is no way a woman can live with man or a man with a woman in such a relationship without wondering about the little things.

My mind was trying to think quickly of our years together and I could not remember ever having any doubts. I had to be naive or something. I don't believe I saw anything and I wondered how he could hide it all these years. Then I remembered watching a TV talk show on this very subject. Wives admitted they were shocked when their husbands came out, husbands basically repeating the same story. One woman said she was married for 41 years, had three children, a happy marriage she thought, until the day her husband told her he was homosexual. He told her he was getting a divorce and was moving in with his boyfriend. Maybe I wasn't so blind after all. Maybe when I think on this later, I might realize I did notice some little things but I didn't believe that.

I saw tears in his eyes. He was totally distraught. He was shaking. He was so sorry to bring this hurt to me now. He wanted nothing left unsaid or undone between us. Deep down he wondered if I would reject him. He needed some sort of acceptance from someone, preferably someone he loved. He wanted to die in peace. Whatever I felt, and I wasn't sure what I felt, I would not hurt him any more than he had been hurt already, by having to live his life a total lie. I vowed that no matter what, whatever time we had together would be spent the way the rest of our marriage had been shared, loving, caring and enjoying each other. I didn't think it was fair of him to tell me now when he didn't have much time left. It hurt me, but I tried to imagine what it must have been like for him. In some small way, I did understand. What a burden for anyone to carry through life. How afraid he must have been, but I didn't want to think about that now.

He wanted to tell the children, but I wasn't so sure it was a good idea, especially with them trying to cope with his illness. I could understand him wanting to be free of this massive guilt he had lived with all of his life, but what would it accomplish? Did the children, or anyone else for that matter, need to know? We had always taught our children to respect others, even if they disagreed with their religion, lifestyle or whatever. I didn't think they would ever turn a friend away if he or she had confessed to being homosexual I didn't think it would make much difference, but he was their dad, that might be quite different.

Sometimes people can accept things as long as they are not directly involved, such as a member of the family. Some people know about family members, but they choose not to talk about it and go on as if everything is alright. I told him there was no need to burden the children at this time. It was enough that he told me. Perhaps in the future, I would be in a better frame of mind to share this with them. I knew he desperately wanted to hear their approval, and I couldn't blame him. What if they were repulsed and he saw that? That would devastate him even more. I couldn't take the chance. I reminded him that being homosexual did not define him and said we needed to concentrate on keeping him as well as possible.

I now felt closer to him than ever before, if that was possible. He had trusted me enough to share this heavy burden that he carried all of these years. How could I let him down? I was deeply touched and proud that he had trusted me with this in the end. He had finally allowed me to share this terrible pain. I was in shock, unbelieving and totally out of the loop but he was my husband and I loved him. He needed to unburden and I was the one he chose to tell. No, I must carry on. Maybe when I have time to think about it, I may see things in a different light but now, I must accept this for his sake if nothing else. The thought crossed my mind that perhaps because he was tired of the charade and all that went with it, he chose not to prolong his life with treatment. Wouldn't that be sad?

Time was racing on now. Bob got steadily weaker. Days passed into weeks. It became more difficult for him to get out of bed. Due to our financial position, we were able to get him private nursing care. Bob was insistent that the family wouldn't be burdened. This also enabled me to keep him at home. Palliative nurses stayed with him around the clock. Paul came into see him almost every day. Anything he wanted or needed was right there. He was kept comfortable and as pain free as possible.

We had visitors including family and friends, but these visits were carefully monitored. He enjoyed their company. His mind was as clear as possible. Daniel told his dad he would be honoured to take over the practice. That gave him such happiness. All the legal documents were signed, all the while Daniel kept insisting to his dad that it wasn't going to happen. I was always at Bob's side. Whenever I needed a little breather, either Beth, Joe, my family, his family, one of the children, or a neighbour would willingly fill in. Everyone was wonderful.

Daniel and Lisa again brought up the subject of them moving in with us for a bit. Help was plentiful and we didn't want to disrupt anyone's life any more than possible. We were so grateful to everyone.

As the end came near, he deteriorated rapidly. I was shocked at how quickly he went down although I shouldn't have been, remembering my hospice volunteering. Oh yes, his illness had gradually taken over his life. There were days when he seemed to be better, rejuvenated even. In the end it was so quick that we were in shock, even though we knew it was inevitable. These days were difficult for everyone but they were also filled with some of the most precious memories for all of us. I told Bob every opportunity I got, how much I loved him, our marriage and what a great husband he was. If he was sleeping, I whispered in his ear. Sometimes he was only closing his eyes, but I told him anyway. I wanted him to know that and also to know his confession didn't change anything. I wasn't totally sure about that, but I wouldn't let him know that.

Eventually he slipped away peacefully and pain free. He died while I was holding his hand. Even though I had months to prepare for this time, I was devastated. I couldn't believe it had finally happened. Most of our families were with us including Beth and Joe. I could not imagine my life without him. He was my rock, my best friend and a perfect husband. Any wife would have felt the same had she been married to him but I happy that he chose me.

XXVII

Why is no one answering that phone? Will somebody please get the phone? What time is it? The phone rang and rang until I awakened and sat up. The ringing had startled me and I had trouble getting my bearings. It was still reasonably light and slowly I realized I was not at home. I was in my cabin on the ship. Now I remembered. I must have been dreaming. How could that be? I wasn't asleep that long, not long enough to have my whole life flash before me, but it was true.

The phone was still ringing. I picked it up. June was on the other end. She was calling to ask if I was ready to meet her in the lounge before dinner. I asked her to give me a half hour to get myself together. I already had my clothes laid out for dinner. I showered before I fell asleep. It wouldn't take long to get ready. We agreed to meet in the lounge where many of the passengers passed some time waiting for the dinner "bon appetito" to come over the intercom. We also preferred this lounge but there were many other places to wait for dinner such as lounges, bars or the casino, etc.

Most of the seats in the lounge were occupied. Even the bar stools were occupied, but we managed to get a couple of seats together. Some of the passengers were up dancing to a trio that was playing for our enjoyment while we waited. June and I had a coffee as we took in all the activity. The floor of this brightly decorated lounge was meant for dancing with bright floral carpeting edging the floor all around the room.

Most of the lounges are on the window side of the ship allowing those sitting beside them to take in a view of the sea. However, other than the odd flying fish, whitecaps and the sun going down, it was water, water everywhere. It was still a lovely view nonetheless.

It was a perfect evening. Comfortable chairs and tables made it easy to relax while enjoying the view outside and activity inside. On the opposite side of the room passengers sat at the bar sipping a cool drink before dinner. I looked around at the happy couples, feeling a tinge of sadness, loneliness and even a bit of guilt because Bob and I had always wanted to take this cruise. It wasn't meant to be, but I know he would have been happy that I decided to take it on my own, more so because I had found this new friend to keep me company. As well as the dancers, some of the passengers enjoyed singing along to the music from our era, which applied to most of the others on the cruise. There were not too many young people on this cruise.

June and I chatted animatedly non-stop. She confessed she had always wanted to travel, but circumstances prevented it. Since she wasn't getting any younger, she decided now was as good a time as any. Her children thought she deserved it. They surprised her with this cruise. I shared that I had been on several cruises, and that

Bob and I had been fortunate enough to get in a few trips once the children were off on their own.

Memories of those trips with Bob were everywhere. That was good. Memories can get a person through difficult times and this was one of those times. I told June that Bob had died recently of cancer, that we had been married for 35 years and had two children. We knew there might be a chance he might not make it, but we decided not to cancel in the hope he just might. I added that I felt the need to take the cruise on my own against everyone's advice. I thought it was the best way to get away, sort out my thoughts, be on my own without family or friends with me and yet I wouldn't be alone. It was the perfect solution. I admitted I had second thoughts a few times and didn't know if I could do it. I told her that meeting her was just what I needed, and also that I planned to tack on a couple of extra weeks at the end to visit Scotland.

June opened up saying she had a terrible life with an alcoholic husband who finally drank himself to death. In the beginning there were happy times. They had three lovely children of whom she was immensely proud and who were the one good thing that came out of the marriage. Most of her married life had been miserable. She wondered aloud why it is that so many marriages start out so full of love but end up with so much anger, hatred and heartbreak. She didn't go into any details and I didn't press for any.

"Bon appetito," was heard over the intercom, signalling passengers that the first sitting dinner was about to be served. A quick gulp of coffee and off we went in the direction of the dining room. June was now sitting at my table as previously arranged. We were both happy with that arrangement. I introduced the newcomer to the tablemates. Everyone used first names because even that was hard enough to remember. What did surnames matter anyway? While our table mates checked over the menu, each gave a little of their background, who they were and where they came from and so on.

An older couple who came from California, had recently married, each for a second time. June and I teased them that we were jealous. They were cute and cuddly, lovebirds for sure. Two former school teachers sat next to the newlyweds, one a widow and the other divorced. Both lifelong friends from Texas who often travelled together. A mother and her adult son sat between the teachers and June and me. The son had recently divorced and moved back in with his mother. When the mother told us that, she rolled her eyes back in her head, wondering how this happened. "Imagine," she said, "a 55 year old moving back home." Colorado was their home. I told them I was recently widowed from Canada, originally from Scotland. June acknowledged she too was a widow. We let them know that we had just met on this trip, were travelling alone for the first time and were happy to have met.

June said she was from London although a slight Scottish accent could be detected. We got a chuckle when the tablemates asked if we knew each other in Scotland. Most people think that because it is a small country, everyone knows everyone else. June mentioned the name of the little town she was from, which was not too far from Glasgow. I almost choked on my water. June patted me on my back. "Just went down the wrong way," I lied. The reason I nearly choked was that the name of the town she was from was the same town where Ian lived. I could not believe it. How likely was that to happen? She probably didn't know him anyway. I decided not to ask her if she knew him, not just yet, maybe I never would.

Later I told June we lucked out with table partners on this trip. Bob and I usually opted for a table for two If it wasn't available we asked for a table for eight because there was a better chance of having one of two compatible travellers out of the bunch. Our tablemates were great. So far this trip was working out to be the very thing I needed.

Several of the diners ordered wine with their dinner but I stuck with water. June had a glass of Perrier as we looked over the menu to see what piqued our fancy. There was light conversation about the shipboard activities, the itinerary and what we thought of the ship. June was the only one at the table who had never cruised before. We all gave her a friendly ribbing and told her she was the baby and we would look after her. Everyone was in a holiday mood and this banter took away any shyness anyone might have felt.

I chose the Caesar salad, marinated chicken breast with garden vegetables and creamed potatoes. For dessert I ordered New York cheesecake. Rolls and bread were always scrumptious, it was hard to refuse but who could? Not me. As I left the dining room I had to pass the table of after dinner mints. There was no way I couldn't take some of them. No Bob to cover for me on this trip. Everything reminded me so much of him.

Elevators were usually busy after the diners left the dining room. We walked up the stairs although that wasn't such a great achievement; it was only to the deck above. After that huge meal, we needed something to work it off.

We wandered through the shops, checking out the beautiful duty free merchandise. Most of the items were excellent quality, but expensive. The casino was next to the shopping area. This was a smart marketing move. Some of the male passengers passed their time away in the Casino with no complaints from their wives. They were happy to spend time and money in the shops. I didn't gamble and didn't care to play the slot machines. Bob wasn't a gambler either, but on our trips, visiting the casino was his entertainment. He usually set aside about

$20.00 for the night. When that was gone, that was it for him. Sometimes he won, sometimes he lost but he usually broke even by the end of the trip. He enjoyed it so why not.

Next stop on our little walk was the International Lounge. A small piano bar was further along this deck. Passengers could join in the singsongs. This lounge, as with the others, was brightly decorated with tables and chairs surrounding a small dance floor and windows all around. Several lounges were spread throughout this large ship. Many guests were relaxing, listening to the sweet music of the young couple who had been playing earlier at the other lounge.

I always had to chuckle when I saw the front rows of the International Lounge already filled. Some passengers nearly knocked others down in their rush to get the front rows of the auditorium. Bob and I usually sat at the back as we thought we had a better view. Those sitting in the front sometimes got picked by the stars for part of their act. Until it was time for the show to start, a small band played for those wishing to enjoy some dancing. Quite a few dancers were up on the floor when we went in. We sat at the back enjoying the various couples dancing and the different styles of dance. Many dancers were as good as professional ballroom dancers. The music was always geared to our age group. It was lovely to sit and listen.

When the band finished their round, the Cruise Director approached the stage. His role was to give passengers information they might need on tours, lifeboat drills, or anything else. He or she always asked how everyone was enjoying the trip so far, and how they liked the ship. Did they have enough to eat and so on. Next day's itinerary was discussed to be sure everyone understood what was available. He took questions. This information was also printed in the daily newspaper delivered to each cabin, but some people still needed to be reminded. The informality of this chatting with members of the audience, generally got them warmed up for the show.

Now it was time for the show and as the lights were dimmed, the entertainer for this evening’s show walked onto the stage. Tonight's show was basically a "one woman" production. Her impersonation of various movie or TV celebrities was excellent. She told a few jokes, a few stories and just reminisced about yesteryear, which was always popular with this audience of mostly seniors. Mingling with the audience, particularly the men, was always a hit and managed to keep everyone's attention throughout the whole show.

XXVIII

June and I went up to the Lido Cafe for a nightcap after the show was over. When I say nightcap, I mean a coffee, tea or cold drink. We were both still quite full from dinner and didn't need anything else to eat. I had a coffee, and June had a tea. We couldn't resist taking one of the tempting goodies. We indulged again.

We had first sitting for dinner, which meant we could go to the first show. Many others preferred the second show although it finished quite late. Other passengers continued on to the disco after that and probably didn't get back to their cabins until the wee small hours of the morning.

The Lido was fairly quiet at this time, most passengers either in the second show, casino or some other activity. We took our snack over to a table by the window. It was dark outside but there was a beautiful full moon and again, we could see the whitecaps on the water as the ship floated ever so easily through the water.

June brought up the subject of her first husband again. She seemed to have a need to tell her story. I was a willing listener but I didn't think I would be sharing my story, not the last part anyway. She said she and her husband had moved many times, finally settling in London where work was plentiful and the money was a lot better. Having an alcoholic for a husband nearly destroyed her family. When he died at a relatively young age, she didn't feel the sense of loss that other widows felt. He died to her many years before. Sometime after her husband's death, she started dating one of the men, Alistair, whom she had met at Al-anon meetings. His wife was the alcoholic in the family.

June and Alistair became good friends but there was no hint of romance in the friendship. They were both angry and bitter at their partners for destroying the family's life. Neither held out any hope at that time of anything getting any better. Even if it did, the love they felt had long been buried. They sat beside each other at the meetings and became friendly, both knowing only too well what the other had gone through. They had a common bond and being able to confide in each other, someone that totally understood, made their lives just a little bit easier. They were not alone. Yes, the others in the meeting all shared a common thread and were there for each other, but it was nice to have someone to personally confide and trust in. Coffee was served at the meetings. June and Alistair often went to a cafe afterwards, just to commiserate and gain strength from one another. There was no romantic link there; just two people who shared a common problem and who felt comfortable with each other.

Alistair divorced his wife before June's husband died but she was not interested in him or any other man for that matter. She was so bitter and angry that thoughts of any romantic liaison with any man, actually made her sick.

She said she could never trust another man. Alistair continued attending the meetings but he was filled with guilt about the divorce and what had happened to the family. He felt guilty that he left his wife but he knew he was not helping her and, in fact, was actually enabling her to continue on with her drinking. It took a lot of strength on his part but it had to be done.

He was continually making excuses for her, keeping up appearances, to say nothing of the drain on the finances her drinking had become. Every time he came home from work, she was passed out in bed or on the couch and the house was a mess. He paid all the bills, bought the groceries and other necessities so she didn't have to handle the money but somehow, she always managed to get enough somewhere for her habit. Even his wife's family, his children and friends, agreed divorce was the right thing to do but it didn't ease his conscience. Al-anon helped.

Memories of living with an alcoholic mother who often wasn't even aware of her children in the house, left them all angry and sad, but he was thankful they all turned out alright. His wife got sober a couple of times after he threatened to leave her but it never lasted, one time a year, second time six months and the last time only days. Maybe if he had allowed her to get to rock bottom, it would have forced her to seek the help she needed and be able to stick with it. His conscience wouldn't let him do that. She knew she wouldn't pay the price.

Finally, he told her there were no more ultimatums. He didn't care if she quit again or not. It was over. He couldn't go on allowing her to destroy their family. He felt he could take it better than the children. I think she went to live with her mother after he told her to leave.

When June's husband died, Alistair was there to help her through some very rough times. Like other partners of alcoholics, June thought she might have been able to make a difference in her husband's drinking. No matter what she tried, said, or threatened, it never changed anything. She finally resigned herself to the fact that alcoholism rests solely with the drinker. Only he or she has the power, the will or the desire to stop. Until they realize that, the drinking continues, ruining their own life and the lives of those around them in the process. When she was thinking clearly, she knew she was not to blame.

Alistair was understanding and helpful. He kept reinforcing that thought in her mind. She didn't know how she could have got through it without him. Oh yes, the family was sympathetic and supportive, but she needed someone apart from family. Who better than Alistair? He had been down the same road and he understood exactly what she was going through.

Eventually she and Alistair went out on dates, but the romance was slow in getting started. Neither ever thought of getting married again, not wanting to get involved again with anyone, no matter whether they drank or not. People change after marriage. It was too much of a risk. They both agreed with that. However, their friendship grew stronger with every passing day and they enjoyed just being with each other. They laughed, they even cried and feelings for each other began to surface. Before too long Alistair let June know he was in love with her and asked how she felt about that. She had to admit that she was flattered and cared a lot for him but she wasn't sure she wanted to get involved again. They talked about marriage, they both had doubts but not about their feelings for each other. Would they be able to put their past marriages behind them? They decided to continue going out with each other and see what happened but they weren't about to rush into anything.

Their marriages were similar as far as the alcoholism was concerned which could work for good if they got married. They knew the pitfalls and could hopefully avoid them. Besides neither was a drinker so alcoholism was very unlikely at this stage of life. While June’s life was hell, she thought Alistair's life must have been much worse than her own. When a mother is not fit, it affects the whole family more than when a father is the alcoholic. The financial loss due to a father's alcoholism or other disease is a real drain, but a mother seems to be able to hold the family together under adverse circumstances.

Alistair and June wanted to be sure that it wasn't loneliness that was pushing them together, but they did feel as though huge weights had been lifted from their shoulders. Eventually, each met the other's family and friends, and everyone seemed to be genuinely happy for them. Everyone knew what pain and sadness they had both endured over many years, and how much they had given up. They encouraged them to seize the opportunity and get some pleasure out of life.

Before too long, they knew they were in love and decided to get married. Those were the happiest months in June's life but as she told this story, her eyes filled with tears. I was surprised to see the tears. I couldn't imagine what would make her cry if the marriage was so happy. All June could get out was that about 10 months after they were married, Alistair died of a massive heart attack. She was devastated, but cherished the time they had together and the wonderful memories Alistair had left her with. I tried to comfort her. I knew what it felt like to lose a loving husband. I told her Bob and I had a wonderful life together for many years and now that he was gone, I missed him so much. Family and friends are great comforts in these times but it isn’t the same. I said I didn’t know if I would ever get over it or get used to living alone.

By now we were both in tears. We dabbed away at our eyes before realizing that other passengers who were filling the cafe, were giving us funny looks. Suddenly it struck us as funny and we started to laugh hysterically. Now the passengers must have thought the two of us were ready for the loonie bin. It was cathartic, and we both needed it.

It was uncanny how quickly our friendship grew. It was strange. Two people travelling alone, drawn to each other, out of all the passengers on this huge ship. We were both originally from Scotland, both recently widowed, both on this cruise alone and both about the same age. A genuine kinship was developing rapidly.

XXIX

We planned on taking the trip ashore the next morning, which meant we had to get up early in order to have breakfast before boarding the bus. We called it a night and walked together along the deck until we had to part ways to get to our cabins. Once in my cabin, I told Bob (in the photograph) about June and how much better I felt having met her. It comforted me to talk to him, even though I knew he wasn't there.

June and I were happy that we hadn't booked any trips through our travel agents, prior to the trip. I wasn't interested in touring alone. Besides, I had already visited some of the ports of call with Bob on previous trips. We rarely took the organized tours, preferring to set out on our own. In some ports where there was so much to see in a relatively short time, it was more advantageous to join the others on the sightseeing trips. For the most part though, we saw the cities as they were, not as tourists.

Because this was June's first trip, she wasn't sure about the organized tours, or which ones she should book in advance. She thought it might be better if she waited until she was on board, chatted with other passengers and the staff to find out what they recommended. Little could we imagine how our decisions would work to our advantage on this cruise. Now we could book together. Normally the cruise lines encourage passengers to pre book the shore excursions, suggesting they might be full by the time they board. I knew from past experience that was not always the case and that's why I waited. June, on the other hand, didn't know what she wanted to do.

The ship docked early in Oslo. Those of us who were going ashore had enough time to get breakfast before heading for the buses. June and I agreed the night before at the cafe, that we would get ready for the trip before going to breakfast so that we wouldn't have to go back to our cabins. We met up at the buffet in the Lido.

Mornings were normally busy and when the tours were leaving, it was especially busy. Everyone wanted to have a good breakfast before heading out. With what most of us ate the night before, we could have fasted for the rest of the trip without feeling any pangs of hunger. June and I chose cereal, yogurt and a piece of fruit out of the large assortment of foods. I had my coffee and June had her cuppa. I told her that our teary eyed session last night kept me awake for a while as I kept going over various things in my mind. I had read a magazine and finally dropped off to sleep. Apart from that, I told her I felt the tears had been good for me. She agreed and said the tears were like a relief valve for her, but she had no problem sleeping. She had a shower, turned out the light and next thing she knew it was morning.

With our breakfast finished, off we went downstairs to the lounge where various tours were being organized. One by one, the groups left the ship by the gangplank and onto the buses waiting on the pier. Passengers were happy, smiling and dressed for the day in tracksuits and walkers. Cameras were in continuous use as pictures of the ship, groups and just about anything the eye could see were snapped. Many of the passengers appeared to be on their own like June and me, but it didn't hold them back. They joined in with one group or another. Even at that, we were happy to have found each other, although we didn't mind if someone joined us. No one did.

A slight breeze felt good on our faces as we boarded the bus. It was a sunny day, warm enough to be comfortable yet not too hot. Perfect for the day ahead. Exploring Vigeland Sculpture Park and the Viking and polar ship museums was included in our tour today. Arriving at the palace, we were just in time to see the changing of the guard. It was impressive, and quite a spectacle. The courtyard and surrounding area was crowded, making it difficult to get a spot for a good view. June and I had both seen the changing of the guard at Buckingham Palace at one time or another so this type of pomp and splendour was not something new, but we thoroughly enjoyed it. I have to admit though, if anyone can put on an excellent show with the soldiers, bands and pomp and circumstance, it was surely the Brits.

By the time we got back to the ship we were a little tired and went straight to our own cabins to relax. Our plan as usual was to meet in the Riviera Club before dinner. I kicked off my shoes. I learned to wear sensible comfortable shoes that would see me through these tours so that I didn't end up with sore feet for the rest of the trip. Although my feet weren't sore or swollen, it was still nice to get my feet up for a bit. I enjoyed the day so much more than I thought I would. Having June made all the difference. This might have been a very different cruise otherwise.

When I made the decision to go on this cruise alone, doubt filled my mind but now I could see it was the right decision. I needed this time away from family and friends, to be by myself. This was no reflection on family and friends. I appreciated having them and for all that they got me through.

After a short rest, I got up, showered and changed into a semi formal beige pantsuit with a brown satin blouse and brown sandals with a little heel. I carried a small purse with me, to keep my cabin key, handkerchief and a few dollars, although I didn't need any money. If I bought anything it was charged to my room. More and more, I felt relaxed, stronger and much better than I had been for the last several months. I left the cabin, locked the door and walked along the deck and up the stairs to the Riviera Club. June hadn't arrived yet. I sat at a table by the window, as we always did. I waited for her before I ordered, not knowing what she might want tonight.

It wasn't too long before she appeared in a black pantsuit with a white silk blouse and black patent sandals. We complimented each other on our outfits and agreed we looked pretty good for a couple of oldies. I joked that we might pick up a boyfriend later but it was a joke, because neither of us was inclined in that way. June shook her head as she laughed. The young couples that were regulars here and in other lounges played the music of our generation with a mix of modern music here and there. These "golden oldies" brought back so many memories. We relaxed and enjoyed the music as we went down memory lane; again! "Bon appetito", signalled it was time to go. We finished our cokes, got up and headed for the dining room.

Evening meals were wonderful, the camaraderie evident, and conversations were mostly about the day's activities, which were different for each of us, depending on which tour was taken. Some of our tablemates stayed on board. Sometimes little bits of our personal lives were discussed but only generalities. Our conversations were mostly about what we did on the cruise.

After dinner we took the stairs again up to the Riviera Deck but not before I got my stash of mints. June didn't slack there either, she helped herself, but unlike Bob, they were for her, not me. We took another stroll through the shops, although we had been in there the night before. It would be our nightly jaunt. There was always something different on display. Daily specials were like magnets to passengers. After that, we walked through the casino. June got a little bit of a gambling bug but she, like Bob, only allowed herself a certain amount of money. She knew that it could be very easy to get hooked. She couldn't afford to take any chances. She didn't have that kind of money, but she got a kick out of the slot machines. Like Bob and many others, sometimes she won, and sometimes she lost. Overall at the end of the trip, she broke even so that wasn't bad.

Our next stop was the International Lounge to watch some of the other passengers dance to the old time music. We sat at the back and waited for the show. This would be our regular spot for the rest of the cruise. There was no fear of us losing them, most passengers preferring seats nearer the stage. We had to admit we felt a little touch of envy at the happy couples dancing, sitting in the seats, or strolling hand in hand as they tried to find a seat they liked. How nice it would have been if our husbands had been with us.

On the other hand, if they had, we probably would not have formed this wonderful friendship. Before every show we had the daily briefing from the Cruise Director. Every night in the International Lounge there was a different production, some more lavish than others. As was our habit, we left the lounge and went to the Lido Cafe for our nightly fix of coffee and tea. Each time we chatted, and a little of our personal stories unfolded.

Copenhagen was our next chosen tour. We agreed to meet at the buffet again before going ashore for the day's excursion. Dressing casually for these outings was a must. We dressed comfortably in slacks, a tee shirt or other top, with a cardigan or sweater, should the weather turn cooler. Sensible walking shoes always completed the outfit.

June had a camera. I didn't. This trip was never about photographs or scenery. I had taken plenty of photos with Bob on other cruises, at some of the same ports this cruise was sailing too. I hoped some passenger would take a photograph of the both of us so that she could send a copy to me. We could get one taken with one of the ship's photographers. They were always buzzing around, snapping here and snapping there.

Copenhagen is another lovely city with lots of places to eat and shop. Our group visited museums, places of interest, and of course the Little Mermaid by the waterfront. Again this brought up memories of Bob. This one tugged at my heart as I remembered the trip we had taken which included Osaka, Japan. A replica of this very statue sat at the waterfront. It also reminded me how badly Bob wanted to go on this trip to Scandinavian countries. I don't know if you could call it guilt that I felt because he wasn't with me. I know he would have loved this trip. I missed him terribly when memories came to mind, but I knew he would be happy for me.

Bob and I couldn't complain about missing out on things we should have done or could have done. We had a full life and travelled as much as we could when the children were on their own. We travelled when the children lived at home but those trips were family oriented, and included Disneyland, Disney World, camping and the cottage. It comforted me to know that we didn't miss any opportunities to do what we wanted, when we wanted. How many can say that? Too often people wait until the mortgage is paid off, the kids are grown or when they retire. Many never make it for one reason or another.

No trip to Copenhagen would be complete without visiting Tivoli Gardens, a magnificent amusement park and pleasure gardens. It was popular with natives and tourists alike. Passengers were given time to walk around the area on their own. June and I stopped to have an ice cream on the way. It was a lovely treat, on a beautiful day in this beautiful park. What more could we ask?

Call to arms. It was time for everyone to get back on the bus for the return trip to the ship. I went down to my cabin, to relax and have time to get ready for dinner again. What a life.

Tonight was one of the Captain's cocktail parties. Dress code for these evenings meant ladies wore formal, cocktail or party type dresses for the occasion. Gentlemen were requested to wear tuxedos or dark jackets, but I saw many different types of dress during my travels with Bob. Some ladies wore dresses that could be worn anywhere while others were dressed to the hilt in gowns covered with sequins. Gentlemen also wore a variety of suits, some with the dark tuxedos, some white tuxedos, some dark suits and others in lighter suits. I think the idea of the dress code was to avoid guests appearing in casual dress on these formal occasions, and it allowed an opportunity to get gussied up. No matter what anyone wore, everyone looked beautiful. As the line moved slowly, passengers were introduced to the Captain before they entered the lounge where cocktails were served, free of charge. On this cruise, there were two such parties on each formal night, one for first sitting and another for second sitting.

June and I chose to wear long skirts and fancy tops. We weren't over the top dressed, but were still tasteful. We thought so anyway. My skirt was white with a red silk top. June's skirt was black with a slightly beaded white top. While we waited in line to meet the Captain, we chatted with others. It was always the same topic of conversation, "how was your day, how are you enjoying the cruise so far, is this your first cruise?" And so on. Moving along, we saw the ship's photographer taking photos of anyone who requested it. An area was staged to give the photos a formal look. I could feel a tear or two coming into my eyes and when I turned to look at June, she was teary too. Bob and I might have had our photograph taken and June surely would have too. I suggested that if we wanted to, we could have one taken of us on the next formal night. It would be a memento for us to take back home with us. June loved the idea.

One of the hostesses stood by the Captain and other members of the crew. She asked for our names and introduced us to all of them. Another hostess guided us to a couple of empty seats where we were served immediately by attentive waiters and waitresses. Another member of the staff kept walking around the room to make sure everyone was being taken care of. Little trays of finger foods were also served. June and I had a soft drink and a few of the little party bites. We didn't want to indulge too much, keeping some appetite for our dinner. When everyone had been introduced to the Captain and staff, the Captain took center stage and welcomed everyone on board. He hoped everyone was having a good trip to which we all applauded. He gave us the statistics on how much food would be consumed during the trip and other pertinent information. He joked about the difference in the weight load of the ship at the end of the trip. It was a pleasant start to our dinner and it was exciting to people watch on this night. The dinner gong sounded and the familiar "bon appetito" told us that dinner was ready. We finished our drinks, ate our little snacks, and along with other passengers, headed off in the direction of the dining room. By now we could have found our way blindfolded.

After another delicious dinner, we thought we might go to see a movie. The billing outside displayed the name of the movie but it didn't appeal to us.

We had checked the daily newspaper and knew what stage show was scheduled for tonight. It was called "Ports of Call", and was a Las Vegas type show. It appealed to us so we headed towards the lounge but before getting settled in our seats, we had to make June's obligatory stop at the Casino.

Anyone who has cruised will tell you that performances put on by staff and guests on stage, were as good as any show in Vegas. It always amazed me how the dancers kept their balance on such a small stage while the ship sailed along, sometimes with a little bump here and there. We never noticed any of the dancers stumbling. Their costumes were exquisite, some of which had been created by well-known designers.

"Ports of Call" was exactly what the title implied. Routines were set in backdrops of various ports around the world. It brought back many happy memories of the times Moira and I used prance in the foyer of the cinema after one of the musicals that we loved so much. In the Paris skit, "can can" girls danced around Paris and under the Eiffel Tower. The New York skit consisted of dancing and singing to the tunes of the famous American composers, dressed in red, white and blue costumes. Dancers in Scotland were dressed in traditional Highland costumes while scenes of Scotland were shown on a screen at the back of the stage. There were no bagpipes. Those were only three of the lands they visited in their dance routines. Each "port of call" they visited around the world was equally as spectacular.

It was still early when the show finished. We weren't quite ready for our nightly fix of coffee and decided to stop in at the piano lounge to see what was going on there. Teams were being organized to play a trivia game and we were in time to get on the last one picked. Thank goodness the others on the team were smart because we ended up winning. Each member of the team received a travel alarm clock with the ship logo engraved on it.

Our next stop, was the Lido for our nightcap. Our usual table by the window always seemed to be waiting for us. We got our "fix" and a little treat and off we went to sit down. Each night we chatted endlessly at our table about our families, friends and told a little of our lives, as well as our likes and dislikes. I told June that I had moved to Canada in the early fifties to join my brother and a few cousins. That's where I met Bob; we eventually married and had two children, Daniel and Lisa. I never mentioned Lisa was adopted because we never considered she was adopted. She was ours the same as Daniel. June was quieter tonight as I spoke. Perhaps she was reliving a small part of her life when her alcoholic husband had upset her. It was easy on this trip to think of things in bygone days because the music alone could stir up memories. It was our music, and most of the passengers were about the same age as we were. To see them dancing and walking together, looking so happy, reminded us of what had been and what might have been. I never asked June any questions, knowing she would talk if and when she felt like it as she had done previously. Besides, I wasn't ready to answer some questions she might ask me.

Midnight was fast approaching. The cafe was filling with guests coming in from the second show, or from wherever they had spent their evening. At this time of night it could get a little noisy with the merrymakers laughing, singing, and kibitzing. It was nice to see such happiness. I got a coffee to take back to my cabin but June didn't seem too interested in getting her nightly cuppa. She appeared to be a little down in the dumps, somber even.

We were to be at sea all day tomorrow, no stops and no ports to visit. It was a day to get involved in some of the other activities or just relax by the pool. We promised ourselves to start our exercise on the first day at sea and made arrangements to start our jog around the deck. I was getting more and more relaxed, falling asleep quite easily now. Sometimes I awakened during the night, still hoping to see Bob come out of the bathroom. Other than that I was doing much better.

June and I have always been early risers so getting up on deck at 7:00 a.m. was no problem for either of us. A few joggers were already running by the time we got there. Coupons were handed out by a cruise assistant every time a lap around the deck was completed. Joggers could collect these coupons and purchase a tee shirt, cap or some other thing at the end of the cruise, if they had enough of them. We managed to make it around the deck four times, marking one mile. That meant four coupons. After finishing our run, we climbed the outside stairs up a few decks to the door of the Lido Cafe. We got additional coupons for that little climb. By the time we reached the cafe we were exhausted. We chose our breakfast and almost collapsed into the chairs.

Every day all kinds of activities were offered. We thought we might try the line dancing. Both of us loved to dance. Anyway, it was good exercise and, hopefully, it would be a bit of fun.

When it was lunchtime again we went back to the buffet luncheon, taking a seat by the pool. Passengers were engaged in various activities, depending on their choice. Some were swimming, some sat in the hot tub, some lay in the sun and others sat reading, playing cards or getting involved in some other activity. In the afternoon I decided I would join one of the table tennis teams. June was not too keen on that. She opted for bingo. We were happy to do our own thing sometimes on days at sea. Other times we joined forces and we always jogged or walked along the deck together. We were proud of ourselves when we earned enough coupons to get a tee shirt and cap at the end of the cruise. It crossed our minds we might have been better buying the items, but we had fun and that's what the cruise was all about. Evenings were spent enjoying each other's company and eating far too much.

Shore cruises included Stockholm, which is known as the Belle of the Baltic. History was everywhere from Gamla Stan to the Palace and the Vasa Museum. Helsinki, the capital of Finland, was next with its broad boulevards, delightful shops and historic buildings. A visit to the quaint village of Porvoo was also on the itinerary. St. Petersburg was a two-day stopover. That meant we would stay on board for the two nights and go sightseeing during the days. Bob and I had visited this city before, but I didn't mind a repeat trip. I was happy to show June around the Winter and Summer Palaces, Hermitage Museum and the Peterhof Palace, with magnificent gardens and fountains. Famous churches, and there were so many of them, were part of the sightseeing, as well as the Kremlin area and Lenin's Tomb, which was guarded by goose stepping guards. We didn't go inside.

Also a must on these trips was the famous GUM store. From the outside it looked like a regular department store but once inside, it contained all kinds of mini stores on several floors. One reason I didn't mind doing the tours again was because the architecture of some of the buildings was magnificent as was the art inside. It was well worth repeat visits.

Docked close by was the Aurora ship, which was used in the revolution. All along the way, Russians traders put up little booths to sell or trade their many souvenirs. Blue jeans were eagerly sought after. Souvenirs included Matruska dolls, army hats, beautiful vibrant floral patterned shawls and Russian dolls. We each bought a few souvenirs for family.

June and I could well understand why there was a revolution in years gone by. The opulence and treasures in the palaces was beyond description, yet there was abject poverty all around. Vast differences between the rich and poor were still very much in evidence in the present time, but it must have been much worse many years ago. Russia seemed to have been a very troubled country. June was utterly flabbergasted by it all.

On the first evening in dock, we took the tour to one of Moscow's circuses. The circus was amazing. Performers were unbelievable. Before we went inside, a vendor had an adorable spider monkey waiting to have his picture taken with tourists. We had to get our picture taken with the monkey. He was too cute. We thought it might help the owner to keep the pet fed.

The next port on the cruise was Tallin, Estonia. We took a guided walk from Toompea Hill in the Upper Town to Palace Square where we passed the Alexander Nevsky Cathedral on the way to medieval Lower Town. This was a clean city. As luck would have it, there was a flea market in the square. It was right up our alley. We purchased some trinkets there for a reasonable price.

Gdynia, Poland was the next stop. It was a short trip from there to Gdansk. We drove by the ship works, made famous throughout the world by Lech Walencza. People were very friendly as we walked through the medieval Old Town, stopping in at St. Mary's Church. The guide was rightly proud of this Old Town. It was remarkable. He told us that during the war this city, which was called Danzig, was destroyed to a total of 95 percent. It was now completely rebuilt and showed no signs of any damage by war.

As we walked through the streets we stopped at jewellery shops, looked in the windows, and finally went into one. Amber gems were everywhere and available in rings, bracelets, necklaces and broaches. Amber is such a beautiful stone. June purchased some earrings for her daughter and I purchased some for Lisa, Beth, Jenny, Bill's wife and my mother. I treated myself to a delicate amber pendant in sterling silver, telling myself that Bob would have purchased it for me, had he been there. That was his gift to me. The guide pointed to tenement like houses, only each housed one family, all joined together. He said that if the houses were single, meaning one window on each floor that meant the people were not too wealthy. Double windows meant they were a little richer, and triple windows meant the residents were pretty well off.

Driving back to Gdnyia, we passed a carnival area. The driver allowed us half an hour to look around. We bought ice cream cones from a vendor and walked through the carnival area like a couple of schoolgirls. We didn't bother playing any of the usual games but enjoyed watching others try to get the ever elusive prizes. Soon our time was up and we met up with the driver and the others. It had been another excellent interesting day with the sun cooperating.

Our evenings during the cruise consisted mainly of our short trip to the shops, June's nightly fix in the Casino and taking in the nightly show. The entertainment could not have been better and each night we saw a different show, including a variety show, an evening of incredible classical piano, a Broadway Show, a Cabaret, an evening featuring America's Music and others. Each one was more spectacular than the one before it. One show that I would never miss on cruises was the passenger talent night. Some of the passengers were talented. Others were not. That didn't stop them and talent or not, they always put on a good show.

I told June about previous shows Bob and I had seen. She couldn't wait to see the acts. Talent night finally arrived but there was only one contestant. It was almost embarrassing. The Cruise Director decided to let him do his thing, because he had auditioned for it. Edelweiss was the song of his choice and he sang it fairly well, but every time we thought he was finished, we applauded, only to find he started all over again. This went on for several minutes. By then, most of us couldn't stop laughing but we did our best to stifle the giggles. The singer didn't seem to be aware anything was wrong.

When he finally finished, he was awarded the first prize. This only made matters worse, bringing on roars of laughter. What could the Director do? He was a contestant, and the only one, so he was entitled to the first prize. Truth be known, he could have claimed the second and third prizes too. It reminded me of the children's song "This is the song that never ends". Apart from being the only contestant, he earned the prize if only for sheer courage, getting up on stage, knowing there was no competition. On the other hand, maybe that's why he had the courage. He knew he couldn't lose. Whatever the reason, it was a most enjoyable evening.

Too quickly this cruise was coming to an end. This was the last evening before disembarking. We both felt a sense of sadness that we would be going our separate ways. Would we ever see each other again? Perhaps June could visit me in Canada or I might take that trip to Scotland that I had thought about. We had become extremely close, were so much alike and thankful that we had met each other. Otherwise the cruise might not have been so pleasant for either of us.

After supper and a show, we walked up to our favourite chatting spot, the Lido. Our table by the window was reserved for us. Maybe that wasn't true but it looked that way. Normally there weren't too many passengers at this time because of other activities but tonight it was almost empty. We put it down to the fact most passengers might be trying their last minute chance to win back some of their losses and others might have wanted to continue any lucky streak they had realized. Some might have been romancing and dancing while the mood was still with them. I thought most of them would probably be packing their luggage. We had finished packing before we left the cabin. The suitcases had to be left outside the cabin for pickup by the stewards to prepare for unloading the next morning. We kept our toiletries and incidentals to tide us over until we got our luggage again.

The waters were calm, the moon was out again, and the swishes of whitecaps were ever present, floating alongside the ship as it sailed towards its destination. Sometimes it was easy to forget we were actually on a ship. Most of the music coming over the p.a. system into the Lido was from the same time frame as the other lounges. It was our music and very good. Almost every song had a memory for either June or myself.

We agreed that this trip wouldn't have been as good, had we not met each other. I was feeling much more ready to carry on when I got home. My decision to sail was the right one, but it might have been a different story without June. Over the course of our friendship we got to know about each other's lives quite well, little bits of information coming out on our evening chats. I told June everything except Bob's deathbed confession. There were times when I was tempted to tell her. She didn't know any of my friends or family. The secret would be safe with her, but then I wondered what the point of that would be. Perhaps I would have been able to judge what the reaction of others might be. I still didn't know if I could ever reveal Bob's story. Only time would tell. Although I remembered June said she originally came from the same town as Ian, I never told that story either.

I don't know whether it was because it was our last night together that we knew of, whether she was coming to terms with her husband's sudden death and like me, she was ready to carry on, or whether she felt like telling her story to someone who didn't know her family or friends. Whatever it was, she wanted to talk and talk she did, baring her soul so to speak. She had previously said I was a good listener when she told me about the miserable life she had with her alcoholic husband but the depths of it were unimaginable. She said that while she had a lot of supporters, most people knew her story because they saw it unfold, but no one knew the whole story. She needed to tell someone from her point of view in order to bring some sense into her past life. No one could understand why she stayed in that marriage and tended not to listen to anything she had to say. In other words, it was her fault if she stayed with her husband. I got a pot of coffee for myself, and tea for her.

She started to cry, tears streaming down her face. It was easy to see she was burdened about something. I reached over, held her hand, and told her to let it all out. She said she was happy for me that I had a good life and a wonderful family. It made her wonder what her life might have been had she emigrated to Canada or Australia like so many others. My life appeared to be smooth sailing and I seemed to have it all. I knew that June's first husband was an alcoholic who died very young. She readily admitted her life was miserable with him, although she never elaborated, and only shared a few things about her children and her own life.

She said she was too ashamed most of the time to let anyone know what was going on behind closed doors. Most of their friends never saw the true man behind her husband's persona, and probably wouldn't have believed the damage the alcoholism had done. Oh yes, their children knew, but even her husband's siblings had no real idea what it was like living with this man, especially when he was consumed by drink. No one can truly know what it's like to live with an alcoholic, unless they have been there.

When her husband drank, he often got loud and obnoxious at various gatherings. His friends dismissed it because they didn't live with it, and probably didn't realize it went on continuously. Most people thought he was a great guy because he could be very charming when he was sober. His family saw a very different picture. Besides, does anyone care about another's problems? Most people have enough to contend with in their own day-to-day life.

She said that she married her high school sweetheart, but that it almost never came about. How many times afterwards, she wished that she hadn't married him, but she was young and so much in love. She thought they could make a good life for themselves. I asked, "What do you mean it almost didn't happen?"

She looked at me and said, "are you sure you want to hear my story?"

By now I was intrigued and told her if she wanted to tell me, if it would help her in some small way to come to terms with whatever, then of course I would listen, and so her story began.

"B.J. and I had been neighbours and friends since school. As we grew older, we began to date. Before long, we were an item. I was ecstatic. Ever since I could remember, all I ever wanted was to marry B.J. Marriage wasn't in our plans until he finished his apprenticeship, but we started saving towards the end. Our courtship was great until one day he came to me and told me he wanted out of the commitment. Stunned didn't fully express how I felt. A ton of bricks falling on me couldn't have done more damage. I thought it was a joke. The look on his face told me otherwise. I asked him why. He told me he had met someone else and although he did love me, he now knew it wasn't true love. He said that because we had been friends for so long, and liked each other enormously, he felt that we had just fallen into the relationship. My mouth dropped, I was speechless and could not take in what he was saying. The thought crossed my mind that perhaps he just needed some space, that it might be good for both of us if we didn't see each other for a while. I tried to reason with him.

B.J. told me he was sorry. He still thought the world of me and hoped we could always be friends. As for marriage, it was not going to happen. I couldn't think of anything to say as my emotions got the better of me. I didn't want him to feel sorry for me and make him change his mind. I believed this was a fling and it would blow over. He would come back to his senses and to me. What else could I do? I had to accept what he was saying. Before I completely lost it, I turned and walked away, my heart totally broken.

Some weeks passed. There was no sign that B.J. had changed his mind. Every time I saw him, my heart fluttered thinking he had come to his senses. He was on his way to tell me he had made a mistake, and that he wanted us to get back together again. That never happened. I was totally devastated.

I hadn't been feeling well for a while. My heart dropped because I thought I might be pregnant. B.J. and I had been intimate once, only once, can you believe that? My parents were out of town and we got caught up in the moment. I knew this when B.J. broke off with me but I didn't want to say anything at the time, still thinking he would make up with me. I also didn't want that to be a reason for him staying with me. I decided not to say anything at that time.

Between that and the breakup, I was physically ill. There was a lot of flu going around. I did not want to consider the possibility that I was pregnant. I was in panic mode.

I wasn't getting any better and started to get sick in the mornings. I just knew that I was pregnant. I didn't know what to do. I didn't want my parents to find out and that added to my stress. Now that I was sure, I had to do something, but what? There was no sign of B.J. making up with me. He had to be told for no reason other than I needed some advice and help. I was on the verge of a nervous breakdown."

My ears perked up and my mouth gaped open. June didn't notice. Her eyes were down and focused on the table. I couldn't believe the similarities in this story and the one I knew all too well. I dismissed it even though I knew June lived in the same town. I knew there were hundreds of stories like this. Besides, her surname was not the same as Ian's. Then I remembered June's second marriage. No, it couldn't possibly be, could it?

"I was sick with worry. What could I do? What should I do? I couldn't ask anyone for help. I knew full well the stigma that was attached to having a child out of wedlock. Both sets of parents were upset at the breakup too but knowing couples have spats, they decided to stay out of it, hoping and believing we would soon be back together. My mother was very concerned about me. Normally an outgoing person and easy to get along with, I had become quiet, solemn and almost unbearable to live with. I wasn't eating, wasn't sleeping and felt I was going into a kind of depression. My mother couldn't broach the subject. Every time she mentioned B.J.'s name, I broke down. My mother attributed my complete change of personality to the breakup with B.J. If only she had known what I was going through. I couldn't take the risk of telling her for fear of being put out of the house. As you know, many young girls who found themselves in the same position as me were totally disowned.

I knew I had to tell him. There was no other way. I waited until I thought he might be at home and knocked on his door. His mother invited me in but since he wasn't home, I didn't bother going into the house. I asked his mother to tell him I wanted to talk to him. His mother, like everyone else who knew us, hoped this was a sign of a make-up. No one knew what caused the breakup. When he arrived home he got the message from his mother. He called on me. I suggested we take a walk over to the little parkette across the street. The very sight of him reminded me how much I loved him, even though he had hurt me so much. I was nervous, shaky and yet excited to see him. I didn't care the reason for the breakup; I just wanted us to get back together. He was the only boy I had loved and with whom I had been intimate.

I asked him how he was and told him how much I had missed him. I asked if he had any change of thoughts. He was quite cold to me, looking annoyed at me bothering his mother to get to him. This was not the B.J. I knew. He told me it was over between us and again said how sorry he was that it had turned out this way. He didn't plan it. It just happened. But he wanted to marry this other girl. I reminded him that we had supposedly been in love, I still was, and we were planning on marriage too. He said that if and when I met someone else and fell in love, I would know what he meant and how he felt. He was getting a little testy and jumpy. He asked what I wanted to see him about. He was meeting the boys shortly for a game of football. He didn't have much time to chat.

I could see that I had to tell him before he got mad and left. I didn't know what to say or how to say it. I just blurted out "I am pregnant." You have never seen such a shocked look on anyone's face as I saw that day. The blood actually drained from his face. He sat or should I say, fell down on the bench in total shock and disbelief. Naturally the first thing he thought to say was "Are you sure?" I told him I had it confirmed by a doctor, but no one else knew. "You know you are the father," I said. He didn't try to deny it. We had been true to each other for most of our lives and other than that one mad moment, we hadn't been intimate. All it took was one time. How many times have I heard that?

I thought he might think I was trying to trap him, but believe me that was the last thought in my mind. I had more to worry about than that. I asked him what he was going to do, but he couldn't answer. I am sure he had all sorts of thoughts going through his mind but I needed help, I needed advice, and I needed his support at the very least. He said this was unexpected and it was difficult for him to think, but he told me he would not marry me. He didn't love me and the marriage would not work. He said he would support me in any other way he could. I knew I could depend on him, but I had hoped that he might realize he loved me and come back to me. He was right; the marriage wouldn't have worked under the circumstances. I knew he would get off a lot lighter than I would. I would bear the stigma of an illegitimate birth. Folks would know he was the father, but it wouldn't have the same stigma tied to him. Sad but true, the woman always paid. His mind was set. I saw no point in discussing it any further, not now anyway. I knew my dad would go off the deep end and my mother would be broken hearted. What a predicament. Just as I did when he broke it off with me, I could only turn away."

I was in a trance listening to this story. It had to be Ian. It was too much of a coincidence. Telling the story upset June. She was visibly shaken and the tears wouldn't stop. I asked if she wanted to continue. She just had to get this story out. Now seemed to be the right time for her. She continued.

"There was nothing else I could do. I had to tell my family and take whatever was coming. My parents' reaction surprised me. Yes, they were disappointed, but they saw what I had gone through since the breakup and now this. They couldn't put any more on my shoulders. They assured me they would be there to support me. Their loving reaction was too much for me. I broke down hysterically but after a few hugs, I was so relieved it was over for now. The thought of having to go to a home for the unwed terrified me. That wouldn't happen.

When B.J.'s family was told of the situation, they were also supportive. Needless to say they, and most everyone they knew were disappointed in B.J. that he wasn't going to marry me. Most thought we could work something out, get married and everything would be okay. His parents were very upset, but in the end they and the others came to realize that marriage was not a solution. I continued on at work because I needed the money more than ever, but I had to resign before the pregnancy showed. As you well know, married pregnant women were seriously discouraged from working when their condition became obvious. It would be unthinkable for an unmarried person to continue working.

I was several months into the pregnancy when B.J. told me that he had broken up with his new girlfriend. I was shocked and happy at the same time to hear the news. I wondered if he had come to his senses about me and the coming baby. That wasn't the way it was. He was shown the door by the girlfriend.

I was not upset to see how it affected him. Now he would know what he had done to me. According to him, his new girlfriend couldn't cope with the thought of him fathering a child somewhere, and not being married to the mother, even though he had committed to supporting the child. I was not interested in marrying him now under these circumstances, or any circumstances for that matter. I was still hurting deeply."

I knew this had to be the same story. After all these years, I was finally finding out what happened to Ian and his girlfriend. No wonder I felt a closeness to June. We both loved Ian, but he had let us down. I continued listening, now more intently, if that was possible. It was riveting.

I asked June why she called him B.J., knowing it was a nickname for something. She said, "Ian (which means John) was his name, but when they were children, there was another little Ian on the street, whom they called L.J. for Little John. Ian, being the older of the two and bigger, got the nickname B.J." That confirmed it. I couldn't believe it, although I wondered why his friends hadn't used the nickname when they were on the train ride. I supposed it was because as people grow up, they don't like to be known by childhood nicknames. Obviously June had a special attachment to the nickname.

We kept refilling our coffee and tea while June continued on. With all the liquids we consumed, I sensed we might spend the night in the bathroom.

"B.J. was true to his word and was there for me and little Morag. My hopes and dreams were put on hold indefinitely until little Morag had grown up a bit, but I couldn't complain because of the enormous support I had. I was still madly in love with him, but had put the thought of marriage out of my mind, contenting myself with the part he was playing in our lives.

Eventually we began to date again to the delight of both parents. At first it was just a night out to the pictures more or less as a break for me, but the romance blossomed. I had always carried the torch for him. I was totally caught off guard the night he asked me if I would reconsider marrying him. This was the day I had dreamed of all my life, but it was dimmed by what had gone on in the past. I knew I still loved him, but what if he found someone else again after we were married? What if his old girlfriend came back into the picture? I couldn't go through that again. I didn't rush into the decision, but in the end I accepted his proposal. He seemed to be overjoyed. I believed he had forgotten his ex-girlfriend. He was such a good father to Morag. He adored his little girl. I convinced myself that he loved me, not because he felt obligated to marry me now. We could just as easily have continued on the way we were, each sharing the responsibility for raising Morag.

Morag was just over three years old when I finally said "I do". B.J. had finished his apprenticeship as an electrician. I knew he could provide for our little family. We had a simple civil ceremony with only close family and a few friends. Not the kind of wedding I dreamed about, but it was nice. Little Morag didn't know what all the hoopla was about, but she was quite proud to be in her party dress. Dinner was held at a local upscale restaurant, after which we left for a short honeymoon, Morag being cared for by the grandparents.

The honeymoon was all too short but it was memorable. I was so much in love with this man, and believed he loved me. We were relaxed as we shared a bottle of champagne. As we consummated our marriage, there was no doubt in my mind that he loved me. I knew this was just the beginning of a beautiful relationship, one that had only been sidetracked momentarily. I was so happy."

I am not sure I wanted to hear these details, but June needed to tell her story. I remembered the many times I envisioned myself married to Ian, knowing how he made me feel when we kissed. I just knew our love would have reached unimaginable heights. I remember how many times we almost crossed the line, how I felt, how he felt, but more so now than ever, I am glad we didn't give in.

"We settled nicely into a small flat just up the street from our parents, a bonus, at least as far as baby-sitting was concerned. Eventually we relocated to a small town in England. B.J. started up his own business. It was not a large operation, but it afforded us the luxury of me staying at home with Morag. At the same time I helped out running the business. He encouraged me to finish my education. I am forever grateful for that, although at the time I thought it might be a waste of time. I never had any intention of working outside the home. Yes, things were turning around, life was good and we were very happy. I was content and he seemed to be too.

In the beginning I had no complaints at all about my new life with my new husband. We had the odd little spat, but then what couple didn't? Two more children joined our family, both boys. B.J. was very proud of them. With Morag, who was the apple of her dad's eye, and now two lovely sons, what more could we want? Our family was complete. Life was good. I continued to stay home with the children during the day, and B.J. stayed with them at night, while I tried to catch up on my education.

As the years rolled by and the children started building their own little lives with friends, school and after school activities, I began to notice a change in B.J. Perhaps I was too busy looking after the family and business, to notice any changes. By now we had moved into a larger house to accommodate our growing family. Instead of coming home after his day's work was done, he began to stop off at the local pub. That didn't bother me because he wasn't a drinker, other than a few beers here and there or a social drink with company.

As time went on, he spent more time at the pub and stayed there until it closed. Workers called me on the telephone to sign out and pick up any emergency jobs that might have come in. I was already responsible for running the office, accounts receivable, payable, payroll, route sheets and so on. I didn't have the same responsibilities with the children now so the extra work wasn't a drain, but I resented being left while he was out drinking or whatever.

I was involved in the cubs, brownies and later on, scouts and guides, school and Sunday school, but B.J. never seemed to be interested. When it was award time, he made an effort but more and more it was begrudgingly, usually leading to an argument. I couldn't understand it because there was no doubt he loved the children, but it was apparent he loved the pub, the drinking and his friends more.

His normally good nature and sense of fair play began to show bouts of nastiness, even anger and meanness. At first I thought it was pressures from keeping the men working, making sure the work was done properly and just generally being concerned about his company. I tried not to over react but when I did, I was sorry I opened my mouth. Both his father and mother were alcoholics and the children didn't have very happy lives. His mother eventually killed his father in a drunken rage. They had both been drinking heavily. He was so aggressive and ugly; she was a more happy drinker. His continued ugliness finally got the best of her. She hit him on the head with a cast iron frying pan. She didn't mean to kill him, but she did.

This was a terrible time for the entire family. His mother went on trial. It was such an embarrassment to all when the real story of their lives came out. Because of the circumstances and the fact she didn't mean to kill him, she got a reduced sentence. Sadly she died in prison, her liver destroyed by years of abuse. B.J.'s siblings were so traumatized by their lives and the ultimate deaths of their parents, that it took them a long time to get their lives back on track. They finally overcame that and went on to have productive lives. None of them would even take a glass of wine. B.J. hadn't been a big drinker, but he appeared to be following in his parent's footsteps. I could never understand why he would do the same thing, knowing how the alcoholism had ruined all of their lives.

I kept hoping things would turn around. I tried to be patient but I noticed other changes in him. He didn't want to eat, he lost interest in his model railroad, which was his pride and joy, he wasn't interested in me or the children. He didn't seem to have any motivation to work; he couldn't remember things and his attitude became more and more belligerent. When he passed out one night I saw what I thought were needle marks. My heart almost stopped. It was one thing to drink too much but drugs? That was an entirely different matter. What could I do, how could I get him the help he so desperately needed?

It was actually better for everyone all around if he did stay away from the office. He was not all that pleasant to customers either. When he was not around, the workers were only too happy to deal with me. Many times, I felt like packing it in, but we needed the money. If I didn't take control, there would have been nothing left. The drinking and drugs took a toll on the children too as they grew. They could never please him. Their reports from school never got a word of praise. If they weren't up to his standards, they soon heard about it. I saw that the children kept out of his way more and more.

Even though his behaviour changed rapidly with his drinking and drugs, there were times when he tried to stop. He wasn't up to doing much work, but he did try to stay away from the pub and his friends. When he was sober, we got along alright. Sometimes we went to a movie, visited with friends, or went shopping, but the bad times were gaining on the good times all too rapidly. He couldn't stay sober for long and it was back to square one again. This happened several times, but the sober times in between got less and less. When he went back to his old ways, he was worse than before.

During the sober times we still had some reasonably good times, but the bouts got progressively worse. He became more and more argumentative, belligerent and obnoxious. More and more he became unpleasant to be around. He was so angry all the time.

Our social life was not all that active, but we occasionally attended dances, the odd house or family party and some other obligatory functions. I began to hate the thought of attending anything with him. They always started out well but before long, he was his usual loud obnoxious self, turning everyone away from him. I got increasingly embarrassed but if I tried to say anything, cautioning him about his health, the business or anything, it turned into an argument. I soon learned that there was little I could do about it.

He tried A.A. at one point, but said it wasn't for him. He managed to stop drinking on his own several times, but each time he eventually went back to the same old pattern, often ending up worse than before. There were so many times when I could have happily hit him over the head with a cast iron frying pan, too many to tell on this trip. One example was when we attended an anniversary party for a couple we knew through the business. As with all the functions, it started out well. I, the eternal optimist, hoped that maybe this night would be different. I bought a new outfit for the occasion, in B.J.'s favourite colour, blue. I was normally thin but with all the stress and worry, I got thinner. I splurged on a new hairdo and had my nails done too. When we arrived at the party held in a party room of the building where the couple lived, B.J. headed for the bar, leaving me to face a lot of people I didn't know. Here we go again, I thought, but he returned right away with a lemonade for me and a juice (with no alcohol in it) for himself. I crossed my fingers.

I had been down this road all too many times. I should have been aware of what the outcome might be, but I still loved him and hoped that one day, he would get the help he desperately needed. As we began to circulate at the party, we got separated. I wasn't particularly worried, I could always see him, and he was never at the bar. However, as the evening wore on, I could tell he was getting his liquor somewhere. The old familiar patterns began to emerge. He was acting loud, obnoxious, argumentative and crude. About this time the food was served. I filled two plates, as I always did, putting his favourites on his plate. I piled it high with sardines, tomatoes, salad, salami and so on. I took the plate over to B.J. and we both sat down to eat. I thought getting food into him might soak up some of the booze. Wrong, I might as well have saved myself the bother. He took a couple of bites then off he went.

Another disastrous evening was about to take place. I knew I had to get him out of there. I knew I had to do it in such a way that would not get him riled up. He was surprisingly cooperative and said he would go if I got the coats. I asked him for the keys of the car but he shrugged me off. Returning a few minutes later with the coats, I approached him again. "Okay, just a minute," he said. This went on for some time. Some of the other guests were trying to help me, but he would go when he was ready, and not a minute before it. I finally told him that if he didn't leave then, I was going home by myself. He could make his own way home. I didn't want to leave him there because he was an annoyance to the other guests. Someone tapped me on the shoulder. I turned around to talk to the other guest who wanted to say goodnight to us. We got engrossed in a conversation and by the time I was ready to tackle B.J. again, he was gone.

I looked everywhere, inside and outside. He was nowhere to be found. No one knew where he had gone. I was totally ticked off by now. I went out to the parking lot to see if he had gone to the car to wait for me. When I got there, the car was gone. I knew he had left without me and in an intoxicated state that could put him into jail. How was I going to get home, and what damage was he going to do in the meantime? Did that even bother him? I had convinced myself by now that what happened to him was his own fault, but I couldn't bear the thought of some innocent unsuspecting person getting injured. What could I do? I went back to the party and spoke to the daughter of the couple the party was for, who offered to take me home.

When I got home I fully expected to see the car in the driveway. It was nowhere to be found. I thanked Julie for the ride and went inside. B.J. was not there either. He arrived in the morning, he never said where he had been and to this day, I do not know where he spent the night. I was just thankful that he hadn't hurt anyone. What bugged me most about all of this was, that if the roles were reversed and I was the alcoholic, there is no way he would have allowed it to go on. If I didn’t get help he would have thrown me out. He wouldn’t be the one to leave. He would have packed my bags and shoved me out the door.

I knew that and should have done the same thing but I was powerless and I don't know why

Over the years that type of situation was replayed many times, too many to tell now. It was always more of the same. Visiting friends for the weekend, he would go out when they were all in bed, and not return until the next day. I was so embarrassed that I tried to keep everything quiet. Never once did he say where he had been. Never once in his life did he apologize, not even at the time of his death.

Once again I vowed that was it but once again, I got over it and life went on in pretty much the same way. Even though B.J. had met a new girlfriend years before when he was dating me, somehow I never thought these absences were because of another woman. His affair was with alcohol.

The boys were now in high school, and his drinking had a terrible adverse effect on them. Poor little Morag seemed to be the target of most of his anger. No one that she brought to the house was ever treated nicely. He ridiculed them all until she never brought anyone home, causing me more anguish because I preferred to see who our children's friends were. Morag married too young and had a couple of children far too early in life, but thank goodness, all of them seemed to be happy. They didn't have much of life's so called luxuries but her husband was a hard worker, holding down a couple of jobs, enabling Morag to stay home with their children. They had a nice little flat, which she kept spotless and between me and the other set of parents, they managed alright. There was genuine love between them. June knew they would survive. There was one rule in that family though, not a drop to drink was ever allowed into the house, ever. Morag's husband's parents were alcoholics too, and he knew only too well the havoc it had wreaked upon his and Morag's families.

The boys, being much stronger, seemed to handle their father's constant badgering better. Most of the time they just ignored him and went to their rooms. It was a miracle that they turned out as well as they did, never having received any praise from their father.

I was caught in the middle. I tried my best to make up for the loss of a father, but I had my own problems. There wasn't anyone I could count on to help me or confide in. That wasn't totally true, I had a wonderful family and many friends. I just couldn't bring myself to admit what I put up with. No one who has never lived through this situation can ever imagine what it's like, and the long lasting damage that it does. The memories of all the terrible things and time wasted never go away. Yes, you can pick up and go on but they are always with you.

The oldest boy, who was the brain in the family, finished his education and went on to university, which was no easy task, considering that money was tight. He studied long and hard, worked to pay for his tuition and eventually became a lawyer. He never got much encouragement from his father either. Even in his continuous drunken stupor, I thought he could at least be proud of our son's accomplishments. The youngest son also went to university and got his teaching degree. They were determined boys and got as much encouragement from me as I could possibly give.

I suffered from guilt because of the effect B.J.'s drinking had on the family. I don't know why I never took a stand. I blamed myself. Both boys always seemed to want the approval of their dad, even after they left home and started their careers. It was sad, but they were strong and rose above all the adversity. I believed that deep down their father loved them and was proud of them. He could just never show it. Perhaps it was because he was raised in a less than loving atmosphere himself, with alcoholic parents. He found it extremely difficult to show any affection, even when he was not drinking. When he was drunk, the coldness turned into hardness, anger and bullying.

B.J. eventually lost interest in everything. He would not take care of his personal hygiene. He had to be told to take baths, change his clothes and even to shave. He gave up on everything but drinking. This once attractive and intelligent man was a mess. I had to run the business, get the men out to work, look after the family and the bills. Often when B.J. did go on the job, he made such a mess of things that the employees and I were happier when he stayed away. He did nothing around the house either to help out. I left the house clean in the morning but by the time I got back at night, he was well on his way to being smashed. Bottles and ashes littered the table and floor. I hated it when he cooked for himself because the grease was splattered all over the stove. Naturally, he never cleaned it up. I purchased an automatic shutoff kettle because he had burned out so many of the regular type. I was afraid the house would burn down. That was all I needed.

He also managed to smash up a couple of cars along the way. Eventually the insurance company would not cover him. That didn't deter him though; he took the vehicle out anyway. He didn’t listen to anyone and he just didn’t care. Thankfully it was only to the store for booze. At least he wasn't on the main roads. He could easily have walked to the store, but it was typical of his bullying, belligerent tactics, that he just had to show he wasn't taking any restrictions from anyone. That was his attitude about everything.

At that time the employees were so faithful to me. They did the best they could but working for B.J., who always managed to stick his nose in somewhere, became too much for them. One by one they went on to other jobs. The work also stopped coming in and eventually we lost the business. I kept my hand in office work by getting a job in the field. It helped greatly.

During those years I had my own battles with weight and self-esteem. I was never very big but what weight I had, just seemed to fall off me. I looked haggard. It was a very difficult time in my life, but I managed to cope and got through it. I never let anyone down and always carried the load."

I was totally engrossed with this story and wondered how he could afford to get drunk all the time. I asked June the question.

"The answer is easy, when an alcoholic wants to get a drink, they always manage to find a way. In B.J.'s case, he was on disability and the cheque was sent to him. He got first crack at it. I tried to get that changed, but was not successful. Sometimes he gave me some of the money, if I was there when the cheque arrived. Otherwise, I was out of luck. He was an avid model railway collector. He had a lot of valuable trains, which gradually disappeared, unbeknownst to me. I never looked over his collection, but eventually it was hard not to notice a lot of the trains were missing. Somehow an alcoholic will get the money to drink. I on the other hand, worked very hard to keep our heads above water, but all I got for it was grief. An alcoholic is the same as a drug user, they don't care where they get the money or whether it causes family to lose everything, they think only of their addiction and themselves.

In the beginning, I gave him credit for the fact that money wise we never seemed to suffer, even with his heavy drinking. Eventually we lost the business, our cars, friends and much more, all because of the alcoholism. I was the one who had to make ends meet with the little I got. Although we had enough to live on, there was an awful lot of money spent on booze. We could have been so much better off. I didn't mind that so much, if only we could have had a happier marriage.

He began to put the alcohol on credit, which opened my eyes as to just how much was being spent. I tried to get the store to refuse him but it wasn't their responsibility and besides, he would just find another store. Our marriage was a sham. Most of our family and friends knew by then about his problem with alcohol, but no one outside of the home knew the extent of it or the damage it was doing. Oftentimes when someone dropped in to visit he was pleasant. He wouldn't drink much when they were there. He could be pleasingly personable. His day started out with a beer after his morning coffee, and from then on it was one after the other. If he had stayed with the beer, it might not have been so bad, but in the evening, his coffees were laced with alcohol. With what little he ate, and the beer he drank before, it didn't take much for him to become verbally abusive and ugly."

June now realized this confession was like reliving her life. She had never stopped to think of all the terrible things he had done to her over the years. Yes, she knew he could be downright ugly but next day he wouldn't be so bad and so she continued on. Was there ever a time when he cared for her? Did he ever do anything to help her? Did he ever let her have her way in anything? She realized she was too blinded by love to notice little things along the way. She would do just about anything to keep him happy and maintain peace in the house. As she told her story, I told her that it was probably just as well she didn't have a flash back like this before. She might have realized what a terrible life she had and moved out. Or would she?

"I was sure he loved his children and maybe even me in his own way, but he never showed it. He adored his grandchildren and they him and he was a good grandfather, except when he had a few extra drinks. It would start out as fun but when he got tired of it, kids being what they are, they wanted him to carry on. That got him mad and the drink didn't help. The parents took the children home, remembering all too well what was next in store.

Being married to an alcoholic is pretty much like being married to a wife beater. It's abuse, although it may not be physical, and B.J. was never physical. While I was going through it, it didn't seem as bad. However, as I look back on my life with him, I cannot understand why I took it. He was verbally abusive and accused me of everything from having affairs to stealing money from him. Some of the names he called me are unprintable. He goaded me into arguments and often in the beginning I fell into the trap, but as the years went by and the children grew up, I just took it and didn't respond. He would come back at me with "what, don't you have any opinions?" "Don't you have the guts?" Sometimes it was too much and I gave him an answer, only to regret it because he went on and on and on.

In the latter years, I felt more and more stressed by all of this. My nerves were frayed. Little things bothered me more and the tears came ever so easily. I couldn't tell anyone because they would suggest I leave him. Our children couldn't understand why I took the abuse, and why I stayed with him. They begged me to move in with them or at least get an apartment. I was in a difficult position. I couldn't understand why I didn't leave him, so why should anyone else?

I hardly got a night's rest with him tossing and turning, pushing me over until I fell out of the bed on many occasions. I got up and went to the other side but he started the procedure again, until I once again slept on the couch. He then came out to the couch and sat on me, forcing me off the couch. How many times I told him the next day that there was nothing I could do about his drinking, and if he wanted to drink himself to death, that was his prerogative. All I asked was that he leave me alone. Why was that so hard for him to do? I had to get control, but how? I also felt guilty about the thoughts in my mind. That only added to my sadness. Many times I felt so alone, even with the good friends I had.

I had another sleepless night and at that time I decided that I had to confront him again because of what was happening to me. I had just fallen asleep when he came to bed. Once again his restlessness had awakened me. It was alright for him because he slept long into the morning hours, and had several naps during the day, but I had to get up and go to work. Every morning I told myself that this was the day when I would face him with the state of the marriage, but somehow I carried on. It was wearing me down. I knew in my heart I had to do something, now. I didn't want to spend the rest of my life like that, but I also knew he would not be able to live on what money he had, considering how much was being spent on booze. I knew that was not my problem, but if anything happened to him after I left I would not be able to forgive myself. I felt trapped.

During the days B.J. was not too bad, but I always felt like I was walking on eggshells. I preferred to do that, rather than cause a scene but as soon as night-time came, it was the same old story. I went to bed and he went to the couch because the night before I had to get up and go to the couch again. I finally drifted off to sleep but was suddenly awakened by a terrific crashing sound from the living room. When I got up to investigate, B.J. was lying on his back, arms and legs stretched out, a candy dish from the small table lying on the rug, with candies everywhere. His coffee had spilled on the table, and of course the eternal bottle of beer capsized and sizzling through the glass on the table to the rug. It was a mess. I thought he must have tripped over the table. When I moved towards him, I could see his eyes were closed but when I said, "This is quite a sight," he opened his eyes and started to laugh. I knew he wasn't hurt so I went back to the bedroom. I felt like kicking him where it would hurt.

Shortly after, not hearing any noise, I went in to check on him again, but by this time he had somehow managed to get himself back up on the couch. I suggested that maybe he should do something about his drinking. He came back at me with his usual retort, "why don't you do something about your ugly face?" I knew not to answer.

I left the room again, but he followed and started his rambling. I knew he would leave the room if I ignored him, so I kept quiet. How much more could I take of this and why was I taking it? Didn't he realize what he was doing to himself and to me? My dream was that one day he would realize all the hurt and pain he had caused. Then he would take me in his arms, apologize, and ask for my help to get him back on track again. I would have gladly done that, in the beginning anyway, but it never happened. After years of this type of abuse, it would have been too little too late. I doubted anything he might do, or how he might change would make any difference in my feelings for him. Never once in our entire married life, did he apologize. Why should he, I thought? He never believed he did anything wrong. If I said I could smell the liquor as soon as I came in the door, his retort was "I can smell your perfume." How can you reason with someone like that?

I knew I had to do something. He was not only killing himself, but he was slowly killing me as well. Depression was never something I felt, or so I thought, but I didn't feel right. Was this just the front I always put on things, keeping it all in, playing the well organized and happy person? There were occasions when I did confront him, but it never made any difference, and more and more he forgot what I had said to him.

This time it was different. I couldn't concentrate on anything and my weight was dropping which only added to my distress. On my annual physical to the doctor, I actually broke down, which surprised both the doctor and myself, because I always joked about everything. The doctor was so kind. He gave me a prescription for a tonic that might build me up. He offered sleeping pills but I wouldn't take them, even if it meant a good night's sleep. What would happen if I went into a deep sleep and he set the house on fire or something?

Two weeks passed but I was no better off. I was beginning to feel I was depressed. Crying came so easily to me now and yet to the outside world, I was the picture of happiness. Discussing this situation with anyone was not an option, because they all told me the same thing "leave him and get some peace and quiet." For whatever reason, I could not do that. I didn't even know why I had put up with this abuse over the years. Why hadn't I left him long ago?

One morning I arose, checked the scale, and was ready to call it quits. I knew I had to do something. This time I would do it. I just couldn't allow myself to be dragged down any longer. After all the wasted money and getting deeper and deeper in debt, after all the sleepless nights, the tormenting, and me just ignoring it and going on the next day, it was time to call it quits. I knew it, but would I have the strength?

We had yet another dreadful evening where he tried to get me involved in an argument. Even though I would dearly have loved to argue back, what was the point? He didn't know what he was saying and wouldn't remember the next day anyway. For the most part I tried to keep quiet, but it was difficult. He went into the bathroom. I heard a thud. I opened the door and there he was lying on the floor absolutely paralytic, trying to get up and falling back down. When I offered to help, he told me to get out of there and pushed me away. What kind of constitution did this man have? He finally managed to get himself up and staggered into the bedroom.

Another night he came into the bedroom where I was watching my favourite weekly TV show. I didn't watch much television as I thought it was mostly nonsense. I had a few favourites, and liked peace and quiet to watch them. When he was ready for bed, I turned off the TV and went into the living room, where I would continue watching TV or read until he fell asleep. Had I gone to bed sooner, it would have been another sleepless night. I would rather wait. Just as I turned on my favourite show on the living room TV he staggered into the room, totally drunk. He was falling all over the place, and in his underwear, even though the front door was open. He didn't care about himself, or anyone else for that matter. He fell down on the chair, and started on about the show I was watching, saying it was garbage and on and on. I got up and went into the bedroom again.

A few minutes later he came back into the bedroom. This procedure went on a few times, all the while he was calling me every name in the book from hypocrite, holier, thou, evil person, and prostitute to name a few. Finally he went to bed and I went back to my TV. A few minutes later I heard a crash. It was the bedroom door being slammed so I knew I would be sleeping on the couch again.

When it came time to go to bed, I went to the bedroom to get a pillow. B.J. was still tossing and turning, but he didn't get up. I made up the couch and finally fell asleep.

XXXI

I was awakened from my sleep by a noisy bang. All the lights were out, so it was difficult to see anything. Coming out of a sleep, I didn't know where the sound came from but I got up, and moved out of the living room into the kitchen to turn on a light. Afterwards I wondered why I hadn't just turned on a table lamp. As I was moving towards the light, I stumbled over something on the floor. I managed to get my balance and reached over to turn on the light. B.J. was flat out on the floor. Even though I was used to this, I couldn't believe my eyes. At first I thought this was just one more time his legs had buckled under him. He just lay there, not moving. How many times had I seen this performance? Although I could have cheerfully smashed him, pity and reason always took over. There was no response from him when I tried to talk to him, although he was breathing. I tried shaking him to no avail. I called the emergency number.

While I waited for the ambulance, I tried to get him to wake up. He didn't need resuscitation because he was breathing. Blood was coming from a nasty cut on his head, which must have happened when he hit the edge of the counter as he fell over. The ambulance arrived and while the paramedics worked with him, I got dressed to go with him to the hospital. When the paramedics got him onto the stretcher and hooked him up to some kind of intravenous, they took off for the nearest hospital. I followed in my car. I waited downstairs while they worked on him, until a nurse told me I could see him in the Intensive Care Unit. I was not prepared for what I saw.

He was hooked up to all kinds of machines with tubes sticking out of him everywhere. An oxygen mask covered his mouth. Even though this brought back many terrible memories of times when I "hated" him for what he put me through, I could only feel pity for him. He was a helpless man who wasted most of his life and almost destroyed others in the process. I knew he wasn't going to make it this time. I held his hand and talked to him, but there was not much of a response. I kept talking to him anyway. At one point it sounded like he said "never again". That was true, because he would never again get the opportunity to fall down on that promise. How many times over the years had he told me that, only to fall off the wagon one more time? What did that all matter now?

I stayed there as long as I could until the nurse finally suggested I go home, call someone or just go for a coffee. Morning light was coming in the windows. I knew it was time to call the children. I telephoned our oldest who in turn called the others. Within a short time they were all at the hospital.

Over the next day or two we all took turns being with B.J. Doctors never gave a name to what his problem was, just that his system had completely broken down through all the alcohol abuse and smoking over a very long period of time. Doctors were actually surprised he had managed to live as long as he did. We were all at his bedside when he died. He had remained comfortable, but never regained consciousness. Strong memories of years of verbal abuse at his hands were very clear in our minds, but we were genuinely upset at his death, probably more so because of all the wasted years. The children had come to terms with their feelings about him long ago, and the abuse they had suffered through his drinking. I am sure that helped them now. While they could never live with him again, and they hated what he did to me, they did love him and were sad at his passing.

Over the years the children had gone their own way and had done very well, in spite of his treatment. Family occasions were always disasters that the children could never tolerate. More often than not, these affairs ended up with his usual drunken stupors, obnoxious and loud rantings and embarrassments. This always made the children leave early, although they didn't like leaving me to face the music. Oh how many times they told me to leave him, and that I didn't have to put up with that kind of life. I deserved better and so on but I could never do it. I didn't know why because the love had long gone out of the marriage, along with any respect we once had for each other. Most of the time I didn't even like him, but I didn't think he could make it on his own, so I stayed with him. I knew I wasn't responsible but I could never bring myself to leaving him, although many times I came close. Now he was gone. I felt badly over the wasted years when it could have been so different, but I could not hate him."

I asked June why she never left him. She thought for a moment but could not come up with an answer. She just didn't know.

"Maybe I believed that one day he would see what he had done and was doing to me, our family and marriage. Then he would magically become a new person or the person I once knew, and we would live happily ever after. The fairy tale never happened and the nightmare never ended. Maybe I was as sick as he was. Some people believe that wives, husbands and even families of alcoholics become sick too, although not in the same way. I just kept going and hoping. I didn't think I could do much else. I can see, reliving this with you, how stupid I have been, and how much time I wasted of my own life in such an unhappy situation. It was a double shame because he could be funny and pleasant at times, but once the drink kicked in, he became an ugly loud mouthed bully and not very loveable.

As they say, he was a cheap drunk, and became totally obnoxious. I always thought or hoped things would get better, maybe I always remembered when things were not quite as bad, maybe deep down I still loved him, although I surely didn't like him. Maybe it was my keen sense of duty, and the commitment to the vows I had made. Whatever it was, it was over and I was determined that for whatever time I had left, I was going to enjoy it. It wasn't that I didn't enjoy life, I had a terrific family and great friends, but times with B.J. were not pleasurable. Everyone told me I had an amazing capacity to rise above it by learning to live with it. I saw it as just getting on with it. Experience had taught me that you never realize how bad things are when you are living through them on a daily basis, but when you relive the times, you see clearly how much precious time had been wasted."

As she told her story to me, she heaved a huge sigh of relief, having this load finally lifted from her shoulders. She said the saddest thing of all was the fact that in the beginning, even before they were married, B.J. was so good to her and Morag, helping her through some rough times. After they started dating and got married, life was good. For many years, they had what she thought was a happy marriage. How could it all go so wrong? What would cause him to give up all thought of his wife, family and even himself to live as he did, slowly killing himself.

No matter how many times she asked herself those questions, she never got the answer. It was just so sad. She wished he could have got the help he so desperately needed. If only he knew how much people cared for him. If only he could have realized that all she wanted was for him to love her and the family, love them by being kinder, considering their needs, and sharing himself with them. It was such a waste, but she knew she was not the only one living through those circumstances. Sad to say, that kind of life is not all that uncommon.

When she went to Al-anon, she met many others who were going through the same thing. Wives, husbands, and children all had different versions of the same basic story. It has been said that living with an alcoholic is like living with a physical abuser, except that it is mental and not physical. She looked at women who had been beaten and wondered why they never left. She was no different. There were some at the A.A. meetings who suffered both physical and mental abuse. June was thankful he wasn't physically abusive. The mental and verbal abuses were bad enough. Would she have left if it were physical? That didn't seem likely under the circumstances.

Alcoholism is such a drain on so many fronts. He was like Alistair's wife in many ways. He never hit rock bottom, something the experts say needs to happen before they can start the road back. Not everyone makes it back, even from the bottom but many do once they hit the skids. B.J. never ran out of money, was never thrown out of the house with nowhere to live and always managed to survive. There was no real threat to him."

I remembered the many times thoughts of Ian crossed my mind, wondering how he was, what would life have been like for the two of us, even though I loved Bob dearly. He was such a wonderful husband. I felt guilty when I let my mind drift back. I knew people often thought back to times past, wondering about old friends, romances and so on. It didn't mean that they didn't love the partner they were sharing their life with, it was just a sort of a "what if". Bob was everything and more to me. Would it have been different for Ian if I had married him? I knew the answer to that was "no", because he would still have become an alcoholic. That wasn't June or anyone else's fault, it was Ian's. A little saying came to my mind that I had heard somewhere. The author was unknown. The saying goes like this: "There were two tears floating down the river, one was shed by the girl who lost him and the other was shed by the girl who got him." How very true and how very sad that saying is.

June and I held each other tightly. She was happy to finally have someone to listen to her story and unburden herself. To be sure, I didn't hear the whole story, but all that was missing were individual incidents and more of the same. The picture she painted was very plain and painful. I wondered how she would have reacted had she known that I was the other girl. I knew then and there I would never tell her about that. She had suffered so much in her life with Ian. Even though it was not my fault, it might have upset June, especially knowing that I had a wonderful married life after dropping Ian. If I had married him, she might have had a better life without him or with someone else. No one would ever know the answer to that one.

XXXII

After making the decision not to tell June, I also decided not to tell our children about Bob's homosexuality. Was I wrong to keep that from them? Was I afraid they would be shocked, or hate their father or hate me for not telling them before he died? I didn't believe that. I felt sure they would understand. I didn't want to taint any memory they had of their dad who was wonderful to them. The fact that I couldn't or wouldn't tell family or friends brought home just how unkindly homosexuals are looked upon. I didn't think anyone should be pressured into accepting another's beliefs or lifestyles. Everyone is entitled to live their lives as they want. It was not up to anyone to push their views on another. Just because someone is different is no reason to hate. In fact, there is no reason whatsoever to hate. Why couldn't people just accept each other? They didn't have to like them. They didn't have to live with them. Why is it so hard for people to accept others' differences? How sad it all was. When Lisa and Daniel were younger and they said they hated someone, Bob and I always discouraged them from using such a strong word. We told them "you may dislike someone and that's okay, but never ever hate anyone for any reason.”

I know that one day the answer will be clear to all of us. Until then it was not up to me or anyone else for that matter to judge. After all, if Bob with his upbringing and beliefs, could be homosexual, it had to be more than choice. There is absolutely no way he would have chosen that life. He was such an amazing husband and father. We were all still trying to deal with the fact he was no longer with us. I felt, at least for the time being, it would not change anything or help anyone if I told the children or anyone else for that matter. He was the best, he was never unfaithful, and he suffered so much inner turmoil while trying to keep it from friends and family alike. Again I thought, "being gay didn't define him." My decision was made. Was I wrong? I am sure many think I was. The only person who suffered was Bob himself, having to keep that secret all of his life. He was gone now. Let him rest in peace. Who knows, maybe down the road I might tell them but then again, I might not.

I changed my mind and didn't take the extended trip to Scotland after the cruise. Most of my family had relocated to Canada and Australia years ago, and my best friend Moira had died. Was the reason I wanted to go to Scotland, just an excuse to find out what had happened to Ian, his girlfriend and their baby? It wasn't a question that I cared for him. I loved Bob, but I was a little curious. Now I knew the story but I wished I didn't, because it was so terribly sad.

I had a lovely trip with my newly found friend, but I couldn't wait to get home to my family and friends who were so dear to me. I was anxious to sit in Bob's chair, to feel his big strong arms around me and tell him that I did have the best life. Oh yes, in life, we were devoted to each other. We appreciated everything we shared together, but this trip and the revelations, had made me see how truly lucky I was. My only regret, if there was one, was that even though Bob loved me and I had no reason to doubt that, his life was never fulfilled. That was sad. Would he have been happier in any other relationship? I didn't know the answer to that. Yes, his physical needs would have been met to his satisfaction but what about love, the love we had for each other? Our love was that and so much more. Surely, it wouldn't have been more than Bob and I had as a couple. True love is in the heart, it's what you give to each other and how you care for each other, and goes far beyond the bedroom.

I thought for a moment about the true meaning of love. One of the descriptions in the dictionary is "a deep, tender, ineffable feeling of affection and solicitude toward a person, such as that arising from kinship, recognition of attractive qualities, or a sense of underlying oneness. A person who is the object of deep or intense affection or attraction; beloved." There is no mention of sex as part of that love. Yes, it is or should be a culmination of love, but so often it is more lust than love and that is what can and does fade with time.

XXXIII

On the last day, June and I were both sad and happy. We kissed and cried before leaving in different directions. We were sad at leaving each other and the fact the cruise was over. From the beginning, we hit it off. We both felt an immediate bond, but didn't know why at the time. There were other reasons, but I think it was because we both loved the same person, who at some point in time loved each of us. We were looking forward to going home to our families with a renewed outlook on everything. I was taking the shuttle to the airport. Daniel, Lisa or Beth would meet me when I landed in Toronto. The trip had been just what I needed, and I was glad I hadn't let anyone talk me out of it.

As for June, she was heading home to her little family feeling much better about herself too, and although she was still devastated at the sudden loss of her second husband, she was glad that she had enjoyed some happiness in the end. The marriage wasn't long enough but the memories and happiness she shared with Alistair would help her to forget the years of pain with B.J. At the same time, she also ached for the years that B.J. wasted through his alcoholism. She took some of the blame for that although she knew she couldn't have changed him, but she could have at least changed her own life.

We exchanged addresses and telephone numbers with promises to keep in touch. Often on trips like this, travellers exchange information but never bother to keep in touch. This time it would be different. We both knew we would never lose touch because of the strange (or not so strange) bond we shared. Some day I might take that trip back home, and June might decide to visit me. Either way, we would welcome the visit. In the meantime, we were friends for life.

My flight home was much brighter than the one I took at the beginning of the trip. I could hardly wait to see the children again. After I cleared customs and walked through the gates the children were there to greet me. What a joyful sight. We ran towards each other and embraced as tears of joy appeared. They remarked right away how well I looked, and said they were glad they hadn't talked me out of the trip. I told them a little of the new friend I had met on the cruise and how we were inseparable, that she too was a widow. I didn't go into the details, only saying we had so much in common it was uncanny. It pleased them that I had a friend to share the trip.

As we drove back to the house, I knew in my heart that I would be alright from now on. Yes, I would miss Bob more than life itself, but I knew I could go on. I knew he would be there with me every step of the way. Beth was waiting in the house for us with the kettle on. She had picked up some groceries. I could see the mountain of mail on the counter top, but I wasn't going to be bothered with that tonight. Chatting over a cup of coffee, I told the kids and Beth about the wonderful time I had on the cruise. They couldn't get over how well I looked, much better than I looked when I left. "Okay, so you were right again," they laughed adding, "it was the right thing to do and we are glad you didn't listen to us this time." Beth brought me up to date on all the local gossip and activity.

After Beth and the children left, I headed to the family room and Bob's chair. I knew what true love was. It was not the hot, tingling, passionate moments that most couples share at first, which usually dulls over time and familiarity. After the fire cools, many find they don't have much in common. Real love is what Bob and I shared, kindness, consideration, genuine care for one another, closeness, intimacy, tenderness and a real desire to make each other happy. He was my beloved soul mate.

As I sat there, admiring the portrait above the fireplace, I knew Bob was with me and said aloud "I love you Bob. You were, you are and always will be the light of my life. I thank you from the bottom of my heart for the wonderful life we shared."

I said "good night" and headed upstairs, glad to be home. I picked up the little scripture card that was placed next to his picture on the night table. "Yes Bob," I said, "some day the pain will be gone and we will know the answers."

As I got ready for bed, I was confident that from now on I would be just fine. Sleep in peace my darling!

The End

Coming Soon...

Two Tears: The Next Chapter

by Rita Smith

It was hardly surprising that on the last day of our cruise, both June and I were sad. We said our good-byes, both of us thinking that our paths might never cross again. We hoped, and honestly believed, that neither one of us would let that happen. Unfortunately, we both knew that, as is all too often the case, we were very likely to get caught up in the routines of our every-day lives and allow the things we vow not to let happen, like lose touch with one another, will end up happening anyway. At the same time we were happy and full of excitement to be going home to our families and friends with renewed outlooks on life. We were full of wonder about what lay ahead for us.

My children, Lisa, Daniel, and even Beth were apprehensive when I told them I was going on a cruise alone. They tried their best to convince me it was a bad idea. In the end they saw I was determined and each of them knew what that meant; I'd go with or without their blessings.

So they backed off and, as it turned out, I was right. I understood their concerns, of course. They feared what might happen when I realized how alone I really was without my late husband, Bob and how far away I really was from family, friends, and everything familiar to me. I honestly can't say that I didn't wonder myself, but I had to get away from everything and everyone close to me. I had to collect my own thoughts and decide for myself what my new life would mean to me. I had to do it without any influence from anyone else.

I also had to come to terms with Bob's big revelation. I was still the only person who knew Bob was "gay". I still wasn't sure whether or not I would tell the children. And if I did, how would I tell them? In my own mind there would never be a perfect time, I knew it had to be done sometime. Maybe not. No matter what I decide the issue would be the most difficult thing I would ever face. It was something so personal, but it would touch all of us in some way. I had to find the right words, the right moment in time, and the right place. One thing I had settled in my mind was that I'd only tell my children, if I told anyone at all. I thought I kind of owed it to them. I felt no obligation to tell anyone else, siblings, friends, or associates. If the children decided afterwards to share with anyone else, that was their prerogative. I wouldn't argue with that, but I would rather not know their decision. I knew, or, rather, hoped that if I finally shared Bob's secret, it would relieve some of the stress I felt about it. But I still wasn't ready to share just yet. I didn't know when I might be ready or if I ever would be ready. Everyone thought so highly of Bob and I did not want to take the chance that anyone might think of him differently. No one within our circle held prejudices that I knew of. We might not all have agreed when it came to other people's choices, but we all believed that everyone has the right to live their own lives as they see fit. Even though

I knew that to be true, I still wasn't ready to share Bob's secret, not yet.

With this huge weight on my shoulders and knowing how alone I would be, I had doubts myself. When I decided to go on the cruise alone, up to and including starting out on the journey the anxiety ate away at me. The closer I got to leaving home, the more the doubts crept in, but I was determined and I couldn't let those who cared about me see any hesitation on my part. I had to show them that I knew what I was doing. Now that the cruise is over, I know I did the right thing. It was what I needed and at just the right time.

It was also what June needed. Meeting up with a complete stranger, June, and the two of us hitting it off right from the start could only be destiny and the feeling that our meeting was meant to happen convinced us both that we were doing the right thing, despite our families' fears. We were both on this cruise alone, June cruising for the first time ever and me travelling without Bob for the first time. An immediate and unusual bond formed between us and as we continued to enjoy each other's company, it became clear that this was a unique friendship that might well continue long after we went home. At the time we didn't know why. Was it because we were two widows travelling alone, both of us in need of some human connection? Or was it because we were both born in Scotland? Whatever the reason we were happy we met and meeting was the thing that made our trip so wonderful. As we sailed to the various ports of call and joined each other for meals, entertainment, and tours, we learned that we were more alike than different. June desperately needed a friend with whom she could share her doubts and problems, and I was happy to be the person she chose.

Over the course of the cruise June bared her soul to me, a little at a time during our heart-to-heart talks whenever we sat down together. I began noticing all the similarities between the both of us. And then there was Ian, the man with whom, as it turned out, we'd both had a relationship. My relationship with Ian was fleeting. June's relationship with the man, however, was far more serious, a true love affair. The revelation that June was in fact Ian's ex girlfriend put me in a very difficult position, one I really didn't want to be in. But what could I do now? What should I, do? I didn't know how she would react if she knew who I was. She might have blamed me for the situation she found herself in. I couldn't risk taking the chance that she might be destroyed all over again. She had been through so much already and besides, I had grown attached to her. I didn't want to lose her friendship now. My lack of complete honesty with her haunted me. She told me every detail of her life with Ian, but I didn't have the courage to admit who I was. I felt I had let her down at a most vulnerable time in her life. When I told her about my happy married life with Bob, I couldn't help asking myself if she discovered I was the one who caused Ian to break off their relationship? She might have blamed me for her disastrous marriage. I knew it wouldn't have mattered who Ian married, he would still have become an alcoholic. That was no one's fault but his own. But I couldn't take that chance or the risk of losing her as a friend, one with whom I'd become so close, and dependent upon even. I didn't know how to handle the situation. How we met and became such close friends almost instantly was unique. Were we drawn together by the similar qualities we saw in each other? Was Ian drawn to us because we we're so similar? There must be something we share in common that attracted both of us to him and he to us.

Ian and June grew up together. People assumed they would marry some day. Even so, he must have loved her at some point in time just as he loved me. June was totally unaware of my connection. In my heart I felt it was better to leave it that way. What would it accomplish now other than more pain for her. I couldn't do that to her. Besides we might never meet again and I wanted her to at least have happy memories of our time together.

Before heading off in different directions we hugged tightly, shed a few tears, and thanked each other for making the cruise so enjoyable. We promised to never lose contact and we meant it sincerely. Passing travellers make the same promise in earnest every day. We meant it. We will never lose touch. Our bond is too strong. Some day I'll take that trip home to Scotland. One day June will visit me in Canada. In the meantime we'll be friends forever.

I travelled by plane back to Canada. June travelled by train through England then by ferry to Scotland. Daniel, Lisa, Beth, maybe all three of them would be waiting for me at the airport when I arrived in Toronto. June was looking forward to seeing her family again too. We were both eager to get our lives into some sort of order, to decide what we would do, and see what our new lifestyles might entail.

Although June was still devastated by the sudden loss of her second husband, she was grateful she had enjoyed some happiness in the end. Alistair did everything he could to help June erase the bad memories of her life with Ian. Alistair restored her faith in humanity and showed her a new meaning of love, marriage, and life itself. June's marriage to Alistair wasn't long enough but the memories and happiness she shared with him would hopefully help her to forget the years of pain with Ian. At the same time, she still grieved over the all-too-many years Ian took from her through his alcoholism. June hadn't yet forgiven herself for her failure to stick up for herself and stand her ground. She blamed herself for being an enabler. Like many in similar circumstances she thought, mistakenly, that by not putting up any argument or trying to change his ways, she could avoid the inevitable arguments that his drinking and downright nastiness led to. It didn't happen that way. It never does. Perhaps if she had threatened him with leaving, it might have opened his eyes. She didn't think that was likely. But now she'd never know. My sincere hope for her was that she'd forgive herself and be relieved of her guilt. Ian's alcoholism was not her fault. Deep down June knows the truth of that, I'm sure. She couldn't have changed Ian no matter what. What she knew now was that she could have changed herself.

My flight home was much brighter than the one at the start of my adventure. I was a mess back then, not sure whether I was doing the right thing, but determined not to let my family know my true feelings. Now I could hardly wait to see the children again.

I cleared customs, walked through the gates, and there they were waiting to greet me. What a sight to come home to. I wondered for a moment if they could see from my demeanour how much my adventure changed my on the inside. We ran towards each other and embraced. Tears of joy and anxiety rolled down our cheeks. Daniel and Lisa remarked right away how well I looked, and said they were glad they hadn't talked me out of the trip. I told them a little bit about the new friend I met on the cruise, how we'd become inseparable, and that she too was a widow. I didn't go into the details, only to say we had so much in common it was uncanny. It pleased them that I found a compatible friend to share the trip. As we drove back to the house, I knew in my heart I was going to be all right. It would take time, but time was what I had plenty of now that I was alone with no one to care for. I would always miss Bob, I miss him more than life itself, but I knew in my fortified heart that I could and would carry on. Bob would expect it and I knew he would be with me in spirit every step of the way.

Beth was waiting for me and my entourage at home when we arrived. She'd already put the kettle on and stocked my shelves with a few of the necessities I'd need until I could get out for a bigger shop. I could see the mountain of mail on the counter top but I wasn't going to be bothered with that tonight. Chatting over a cup of coffee, I told the kids and Beth about the wonderful time I had on the cruise. They couldn't get over how well I looked, much better than when I left. "Okay, so you were right, again," they laughed adding, "it was the right thing to do and we are glad you didn't listen to us…this time."

My children took turns getting me up to date on all the local gossip and goings on and when they finally said their good-nights and left, I breathed a sigh of relief. I sat myself in Bob's chair—that would be my favourite relaxing spot from now on, my new fave chair—and went about putting to bed all the deep thoughts I'd been shuffling around in my head during the long voyage home. I knew what true love was. It was what Bob and I shared, kindness, consideration, genuine care for one another, closeness, intimacy, and tenderness. Our prime purpose in life was to make each other happy and that's what we did. He was my soul mate. I know I was his. Sadly, and all too often, married couples miss out on that for one reason or another. I was truly blessed. I had so much to be thankful for. Bob's secret did not change that.

As I sat there admiring the portrait above the fireplace. I knew Bob was with me when I said aloud, "I love you Bob. You were… You are and always will be the light of my life. Thank you from the bottom of my heart for the wonderful years we shared. I miss you so much, always will! The memories of our life together are what will get me through the rest of my life without you."

Before I went upstairs, I made sure the doors were locked, did my usual round of checking that everything was secure before turning on the outside light. I switched on the hall light and would turn it off when I got to the top of the stairs. Daniel had taken my suitcases upstairs and put them in the bedroom. I was happy to be back home. I looked at the little scripture card again the one the Pastor gave me at Bob's funeral.

"Yes Bob," I said, "some day the pain will be gone and we will know the answers."

As I got ready for bed, I was confident that from now on I would be just fine. I will have good days and not-so-good days, it will take time but I was confident that I would be alright.

The trip home as well as the excitement of being back among my family tired me a little. I couldn't be bothered to empty the suitcases. I took my small night case holding my toiletries into the bathroom. I was too tired to shower. A bath might have been lovely but I was afraid I might doze off. With no one at home, that was a little risky. I washed, changed into my goonie, turned off the bathroom light, slipped the quilt off the bed, turned down the sheets, and sat down on Bob's side of the bed. This is where I want to sleep tonight, I thought and somehow I knew I'd sleep in that spot from now on. Call me crazy but doing so brought him closer to me and I wanted that, I needed that. I spoke to his photograph, closed my eyes, and gave thanks to the Lord for all the care he's given us throughout the years.

Goodnight Bob.

I got into bed, pulled up the covers, closed my eyes, and before I knew it, the night passed and a new day was dawning. What would it hold for me? Whatever lay ahead, I was ready for the next chapter. Whatever my new life without Bob in the flesh might hold for me, I knew he would be with me every step of the way forever in my heart...